Prey for the Shadow

A Terra Alta Investigation

JAVIER CERCAS

Prey for the Shadow

A Terra Alta Investigation

Translated from the Spanish by
Anne McLean

MACLEHOSE PRESS
A Bill Swainson Book
QUERCUS · LONDON

First published in the Spanish language as *Independencia*
by Editorial Planeta, S.A., in 2021

First published in Great Britain in 2023 as
A Bill Swainson Book by MacLehose Press

This paperback edition published in 2024 by

MacLehose Press
An imprint of Quercus Editions Limited
Carmelite House
50 Victoria Embankment
London EC4Y 0DZ

An Hachette UK company

A CIP catalogue record for this book is available from the British Library.

ISBN (MMP) 978 1 52942 251 1
ISBN (Ebook) 978 1 52942 250 4

1 3 5 7 9 10 8 6 4 2

Designed and typeset in Sabon by Patty Rennie
Printed and bound in Great Britain by Elcograf S.p.A.

Papers used by MacLehose Press are from well-managed
forests and other responsible sources.

For Raül Cercas and Mercè Mas,
my Terra Alta

Prey for the Shadow

Melchor burst into the place and, pushing his way through the customers, walked straight to the bar, sat on a stool and ordered a whisky. The bartender looked at him as if he had landed from outer space.

"What are you doing here?" he asked.

"Don't worry," Melchor said, "I come in peace."

"In peace?"

"That's right. Are you going to pour me a whisky or not?"

The bartender was slow to answer.

"Neat or on the rocks?"

"Neat."

It was past three in the morning, but the place was still quite busy. Several girls were dancing naked or half-naked on the illuminated catwalk that ran through the middle of the main room, bombarded with strobe lights, while a few men watched them with hungry eyes; here and there, other girls, alone, in pairs or groups, waited for the night's last clients. Or the end of the night. *Like a Virgin*, an old Madonna song, was playing over the speakers.

"If I wasn't seeing it with my own eyes, I wouldn't believe it," Melchor heard behind him.

While the bartender poured his whisky, the man who had just spoken sat on the stool next to Melchor's. He was a bald, tough-looking, mixed-race guy in a dark suit, at least two metres tall. The police officer took a long pull of his drink and the guy pointed to it.

"Have you kicked the Coca-Cola habit?"

"Yeah," Melchor said. "I'm celebrating."

The guy showed two rows of very white teeth.

"You don't say?" he said. "And what are you celebrating? That the judge believed we were right and left you high and dry?"

"The judge didn't believe you, dickhead," Melchor corrected him. "He just said there wasn't enough evidence against you. But don't worry, I'll find it. Pour me another shot."

The bartender, who had not left their side, still had the bottle in his hand, and poured Melchor another whisky. The big guy spun his stool around, rested his elbows on the bar and leaned back on it, watching the dancers on the catwalk and smiling. Melchor took another pull of whisky.

"Do you know why I like this place so much?" he asked.

The guy didn't say anything. Melchor brought the glass back to his lips.

"Because it reminds me of my childhood," he said, after he swallowed. "My mother was a hooker, you know. So I grew up in places like this, surrounded by whores like her and pimps like you. That's what I'm celebrating: a homecoming."

The Madonna song ended, and the man's laugh resonated loudly through the growing silence of the brothel. On the sound system, Rosalía replaced Madonna, and two or three girls started dancing among the customers and their colleagues. The man placed one of his huge hands on Melchor's shoulder.

"That's what I like to hear, *poli*," he said. "A man's got to know how to lose." He stood up and, winking at the bartender and nodding towards Melchor, added: "On the house."

Melchor carried on drinking without raising his eyes from his glass and, although all the girls knew him, none of them approached. When he ordered a third whisky, however, one of them sat down beside him. She was Spanish, dark-haired, mature, full-figured, wearing a black corset and bare breasted. She held a hand to her throat and asked for a glass of cava. The waiter warned Melchor:

"Drinks for the girls aren't part of the boss's invitation."

Melchor nodded his assent and the bartender poured her cava. They drank as they waited for him to move away from them. When he went to serve someone at the other end of the bar, Melchor asked:

"Are we going through with it?"

"Of course," she answered.

"You sure?" Melchor insisted. "If they catch us, you'll be in trouble."

The woman looked indifferent.

"I don't get scared anymore, kid."

Melchor nodded without looking at her.

"OK," he said. "Let's wait a bit. When you see me go upstairs, you go to their room. Leave the door open and tell them I'll be right there."

"They're really frightened. Do you want me to stay until you get there?"

"No. Calm them down. Tell them nothing's going to happen. Tell them I'll be right there. And then open the other two doors, the ones to the balcony, and go home or come back here. No, you better go home." He paused for a moment. "Understood?"

"Yeah."

Melchor nodded again, but this time he looked at her.

"Be careful," she said.

"You too," Melchor said.

The woman stood up and, leaving half the glass of cava on the bar, walked away.

Melchor kept drinking without talking to anyone except the bartender, without moving from his stool, except to go to the toilet. When the place was almost completely empty, the big guy reappeared and smiled unpleasantly when he saw Melchor.

"You still here?" he asked.

"He's had six whiskies," the bartender answered for him. "Too bad it wasn't six Coca-Colas: he'd be dead."

"I need to see your boss," Melchor announced.

The big guy wrinkled his brow; his smile had disappeared, swallowed by his full mauve lips.

"He's not here."

Melchor clicked his tongue.

"You think I'm stupid? Of course he's here. He never leaves till you've closed: he's not going to let you steal the takings."

The guy looked at him with a blend of curiosity and suspicion.

"What do you want to see the boss for?"

"That's none of your business."

"Of course it's my business."

"He says he's come in peace," the bartender chimed in.

The big guy's gaze jumped from the bartender to Melchor and from Melchor to the bartender, who shrugged.

"I want to apologise," Melchor said. "For the trial. For the trouble. Well, you know."

The guy seemed to relax.

"Sure. That's great. But you don't have to see him for that. I'll tell him. Consider yourself forgiven."

"I also want to make a proposal."

The guy became wary again.

"What proposal?"

"That's for me to know . . ."

"Then you can forget about talking to him."

"If you say so. But the proposal is a good one and he'll be interested." He looked at the bartender and added: "I don't think he'll be pleased to hear you wouldn't let me tell him about it."

Now the big guy seemed doubtful; he looked back at the bartender and, scrutinising Melchor, after a few seconds stepped away, just far enough to speak on the phone without being overheard. When the call was finished, he gestured unenthusiastically for the policeman to follow him.

They crossed the deserted dance floor, and walked up two narrow flights of stairs. When they got to the second landing, the man opened a door and told Melchor to step inside. In the office on the other side was the boss, who did not stand up when he saw Melchor come in. He didn't shake hands either. He was sitting behind a rickety old desk, with his hands in sight and a mocking glint in his eyes.

"Why didn't you tell me you were here?" he said, motioning to a seat in front of him. "I would have come down to say hello."

Melchor did not sit down. The boss was an overgroomed man in his fifties, his hair slicked back, neat beard speckled with grey, hands swarming with rings; he was in shirtsleeves, wearing braces and a silver chain with a large gold medallion. His name was Eugenio Fernández, but, for reasons unknown to Melchor, everyone called him Papá Moon.

"I hear you want to apologise," he said. "I also heard you've been drowning your sorrows in whisky. Well done. In any case, I already warned you that you were getting yourself into a mess. That's the advantage of living in a democracy, kid: here we are all innocent until proven otherwise. Including me, who does not read books, like you do. But I got this far. You won't sit down?"

Melchor didn't answer. Papá Moon directed a questioning look towards his henchman, who was standing behind the policeman and shrugged. Behind him was a standard lamp, and in front, on the desk, a table lamp; they both cast a feeble light around the room. Fitted into a panel at the back, facing the desk, a flat-screen TV with the volume turned way down was showing an NBA basketball game.

"Aren't you going to say anything?" Papá Moon asked again.

"I have a proposition for you," Melchor finally said.

"That's what Samuel told me," Papá Moon said. He swivelled around in his chair and opened his arms in a welcoming gesture. "I'm all ears."

Melchor turned to look at Samuel for an instant and then back to his boss.

"Don't worry," Papá Moon tried to reassure him. "You can say whatever you like. Samuel is completely trustworthy."

Melchor did not take his eyes off Papá Moon, who after a couple of seconds sighed and, moving his head slightly, indicated that Samuel should leave. After a moment's hesitation, the big guy patted Melchor down. Melchor let him, as he was not armed; he only had a couple of pairs of handcuffs in his pockets. Then Samuel asked:

"Are you sure, boss?"

Papá Moon nodded.

"Start closing up," he ordered. "I'll be right down."

Reluctantly, the henchman left, closing the door behind him.

"OK." The boss leaned back in his chair. "Let's hear it."

Melchor took two steps forward, leaned his knuckles on the desk and, stretching his torso across it, moved in very close to Papá Moon, as if he wanted to whisper something to him.

"It's about those young girls," he said.

The boss looked bored.

"Still on about that?"

Melchor stared at him. Papá Moon asked: "What is it about the girls?" There was another silence, until the man's expression began to give way to a complicit smile. "Let's get this over with," he said. "You like them too, don't you?"

He was about to add something, but he couldn't: Melchor head-butted him and, without giving him time to react, grabbed him by the back of the neck and smashed his skull against the desk. It crunched as if he'd broken it. Then he circled the desk, lifting Papá Moon up by the neck, and started hitting him again, first a punch to the stomach and then a kick to the testicles. Papá Moon fell to the floor with a shriek.

"Don't yell," Melchor warned him: he'd grabbed the silver chain and was pulling it tight against his Adam's apple, as if wanting to choke him. "If you yell again, I'll break your neck."

Papá Moon was kneeling, gasping for breath.

"Have you lost your mind?" he managed to whimper, his face as red as a tomato.

Melchor banged Papá Moon's head again, this time against the side of the desk, then slapped him and twisted his arms behind his back while searching with the other hand until he found his mobile. He smashed it underfoot.

"Where's your pistol?" he asked.

"You're breaking my arm."

7

"I said, where do you keep your pistol."

"What pistol?"

Now Papá Moon's face was slammed against the floor. When Melchor pulled it up again, a trail of blood was dripping from his nose onto his beard. Melchor repeated the question. The boss answered it and, without letting go of him, Melchor opened a drawer, took out a pistol and checked to make sure it was loaded. Then he forced Papá Moon to his feet.

"This time you've lost the plot, *poli*," he managed to splutter. "Your career ends here."

Melchor twisted his arm harder and put the barrel of the gun under his jaw.

"We'll talk about that later, boss," he said. "Right now we're going to walk out of here and you are going to fucking behave yourself." Then he warned him, rubbing the pistol against his face: "If you shout, I shoot. If you do anything stupid, I shoot. Is that clear?" Papá Moon kept quiet. Melchor twisted his arm again and the man nodded. "Very good," Melchor said. "Let's go."

They walked out of Papá Moon's office as one, and down the stairs Melchor had come up. At the first landing, the policeman pushed the door open a little and peered around it. He could see a sort of balcony, actually an outdoor corridor that ran the length of the brothel and overlooked the entrance and the car park where there were still several vehicles. They walked at top speed along the balcony, past a stairway that went down to the car park and, at the end, Melchor half-opened another door and made sure again there was nobody on the other side of it. That done, he opened the door and they walked into another hallway, this one interior and harshly lit, lined with a series of doors, through some of which came voices, noises, the odd burst of laughter. Melchor opened the last door. Inside, three adolescent girls waited: two of them were huddled on the bed and the other stood in the middle of the room; all three had ebony skin and looked at the recent arrivals with expectant, panic-stricken eyes. Melchor closed the door behind him, looked at all three of them and asked if they were ready.

Only the one who was already on her feet nodded, but the other two stood up immediately. Melchor knew all three of them. They'd been born in Lagos, and their stories were basically the same. All three had arrived in Madrid years earlier, fleeing poverty and believing they would be able to study in Spain. On arrival they were deprived of their passports and mobiles, forbidden to contact their families or go outside, told they owed sixty thousand euros for travel expenses and, to terrorise them even more, submitted to a ritual that consisted of cutting their nails and hair, shaving their underarms and pubic hair and forcing them to drink a liquid hallucinogen. From then on, they were forced into prostitution. That's how they began a tour of strip clubs across half of Spain, working from five in the evening until four in the morning in order to pay off the debt that, in theory, they had contracted with the organisation that had in fact kidnapped them. A tour that Melchor had resolved would end there, that night.

He forced Papá Moon to sit on the floor, beside the teenagers' bed, took out the handcuffs and locked his right wrist to one leg of the bed, and with the other pair locked his left wrist to another.

"You've gone crazy, *poli*." Papá Moon raged. "You're going to pay for this."

It was the last thing he said: Melchor stuffed a scarf in his mouth and shoved it down his throat. The three adolescents watched the operation from the door, trembling with fear.

"Now listen carefully, you piece of shit," Melchor said,

crouching in front of Papá Moon. "We couldn't do it by fair means, so we had to do it by foul. These girls are coming with me. Don't you dare bring any more. And don't even think of reporting me. Do you know what will happen if you report me? Listen hard, because I'm only going to tell you once. If you report me, I'll burn this joint down. I'll kill your children and your wife. I'll kill your whole family. And then I'll kill you. That's what will happen. You understand that, don't you?" The rage in Papá Moon's eyes had now turned into a frenzied, animal fear. Melchor moved his face even closer to add: "Tell me you've understood, yes or no?" Papá Moon moved his head up and down; Melchor gave him a satisfied pat on the cheek. "Splendid."

He stood up and turned to the girls. The effects of the whisky had worn off; his head was clear, and he felt light and happy.

"Ready?" he asked.

All three nodded. Their names were Alika, Joy and Doris. Alika and Joy were sixteen; Doris, eighteen. They looked like they'd dressed to take part in a community run or a political demonstration: dark T-shirts, cheap jeans and trainers. The three of them looked at him with wide, imploring and frightened eyes, as if a meteorite was about to fall on the brothel and only he could save them from the catastrophe. Melchor pushed the door open an inch, checked to make sure there was nobody in the hall, stuck the pistol in his belt and took the two younger ones, Alika and Joy, by the hand.

"Don't worry," he said. "Stick with me and everything will be fine." He opened the door the rest of the way: "Let's go."

Part One

Part One

1

Melchor changes the water in the vase, throws out the wilted flowers and replaces them with fresh ones, takes out a cloth and cleans the stone, where it says: "Olga Ribera, Gandesa, 1978–2021". Then, as on every Saturday morning for the last four years (except when he's on duty), he spends a while there, at his wife's grave, telling her about Cosette and commenting on the few events of the week.

The cemetery lies on the slope of a hill on the outskirts of Gandesa. Melchor hears only the chirping of birds and, every now and again, the distant sound of a car snaking its way towards Vilalba dels Arcs and up La Fatarella, the peak of which stands out against the immaculate blue sky to his left, studded with white wind turbines turning sluggishly in the still heat of the July morning.

Half an hour later, Melchor slings his bag across his shoulder and leaves the grave behind. He passes the Adell family vault, a sumptuous tomb of black marble mottled with white, and walks up a narrow little road, shaded by cypress trees and flanked by burial mounds. When he leaves the cemetery he takes a footpath and soon comes out at the roundabout that leads into Gandesa. In the middle of the roundabout, sitting on a step under a stone cross, he is not surprised to see Rosa Adell.

"I was just thinking that I never go to the cemetery," she says in greeting.

Melchor walks over to her. Rosa is wearing a dark blue, sleeveless blouse, very thin brown trousers and sandals that reveal her tiny feet, her toenails painted red. Melchor cannot see her eyes: a pair of dark sunglasses hides them.

"And I've got my whole family buried in there," Rosa adds. "Should I feel bad?"

Thinking of the Adell family mausoleum, Melchor answers: "Dreadful."

"Are you serious?"

"No. What's in there has nothing to do with your parents."

"What about Olga?"

"Her neither."

"So why do you go?"

Melchor shrugs. Rosa Adell looks at him for a moment, then makes a puzzled face and, brushing the dust off her trousers, stands up.

"Where's Cosette?"

"In the pool." Melchor gestures vaguely towards a building fifty metres down the road, between the fire station and the sports complex. "She'll be out at twelve."

Rosa looks at her watch.

"Just time for a coffee."

They head for the Hotel Piqué down avenida Joan Perucho. They walk in silence, as if the increasingly intense heat of the sun dissuades them from talking, and in silence they walk past the Terra Alta middle school and the faux neoclassical facade of the courthouse.

In the last few months the two of them have seen a lot of

each other, sometimes by pure chance, other times by chances not so pure, always or almost always instigated by Rosa, who has taken up the habit of waiting for him every Saturday morning by the cemetery gates. Like everyone else, Rosa is ignorant of Melchor's actual role in the resolution of the Adell case, which shook Terra Alta out of its perpetual slumber four years ago and since then has kept Albert Ferrer, her ex-husband, in prison, as well as Ernest Salom, former police corporal, Ferrer's best friend and Melchor's colleague at the Gandesa police station, the first convicted of inducement to murder the Adells and their Romanian maid, the second of collusion in the murder and accessory after the fact. And, although it's true that Rosa sensed early on that the official version of events did not entirely coincide with reality, and that Melchor was hiding things (or that's what Melchor himself sensed), the truth is she had never felt like questioning him about it. In fact, they rarely mention it, despite having met because of it, and Melchor has heard almost none of what he knows about Rosa's reactions and the consequences she has faced directly from her. What Melchor actually knows is sketchy and piecemeal: that Rosa has not seen her ex-husband since his trial, for example; or that all four of her daughters, aware that it was their father who ordered the murder of their maternal grandparents, have disowned him. Apart from that, Rosa Adell lives alone in the refurbished farmhouse near Corbera d'Ebre she shared with Albert Ferrer four years ago – her four daughters are working or studying in Barcelona now – and she has tried or is still trying to get over the murder of her parents and the conviction of her husband by devoting herself body and soul to leading the business empire created out of nothing by her father, with Gráficas Adell at the heart of it. She works a lot, travels a lot, spends occasional weekends in Barcelona with her daughters, but for some time now, when she is in Terra Alta, she ends up calling Melchor on the phone or, of late, going to look for him on his way out of the cemetery.

They pass the bus station on their right, cross the road and the area in front of the Hotel Piqué and go into the café, which at that time of day is occupied by a group of excited tourists at the bar, a pair of cyclists and an older couple. Rosa sits down at a table beside a big window overlooking the car park, while Melchor waits his turn at the bar; when he finally manages to get served, he brings their two cups of coffee to the table.

"I've heard things are going well," Melchor says as he sits down across from Rosa.

In the hubbub of the café inundated with sunshine, Rosa has taken off her dark glasses and looks at the police officer with her serene, brown, oval eyes, while stirring her coffee.

"News travels fast in Terra Alta," she says. "You've already heard about Medellín?"

Melchor nods.

"It was Señor Grau's idea," Rosa says, downplaying her own importance, a gleam of carmine lipstick shining on her full lips. "Colombia is a country that works really well, ideal for investors, and setting up a factory there has been wonderful for us. Besides, Medellín is a great city."

"How's Señor Grau doing? I haven't seen him in ages."

Rosa Adell squints, smiles half-heartedly and sips her coffee.

"He's old," she says without melancholy. "But there he is, still ready for anything. The truth is I don't know what I'd do without him."

Melchor nods again. The image of Gráficas Adell's eternal manager has just flashed through his mind: a fierce old man, with proven business acumen, pale, cultured and short-sighted, scrawny with thin hair, who, at the age of ninety, continues to show up every day at his office in La Plana industrial estate, on the outskirts of Gandesa, always impeccably dressed and ever more hunched over, still at the helm of the flagship of the Adell empire. He also remembers, with amazement, that this paragon of managerial probity and personal loyalty to the man he'd worked for almost his entire life had been, while he and Salom were investigating the Adell case under the orders of Deputy Inspector Gomà, the main suspect in Rosa's parents' murder.

"Well, you should probably start thinking about that," Melchor advises her.

"I know," Rosa admits, looking out of the window. In the hotel car park, there are only a couple of cars and a delivery van, protected from the sun by a thatched roof; there is little traffic on the way into Gandesa. "By the way –" she turns back to Melchor all of a sudden – "Señor Grau is coming for lunch today. Why don't you and Cosette come too? I'm sure he'd love to see you."

"Thanks, but I can't. We're watching a movie at home. Besides," he says, patting his bag, which he'd hung over the arm of the chair when he sat down, "this afternoon I have work to do." Rosa looks at the bag and then at Melchor, who clarifies: "They're manuscripts for the literary competition."

She smiles broadly: a luminous, teasing, open smile.

"So they finally convinced you to be on the jury."

Melchor looks away but doesn't find anywhere else to direct his gaze.

"Apparently there was nobody else and . . ." Flustered, aware the phrase was headed in the wrong direction, he starts another. "And that's not the worst thing."

"No?"

"No. The worst part is I have to give a speech at the prize ceremony. They've asked me to say a few words about reading.

17

Or about literature. Or about the novels I like. Something like that."

"That's a lovely idea."

"Charming. Except that I've never given a speech in my life."

"Don't tell me you're scared."

Melchor turns back towards Rosa.

"Not scared," he confesses. "Panic-stricken."

She laughs wholeheartedly.

"Don't be silly," she says. "You'll do a great job, *poli*."

"Sure."

"I'm serious. Do you want me to help you prepare?"

A hopeful spark flares up in Melchor's eyes for an instant, which goes out as soon as he decides that despite her claims to be serious, his friend is joking.

Before Rosa can assure him that she's serious, Melchor stands up to order two more coffees. He comes back with them a minute later and, although he flatly refuses to return to the subject of his speech, they do talk about the literary competition for a while. The library and the high school are organising it, and the jury consists of two teachers, a local poet, the head librarian and Melchor; the prizes are set to be presented at the beginning of September, during first assembly of the school year. Melchor tells her about a science fiction story he'd just read and liked a lot; he sums up the plot for Rosa, who – despite not being a big science fiction fan, or even much of a fan of literature – agrees it sounds good. They also talk about a proposal the mayor of Gandesa has made to Rosa, that she expand the main Gráficas Adell factory in La Plana, and about a business trip she has coming up to their Romanian subsidiary in Timisoara. Then they discuss the plans each of them has made for their holidays: Rosa is going to take her four daughters to the United States for two weeks, and Melchor, at the beginning of August, is intending to do the same thing as the previous summer, when he and Cosette spent a few days in Molina de Segura, staying at the house of his mother's last friend, Carmen Lucas, and her husband Pepe.

"You're going to melt in the heat down there," Rosa predicts.

"Last year we had a really good time," Melchor says. "Do you know what Cosette liked best? That all the little girls called her Cosé."

Rosa is still laughing when Melchor's phone rings. He looks at it and lets it ring.

"Aren't you going to answer?" Rosa asks.

"It's Vivales. I'll call him later." Now it's Melchor's turn to look at his watch. "Cosette must be almost done. Shall we get going?"

Rosa Adell doesn't know much more about Domingo Vivales than she does about Carmen and Pepe. Melchor introduced him to her a while ago, when Vivales was visiting Gandesa, but she hadn't understood the relationship between two men of such disparate ages they might easily be father and son. In fact, almost the only thing she knows about the lawyer is that, just like Carmen Lucas, he was a friend of his mother's, and that Melchor inherited that friendship the way some people inherit furniture. The policeman hadn't told her any more than that; she didn't ask either, because the first unwritten rule of their friendship concerns the careful obligation to respect each other's privacy.

While Rosa pays for the four coffees – here is another unwritten rule of their friendship: she always or almost always pays – a WhatsApp alert chimes on Melchor's phone. It's Sergeant Blai, who is no longer a sergeant but an inspector and stationed not in Terra Alta but at headquarters, in the Egara complex, on the outskirts of Sabadell. "What's up, *españolazo*?" Blai texts.

"Where are you?" "Hotel Piqué," Melchor replies. "Shaggin'?" Blai writes back. "Ha ha, just kidding. I'm at my in-laws' place. We have to see each other as soon as possible. This afternoon."

"Don't worry," says Rosa Adell, putting her sunglasses back on and joining Melchor at the hotel door. "Speak to whoever you have to speak to."

They walk across the grounds and, while waiting to cross the road, Melchor types on his phone: "I can't." "For fuck's sake, man, now you can't even count on your friends?" Blai immediately replies, and texts again a second later: "It's serious. We have to talk. It's urgent." They are walking down avenida Joan Perucho under the blistering midday sun.

"Is it work?" Rosa Adell asks.

Melchor says it is.

"I leave my work mobile at the office on weekends," Rosa says. "Is it important?"

"I'm sure it's not, but he thinks it is."

When they reach the courthouse, Melchor texts back: "I'll call you later." "Soon," Blai replies. "I've got a big family meal at seven. I need to see you before that." Melchor sends him a yellow thumbs-up emoji in reply.

When he looks up from his phone, Rosa Adell has just opened her car door.

"Are you sure you don't want to come over for lunch?" she says.

"I'm sure. Give my regards to Señor Grau."

They say goodbye with a kiss on each cheek.

There is a change of plans. When she comes out of the municipal swimming pool, Cosette asks if she can eat at her friend Elisa Climent's house and spend the afternoon with her, and

Melchor, after talking to the little girl's mother and negotiating with Cosette, agrees. "I'll pick you up at six," he says. As soon as they leave it occurs to him that he could call Rosa Adell and have lunch with her and Señor Grau, but he immediately dismisses the idea and heads for the plaza. He spends the rest of the morning there, sitting on the terrace of the bar, drinking Coca-Cola and reading several of the stories entered for the competition: he puts a minus sign on those he doesn't like much or doesn't like at all, a plus sign on those he likes and two plus signs on those he likes most, intending to reread them later and make his shortlist from among them.

At around two he goes home. He makes himself a salad with cheese and nuts, grills a steak and eats at the kitchen table, along with that Saturday's third Coca-Cola, while looking every once in a while at the empty seat on the other side of the table, where Olga used to sit.

Four years have passed since she was hit and killed by a car Albert Ferrer had rented the previous evening in Tortosa. According to what he said to the police interrogators and at his trial, he had not meant to kill her but to intimidate Melchor, force him to abandon the investigation into the murder of Ferrer's in-laws, which he insisted on pursuing of his own accord and at his own risk despite the case being officially closed. Be that as it may, barely a day has gone by since Olga's death without Melchor thinking about her. When that happens, when he forgets his wife for a bit, he feels bad, although he doesn't know why. He has tried to reconstruct in neurotic detail, week by week, day by day, hour by hour, minute by minute, the three and a half years lived with his wife, but he has not been able to, and sometimes he harbours a contradictory feeling towards that happy time of his life when, after arriving in Terra Alta, he met Olga and fell in love with her, and they married and had

Cosette: on the one hand, it seems entirely unreal, as if, rather than having lived through it, he'd seen it in a film or dreamed it; on the other hand, it seems like his life with Olga has been the only real thing that's ever happened to him. At first, after his wife's death, he was always wondering what she would have said about this, that and the other, but after some time he managed to escape that irrational torture. However, he is still unable to talk about her with anyone, not even Cosette, and, when the little girl asks about her mother, whom she barely remembers, he doesn't know how to answer and changes the subject.

The early stages without Olga were very hard. He could not get her death out of his head; nor could he stop thinking that he had failed her: he had read somewhere that as long as there's remorse, there's guilt, and he was constantly being eaten away by regret. Both things explain why, after a few months, he decided to get away from Terra Alta, in the hope that leaving behind what had become his home thanks to Olga would help him to overcome her death. By then it had been five years since the Islamist attacks of 2017, many of his co-workers knew it had been him who shot four terrorists in Cambrils and the commanders were aware that, at least within the force, he had become a symbol; so, making use for the first time of his privileged position, he called Commissioner Fuster and asked for a transfer.

Fuster's reaction was what he'd expected. The commissioner didn't ask why he wanted to relocate, just where he wanted to be posted. Melchor, predictably, answered Barcelona. Predictably because, despite having spent so much time away from the city, he knew it was still his home: he had never lived anywhere else until they posted him to Terra Alta in order to protect him from possible Islamist reprisals. In Barcelona, moreover, he had

Vivales, who had been a constant support since his mother's death and who, he was sure, would help him raise Cosette. "Do you want to stay in criminal investigation?" Fuster asked, as obliging as ever. "I don't know how to do anything else," Melchor answered. "Well, you're in luck," the commissioner congratulated him. "I just spoke to the chief of the DCI and he told me that the Abduction and Extortion Unit is short-staffed. What do you think of the idea of coming here, to Egara?" "Great," said Melchor, so impatient to leave Terra Alta that he would have accepted the worst job in the worst hovel in the worst station. "Hey," Fuster warned him. "Don't expect it to be cushy. The unit is very demanding. You won't get bored, you'll learn a lot, but you'll work your socks off." "Perfect."

He meant it. Melchor was certain the relative inactivity and rural tranquillity of the Terra Alta station, which had been so good for him when Olga was alive, was now killing him; the more absorbing his work, the better off he'd be. He knew that Cosette was a curious and energetic child, but also adaptable, and that Olga's death, far from making her faint-hearted, had made her more resilient. So, even though Cosette's roots in Terra Alta were as deep as his and perhaps at first she wouldn't want to leave the region, he was convinced that she would embrace the change of place and school, the novelty of the capital and the challenge of making new friends as an adventure; he was also sure she would love having Vivales closer.

The Central Abduction and Extortion Unit was part of the Central Jurisdiction of Personal Investigation, which in turn belonged to the Division of Criminal Investigation (DCI), and, when Melchor joined it, he realised that Commissioner Fuster had also meant what he said. What Fuster hadn't warned him about, however, was that, as well as being a demanding unit, Abduction and Extortion was a singular unit. At that time it had a staff of twelve, nine men and three women who worked under the orders of Sergeant Vàzquez, a hyperactive, muscular man in his forties with a shaved head, a passing resemblance to a bulldog and a reputation for being a strict, argumentative cop. It was true that Vàzquez was always complaining to his superiors about the shortage of officers in his unit, but he complained for a reason: it was not for nothing that Abduction and Extortion worked twenty-four hours a day, all year round, and covered the whole of Catalonia. However, what made it singular – what demanded that it operate like no other, resemble no other – was its obligation to be the most discreet unit in the force; reserve was in fact the key to its success: the first thing Melchor learned when he joined Abduction and Extortion was that, the fewer people who knew they were trying to solve a case, the higher the probability they would be able to do so. Another thing that made the unit singular was its members' high degrees of specialisation, which forced Melchor to gain new skills as quickly as possible. During his first months he took four courses: one in negotiating, one in abductions, one in organised crime and another in advanced investigation. They were exclusive courses, on which only select people could enrol (members of the unit, or similar units of the Guardia Civil, the National Police or the Basque Ertzaintza), and where it was required that everything taught there was to be kept secret to the point that, to prevent leaks, there was no written documentation. "If the bad guys find out how we fight them, we're fucked," Vàzquez used to advise those who were preparing to take a course. "So, other than here, not a word of what you learn there. As a wise man once said, silence is invincible."

At first, Melchor enjoyed his new posting. He worked hard, looked after Cosette, read novels and talked to Vivales (who helped him look after Cosette). He was still an intense reader, but now he divided his reading between his own books and the ones he read to his daughter at bedtime. She acclimatised to the big city with the enthusiastic ease he had predicted. Of course, Melchor knew the little girl missed Terra Alta, but he never heard her say so; he sometimes missed it too. It didn't take him long to realise that no matter how hard he worked, no matter how far away from Terra Alta he moved, he was not going to get Olga's death out of his head, and he ended up accepting that he would have to live with that poisoned memory for life.

To his surprise, the return to Barcelona awoke another memory, no less poisonous, that had lain dormant for years: the memory of his mother's murder. While he lived in Terra Alta he thought of her once in a while, but never or almost never of her death; the reason for this lucky omission was probably that, after having spent years trying obsessively to solve that crime on his own in his spare time, violating some of the most basic rules of policing in the process, just before moving to the region he had discovered by chance that the woman who was with his mother that fateful night was called Carmen Lucas, he had tracked her down to a vegetable-growing district in Murcia, and had travelled there and interrogated her for two days without gaining a single lead that might help him find the killers, all of which had eventually persuaded him the crime would never be solved. Now, however, that memory had returned, solid and tenacious, as if going back to Barcelona meant going back to running into that memory and all the atrocious associated memories: his mother prostituting herself around the Camp Nou, along with Carmen Lucas and their unfortunate companions; the memory of a brown BMW or a dark Volkswagen or a black Skoda, depending on the witness consulted, which his mother had first refused to get into after a fruitless negotiation

25

with its occupants ("A gang of rich kids out for a good time in papá's car," she'd told Carmen), only later to relent, propelled by the desperation of a night with no customers; the memory of his mother's corpse found at dawn the next day on some waste ground in Sagrera, in Sant Andreu, her skull smashed. All those partial memories made up a lacerating recollection that now returned with a vengeance, as if some impregnable corner of Melchor could still not accept that this long-ago murder had gone unpunished. In short, he had escaped Terra Alta fleeing from a solved crime, and in Barcelona he had been trapped by two, one solved and the other unsolved.

When he understood that, as much as he wanted to part with his worst memories, his worst memories did not want to part with him, he decided to return to Terra Alta. He waited to request the transfer until the school year finished, which coincided in time with an event that effectively broke up the Abduction and Extortion Unit.

It was the kidnapping of the daughter of a Venezuelan drug trafficker who lived with his family in a villa in Ampuriabrava, a seaside village near the French border. The victim had been abducted by a rival gang, who the Venezuelan had tried to rip off, and who were demanding, in exchange for her liberation, a sum of money he was in no condition to be able to get together. For months, the entire unit worked on the case, with Vàzquez as the main negotiator between the narcos. It was a surly negotiation, during which the Venezuelan narco received at his house, one after the other, three small fingers amputated from his five-year-old daughter's hand. Finally, Vàzquez thought he'd found the girl in a warehouse on the outskirts of Molins de Rei and pulled together a rescue squad of eighty people, including civil guards and National Police. The operation failed. There were three arrests and one man was killed, but they did not manage to save the narco's daughter, and the most vivid memory Melchor retained of that day was the image of Vàzquez sitting in a pool of blood on the concrete floor of the warehouse, with the little girl's severed head in his lap, his eyes popping out of his head, trembling and shrieking like a man possessed.

They had to prise the head out of his hands, and Vàzquez was admitted to hospital that very day and not discharged for a week, and when he was it was not to return to Abduction and Extortion but to a posting at the Seu d'Urgell station in the Lérida Pyrenees, where he was from. Melchor learned all this gradually, back in Terra Alta by then. He did not leave there again in the years that followed, which he devoted to his daughter and his work. He filled his abundant free time by lending a hand at the library where Olga had worked and studying for a degree in Information and Documentation at the Open University of Catalonia; also, of course, with reading novels, although since Olga's death he had avoided rereading *Les Misérables*, which until then had been, as well as his favourite novel, the mirror he looked into and the weapon with which he defended himself from life's abuse. He had been unable, however, to overcome another of his vices, this one more or less secret. Whenever an individual was accused of hitting a woman in Terra Alta he would receive a beating, and, at least at the station, everyone knew who'd done it, and everyone was obliged to look the other way.

When he finishes his lunch he washes the dishes, makes a coffee and carries on reading manuscripts sitting on the sofa. At five on the dot, with professional punctuality, Inspector Blai shows up.

"These Terra Alta women are incredible," is the first thing he says, bursting into Melchor's house. "There's no way to uproot them."

It's the same regret that Melchor has heard a thousand times from the former boss of the Terra Alta Investigations Unit since he moved to Barcelona: that his wife cannot adjust to living so far away and, for that reason, every weekend the family returns to her parents' house, in La Pobla de Massaluca. Melchor offers his friend a coffee. Blai accepts and, while Melchor starts to prepare it, carries on complaining, leaning his bulk against the kitchen doorframe.

"I spend all week working my balls off and, as soon as the weekend arrives, get in the car and risk our lives on these god-forsaken roads to get back to Terra Alta as fast as possible, as if the world was going to end. And then, instead of relaxing like a normal person, here I am every Saturday and Sunday, up hill and down dale, so the kids will know their mother's land and not lose their roots. I shit on their fucking roots: when we lived here, nobody cared about their roots, especially my wife. And that's without even mentioning the fucking in-laws, of course. I won't even tell you about the kids: they're unbearable. By the way, where's Cosette?"

"At a friend's house."

"How is she?"

"Great."

"And you?"

"Me too."

"Come on, man, give me some good news, go on. Tell me you've got a girlfriend. Brighten my day, it really needs it. I am going to give you some advice, though: if you do get a girlfriend, make sure she's not from Terra Alta. There's no way to get them out of here."

"What you should do is come back," Melchor advises him. "By the way, you know we've been without a chief since May, don't you?"

"Do I know?"

The coffee machine has just ground the beans with a sound like crunching gravel and, before pressing a blinking button so the liquid will begin to flow from two stainless steel tubes, Melchor turns towards Blai, who has moved closer.

"Can you keep a secret?" the inspector asks.

Melchor has just read a G.K. Chesterton novel in which a character asks the same question and is told: "If you're not able to keep a secret, how do you expect me to?" But he doesn't want to irritate his friend, so he says:

"Of course."

"They've offered me the post."

"Station chief?"

Blai nods with a sad expression. Melchor asks:

"And what did you say?"

"What do you think I said?" snorts Blai, gesticulating. "After the trouble it took to get me out of this hole . . ."

It's true. Two and a half years earlier, when he was still a sergeant and head of the Terra Alta Investigations Unit, Blai passed the inspector's exams he'd sat on the advice of his superiors. They considered that the corps could benefit from his reputation as a criminal investigation ace, acquired thanks to the numerous radio and TV appearances resulting from the resolution of the Adell case, for which public opinion gave him credit. Neither Blai nor anyone else at the Terra Alta station had the slightest interest in dismantling the official version of the case, according to which he and not Melchor had solved it. At first, this made Melchor uncomfortable, because he thought deep down Blai would consider himself an impostor;

but he stopped worrying about it when he realised that, after explaining in minute detail how he had solved the Adell case innumerable times in public, his old boss had completely forgotten the truth and, except when he recalled the case one to one with Melchor, he seemed convinced that it had indeed been him and not Melchor who had identified those responsible for the triple homicide.

Blai insists that his friend keep the secret he's just confided in him ("Do me that favour, won't you, *españolazo*? You know what my wife's like: if she finds out I turned down that post, she'll cut my balls off.") and he goes on ranting and raving about his divided life, with one foot in Barcelona and the other in Terra Alta. Until, once Melchor has given him his coffee and gestured to Olga's chair, he sits down and asks:

"Do you know what the only thing that makes up for all this shit is?"

Melchor guesses the answer because he knows his former boss as well as his former boss knows him.

"What?" he asks anyway.

What lightens Blai's load of family annoyances is not, as far as Melchor knows, that the bigwigs encouraged him to sit the exam and muttered promises of help and were true to their word and promoted him to inspector; nor the fact of having obtained that promotion by skipping a step up the ladder, without spending any time on the intermediate rung of deputy inspector; or even that, despite that scandalous string-pulling, he had wasted no time in demonstrating that he was a competent professional and deserved the promotion, to the extent that not long after he was promoted he was put in charge of directing the Central Area of Investigation and posted to headquarters in Egara, where he had always dreamed of working, because it is the place where all resources are available and all important decisions are made.

No: Blai's compensation is something else.

"Running into Gomà every day," the inspector proclaims, bringing his cup to his lips, less to savour the coffee than the phrase he has just uttered. The two policemen have sat down facing each other, at either end of the table, which still has various items of Cosette's usual breakfast on it: a box of Kellogg's cereal and a packet of chocolate corn cakes endorsed by a TV chef. Still holding his cup, Blai smiles happily. "Brushing past him in the corridors, seeing him in meetings, having coffee next to him," he lists. "God, what fun! Who would have told that cocky bastard four years ago, eh? Who would have said that the same sergeant he'd arrogantly pushed aside from the Adell case so he could take all the glory of the triumph, would now be his superior officer at Egara and he would still be a fucking deputy inspector, because he flunked the same exams I passed? And who could have imagined that this would happen to him specifically because he sidelined me from the Adell case, because he was unable to solve it and I had to step in to get him off the hook? Yes, yes, I know you'll say they haven't promoted me just for solving the Adell case, that before the Adell case I'd already done enough to deserve to be an inspector, but . . . The way the world turns, eh, *españolazo*? Hey, by the way, have you heard about Salom?"

Melchor looks up from the chequered tablecloth, and studies Blai.

"I don't know anything about Salom," he says.

Blai doesn't seem surprised; he gulps down his coffee and sets the cup down on the saucer. He's about to turn fifty and, despite not having a single hair on his head, his lean body with its gym junkie's muscles make him look ten or fifteen years younger; he's six foot three, wears very tight sports clothes and his blue eyes drill into his interlocutor.

"You never went to see him at Quatre Camins in the end, did you?" he asks.

Melchor shakes his head.

"You shouldn't be spiteful. He was your best friend, after all."

"I'm not spiteful. I just don't have anything to say to him."

"But he does have things to say to you. That's why he asked me to get you to go. I think he wants to apologise."

"He already did."

"He wants to apologise for real. He's sorry." Blai pauses theatrically. "We all make mistakes, don't we?"

Melchor smiles. "Are you going to give me a lecture?"

"Go to hell, *españolazo*."

Melchor lets the smile linger on his face while the two men look at each other for a second. Sharp children's voices reach them from calle Costumà, and Melchor wonders if Blai wanted to see him so urgently just to talk about the ex-corporal.

"What's going on with Salom?" he asks.

"Nothing," the inspector says. "The other day I ran into the penitentiary surveillance judge in charge of his case and he told me his sentence has been reduced again. In a couple of years he'll be out. Maybe sooner."

The children's voices have gone, and an embarrassing silence engulfs the kitchen.

"I'm happy for him," Melchor says. "And for his daughters."

"Do you see them?"

"Once in a while, especially Claudia. She teaches at the high school." After a pause, he adds: "But neither of them speak to me."

Blai sighs, shakes his head, clicks his tongue.

"That's understandable, don't you think?" he says. Suddenly the children's voices liven up the afternoon again. "Their mother dead, their father in prison and all their dreams in the bin. Twenty-odd years old. It's always the same story in Terra Alta, that's why I wanted to get away from here . . . Their lives are fucked."

"We're the ones who fucked them up. Or finished them off."

"That's bullshit. The one who fucked it up was their father, for doing what he shouldn't have done."

"That's as may be, but the ones who threw the book at him were us. Besides, what he did, he did for them. And you and I both know it."

"What? Help that brainless Ferrer kill the Adells? He did that for his daughters? Come on, man! He did it because he felt like it, because greed kills the golden goose, or whatever they say."

"A minute ago you were defending him."

"It's one thing to defend him and quite another to say he's not responsible for his actions. Look, I don't know why he did what he did, but the thing is he did it. I'm glad he's sorry, but he did it. Full stop." A little angry, Blai looks away from Melchor, but soon looks back, suddenly curious. "Hey, you don't regret arresting him, do you?"

With a discouraged gesture, Melchor pushes the Kellogg's box against the wall and stands up.

"Enough with the regrets," he says. "Another coffee?"

Blai nods and Melchor switches the coffee machine back on. While the kitchen fills with the sound of crunching gravel again, Melchor wonders if Blai is worried about Salom getting out of prison.

"Is this what you were in such a hurry to tell me?" he asks.

"No," the inspector says in a different tone of voice, standing up and walking around the kitchen. "I'm here because I have a problem."

Melchor waits for the machine to finish grinding the beans, places a cup under the steel tubes, presses the illuminated button and the dark liquid pours out.

"What problem?" he asks without turning around.

"I'll tell you if you promise to give me a hand."

The dark liquid stops flowing, Melchor takes the half-filled cup away, places an empty cup in its place and presses the button again.

"You want me to lend a hand with a case?"

"That's right."

"You want me to go back to Abduction and Extortion?"

"Yes. Just for a few days. Long enough to resolve the matter."

The kitchen is silent again, apart from the electronic buzzing of the coffee machine, which is still dispensing coffee. They haven't heard the children's voices for a while.

"I'm not going to help you," Melchor says. "I'm leaving the force. And besides, I don't know anyone there anymore."

"You're wrong. Vàzquez has come back."

Melchor turns towards him, raising an inquisitive eyebrow.

"Almost a year ago," Blai explains. "The new Criminal Investigations commissioner convinced him. It wasn't too difficult: seems he was bored to death in Seu d'Urgell."

"You didn't tell me."

"You didn't ask."

Melchor makes a vague gesture of approval and turns his back on the inspector again.

"Well, I'm glad to hear that, because it means you don't need me," he says. "Vàzquez is really good."

"I know, but he's mad as fuck. You know him: he does his own thing. I can't rely on him, not in this case, at least. That's why I need you."

"Forget it."

"It won't be for long, with a bit of luck we'll wrap it up in a week. Besides, I already told Vàzquez you'll be coming. He's really happy."

"Well, you lied to him."

"Don't fuck with me, *españolazo*."

"I'm not fucking with you. Just don't insist: find someone else."

Blai protests, swears, huffs and puffs. The coffee is ready again, and Melchor stands for a few seconds holding one of the cups out to his friend, who does not seem prepared to take it, as if that refusal were emblematic of another: the refusal to give up the dispute as lost. Finally, he seems to capitulate, accepts the cup, takes a sip, then another; eventually he asks: "What was that about leaving?" His off-hand tone does not deceive Melchor: Blai has not given up; he has just changed his strategy. "Are you thinking of retiring or what?"

His own cup in hand, Melchor says: "More or less. As soon as a librarian's position opens up, I'm going to apply and I'll leave the force."

Blai looks at Melchor as if he'd just told him he was going to undergo a sex-change operation.

"Are you crazy, or what?"

Melchor downs his coffee in one, leaves the cup in the sink and switches off the machine.

"I thought I told you I was studying librarianship."

"Yeah, but . . ."

"Actually, I don't even need to complete the course. Well, only if I want to be a head librarian. So, as soon as an assistant

35

librarian's position comes up, I'll apply. I'll earn less than at the station, but it'll be enough. Cosette and I don't need very much to get by."

Blai's mouth is still hanging open.

"You're pulling my leg, aren't you?"

"No," Melchor says.

Now, the annoyance visible on Blai's face is joined by incredulity.

"You've gone crazy, man," he says, shaking his head. "You, a librarian? What the hell are you thinking? Taking Olga's place, or what?"

"Of course not," Melchor says. "How could you think that?"

"Forgive me for reminding you, kid," Blai goes on, as if he hadn't heard his friend. "But your wife is dead, she died four years ago, it's about time you got that through your skull." Although Melchor tries to interrupt, he can't; Blai is fired up. "Besides, you'll suffocate outside the station. It's one thing to help out once in a while at the library but spending the whole day there is something else entirely, shelving novels, looking after old folks, reading stories to children and taking books on trollies to the swimming pool, let's see if you can persuade teenagers to read when all they can think of is shagging, I can tell you, I have a bunch of them at home. Anyway, you won't last a week. If my name isn't Blai. But you're the most cop-like cop I've ever seen in my fucking life, man!"

"Not anymore," Melchor manages to get in. "That was before."

"Oh yeah? What happened, now a vocation gets cured with time, like conjunctivitis?"

"A vocation's a fairy tale, Blai."

"Yeah. And I almost fucking believe you."

Standing beside the kitchen counter, the two policemen stare at each other for a moment. Blai's fists are clenched, his forearms trembling and his jaw about to explode, as is usually the case when he gets irritated. For his part, Melchor feels what sooner or later he ends up feeling every time he talks to the former boss of the Terra Alta Investigations Unit lately: that he misses his tantrums.

"Go on, drink your coffee," he says. "It's going to get cold."

Frustrated and reluctant, not knowing what to add to his rebuke, Blai drinks his coffee, and Melchor looks at the apple-shaped clock on the kitchen wall. It's after six.

"I'm going to pick up Cosette," he says. "Are you coming with me?"

Blai grabs Melchor by the arm.

"Do you know why I need you to help me?"

The coffee has Blai on edge: his hand is a claw.

"Because I don't trust anyone." He answers his own question, anxiously searching for Melchor's eyes. "Egara, the great Egara, but the place is full of spoiled brats and show ponies; not many real police officers. Besides, what they've assigned me is an important case. No, not important, exceptional. My bosses are beginning to think they made a mistake with me. They don't say so, but I can tell, Melchor, it's like when your wife goes with someone else. They're starting to wonder if the Adell case wasn't a fluke, if I wasn't bluffing. I'm worried, you understand, don't you?"

"Well, you shouldn't be," says Melchor.

Blai's expression changes all of a sudden: it's no longer one of anguish but of curiosity, genuine curiosity.

"You don't think so?" he asks.

"Of course not," Melchor says. "You've always been a very good cop."

The compliment puffs Blai up like a turkey, but he tries to hide it.

"Yeah, yeah," he says.

Melchor understands his friend's vanity is not yet satisfied; and that it never will be.

"Besides," he adds, resolved not to puff him up any further, or deflate him, "if they kick you out of Egara you can come back here. And your domestic problems will be over."

As if he's just received an electric shock, Blai lets go of Melchor, who smiles with his eyes, but not with his lips.

"You know what I say to you, *españolazo*?" Blai says, shaking his head and clicking his tongue again. "The day you least expect it I'm going to smash your face in."

Outside, the two men walk together along calle Costumà, where there is no longer any trace of children. Defying the summer heat, they head towards the church without seeing a single soul, cross the plaza, skirt round the Farola roundabout and carry on up avenida de Catalunya. They have started talking about Abduction and Extortion again, because Melchor has asked after Vàzquez.

"He's a dynamo," Blai says, then goes on to ask: "When you were there did he spend all day swearing about his need for more people?"

"Yeah," Melchor says.

"Well, he still does," Blai says.

Just before reaching the Hotel Piqué they turn right. Melchor's phone rings once more: Vivales again. Melchor does not answer this time either and, when they are about to arrive at Elisa Climent's house, Blai goes back on the offensive and asks, in a tone of offended incredulity, if he really isn't going to lend him a hand. Melchor is not surprised: he worked under Blai's orders long enough to be sure that, if the inspector is still there, it's because he trusts in his powers of blackmail or persuasion, because he hasn't given up yet. They have stopped under the awning of a grocer's shop.

"It's the last favour I'll ever ask of you," Blai insists, and his voice sounds too strident in the Saturday silence of the sweltering, empty streets. "The last. Just think it could be your last real case as well, if you're serious about this library thing. Come to Barcelona with Cosette for a few days on assignment, and then you can come back here and stay with your old folks and children."

Melchor thinks Blai is not talking nonsense, that he's not asking him for something impossible. In his friend's eyes there is a gleam of supplication.

"Don't you even want to know what it's about?"

"What's it about?"

As soon as he asks the question, he knows he has made a mistake, but it's too late to take it back, or perhaps he doesn't want to. Nor can he, because Blai hurries to tell him:

"Someone's blackmailing the mayor of Barcelona."

It's a little after six when the two of them collect Cosette from Elisa Climent's house. Blai walks back with them as far as the centre: his car is parked near the plaza, next to the Town Hall. They say goodbye to him there, and, when they get home, Cosette starts watching a film on television; meanwhile Melchor makes dinner. While they eat they watch the end of the film, which is about a group of children who start a rock and roll band with the teacher of their rural school, triumph in the music business, get disappointed by it, fight among themselves, make up and go back to their village, where the teacher is waiting for them, still there, teaching their former classmates.

When the film ends, Melchor and Cosette take their plates into the kitchen.

Melchor washes up while his daughter changes into her nightie and gets into bed. Once he finishes tidying up the kitchen, Melchor lies down next to Cosette and, as he does every night, reads to her for a while. For the last few days they've been reading *Michel Strogoff*, by Jules Verne, and they've reached the part where the Czar's courier – who is travelling to Irkutsk under the false identity of a merchant called Nicholas Korpanoff, with the mission of warning the governor, the Czar's brother, of ex-colonel Ivan Ogareff's treachery – meets his mother in Omsk, his hometown, after having met Nadia Fedor and fallen in love with her. The story has Cosette completely absorbed, but, when they finish the chapter, she admits:

"There's one thing I don't understand, Papá."

"What's that?"

"If it's so dangerous to go to Irkutsk and warn the Czar's brother, why is Michel doing it?"

"Because it's his duty: the Czar has ordered him to."

"I know that. I'm not stupid. But it's a very dangerous mission. The Tartars could catch him, and if they do they'll kill him. Why doesn't he run away with Nadia and his mother and marry Nadia?"

"Because he can't."

"Why can't he?"

"Because. Everyone has to do what he has to do. And Michel is courier to the Czar and he has to get that message to the Czar's brother."

"Yes, but why does it have to be Michel who takes it to him? Why can't someone else do it?"

"I told you: because the Czar has ordered him to."

"And why has he ordered him?"

Melchor thinks, trying not to get impatient. It's not the first conversation like this they've had. Before he had a daughter, he had heard that children ask uncomfortable questions, but only when he had her did he discover that those were the best questions and the hardest to answer. After a few seconds he ventures a reply.

"Because Michel is the best courier he has."

"You think Michel is the Czar's best courier?"

"Of course. If not, why would he have assigned him the mission?"

Cosette thinks for a while, as if she feels her father's argument is weak; in any case, she doesn't seem entirely convinced. Melchor tries to continue reading, but he stops himself. He notices his daughter's body next to his, warm and familiar, and sees the profile of her tanned little face against the white wall. Cosette turns towards Melchor and looks at him with her big brown eyes.

"Maybe nobody wanted to do it," she says.

"Take the message?"

The girl nods.

"That could be," her father agrees. "And if Michel doesn't take the message, nobody will. And, if nobody takes it, the bad guys win. And you don't want the bad guys to win, do you?"

Cosette shakes her head back and forth with scandalised emphasis. After a few seconds she takes up the interrogation again:

"Is that why you became a policeman? So the bad guys wouldn't win?"

Caught off guard again, Melchor remembers Javert, the inflexible policeman who inflexibly pursued Jean Valjean all through *Les Misérables*, and he also remembers that Victor Hugo's novel awoke in him when he first read it, still a boy locked up in Quatre Camins, a furious desire to join the police, to find his mother's murderers. He also remembers a long-ago swim in the summer dawn off the Barceloneta, after a Terra Alta-born Mexican tycoon had revealed, over the course of an endless night, the reasons why, with the help of Albert Ferrer and Salom, he had ordered the murder of Francisco Adell; and he remembers feeling Javert's ghost dissolve in the chilly waters of the Mediterranean, as if it had been the ghost of the father he never knew. Now his daughter's question forces him to wonder if Javert has really disappeared for him, if that illusory father really no longer exists, if this afternoon he was being sincere with Blai when he told him that vocation was a tall story and he no longer felt like a police officer.

"More or less," Melchor answers.

Cosette has stopped looking at him. Now she's staring into space.

"And what if the bad guys catch you one day?" she asks.

"They're not going to catch me," Melchor says. And he takes Cosette's hand, an assembly of little bones wrapped in velvet skin. "Besides, in a little while I won't be a policeman anymore, and I'll work in a library."

"Like Mamá?"

"Exactly."

"But if you stop being a policeman, the bad guys might win." She pauses and then adds: "Don't you care if they win?"

"Of course I care. But they won't win: there are other good police officers. Blai, for example."

"I know," Cosette says, turning back towards him. "But you're the best."

His daughter observes him with an almost adult gravity.

"Come on," Melchor says. "Don't be a toady."

Cosette takes a second before she laughs; then she asks her father to read another chapter of *Michel Strogoff*. Melchor agrees, and when he gets to the end announces that the reading is done for tonight. Cosette asks him for something else: that he stay by her side while she falls asleep. Melchor gives way again and turns off the light. Almost dark, with only the faint light from the hall seeping into the room, they lie side by side, holding hands, listening in silence to the sounds that come from town. Cosette still has her eyes open when Melchor asks her in a whisper if she'd like to spend a few days in Barcelona.

"At Vivales' house?" she murmurs.

"If he'll have us . . ."

"Cool."

It is the last word the child speaks that night. Melchor doesn't want to get her hopes up in vain, so tries to warn her that it's not for sure yet, but his daughter has already begun to slide into sleep and he realises she hasn't heard his warning or she heard it wrapped in an indecipherable fog, and most likely has taken the possibility and turned it into a fact.

When he's sure Cosette is asleep, Melchor gently lets go of her hand, stands up without making the mattress creak and, pulling her bedroom door half-closed behind him, goes to the dining room. For a while he tries to read on the sofa – *The Illustrious House of Ramires* by Eça de Queirós – but he can barely concentrate, and finally he phones Vivales, who does not answer. A minute later, the lawyer phones him back with his usual question, in his gravelly, tobacco-ravaged voice: "Everything under control?"

Melchor answers yes. He hears the deep, syncopated din of a nightclub in the background.

"Where are you?" he asks in turn.

"Here," Vivales says. "Having a drink. Wait a moment." Melchor waits a few seconds. "There we go." The noise has stopped: it's obvious that, wherever he might be, Vivales has gone outside. "How're things? I've been calling you all day."

"Yeah, I know."

"Is Cosette there with you? Put her on the phone, come on."

"She's asleep. Do you know what time it is?"

There's no answer.

"Vivales?" Melchor says.

"Wait one more moment, please."

Indistinctly he hears something that initially sounds like a civilised dialogue, then a heated argument and finally a drunken row, all culminating in a sort of human barking.

"Sorry, Melchor," Vivales comes back on the line. "What were you saying?"

"What's going on?" Melchor asks.

"Nothing," Vivales says grudgingly. "The owner of this dive, who's a bit of a snob, keeps coming and going telling me I can't take my glass outside. I'm not kidding. I've threatened to sue him. Barcelona is getting unbearable, kid: as filthy as Naples and as puritanical as Geneva. The worst of both worlds. What were we talking about?"

"Nothing," Melchor says. "But I was thinking about something. What do you think about Cosette and me spending a few days at your place?"

"You don't even have to ask, man. When are you coming?"

"It's not for sure yet. And it won't be for long."

"As long as you want. My mouth hurts from telling you my house is your house so many times. Besides, with the excuse of having you two here I could take a few days off: I've been up to my balls in work."

"Don't do it for us."

"It's not for you. I'll do it for me."

"Thanks. Tell me something else. Do you know anyone at City Hall?"

"At City Hall? Who do you take me for, kid? I only deal with honourable people, and it's easier to find a fucking virgin than an honourable man at City Hall."

"I don't mean politicians, Vivales. Well, not only. I'm interested in civil servants as well, people who work for the institution . . ."

"Oh, well then. There are a lot of thieves and a lot of scoundrels, but there's also my friend Manel Puig."

"Puig?"

"The guy you gave a black eye to when he was guarding my door that time you came to pick up Cosette, when the Adell case was finished. Do you remember him?"

"Of course I remember. You're the one who doesn't remember. We saw each other not long ago at your place, with the other guy . . . What's his name?"

"Chicho Campà."

"That's it. Though I didn't know Puig worked at City Hall."

"He doesn't work there. But he's an architect, and sometimes his studio does projects for them."

"And does he know the mayor?"

"I have no idea. Why don't you ask him? Do you want me to arrange a dinner to celebrate your visit to Barcelona?"

"That would be perfect. And tell Campà to come too."

"Don't worry. Those two go everywhere together, like Ortega y Gasset."

"Who?"

"Nothing. So, when do I expect you?"

"Soon. Maybe we'll be there by tomorrow evening. I'll call you as soon as I know."

"Fuck, what great news, kiddo. I'm going to knock back a huge shot to celebrate right now. So long."

2

"All three of them are sons of wealthy families. Sons of bitches as well, of course, but mainly posh brats. They were born like that and they'll die like that . . . Rich people are another species. Have you never heard that? Well, it's the truth. I'm telling you. The world is divided into two types of people: the rich and the rest, including those who aspire to be rich, who are the majority. Here you have a perfect example: I was one of them.

"My father said that Catalonia has always been under the control of a handful of families. They ruled before Franco, they ruled during Francoism, they ruled after Franco and they'll rule when you and I are both dead and buried . . . Money is magic, immortal and transcendent. Money is the best. It's much stronger than power, because power depends on it, and it also survives everything, starting with changes of power. Well, so my three friends belonged to that handful of Catalan families. That's why I tried so hard to be their friend. And that's why I disgust myself . . . Sure you don't want a drop of whisky?"

"I'm sure. Go on."

"I'll go on . . . Though, thinking it over, I don't know if I should. I don't really know why I'm doing this. I don't know what I'm going to get out of this . . ."

"Sure you do. We've made a deal."

"You're really going to help me?"

"I already told you I will. I told you I'll do what I can."

"What do you want to know about them? Where should we start?"

"I told you that too: start at the beginning. When did you meet them?"

"When did I meet them . . . ? Many years ago, at Esade, the business school where the Catalan elite send their kids to learn how to make money. And how to keep it . . . The three of them all knew each other before, of course, had known each other their whole lives, because the handful of families who run Catalonia all know each other. Casas and Vidal lived near each other, on avenida Pearson. Rosell also lived in Pedralbes, I can't remember exactly where, I didn't go to his house much, a lot less than the other two . . . Anyway, the three of them had gone to the same places since they were kids, the Barcelona Tennis Club, which was near where they lived, or Cerdanya, which was where they went for Christmas and summer holidays. They were the same age, born in the same year, the same as me, and they'd been students at Aula, another school for elites. And all three of them had lots of brothers and sisters; I, however, am an only child . . . None of the three was a great student, that's true, but Casas and Vidal read a lot and were intelligent, even very intelligent, which is not something you could ever say of Rosell, who ended up in politics because his family thinks he's too slow for business."

"Vidal is a politician too."

"Yes, but he didn't go into politics because he had no other choice, like Rosell. He got into politics because he wanted to,

47

because he understood straight away that politics is an extension of business . . . That's how these people have always understood politics. Although they wouldn't say as much."

"And Casas?"

"Casas is different . . . If the question is whether he is also involved in politics, the answer is yes. But he's involved in his own way because Casas has always thought it preferable to practise politics without getting his hands dirty . . . In the shadows . . . Through someone else."

"You mean the mayor?"

"Until he separated from her, yes."

"Is that what you deduce or did he tell you?"

"He told me. The last time we saw each other, in a restaurant called the Santa Clara, not long after he and the mayor had split up."

"Casas told me that you two hadn't seen each other since university."

"Well, he lied to you. I'll tell you about that lunch later, you'll be interested . . . That day Casas told me something that stuck with me. He told me, in today's world, what distinguishes you, what gives you power, isn't being in the media, but rather not being in the media, and so the people who really run things should never be seen out anywhere . . . 'I have to stay in a discreet position, in the shadows, in the background,' he told me. 'Let the poor wretches who can't choose be the ones on television and in the papers, and get scorched by the spotlights. We, meanwhile, will do our thing . . .' Smart bastard, isn't he?"

"Maybe . . . But tell me, what were you doing at Esade?"

"What do you think I was doing? The same as them: learning how business operates, how to pile up cash, how to get rich."

"But you weren't rich."

"Precisely: I told you before that I aspired to be rich, so I had to learn how to be. And my father also wanted me to be rich. He, especially . . . Well, you know how parents are . . . Have you got kids?"

"One daughter."

"What's her name?"

"Cosette."

"Cosette? Your wife's French?"

"No. Let's get back on track. You were telling me about your father, although I don't see how your father has much to do with—"

"He has everything to do with it."

"Go on, then."

"He died a few years ago, maybe if he hadn't died . . . My father and I had a special relationship, or maybe not so special, the thing is we always loved each other, he wanted me to be rich and have the best, live the life he hadn't been able to, what all parents want, I suppose, but I think he wanted it more, he wanted me to become part of the Catalan elite, which was beyond his reach, that handful of families he hated and admired at the same time . . . That's why he did everything possible to convince me to enrol at Esade, and that's why I let him convince me. And also because I was a good student, I hadn't gone to Aula but Salle Bonanova – it's not an elite school but it is a good school, my teachers and classmates expected the best of me, everybody expected the best of me, and here I am, hidden away like a maggot in this corner of the world . . . I'm glad my father didn't live to see this."

"You were saying that he's important to this story."

"And it's true . . . My father wanted my life to be better than his, as I said, but in the end it hasn't turned out that way, in the end his life was better than mine. Much better . . . Or at least it was for years. Then . . .

49

"He was a special man, my father . . . In the United States they would have said he was a self-made man, that thing Americans admire so much and seems so ridiculous and mendacious to us, right? So fake and so tacky . . . He was poor, that is true, I mean he was born into a poor family. Really poor . . . As a boy he emigrated to Catalonia with my grandparents, who didn't have a pot to piss in in Albacete, and at the end of the dictatorship and the beginning of the Transition, he was involved in the workers' struggles in Hospitalet. That was the best time of his life, he always said . . . And I believe him. He was still young then, and there was the romanticism of underground activism, forbidden gatherings in smoke-filled basements, running away from the fascist police, all the clichés of the era, which turn out to be true, because my father lived them. Later, when he met my mother, and I was born, he got into union politics and held positions in the UGT, increasingly important positions, until in the 1990s he was a member of the Catalan parliament. Diputado for the Socialist Party . . . He was there for eight years, two legislatures, and he became very well known as a scourge of corruption. That's how he dug his own grave.

"What's so bad about being known as a scourge of corruption, you'll be wondering. Nothing, in theory, but in practice . . . Look, that was a time when nobody talked about corruption in Catalonia. All the journalists, the whole political and economic world, knew the autonomous government was up to its neck in shit, but nobody or almost nobody said anything . . . My father's mistake was daring to say it. That turned him into a controversial person with a righteous reputation, with many supporters and many detractors. And many enemies. And that also caused him many problems . . . For a start, with his own party, in part because they couldn't see his strategy clearly and thought he was a sort of kamikaze, and in part because they were afraid that his denunciations would end up tainting them as well ... The fact of the matter was that, by the time I started studying at Esade, the Catalan Socialists had got rid of him, they kicked him upstairs and sent him to Madrid. That was probably why he was so obsessed with me learning how to earn money and ingratiate myself with the elite. Because he had just discovered that money isn't a form of power. It *is* power. And because he'd also discovered that without money you can only be a slave ... But I'm getting off track, aren't I?"

"Yes. You still haven't told me how you met your friends."

"If you mean how I started talking to them and stuff, how we became friends, the truth is I don't remember exactly ... What I do remember is that, when classes began at Esade, they caught my attention. Mine and everyone's ... I didn't know who they were at first, of course, didn't know that they were part of the famous handful of families my father spoke about, but I noticed them because they went everywhere together, because they sometimes skipped classes and, most of all, because they were always laughing, as if they were making fun of everyone or as if they smoked marijuana non-stop. And I also noticed them because the atmosphere at Esade was so formal, so conscientious, and those three dressed any old way, sort of like hippy rockers: they wore their hair long, baggy clothes, trainers, things like that ... And all that stood out on a course where there were a lot of sons of provincial businessmen, quiet, responsible kids who slept in the school's residences or in rented flats in Sant Cugat ... And, now that I think of it, that was probably precisely what brought us together there, my three friends and me: that all four of us were a bit out of place, that neither they nor I fitted in with our classmates, even though they didn't fit in from above and I didn't fit in from below, they had too much and I had too little. I don't know if I'm making sense . . ."

"Perfect sense."

"So I must have approached those three bit by bit, because I was quite shy and not very good at making friends. Also, none of the three seemed that interested in what their classmates did or didn't do, the truth is they didn't have much to do with us, it was as if they were blinkered or as if they didn't need us . . . One day I told my father they were on my course. I think I expected him to be pleased or impressed, but he seemed neither impressed nor pleased, he just spoke to me, in quite a cold, quite a neutral way, of their families, of the fortunes and privileges and wangles and barbarities and fiddles of their families. And in the end he said something that stuck in my head: 'Surround yourself with good people and you'll become one of them,' . . . I don't know where he got it, don't know if he made it up or had read it somewhere, but I interpreted it as his way of encouraging me to make friends with my new classmates, although now I'm not so sure, maybe there was a warning there or sarcasm that I missed at the time . . . Another thing that's stuck with me is the first time the four of us went out together . . . Shall I tell you?"

"Sure."

"It was also the first time I went inside Vidal's house. We had a project to do together for a class called Applied Mathematics for Management, and we arranged to meet to finish it. It was a Saturday evening, I remember very well because the assignment was due on the Monday, but especially because of what happened at the end, that I'll never forget, it was like my baptism of fire, or whatever, and also when I realised what kind of people they were . . . Although I also remember it because during those hours I had the impression several times of having entered a different dimension, a dimension I hadn't even known existed . . .

"Anyway that Saturday I showed up in the early evening at his house, a three-storey villa surrounded by a wrought-iron fence covered in ivy. Through the gate I could see a garden that looked unkempt, but later I learned that it was an English garden . . . I rang the bell, the gate opened, I walked up a path and ran into a man wearing a uniform and white gloves who I thought must be the butler, but who was actually Vidal's father's chauffeur. I asked for my classmate and the man gave me some directions. A little intimidated, I crossed a large vestibule, climbed two sets of stairs, walked down a hall and, when I was already lost, a pair of twelve- or thirteen-year-old twins appeared. They were Vidal's little sisters . . . I asked them where their brother was and they answered giggling: 'Tito? He's in his room.' And they pointed me towards the last door down another corridor.

"I knocked on the door, but nobody answered . . . I knocked again with the same result, and, when I was about to go back the way I came, the next door opened and Vidal's grandfather appeared, an old man in a dressing gown and slippers, dragging his feet. The old man didn't even look at me, so I called after him and asked after his grandson, though I didn't know he was his grandson then . . . I had to ask him two or three times before he pointed at the door I'd been knocking on. I thought he was encouraging me to go on in, so I walked in without knocking and there was Vidal, sitting on his bed, cross-legged and with headphones on. He didn't take them off when he saw me, but gestured that I should wait until the song he was listening to ended.

"I waited . . . Vidal was moving on the bed to the rhythm of the music, which was coming from a spectacular stereo system;

I had never seen anything like it outside of a nightclub or a music venue, and I looked around at the adolescent lion's den, a bedroom illuminated by a window that looked out on part of the back garden with a pergola and a little pine forest, a very large square, with very high ceilings, showing all the signs of solid, ancient wealth, even though disguised, or as if they didn't matter, or precisely because of that, the magic and immortality of money stands out even more if you try to hide it, authentically rich people never flaunt their wealth . . . As soon as the song ended, Vidal took off his headphones, jumped off the bed, apologised and told me the title of the song and the name of the group – I'd never heard of either. For a while we talked about music, which for Vidal meant talking about rock, and I tried to appear less ignorant than I actually was, without much success . . . Then Vidal asked: 'Well, shall we get to work?'

"Vidal was good at maths and had a good grasp of the basics, there's nothing like an elite school for solid foundations. So, even though he'd missed several classes, he wasn't that far behind and we finished the project sooner than we expected. Then I said I was going . . . Vidal asked me: 'Are you in a hurry? Are you meeting someone?' I told him the truth: that I wasn't meeting anyone and had no specific plans for that Saturday. And I hoped with all my soul that he would answer the way he did: 'Then, why don't you stay?'

"We spent the rest of the evening listening to music and talking, though we were only alone for a little while before Rosell showed up. Then Casas . . . Neither of the two seemed surprised to see me, so I thought Vidal had told them, that both of them had come over to his house knowing I would be there. I still think so . . . What I mean is that I don't believe it was a coincidence, but that they planned it. That it was something like an ambush: the three of them chose me to do what they needed done, thinking I was the ideal companion or helper for them, the perfect person, I'm sure it was blatantly obvious how much I wanted to be their friend and that I was ready to do whatever it took. And then keep quiet about it.

"If that is really what they thought, they were right. And how . . .

"Around nine or nine-thirty, when we left Vidal's house, all three of them insisted I come with them to get something to eat. We went to Jumilla, on calle Artesa de Segre, near paseo de la Bonanova . . . I especially remember three things about that first dinner . . . The first is how good I felt with them, because they were who they were or who their fathers were, but most of all because I was an insecure kid, a bundle of nerves, and those three guys my age acted as if they had absolute confidence in themselves, as if they could do whatever they wanted or as if they were the lords and owners of Barcelona, so at their sides my insecurity and nervousness seemed to evaporate. The second thing I remember is that I got confirmation of something I had intuited at first sight, something anyone would have guessed no matter how little they noticed them, and that is that Casas and Vidal were the two top dogs of the trio, not only the smartest but the ones who ruled the roost, that night I also discovered that they challenged each other non-stop and got a crazy amount of enjoyment competing against each other, as if they had to demonstrate all the time who was the funniest, the most ingenious, the cockiest and the one who knew the most, while Rosell was just an extra, the spectator that any artistic duo needs to turn their spectacle into a spectacle . . . And the third thing I remember is what most surprised me, and it's that at a certain moment they started talking about politics . . . I was surprised they did and surprised by the way they talked. I was surprised that they did because in those days people my age were not political, especially Esade students, who seemed interested only in making money. And how they talked surprised me because, well, I had heard my father and his friends and other people in the Socialist Party talk a lot about politics, but I'd never heard anyone talk politics like that, the way those three did, which must have been how they'd always heard it talked about, I suppose, how they must've talked about it in their families."

"How?"

"I don't know . . . With a contemptuous irony. With an icy passion. Something like that . . . As if political struggles interested them but had nothing to do with them. As if politics provoked the same kind of curiosity an aristocrat might feel for his servants or a predator for his victims . . . Anyway, at some point, while Casas and Vidal were talking politics, I told them who my father was. It was inevitable, I guess, and the news brought me into the centre of the conversation for a few minutes. They knew who my father was, of course, at the time everyone in Catalonia knew who my father was because his name was always in the newspapers, but it had never occurred to them that he might be related to me . . . They asked me about him, about his corruption reports, his move to Madrid, about everything, and when they got tired of asking and we finished dinner we went to Up&Down, that nightclub on Diagonal . . ."

"The posh one."

"It had that reputation till they closed it . . . I had heard a lot about it, but I'd never stepped inside. For my friends, I noticed immediately, being there was like being at home, better than being at home, because at Up&Down they didn't have to give explanations to their families . . . I, however, felt like a fish out of water, and after a while decided to leave. And I was just about to go when Casas appeared beside me, grabbed me by the arm and asked me where I was going. 'Home,' I said. He laughed. He'd had a lot to drink, but Casas didn't need to drink to laugh at anything, I think I told you already . . . He said: 'Don't go. It's still early.' I told him it wasn't that early and I had to get going. Casas insisted I stay. 'Don't be silly,' he said, charmingly: when he wants to be, I assure you, Casas can be charming . . . And then he added: 'Stay. The good bit's about to begin.'

"I thought it was just an expression, but his insistence must have flattered me, must have made me feel important, because I stayed. I soon discovered it wasn't just an expression . . . a short time later we left Up&Down, got in the car and drove out of Barcelona in the direction of the airport. I asked where we were going and they told me not to worry, that I'd soon see. I wasn't worried but intrigued, actually I didn't mind continuing the night, just the opposite, but I didn't say anything . . . Half an hour later we arrived in Viladecans, pulled into an industrial estate and parked in sight of a packed crowd in front of an enormous warehouse with a big sign on the door that said: SOUVENIR. It was another nightclub, actually a nightclub and an after hours club, maybe you've heard of that one too, it was very famous in its day . . .

"We went in after standing in line for a while. The place was so packed that I soon lost sight of my friends. I figured they wouldn't leave without me and wouldn't leave me stuck out in that godforsaken place in the early hours, so I didn't bother looking for them, but went to the bar, ordered a beer and turned to watch the hysterical swarm on the dance floor, which was roiling with people dancing in that darkness bombarded with streams of light in every colour . . . I don't know how long I spent there on my own, but after a while Vidal showed up, ordered a beer and stayed there at my side. We shouted into each other's ear every once in a while, the only way to make ourselves understood in all that noise . . . Then Casas and Rosell arrived. There was a girl with them. I remember her very well: she was short, dark-haired, probably South American, with a nice body, quite good-looking. They didn't tell me her name, but Vidal ordered a cocktail for her at the bar. While they were getting it, Casas and the girl were kissing and Vidal slipped a crushed tablet of Rohypnol into her drink . . . I know that now, of course, at the time I only noticed that Vidal held the glass for longer than normal, maybe that he did something weird to it. When Casas and the girl stopped kissing, Vidal handed the cocktail to the girl, who was smiling and seemed very happy to be with us, and, when she finished drinking the cocktail, Casas took her back out on the dance floor, Vidal and Rosell followed them and the four of them were dancing for a while, but this time I made sure not to lose sight of them and kept an eye on them from a distance . . . Until, after a while, not much later, they came back to the bar with the girl and signalled to me that it was time to leave.

"We got back in the car. Vidal was driving, as he had been before, but now I was in the front seat with him; the girl was in the back, huddled between Casas and Rosell . . . I spied on them every now and then in the rear-view mirror, and once I thought I saw that, as well as kissing Casas, the girl was kissing Rosell, or Rosell was forcing her to kiss him, though I immediately thought I was mistaken . . . We drove back into Barcelona and, as we were heading uptown, I asked Vidal to drop me near a metro station. He didn't answer, he seemed to be concentrating on the song that was playing in the car, and I took advantage of a pause in the music to ask where we were going. He answered to finish off the night. He said: 'You'll like it. You'll see.' Or something like that . . .

"The place we ended up at was an old building that belonged to the Casas family. It was on León XIII, a street parallel to Tibidabo, very close to the ronda de Dalt ring road, and nobody used it except for those three, though I only found that out later . . . We parked in a weed-choked garden, and the first thing I noticed when we got out of the car was that the girl was zigzagging as she walked. We went up a set of stairs, entered that ramshackle house, some parts of which looked like an old factory with lots of big spaces and others like a hastily abandoned palace, and walked through several rooms almost in the dark: some practically empty, others full of old furniture and junk . . . Until finally we came to a room that gave the impression of being occupied, or at least somewhat lived in, or at least once in a while. It was relatively small, with no windows, but with two lamps that shone with a creamy light. The floor was covered in mats, cushions and mattresses, and the walls were papered with posters of rock bands and movie stars . . . The girl flopped down on a mattress, or they pushed her, she was laughing and mumbling incomprehensible phrases and I noticed she spoke with a Latin American accent (Colombian or Peruvian or Ecuadorian). Vidal and Rosell fell down with her, and Casas took me by the arm again and asked me to come with him.

"I followed him down a hallway to an even smaller room, that looked like it might have been a pantry or maybe a servant's bedroom; in there was nothing but a tripod and a video camera focused on the back wall. The paint was peeling off the walls and there were damp stains, a bare bulb hung from the ceiling and the stale air smelled of a mixture of dust and mould . . . Casas pointed at the camera and said: 'We're going to make a film. We are the actors and you are the director, well, the director and the cameraman. What do you reckon?' Since

I didn't know what to say, I smiled. I probably thought he was joking . . . 'A film?' I asked. 'That's right,' he said. 'Couldn't be easier. All you have to do is record everything you see.' The camera's viewfinder was pressed up against a hole they'd made in the wall, and Casas walked over to it and showed me how it worked. When he finished his explanation, he said: 'Simple, right?' I said yes and asked what was going to happen on the other side of the wall, what was it I was going to film. 'It's a surprise,' he answered. 'You film it and forget about the rest.' That's what I did. I didn't ask for further explanations. I didn't ask any more questions . . . That's what they had expected, I have no doubt about it now. The three of them must have thought I would be too delighted to be in their company and enter into their magic world of money and power to refuse to do anything they asked of me . . . And they were right, of course. That's the effect money has on many people: it makes them servile. Casas, Vidal and Rosell had known that since they were born, knew it without anyone having to teach them, and I'm sure that's why they invited me to go out with them that night. Because they had read on my face that I was one of those people. And they knew they could use me . . .

"The fact is I stayed alone in that room and did exactly what they told me . . . I'm not going to tell you what I filmed because I'm sure you can imagine. They did everything to that poor girl. At first, I thought she was aware of what was going on and tried to persuade myself that she accepted it, even that she was enjoying it, but it was difficult to hold on to that illusion for very long and, when it was all over, I had no option but to face the fact that I had just witnessed a full-blown rape . . . And I hadn't lifted a finger to stop it.

"I didn't protest . . . I just pretended that what had happened had not happened. We left the girl in one of the alleys off paseo de la Bonanova . . . She was awake and crying . . . I said goodbye to my friends at the Reina Elisenda metro stop. Dawn was breaking, and before I got home I threw up . . . 'Surround yourself with good people and you'll become one of them,' I might have thought while I vomited. But throwing up was enough to deal with.

"That night changed everything. From then on the trio of friends turned into a quartet, or that's what it seemed like over the two and a half years that followed . . . Or that's what I wanted to believe . . . Naturally, now I know it was false and deep down they never considered me a friend. Why would they, when they're a different species? But it doesn't matter . . . As I say, from then on things were different, and we became inseparable. My father knew it right away. I don't know if he was happy or not, but I've always thought that must have been the best stage of his life: him in parliament in Madrid, at the centre of political power, and his son at Esade, hobnobbing daily with the Catalan elite, with the sons of that handful of families who are in charge here . . . What more could a Ramírez from Albacete hope for, having arrived not long before in Hospitalet with nothing in his hands but his nuts?"

"You were saying you became inseparable from your friends. What does that mean?"

"That we came and went to Esade together. That I tried to blend in with them, talk like them, even laugh like them . . . The only thing I didn't do like them was shirk my studies. I continued to be a good student, never skipped classes, which was handy for them, because I'd lend them my notes, explain what they didn't understand, get the books they needed, and discuss or research or ask questions for them. In exchange we went out together almost every Saturday night."

"In exchange?"

"I already told you, I suppose I felt that the payment for doing everything I did for them was to be their friend, hang out with them on Saturday nights and stuff . . . It's disgusting but that's how it was."

"And did you do the same thing as the first time?"

"On Saturdays? Pretty much . . . We'd meet up at Casas' or Vidal's house, go for dinner at Jumilla or Bar Bero or Flash-Flash, spend some time at Up&Down and in the early hours we'd head out to the nightclubs or bars on the outskirts. Or in the old part of the city."

"Did you always finish off the night by picking up a girl and taking her to the place on León XIII?"

"Not always."

"What did it depend on?"

"What we felt like . . . And the girls that let themselves be picked up, of course. As you can imagine, it wasn't always as easy as it was the first night."

"Did you participate in the pursuit? Directly, I mean."

"If the opportunity presented itself."

"And in the rapes?"

"We called them orgies."

"You're the one who used that word."

"Because that's what they were."

"Did you participate in the rapes?"

"Sometimes."

"And that disgusted you . . ."

"Yes. But one gets used to anything, even what disgusts you. That's the truth."

"Who did the filming?"

"Most of the time, me . . . Actually, almost always."

"And the girls?"

"What about the girls?"

"Were they aware of what was happening?"

"That we were filming them? Of course not."

"That you were raping them?"

"Not always. On that first night . . . That one, after taking the Rohypnol, she didn't know much of anything. She probably didn't know anything about it, at least until it was too late. That was the usual way, though there were all sorts . . . Some did know, and sometimes even started to enjoy it, but, when they put up a fight, scratched and bit, then things got rough . . . Sometimes, really rough . . . Others resisted from the start. And there were also those who, as soon as they realised what they'd got themselves into, let it happen or even tried to make us think they were enjoying it, because they sensed that resistance was dangerous and that way we wouldn't hurt them . . . The majority were poor girls, workers, chambermaids, waitresses, things like that, young and not so young, mostly immigrants, girls who went out dancing on a Saturday night and were spellbound by us, to them we must have seemed like knights in shining armour about to rescue them from their miserable lives . . . Or something along those lines."

"There's one thing I don't understand."

"What's that?"

"None of them reported you?"

"How would they report us . . . ? Didn't I just tell you that half of them, more than half, didn't know we were raping them?"

"And the other half?"

"They were too scared to report us. Some of them we threatened before letting them go, but with most of them we didn't even have to, they had noticed on their own how we used them, that if they reported us it would be them who got into trouble . . . I've already told you about my friends' mindset:

they were the lords and masters of Barcelona, they could do whatever they felt like, they were untouchable. That's what they thought, and they were right . . . The proof is that not a single one of those women reported us."

"Tell me something else: did you film all the rapes?"

"Almost all of them. If not, it took the fun out of it . . . At least, part of the fun."

"And what did you do with the recordings?"

"We kept them there, in the place on León XIII. And every once in a while, when we had time and we felt like it, we watched them. Normally, in La Pleta de Bolvir."

"La Pleta de Bolvir?"

"The poshest place in Cerdanya. Vidal's family has a little house up there, in the mountains. Or they had . . . It's not far from here, near Puigcerdà, for years it had been Vidal's father's bachelor pad. That's what Vidal told us. In any case, his father had stopped using it, or maybe he'd handed it over to his son, the fact was it was free and we used to go up there once in a while, some weekends . . . It was kind of like a cabin, though it was full of luxuries, among them a big screen on which we could watch our videos. Sometimes we'd spend whole nights watching them. Up there . . . In the middle of nowhere . . . The four of us alone . . . Surrounded by snow . . . Crazy, eh?"

"And one of those videos was of the mayor?"

"Of course."

3

Melchor shows his ID at the security gate and, once the barrier is raised and he's driven through, parks his car, gets out and walks towards the glass and steel facade of the vast complex that houses the general headquarters of the Mossos d'Esquadra.

It's Monday. Two days earlier, in Gandesa's empty streets, Blai had told him that Commissioner Vinebre, the new chief of the force, had called that very morning to tell him that the mayor of Barcelona was being threatened with the disclosure of a sexually explicit video recording and that, if she did not want it disclosed, she should pay 300,000 euros. Blai suspected that the news came from the justice minister of the autonomous government, who, as was public knowledge, had a good relationship with the mayor, even though they were members of rival parties. That detail, however, was incidental. The essential fact was that Vinebre had put Blai in charge of the case and had urged him to solve it as soon as he could and with maximum discretion. Blai had also told Melchor that he was going to assign the case to the Abduction and Extortion Unit, and he wanted the head of the unit, Sergeant Vàzquez, to handle it personally; but he had insisted that he didn't entirely trust the sergeant. "You know him," he said. "He goes his own way. Also, right now he's very busy with the kidnapping of a drug trafficker's wife, in Santa Coloma de Gramenet. A case that, between you and me, is not looking good." That's why he'd turned to Melchor, Blai told him: so he could shadow Vàzquez closely, make sure he takes the matter seriously, and keep Blai informed. Furthermore, he had insisted that the case was fundamental, that he couldn't trust anyone at Egara and he needed him. Melchor had not said yes immediately; but Blai figured that his reply would be affirmative as soon as he promised to think it over, and that he would tell him the next morning.

He wasn't wrong.

Two colleagues from the Central Narcotics Unit, whom he'd worked with years before, when he was stationed at Egara, say hi to Melchor as he crosses the courtyard that separates the four buildings of the complex, joined by enclosed footbridges and separated by green spaces. They ask if he's back working at headquarters and Melchor says no, he's just come back on assignment and he won't be around for long. Then he goes up to Blai's office, which is next to the Central Abduction and Extortion Unit; beside the door, a sign says HEAD OF THE CENTRAL JURISDICTION OF PERSONAL INVESTIGATION. The door is ajar; Melchor pushes it: sitting at the desk in his office, Blai is talking on the telephone.

"Speak of the devil," he announces and points Melchor towards a table with a number of chairs around it. "Don't worry, Commissioner, he'll be right there. Anything else I can do for you?"

While Blai is still on the phone, Melchor stands in the middle of the office. It is much more spacious than the one Blai had in Terra Alta, and is just as Melchor remembers it: two big tables – one, his desk, the other for meetings – the metal filing cabinets, the anodyne paintings hanging on the walls and the big window overlooking the interior courtyard of the complex, through which summer light floods in; the only detail Blai appears to have added to that interchangeable décor is a photograph of him and his wife and their four children, all smiling and dressed in hiking gear, with an unmistakeable rocky Terra Alta landscape in the background.

Melchor stands looking at the family photograph while Blai keeps talking on the phone.

"News travels fast here in Egara," the inspector says after he hangs up. "Do you know who that was?" He stands up and walks over to Melchor. "Commissioner Fuster."

After the Islamist attacks in Barcelona and Cambrils in August 2017, with Melchor under threat due to his role in that incident, Fuster was the commissioner who took charge of his security. It was Fuster who had suggested he lie low for a time in Terra Alta and who, since then, had periodically taken an interest in his situation. By this point however, it has been a long time since the two men have spoken, in spite of the fact that in recent years certain politicians and media outlets have been constantly on the alert about the new outbreak of radical Islamism in Catalonia.

"Is he still in Information?" Melchor asks.

"He's put down roots there," says Blai. "He heard you'd arrived. I don't know who told him, not me, obviously. Go see him when we're through here: he wants to talk to you." He takes Melchor by the shoulders. "Have I thanked you for coming?" Before he can answer, Blai adds: "And, by the way, where have you left Cosette?"

"With Vivales," Melchor says. "We're staying at his place. We drove up last night. Vivales has already found her a summer camp at a community centre. She starts tomorrow."

"Great." He sits down at the meeting table. "You'll see: this will be like a holiday for her. And for you too. So much time in Terra Alta . . . it's nothing but rocky ground, for fuck's sake. Besides, I bet we'll wrap this matter up in two ticks."

"You're scaring me, Blai," Melchor hears behind him. "What is it we're going to wrap up in two ticks?"

He has recognised Sergeant Vàzquez's voice and, when he turns round, the head of Abduction and Extortion cannot hide his surprise.

"Well, well, well," says Vàzquez. "What on earth is the hero of Cambrils doing here?"

The sergeant sets his motorcycle helmet down on the table and the two men hug. As he feels Vàzquez's rock-hard muscles against his body, Melchor relives the image of the sergeant sitting in a pool of blood on the floor of the warehouse in Molins de Rei screaming like a lunatic, with the decapitated head of the Venezuelan drug trafficker's daughter in his lap, his clothes covered in blood and his eyes popping out of their sockets. When he steps back from the sergeant, Melchor realises that Blai lied to him on Saturday, and that he hasn't told Vàzquez of Melchor's temporary redeployment. Blai must be reading his mind, because he hurries to explain to the recent arrival:

"Melchor has come to give us a hand."

"Hallelujah!" Vàzquez exclaims, putting his backpack down on the table as well. Physically at least, he has barely changed in those four years: he still has his ferocious bulldog look and the same shaved head; his sporty attire hasn't changed either: frayed jeans, blue T-shirt, trainers. "We can sure use it: I've got a hell of a mess on my hands and I don't have half the men I need." Turning to Melchor, he says: "You've been missing the rock and roll, you bastard? Like I always say, what we do's addictive. When do you start?"

"Right now," Blai answers for him. "But he's not staying long. He's here on assignment."

Vàzquez looks jumpily from one to the other, until Blai says: "Sit down, please."

All three of them sit. The sergeant arranges his two mobile phones on the table in front of him, parallel to each other, and the inspector sums up the situation: the mayor of Barcelona is currently the victim of "sextortion"; she is being threatened with the release of a compromising video; the blackmailers are demanding 300,000 euros in exchange for not broadcasting the images; Commissioner Vinebre has put him in charge of the case. Vàzquez listens attentively to Blai, now and then sneaking looks at his phones, which do not stop vibrating, though he doesn't respond, just checks to see who's calling or texting. Melchor notices the sergeant's lower lip is trembling, and that his expression turns bitter now and then. When Blai finishes speaking, Vàzquez mutters:

"What a drag." He shakes his head back and forth. "When politicians are involved, it's always bad news."

Blai nods. "I know."

"Those people are full of shit," Vàzquez says. "And they lie through their teeth."

"Precisely why we have to look after the case," Blai says, backing himself up. "That's what the chief must've thought. And he wasn't wrong. This can't be handled from a station."

"I don't see why not," the sergeant replies. "And, if it can't, the Vidal Boys should handle it."

"Who are the Vidal Boys?" Melchor asks.

"Don't tell me news of the Vidal Boys hasn't reached Terra Alta!" Vàzquez sounds surprised, or pretends to be surprised. "You don't know how easy you've got it, man! I'm thinking you should run the fuck straight back there."

"The Vidal Boys are the praetorian guard that has been set up at City Hall with people from the Guardia Urbana," Blai explains, displaying a didactic spirit Melchor doesn't remember having noticed before. "They've been installed by the deputy mayor, Enric Vidal. That's why they're known as the Vidal Boys. They report only to Vidal and do whatever he commands, including some pretty shady things."

"Pretty shady?" Vàzquez smiles sarcastically. "Very dark things! Pure trash." He turns back towards Melchor. "Those people are the sewer rats of City Hall, kid. Everyone knows it, but no-one dares to get in their way. What a gang."

"Vidal has put together the worst of the worst." Blai sighs. "In any case, a matter like this is not one they should be handling."

"Yeah right," says the sergeant. "As if the Vidal Boys only handle what they should."

"Most likely it will have to go to court," Blai insists on arguing. "And they are not judicial police."

Vàzquez emits a sort of sardonic rasp.

"As if they cared," he objects. "In any case, I don't see why Vinebre had to put you in charge of it, or why you have to put me in charge of it. Because she's the mayor? I don't care if she's the Dalai Lama. I have much more urgent things to do, as you know better than anybody. Have you told Melchor? Have you told him about the wife of the crook from Santa Coloma? That could blow up in our faces at any moment, and I don't plan on letting it." Out of breath, with an angry vein throbbing in his neck, Vàzquez stands up, taking his helmet and backpack. "That's what's what, boss. If the mayor let herself be filmed shagging some lad who now wants to bleed her dry, then she's screwed. She should have been more careful, for fuck's sake."

Blai turns to Melchor as the sergeant throws the backpack

over his shoulder. His expression clearly says: *You see?* Or maybe: *I warned you.*

"Vàzquez," Blai says softly.

Vàzquez turns expectantly.

"In one hour we have a meeting at City Hall," Blai informs him gently, looking at his watch. "The three of us are going to see the mayor: you, me and Melchor. I will go because the chief asked me to. To reassure her, to let her see we are taking her problem seriously. Because we are going to take it seriously. The proof is that you are going to take charge of the case. Personally. You don't have to stop working on everything else, but you are going to be the main negotiator; Melchor will be your backup. I want us to solve this as soon as possible. And keep me informed by the minute." Finally, he looks up at the sergeant and adds: "Is that clear?"

"Damn it all to hell," Vàzquez curses in the hall, opening the door to the Abduction and Extortion office. "Dropping that shit on me, with what I've already got piled up on my plate . . . At the very least he could have made you the lead investigator."

"I'll do it if you want," Melchor offers, admiring how much Blai's command skills have improved since he's been working at Egara.

"No," Vàzquez says immediately, not yet all the way in the office. "You've been away too long. I'll do it, at least to start off. Later I might pass it to you, so long as Blai doesn't find out." Melchor motions vaguely towards the other end of the hallway and starts walking that way. Taken aback, the sergeant asks: "Where are you going? Aren't you starting now?"

"Commissioner Fuster called. He wants to talk to me."

The sergeant seems surprised.

"Are they still on about Cambrils?"

"I don't know." Melchor shrugs. "I'll tell you later."

Fuster's office is on the top floor of the building, very close to that of the force's chief, and Melchor barely has to wait to see the commissioner. He receives him with a cheerful handshake that doesn't seem feigned.

"Tell me, Marín, when did you get here?"

"I got to Barcelona yesterday. To Egara, half an hour ago."

"I heard you're here on assignment."

"That's right."

"Did Blai call you in?"

Melchor says yes.

"Have a seat, please."

They don't sit at his desk, but on a leather sofa. When Melchor first met him at the end of the summer of 2017, in that same office, Fuster was a young commissioner recently promoted to the highest rank; now he's a veteran, longer-serving than almost all his colleagues, including the head of the force. His physical appearance, however, has hardly changed: he has neither gained nor lost weight, still has that stiff, curly red, close-cropped hair, which he hardly needs to comb; the years have not dimmed his cordiality or dynamism either. Now, seeing him cross his legs in front of him, it suddenly occurs to Melchor that Fuster has summoned him to talk about the blackmailing of the mayor.

He hasn't. In fact, the commissioner does not even ask the reason for his presence at headquarters, and launches straight into the speech that, with slight variations, he inflicts on him every time they see each other: he assures Melchor that he is still a vital symbol for the force, reminds him that he is there for whatever he might need, repeats that he shouldn't let his guard down.

"How much time has passed since the attacks?" Fuster wonders out loud, stroking his goatee. "Eight, nine years? It doesn't matter. Many people in the corps know about you and what you did, and, if your face were made public, the next day your photo would be on all the jihadist websites and you would become a target. Why am I saying target: you'd become a trophy. It's true that right now there is no reason to think you're in danger, but you can be sure the jihadists haven't forgotten you."

"I thought the Islamist risk was higher now than it was five or six years ago."

A disbelieving sneer creases the commissioner's face.

"That's what some politicians are saying."

"The mayor of Barcelona," Melchor points out, "for example."

"For example."

"And it's not true?"

"Not as far as we know. As a matter of fact, never in recent years has there been less immigration to Catalonia from Muslim countries. And never have we had fewer signs of Islamist activity. And what we do have is under surveillance."

"So then?"

The commissioner blinks several times and his facial expression changes again, although, this time, rather than disbelieving, he appears indifferent.

"Political stuff," he says. But he hurries to add: "Which does not mean a lone wolf might not show up and all hell could break loose . . . Besides, Barcelona is not Terra Alta. There still aren't very many Muslims out there, here there are a lot. That's why I wanted to talk to you as soon as I heard you were coming back. Do you want us to assign you protection? Do you want us to protect your daughter?"

"You just told me there's no danger."

"Don't put words in my mouth," the commissioner says. "What I said was that the danger is the lowest it's been since 2017. Not that there isn't any. I also said that Barcelona is not Terra Alta and that we cannot guarantee your safety. That's what I said. What do you say, should we give you protection or not?"

Melchor thinks for a moment. He tells himself that what Fuster has just explained is not in fact very different from what he explained a few years back, when he returned to Barcelona fleeing Terra Alta or Olga's ghost in Terra Alta, and that there is no reason to give him a different answer.

"It's not necessary," he says.

The commissioner nods in acquiescence and, leaning his hands on his knees, stands up.

"As you wish." They shake hands. "I thought you'd say that. But, while you're in Barcelona at least, do me a favour: be careful."

Melchor is barely out of the door when he hears at his back:

"By the way, Marín."

He turns around. Fuster is still standing beside his desk, but now his features reveal vexation or embarrassment, as if he's striving to select the words he must say next.

"You'll have heard about the novel by now, no?" he finally says.

Melchor is slow to answer.

"Novel? What novel?"

"The one about you." For a couple of long moments, the two policemen remain silent. "*Even the Darkest Night*, it's called. The author's name is Javier Cercas."

Although Melchor had heard of a novel with that title, he hadn't read it – Melchor does not read contemporary fiction

– and he doesn't entirely understand. The commissioner tries to explain, but his explanation is confusing, and Melchor only manages to discern, overwhelmed by the feeling that he has lived through this instant before, or that he has dreamed it, that he has turned into the protagonist of a novel called *Even the Darkest Night*.

"My wife read it," Fuster says, perhaps because he doesn't know what else to say. "She says it's not bad."

Melchor says he knows nothing about it, and the two men go back to looking at each other in silence both perplexed, neither knowing what to say, until, eyebrows raised and with a wan smile playing on his lips, the commissioner dismisses him:

"Anyway, like I said. Be careful."

The office of the Central Abduction and Extortion Unit has not changed much since he last worked there either, except for the people who, caught up in the habitual hectic atmosphere, hammer away at computer keyboards, listen in to tapped telephones, search the internet, study documents, make phone calls or talk to each other. It's a big rectangular room at the back of which Vàzquez's glass-walled office is hidden, with his desk, computer, metal filing cabinets; the space is illuminated by an oblong window, the walls covered in tree diagrams and photographs of criminals and suspects. At that moment four men and one woman, three of them wearing headsets, are sitting at their computers. Vàzquez comes out of his cubbyhole to meet Melchor while calling for everyone's attention, and they all stop whatever they were doing. Five pairs of eyes lock onto both men.

"This guy is called Melchor Marín," the sergeant announces into the sudden silence, pointing to the recent arrival with his thumb. "You'll have heard of him. He worked here a few years ago. How many?"

"Two and a bit," Melchor calculates out loud.

"Two and a bit," Vàzquez says. "He's come back to give us a hand, which we really need. He's good; a pain in the ass, but good. Don't trust him though: he comes from Terra Alta, same as Blai. That lot are worse than the Corleones."

There are smiles, nods of approval, murmurs, and, while Vàzquez goes back to his den, the five come over to welcome Melchor; one after the other they introduce themselves: Roig, Cortabarría, González, Torrent, Estellés. Then Melchor goes into Vàzquez's office and takes a seat.

"I'm going to fill you in."

Without further ado, the sergeant starts to outline the cases the unit has on their hands. The main one, he warns him off the bat, is a settling of scores over drugs they've been bogged down in for weeks: the kidnapping of the wife of a cocaine trafficker originally from Saudi Arabia, who lives in Santa Coloma de Gramenet; as well as being the main case, it's the one that worries him most and the one on which most of the unit's energy has been concentrated, among other reasons because, after being in contact with the kidnappers for some time, he feels the negotiation is about to change course. Vàzquez also offers details of other ongoing investigations, including several cases of extortion, and tells Melchor about tapped telephones, stakeouts, suspects being followed and a handful of agents from other units, who he has under his command at that moment, collaborating with his unit.

"That's more or less what we've got," Vàzquez concludes, after almost three-quarters of an hour. "If you want more details, that's up to you. Anyway, for the moment, you better stay on the mayor's case, which is why you're here, right?"

Melchor doesn't answer, and Vàzquez lets a half-smile escape. "And speaking of our lady mayor." He looks at the time on one of his phones and, banging his hand on the arm of his chair, stands up. "Let's go. Blai must be waiting for us."

It turns out they have to wait for Blai. When he finally arrives at the garage, the three of them get into a Seat León and head towards Barcelona. Blai drives, Vàzquez sits beside him, with Melchor in the back. Blai has just come out of a meeting with other area chiefs of the Criminal Investigations Division. He tells them that the chief inspector had brought up the personnel problems at a departmental meeting and the boss had promised that at the beginning of autumn the vacant positions would be filled, three of which were attached to Abduction and Extortion.

"Let's hope it's true," Vàzquez grumbles. "When I returned to Egara you promised me—"

"I never promised you anything," Blai cuts him off.

"The commissioner promised me—" Vàzquez says.

"I'm not the commissioner," Blai says. "I don't know why you always have to be complaining so much."

"Because I fucking feel like it."

Without any embarrassment, as if the sergeant's rude remarks were water off a duck's back, Blai informs Melchor that the chief inspector restructured the Criminal Investigation Department a few months ago and that, as a result, he now has under his direct command, in addition to Vàzquez's unit, another five: Missing Persons, Computer Crimes, Homicide, Sexual Crimes and Juvenile Gangs. Then he asks Vàzquez how things are progressing with the kidnapping of the Santa Coloma trafficker's wife.

"Like shit," the sergeant replies.

Vàzquez explains to his immediate superior what minutes

earlier he had been telling Melchor in his office: that they are almost certain that, even though the person who ordered the kidnapping was Saudi Arabian – probably a relative of the kidnapped woman – all or almost all those who are guarding the victim are Romanians. Blai asks why they are so sure of that; Vàzquez explains: he tells him of a telephone conversation they caught by chance and about a WhatsApp group, tells him about accents, allusions and spelling mistakes. Then he assures him that the Arab is a tough negotiator.

"A real son of a bitch," he claims. "The Romanians are different."

"Different?"

"More flexible," Vàzquez says. "I reckon they only want the money, to get rid of the package and clear off as soon as possible."

"Divide and rule," Blai says. "In other words: forget about the Arab and negotiate with the other guys."

"And what do you think we're doing?" Vàzquez asks. "We're attacking that flank, trying to soften up the Romanians. They're the weakest link in the chain. As soon as we catch them, we'll go after the real bad guy. That's the idea."

"Sounds like a first-rate plan."

"And it would be, if I had the people to carry it out. But, since I don't, because half of them are out there working on bullshit, it's a shitty plan."

"I imagine that you'd include the blackmailing of the mayor among that bullshit."

"What do you think?"

Traffic on the Meridiana is moving, but gets clogged up when they turn towards the city centre on calle Aragón. Only when they turn towards the sea on Pau Claris do they start moving freely again. Finally, near plaza de Sant Jaume which is being renovated, they leave the car in an underground car park: scaffolding completely covers the facade of the Generalitat palace, where a team of construction workers has been carrying out restoration work for months. At the main entrance to the old City Hall building, they have to show their ID, state their destination and pass through a security check.

"This we should have skipped," Vàzquez grumbles. "If anyone sets eyes on us, we're fucked."

As they walk up through the old carriage courtyard to the Gothic balcony by way of a solemn stone staircase, Blai nods in agreement with the sergeant, but explains that the mayor has only granted them a few minutes there. The sergeant huffs again.

"Fucking great."

A secretary announces that the mayor will see them shortly and leads them to a room. When the woman leaves, Blai and Vàzquez sit down on the sofa and start typing on their mobile phones. Melchor remains on his feet. It is a majestic room with crystal chandeliers and lamps with cream-coloured shades, and windows that do not allow a single sunbeam through; the floor is parquet, and the walls and ceiling, adorned with gilded mouldings, display large frescos of biblical scenes in which shiny blues and reds dominate. In the centre, on a scarlet rug, there is a small wooden table, two imitation leather armchairs and two sofas, one of which the sergeant and inspector are occupying. Melchor looks at the fresco above their heads. It is in the shape of a medallion and shows a woman naked from the waist up, sitting on a fluffy cloud, with a tiny brigantine on her lap. Around her are other women, as well as cupids and seagulls. Crouched down in one corner of the fresco, almost hidden behind some rocks, a man who resembles a satyr blows on a horn, surrounded by other men; he seems to be heralding the imminent assault of the half-naked woman. The image brings to Melchor's mind the blackmailing of the mayor; a second later, the murder of his mother. Immediately, anguish catches in his throat.

At that moment the door opens and the mayor walks in. Blai and Vàzquez stand up and shake her hand; Melchor also greets her.

"Thank you for coming," the woman says, occupying one of the armchairs and leaving a manila envelope and a grey leather briefcase with black handles on the table. Blai and Vàzquez sit back down; Melchor sits opposite them. "I'm in a bit of a hurry, so I can't stay long. In any case, there's not much to say."

Without wasting a second, the mayor picks up the manila envelope and hands it to the inspector, who, before touching it, puts on a pair of rubber gloves. While Blai takes a piece of paper out of the envelope and reads it, Melchor concentrates on overcoming his anguish and on observing the mayor. She is about forty years old, tall, solidly built, with green eyes and fine, sharp features, and Melchor feels having her near just what he feels every time he sees her on television: that she is one of those women you have to look at with care to discover their beauty. Although he also feels something a bit contradictory to that, and it is that this uneasy and restless woman, who fiddles non-stop with her recently manicured fingers, does not seem to have much in common with the politician brimming with self-assurance who, at least since she took office, has largely monopolised the Catalan media (and who, judging by the electoral results she reaps, successfully hides her natural haughtiness behind a tireless deployment of smiles). Her lips and fingernails are red, and she wears a close-fitting dark grey jacket, a white blouse and an elegant pair of high-heeled grey shoes.

When Blai looks up from the paper, the mayor picks up the

briefcase and, before the inspector can get a word out, hands it to him.

"Here's the money," she says. "Pay these people and let them leave me in peace."

Blai does not touch the briefcase.

"When did you receive this?" he asks, waving the piece of paper.

The mayor seems not to understand. The inspector repeats the question.

"Friday," she says.

"Where did you receive it?"

"Here. At City Hall."

"Did it come in this envelope?"

"Yes."

"Who has touched it?"

"I don't know. Me. My secretary. I don't think anyone else has. Why do you ask?"

Blai brandishes the paper again, this time close to its envelope.

"The next time you receive anything like this, don't take so long to get in touch with us," he answers. "Better yet: call us straight away."

"There won't be a next time," the mayor says. She stops fidgeting, holds the briefcase out to the inspector and adds: "I want you to pay up and put a stop to this matter as soon as you can."

The inspector stares at her without taking the briefcase. After a moment of surprise, the woman turns to Vàzquez and then to Melchor, searching the eyes of each of them for the explanation she is not finding in Blai's. The anguish begins to loosen its grip on Melchor's throat as he tries to concentrate on what he is hearing.

"It seems you have not understood your situation, Señora Oliver," Blai says: he places the envelope and the piece of paper on the table and takes off the gloves. "If you pay the money they're asking for, they will most likely ask for more. And more still if you pay them again. In fact, you've already paid once, haven't you?" The mayor does not answer; she has stopped offering the briefcase to the inspector and is listening to him with guarded attention. "Look," Blai goes on, "right now you have no guarantee the blackmailers have what they say they have, or if they're going to give it to you if you pay, or that they won't keep blackmailing you until doomsday. So the best idea is not to pay."

"So what do I do, then?" the mayor asks.

"Leave it in our hands," the inspector says. "Do what we tell you. Trust us." Without looking at him, he points to Vàzquez, who, at his side, is holding the piece of paper in gloved hands with all five senses concentrated on reading it. "This is the first time something like this has happened to you, but the sergeant deals with cases like yours on a daily basis. Let us do our work, listen to us, trust us. Don't worry and everything will be fine."

Now the mayor is the one staring at Blai: obviously she is weighing up his words. For his part, Vàzquez has handed the blackmailer's message to Melchor, who has also put on gloves. It is a sheet of A4 paper folded in half; in the top half of which, hand-written in minuscule black capitals, with a ballpoint pen, he reads:

YOU SAW IN GAVA WHAT HAPPENS WHEN YOU PLAY THE FOOL. DO NOT DO THAT AGAIN. IF YOU DO NOT WANT EVERYONE TO SEE THE VIDEO, PAY US THREE HUNDRED THOUSAND EUROS

IN MONEROS. HERE IS THE ACCOUNT NUMBER
WHERE YOU SHOULD DEPOSIT IT:

4GdoN7NCTi8a5gZug7PrwZNKjvHFmKeV11L6pNJP
gj5QNEHsN6eeX3DaAQFwZ1ufD4LYZKArktt113W7
QjWvQ7CWGQvrZnnmQ5ZHduiH.

WHEN WE RECEIVE THE MONEY WE WILL RETURN
THE FILM. AND ALL'S WELL THAT ENDS WELL. SO
LONG AS YOU DON'T DO SOMETHING FOOLISH
AGAIN. AND DO NOT TALK TO ANYONE. START-
ING WITH THE POLICE. YOU HAVE BEEN WARNED.

"And what happens if it doesn't work out?" the mayor asks.
"What if they carry out their threat?"

"They won't," Blai says. "They don't want to broadcast the
film. What they want is your money: that's why they've con-
tacted you. And you want the film, so they will leave you alone.
So they have what you want and you have what they want.
Which means that you're obliged to come to an understanding.
That is, you're both obliged to negotiate. Is that clear?"

While he is gradually mastering the anguish he feels,
Melchor realises that, although Blai is explaining it clearly, the
mayor has not understood. Vàzquez is visibly suppressing his
impatience, keen to interrupt; on his thighs he balances his two
mobiles, which are constantly vibrating; his nostrils flare and
his jaw muscles look like they are about to explode. Taking
advantage of the mayor's uncertainty, Blai presses the point:

"Allow me to be frank. You already have your problem. The
problem is that you did what you did and let yourself be filmed
doing it. That we cannot fix. Not us, not anybody. What I mean
is that, whether or not you give in to the extortion, whether or

not you pay what they're asking, the blackmailers can make that film public at any time. Right now. While we're talking. The fuck-up, if you'll forgive the expression, has already happened. Now what you have to decide is whether or not you'll try to handle it with the people who know how to handle it. And the people who know how to handle it are us. Nobody else. We have resolved hundreds, thousands of cases like yours, we do it all the time, we're the best, we are one hundred per cent effective. I'm not bragging: it's simply a fact. But, if you want us to solve your problem, you have to listen to us, you have to trust us blindly. If you do, Sergeant Vàzquez will set up an investigation team to work on your problem, collect evidence, find out who the bad guys are, arrest them and make them pay for what they've done. Have no doubt. If you do what we say, we'll solve your problem; if not, it won't get solved: it will multiply. You choose."

A solid silence follows Blai's ultimatum. Still with the briefcase of money in her hand, the mayor seems to be trying to take on board what she has just heard, eyes fixed on the inspector and the line of her lips hardened by concentration. It is obvious that she is much calmer than when she came in. All of a sudden she looks away towards the door, as if expecting someone or as if someone just came in, but she soon looks back at Blai, sighs deeply and sets the briefcase down by the table leg.

"Alright," she concedes. "Tell me."

Blai has no need to hand over to Vàzquez, who leaves his two telephones on the table and, in a didactic tone, begins:

"For a start, the most important thing is that you do what the inspector has told you. Trust us. Us and nobody else. No-one must know that we're working on this matter, no-one must find out that we're advising you. That's the main thing. Do you know why?" The mayor listens without blinking or leaning back on the sofa. "Because secrecy is the most important thing in our toolbox. The fewer people who know what's happening to you, the better. So now, tell me: who does know what's happening to you?"

"No-one, as far as I know. Well, yes, Gabau, the justice minister. He's a friend of mine. He's the one who spoke to Commissioner Vinebre."

"Apart from those two?"

"Nobody."

"Are you sure?"

"Yes."

Vàzquez looks at the mayor for a second, then turns to his boss, as if asking for an explanation, and clicks his tongue in annoyance, meaning: *Off to a bad start.*

"It would be best if you told us the truth," the inspector intervenes. "If you lie to us, we won't be able to help you." He leaves a pause for the mayor to reflect and then continues. "Tell us: who else knows? What happened in Gavà? Why does the message say you played the fool? You've already paid them, right?"

Someone has just knocked on the door; without taking her eyes off Blai, the mayor gives them permission to enter. It is her secretary, who says people are waiting for her in her office. After a few seconds, during which there is no reaction from the mayor, she turns to her secretary and asks her if they can delay the meeting for a few minutes. The secretary says yes.

"I hired a detective agency," the mayor confesses, once her secretary has closed the door behind her. "It's called Sayen. I was told it's a good one."

"It's bad," Vàzquez says. "But there are worse."

"The thing is, it didn't go well," the mayor admits.

Blai asks what happened and the mayor tells them. A few weeks earlier, when she received the first message, without discussing it with anyone, she decided to go to a detective agency. She says that in the first message the blackmailers asked for three hundred thousand euros in exchange for not broadcasting the film, and that it should be paid in fifty-euro notes, which she should personally bring, on a particular day, at dusk, to a particular spot on the beach at Gavà, very close to the shore, where she would find a lunchbox in which the blackmailers would leave the video, once they received the money. She says that, following the private detectives' instructions, she did what they asked and, after leaving the money in the lunchbox she found on the beach, the detectives kept watch, waiting for the criminals to collect the money, to catch them in the act. She says the detectives lay in wait for hours, spent the whole night there and no-one showed up, and that, at dawn, when the sun lit up the beach, the lunchbox had disappeared.

"It was taken by a diver," Blai guesses. "The lunchbox was tied to a cord and the diver pulled the cord from under the water."

The mayor looks open-mouthed at the inspector.

"How do you know?" she asks.

"Because it's the oldest trick in the book," Vàzquez answers. "I'll tell you one thing: those muppets might've fallen for it, but we wouldn't."

"You see now why we're the ones you should trust?" Blai stresses.

"Four things," Vàzquez hastens to specify, holding up four energetic fingers. "Two we've already said. The first –" with his left hand he holds his little finger – "trust us and only us. The second –" he grabs his ring finger – "don't tell anyone anything. These two are the basics."

"What's the third?"

"Swallow your fear," Vàzquez replies, holding his middle finger. "Blackmail is based on intimidating the victim. The blackmailers want you to be afraid, want to pressure you and isolate you so you lose your nerve, so you get bewildered and can't think straight and end up doing what they want you to do. And don't tell me you're not scared." Vàzquez anticipates the mayor's objection: he hasn't let go of his finger, but he is no longer displaying it for emphasis. "Because we know you are. If you weren't, you wouldn't have turned to us. If you weren't, you wouldn't be brave, you would be reckless. And you're not reckless, are you?"

The mayor scrutinises Vàzquez while appearing to search for a reply, and Melchor guesses that the woman has just realised that the sergeant is more intelligent than she'd thought.

"Go on," she says.

"Swallow your fear," the sergeant repeats, holding on to his middle finger. "That's what you have to do. And when you get nervous, when you feel that fear is about to take over and you might do something stupid, call me. From now on I'll be your confessor, your confidant, your guardian angel." He points to Melchor and adds: "If you can't get hold of me, call my colleague. Take our numbers." The three of them exchange phone numbers. "Call me whenever you need to. Don't be shy: I'll be available twenty-four seven. Agreed?"

The mayor nods.

"What else?" she asks.

"One more thing," Vàzquez says. "The fourth and most important." He holds his index finger and stretches his lips into a shrewd smile. "We have to dance."

The mayor's face reflects total confusion.

"Dance?" she asks.

"The dance is the negotiation," the sergeant clarifies. "We have to dance. As the inspector said before: your blackmailers are obliged to come to an understanding with you, because they have something you are very interested in, and they know you are prepared to pay for what they have. Therefore, if it's true they want to collect, they'll have to do things to make it happen. And to do them they'll have to move. And when they move they'll make mistakes. And as they make mistakes they'll leave clues. And those clues will lead us to them, and we'll catch them. You can be sure of that."

"Of course, it might also be the case that the blackmailer backs off," Blai interrupts. "They might decide things are getting too complicated, or they might get scared and stop blackmailing you."

"Then what happens?" the mayor asks.

"Then it's over," Blai says. "Good riddance to bad rubbish. Unless you want us to pursue them. But, as far as we're concerned, it's over. We're not going to cause you problems just to catch the bad guys. We're here to fix problems, not create them."

"That's right," Vàzquez says. "Only I suspect these ones aren't the kind to flee. Not without at least getting something out of it. They're not amateurs. What happened in Gavà is not something amateurs do." Blai half-closes his eyes in a gesture of agreement. "So we'll have to dance. We will put pressure on the bad guy, and you will have to stand firm, so we can provoke him into a misstep. You have to be patient. If he doesn't move, we wait; he'll move eventually, he'll say something. This is a chess match, a long-distance race, whatever you want to call it. But in the end the bad guy will make a move and make a mistake. And then he'll fall. Don't have the slightest doubt about that. Because we are smarter than he is." After a pause, he composes a twisted smile and adds: "And, if we have to be, meaner. You understand, don't you?"

The mayor nods again, unsure at first, then unreservedly. Then she asks, as if making a statement, addressing the inspector:

"This is everything?"

It is Vàzquez who answers.

"No," he says. "This is just the start."

From that moment on the sergeant submits the mayor to a systematic interrogation, which Blai only interrupts every once in a while, in order to correct or clarify or qualify or amplify or stress some point. As for Melchor, he confines himself to doing what he has been doing all along: observing the woman with great care.

Vàzquez asks if she kept the first message from the black-mailers; the mayor says no, that she got rid of it immediately, fearful that someone might find it. Then Vàzquez explains that, for them, the messages from the blackmailer represent a precious source of information, and begs her to try to remember who has touched the second one; the mayor answers that, just as she'd told Blai at the beginning, only she and her secretary have. Vàzquez asks a few more questions about the messages and then redirects the interrogation towards the content of the video with which they are blackmailing her, which provokes the mayor to start fidgeting with her fingers again, wringing her hands and showing renewed signs of anxiety. At one point the sergeant asks how she knows that the film contains sexual images, and, after making him repeat the question, the mayor says because the blackmailers told her in the first message. Vàzquez asks if she has any idea what images the video might contain, to which the mayor replies no, and then he asks her why she is so afraid if she doesn't know what they are.

"Precisely because I don't know," the mayor answers. "If I

knew what they were, I might fear them or not. Since I don't know, I can only fear them."

Vàzquez acknowledges the flawless logic of the reasoning with a slight nod, and then asks the mayor if, before the attempt to blackmail her, she was aware of the existence of any such images of her, and if it were possible there might be others; the mayor answers no to the first question and that she doesn't know to the second. Then the sergeant tries a feint.

"You and your husband are separated, aren't you?"

Instead of flustering her, the question seems to restore some of the mayor's composure, and she answers yes.

"How long have you been separated?" the sergeant asks.

"Officially, a little over a year," she answers.

"What do you mean officially?"

"It means that for slightly more than a year we have not been functioning as a married couple."

"Do you have a partner now?"

"No."

Vàzquez shakes his head again. On the table, near the manila envelope, his two mobiles vibrate now and then as messages come in, but, focused on the interview, the sergeant has stopped paying attention to them: he doesn't even look to see who is texting or calling anymore. While Melchor and Blai exchange a furtive glance, Vàzquez asks the mayor if she thinks the images she is being blackmailed with are from her marriage or previous to it, and she answers that she already told him she doesn't know. Then the sergeant wants to know if, while she was married, she had any extramarital relationships. A little annoyed (or that's the impression Melchor gets), the mayor asks Blai if she has to answer that and, with a vaguely regretful gesture, the inspector gives her to understand that she should. The mayor reflects for a moment.

"None," she answers.

Considering her initial annoyance, Melchor has a feeling this moment of reflection (or doubt) might be eloquent.

"And before your marriage?" Vàzquez asks.

"What do you want to know about what happened before my marriage?"

"Whether you had a lot of relationships."

"Some. I married relatively late."

"Were they normal relationships. I mean . . ."

The sergeant does not finish his clarification, and Melchor feels that what has terminated his colleague's sentence is the smile playing on the mayor's lips.

"Are you asking me if I've slept with women?" she asks. "If I've participated in orgies? Is that what you're asking?"

Vàzquez's Adam's apple visibly rises and falls before he manages to answer yes. The mayor smiles openly: an ironic smile, almost mocking, but not aggressive.

"Look, Sergeant," she says in a different tone, which, rightly or wrongly, Melchor identifies with the one she uses in front of journalists' microphones. "I have made many mistakes in my life. Many. But I have learned from them. I have evolved. At the age of twenty I was one type of person; now I am another. At twenty I believed in some things and now I believe in others: back then I did not believe in marriage, and now I do believe in it; back then I did not believe in the importance of marital fidelity, and now I do believe in it; back then I didn't believe Christianity was important, and now I believe that it is, and very much so . . . As Keynes said: 'When the facts change, I change my mind. What do you do?'" After a pause, she goes on: "I have changed because the world has changed. People who always think the same way don't think. And I think a lot, so I've changed a lot. There is only one thing constant in me:

I am a free woman. I was when I was young and I still am now, when I'm not so young. Gregariousness is not my strong suit. Nor is political correctness. I think in my public life I have shown more than enough signs of that. As for the rest, let me say that, at your age, you should know by now that there's no such thing as normality. It's a scam. When it comes to sex or to anything else."

Another solid silence follows these words. The smile has disappeared from the mayor's face, replaced by an expression of self-satisfied dignity. The sergeant clears his throat.

"Shall I interpret from your answer—"

"Interpret what you like."

One of Vàzquez's two mobiles begins to buzz, and so does the other, almost immediately, but the sergeant does not even glance at them. He changes the subject. For a while he questions the mayor about how much money she has available, about her friends, about her two daughters and about her ex-husband, Daniel Casas, principal shareholder and proprietor of various companies, the best known of which is Clave Barcelona, a consultancy firm specialising in reputation enhancement, corporate communication and advising private companies in the technology sector. The interrogation is still not finished when the secretary appears again and announces that the postponed meeting is starting in five minutes and she can't push it back any further.

"I'll wrap up," Vàzquez promises once the secretary has left. "Look, we have two instruments to catch the criminals. The first is this." He picks up the message from the blackmailers and shows it to the mayor. "With your permission we'll keep it. We'll try to find out who the monero account belongs to and study the piece of paper for clues. We'll find something."

"And if you don't?"

"That's what the second instrument's for. The proof of possession."

The mayor wrinkles her brow.

"The bad guys need to show us they have what they say they have," Vàzquez explains. "I mean the video, of course. They have to show us that they have it and you have to ask them for it."

"And how do I ask for it?"

"Don't worry about that. If you're not in a hurry, if you have patience, they'll get in touch again. No doubt about it."

"Why are you so sure?"

"Because, if they don't, they won't get what they want."

"And how will they get in touch with me?"

Vàzquez shrugs.

"Ah, that we don't know yet," he admits. "All we know is that they will. And, when they do, we'll have more clues. And one of those clues will lead us to them. And we'll catch them. You can be sure of that."

The mayor's forehead has smoothed out again: the sergeant's words have got her back onside. Melchor and Blai exchange another furtive look. The mayor asks:

"What do I have to do when they get in touch with me?"

"Let us know immediately," Vàzquez replies.

"What if they phone me?"

"Then things change." The sergeant turns on the sofa. "Then the first thing you have to do is try not to get nervous. And, the second, tell him the following: 'Look, for years people have been threatening to publish sex tapes featuring me, there are tons of hoaxes like this going around, so how do I know this isn't just another one? How can I know you have that video? How do I know I can trust you? Give me some proof and I'll do what you say, because I'll know you're the person I have to negotiate with to sort this out.' Anyway, that or something along those lines, is what you have to say. In any case, something that forces him to make a move, to get in touch with you again and make the mistake that will allow us to catch him. Got it?"

The mayor does not answer straight away; she has her eyes fixed on the briefcase with the ransom money resting on the table beside the sergeant's mobiles.

"What I don't understand is how we are going to force them to contact me," she says, turning back to Vàzquez.

"We're not going to force them. If they don't want to, they won't, but they won't get another cent, and, as the inspector said before, good riddance to bad rubbish. But, if they do, if they do want to get in touch with you, and it is very likely that they will, we'll be waiting. There's no rush. Quite the contrary: we have all the time in the world, as the song goes. That's why I said you should arm yourself with patience. Patience, and trust in us. That is the key."

The mayor finally seems to agree, nods, adjusts the jacket of her suit by tugging on the lapels with both hands and looks in turn at all three policemen, as if making sure no-one has anything to add to what the sergeant has said. It is clear that she is no longer the apprehensive and uncertain woman who walked into the room three-quarters of an hour earlier.

"OK," she resolves, taking the briefcase with the money and standing up. "I'll follow your instructions to the letter."

She shakes hands with Vàzquez and Melchor by the door; when it comes to Blai's turn, he holds on to the mayor's hand and does what he usually does at the end of this type of interview: remind the victim of the essentials.

"Don't speak to anyone," he reiterates. "Don't get nervous. Call my men for anything you need. Most of all, call us if the blackmailers call you, if they contact you. Trust in us and everything will be fine."

The mayor again assures him she'll do as they advise, thanks them and opens the door to leave along with them; she hasn't opened it all the way when she closes it again.

"What happens if I don't pay and they release the video?" she asks, anxious again.

Melchor thinks the strange thing is not that the mayor should ask that question, but that she hadn't done so before. Again, it is Sergeant Vàzquez who answers.

"They won't," he assures her. "Because, if they do, they won't get what they want, which is your money. But, in the unlikely event they do go ahead, we can always counteract the publication of the video."

An expression of interest replaces the worry on her face, or a mixture of interest and surprise.

"You can? How?"

"Many ways," Vàzquez explains. "It depends how and when it's released and who releases it. If it's on the internet, for example, you can hire a company that erases content or that can send the video into Google hell so nobody ever sees it. If they release it on TV, we can send people to cast doubt on the veracity of the images, people who'll say the video is false or something like that. As I say, it depends."

"And you would do that?"

In reply, Vàzquez lets out a cheerless, dry guffaw.

"You think we're going to spend public funds on that?" he asks. "Are you kidding?"

The mayor is taken aback.

"What the sergeant means is that we can't do that sort of thing," Blai says, coming to the rescue. "We can only punish criminals and protect victims. Nothing more. And here the crime is extortion; the fact that they filmed you and could release the images as they please, that we can't prevent, that cannot be fixed, the fuck-up, as I said, has already happened. Although, of course, if necessary, we can advise you on the steps you need to take so the broadcast of those images damages you as little as possible. From then on it will all depend on you, that is, on your means. But don't worry," the inspector concludes, acting as if the misunderstanding were cleared up and indicating the exit from the room with a little bow. "None of that will be necessary. Do what we tell you and it will all be sorted out."

"You're such a loudmouth, Vàzquez," Blai scolds him. "You could have spared us the bit about whether or not the mayor was kidding."

"What you could have spared us is this entourage," Vàzquez replies, indicating the three of them with a caustic gesture. "She's not the bloody Queen of Sheba. And anyway, is she off her rocker? Did she really think we were going to go around cleaning up her fuck-ups with taxpayers' money?"

"She didn't ask for anything," Blai reminds him. "It was just a question."

"What do you mean, a question?" Vàzquez says. "A request in every sense of the word, that's what it was. And who was the Queen of fucking Sheba, anyway?"

Blai deflects this question with one of his own.

"How did the mayor seem to you, Melchor?"

They had left City Hall, crossed the plaza de Sant Jaume and walked down to the underground car park without saying a word to each other, while Blai argued over the phone with the chief of the Central Organised Crime Branch and Vàzquez typed WhatsApp messages at supersonic speed, and only started commenting on the interview with the mayor as they drove out into the perpendicular midday sunshine.

"Fine," Melchor answers. He sits up in the back seat, rests his arms on the front seats and, observing the traffic on all sides as they drive up vía Layetana, adds: "But she's lying."

"No fucking kidding," says Vàzquez. "Have you ever heard a politician tell the truth?"

"How do you know she's lying?" Blai asks, looking into his friend's eyes in the rear-view mirror.

"Because, as soon as Vàzquez started talking about the images on the video, she got more nervous than she already was. I also think she lied when she said she hadn't been unfaithful to her husband."

"Could be," Blai says. "In any case, I think she's a woman who can stand up to pressure. A woman with fortitude. That's what everyone says about her, isn't it?"

"All clichés are lies," Vàzquez proclaims.

"All clichés contain some truth," Blai counters. "Otherwise, they would never have become clichés."

"I'm not saying she won't stand up to pressure," Melchor chimes in. "I'm just saying that her nervousness spikes when she talks about the video. I think she's lying about that. And about the other thing as well."

"You think she knows who filmed her and when?"

"I think she knows more than she's told us."

"Now that you mention it," Vàzquez says, "I had the same impression."

"There's another thing I don't understand," Melchor says.

"Only one?" Vàzquez asks.

"If that woman is as free as she claims," Melchor says, "if she doesn't care about political correctness and all that, why is she so worried about a sex tape going public?"

The question hangs for a few seconds in the silence that reigns in the car, emphasised by the urban noise outside.

"Well, because she's not as free as she says she is," Vàzquez finally answers. "Don't you see? That woman is all affectation: as fake as a three-euro note."

"Or because she really does know who recorded the video and when and is sure that those images getting out would finish off her political career," Blai ventures. "Who knows. Whatever the case, you're right: it doesn't add up."

"I have a question," Vàzquez says.

"Fire away," Blai says.

"Are we going to tap her phone?"

Blai lifts one hand from the steering wheel and cuts the air with it.

"Forget it," he says. "No judge who would go for it, at least for the moment. And much less with the mayor involved."

When they get back to Egara, Vàzquez calls a meeting in Blai's office. All the Abduction and Extortion officers who are on duty attend: Torrent, González, Cortabarría and Estellés. Blai describes the case succinctly, and then gives the floor to Vàzquez, who, while listening to his superior, has put on a pair of gloves, taken the envelope with the blackmailers' message out of his backpack and placed it on the table, but he only has time to pronounce one formulaic phrase ("OK, guys, we're going to chip away at this") before one of his two mobiles vibrates again. As usual, he glances to see who is calling or texting; unusually, this time he grabs the phone and stands up.

"Fuck me, it's the Queen of Sheba," he says.

The meeting is paused while Vàzquez talks to the mayor, or rather answers her questions and tries to reassure her. All those around him listen in silence, trying to guess the contents of the conversation; as if to prevent that, Vàzquez paces up and down the office, from the door to the window and from the window to the door.

"She's shaking like a leaf," he tells them when he hangs up, with an irritated look on his face. "Much worse than when we left her."

"Understandable," says Blai. "As soon as you're on your own, it starts going round and round in your head. What did she tell you?"

"Nonsense. But it seemed like she'd overheard our conversation in the car." Vàzquez sits back down at the table. "She asked if we were going to tap her phone. Calm down: I told her not to worry. That we weren't going to tap it. That we didn't need to at the moment . . . And I'm a monkey's bollocks. It could work wonders for us."

"I told you to forget about it," Blai reminds him. "Right now, no judge is going to let us do any such thing. Unless she agrees to it, of course."

"To us tapping her phone?" Vàzquez replies. "No way. That's precisely why she called me: she's probably terrified at the possibility of us finding out about all her skulduggery. We really will have to forget it."

"Forgotten," says Blai. He gestures around him and reminds Vàzquez: "You were telling these people how we're going to have to chip away."

"There's no alternative," Vàzquez says regretfully. Still wearing the gloves, he takes the piece of paper out of the envelope and shows it to them. "This is the stone we have to chip away at, or the two stones: the envelope and the paper. González, I want forensics to study every millimetre: traces, prints, DNA, everything. Apart from the blackmailers, the only people who have touched the envelope are the mayor and her secretary, so this afternoon, Ricart, you head over to City Hall and take their prints and DNA. You go with him Cortabarría. Find out where the City Hall cameras are; if there are none over the letterbox, we'll have to put one there, in case they leave another message. And one at the mayor's house, in case they decide to send a message there. We also need to ask the City Hall people for all the footage their cameras recorded last Friday, when the mayor received the envelope. If necessary, ask for all the recordings around City Hall, from that day I mean, and you and Ricart go through them. See if anything strange shows up. And the main and most important thing." Vàzquez hands the blackmailer's message to a burly and slightly slovenly police officer, who hides his boyish face behind plastic-framed glasses and a thick beard; he's the only one who's been listening to his bosses standing up, leaning on a filing cabinet, and before taking the paper he puts on a pair of gloves. "The blackmailers want the mayor to pay in moneros, which suggests they're professionals. There's an account number where she's supposed to deposit three hundred thousand euros. Take it down, Torrent, and go to Financial Crimes and ask them to find out who the account belongs to as soon as possible. Melchor, you take charge of writing up the crime brief. Excel yourself, eh! Let the judge know you're back." Vàzquez elbows Melchor while winking at everyone else. "For those of you who don't know, our Terra Alta guy here is a bit literary, aren't you, Melchor?"

"What else?" asks Blai, who's not in the mood for jokes.

"That's it as far as I'm concerned," Vàzquez replies. As he takes his gloves off he says: "Any questions?"

"Has this got top priority?" asks an extremely muscular blond guy, with green eyes and a cleft lip: this is Cortabarría. "I mean we're already up to our necks in work and—"

"Tell me about it," Vàzquez cuts him off. "Top priority, absolutely not. Do what I've just told you, and, when it's done, we'll see if any clues have turned up or not. If they do, we'll follow them; if not, we'll wait for the criminals to show their hand, and see if we have more luck then. But, meanwhile, we stick to our guns, we're getting warm, very warm on the Santa Coloma kidnapping. This is just pissing about."

"This is not pissing about, Vàzquez," Blai corrects him curtly, turning to address the whole team: "We're talking about someone blackmailing the mayor of Barcelona, so it's not exactly a joke. I'm not saying drop everything you're doing to look after this. But pay it maximum attention, please. It's important that we resolve it as soon as possible." Blai pauses. He seems really irritated. "Have I made myself clear?"

Everybody nods, including Vàzquez, who does so reluctantly, and Blai wraps up the meeting ("Tomorrow morning I want to see results," he says). While the whole group leaves his office, Blai asks Melchor to stay, and he sits down at his desk.

"Vàzquez is a pain in the arse," he says when they're on their own, leaning back in his chair and rubbing his shaved head. "Now do you understand why I need you here?"

Standing in front of him, Melchor stares inexpressively. Blai leans forward slightly in his chair and starts to open his mouth, as if ready to begin an explanation; finally, however, he gives up.

"It doesn't matter, *españolazo*." He waves his hand as if swatting away a fly. "Don't let Vàzquez out of your sight and keep me informed. I'm counting on you."

Part Two

1

"Well," Sergeant Vàzquez says the next morning, putting his two mobiles on the desk and fixing his gaze on González, a lean thirty-something with tattoos all over his arms, "what have we found out on the mayor's case?"

It's ten o'clock and the full morning shift – González, Torrent, Ricart, Roig, Cortabarría plus Melchor – are meeting in Vàzquez's office. The square room has bare walls and the obsessive order of a monastic cell – there is not a single slip of paper out of place, no uncapped pen or unsharpened pencil in sight – as if it were occupied by an ascetic or a fanatic dedicated to his dogma; that is, in fact, the sergeant's reputation at Egara, where otherwise very little is known about his personal life. In fact, Melchor only knows that he has two teenage sons and that, after the crisis that broke up the unit two and a half years ago undid his psychic resistance and sent him home to Seu d'Urgell, he separated from his wife and now lives alone. Bright sunshine blazes through the window and floods the office.

"Nothing from us," González answers. "The forensics guys studied the blackmailers' message and found only the mayor's prints."

"And on the envelope?" the sergeant asks.

105

"There were two others there," Ricart says, pointing to the report he has in front of him. "But they belong to her secretary and the doorman."

"Nothing else," González insists. "No other prints, no traces of anything."

"We haven't had any luck either," says Cortabarría, before the sergeant asks. "There are no cameras overlooking the City Hall letterbox, or the mayor's house, but we've requested they be installed. I also requested the recordings from the City Hall cameras and others in the neighbourhood for the hours when the message must have been delivered, and split them with Ricart."

"There's nothing strange on them," the latter adds.

Vàzquez takes a deep breath and says "Torrent," who looks up from his notebook.

"The Financial Crimes people have found a couple of things," he says.

"Thank goodness." Vàzquez exhales. "Anything to sink our teeth into?"

Torrent nods.

"The alphanumeric code of the account where the black-mailers want the mayor to deposit the cash is attached to a SIM card with the number 696519382 and registered in the name of a Farooq Hoque," he says.

"Sounds Pakistani," Vàzquez guesses.

"Precisely," Torrent says.

"Have you got his address?" Vàzquez asks.

Torrent names a street in the Raval neighbourhood.

"I've also found out the IMEI code of his phone," he adds. "It was purchased at the MediaMarkt on Diagonal Mar."

"Great," Vàzquez says. "Anything else?"

"We haven't been able to identify the phone's IP address," Torrent says.

"Why not?" Vàzquez asks.

"Because it's been camouflaged with an app," Torrent says. "It's called Tor. They explained how it works. It's complicated, but if you want—"

"No need," Vàzquez cuts him off.

"They told me they could try to identify it again," Torrent says. "But the blackmailers would have to connect to the account again for that."

"In other words, if the mayor pays, we can catch them."

"If the mayor pays and they collect, we can try," Torrent qualifies. "It's not certain that we'll catch them. It looks like these guys are really good. Not amateurs at all. First class. That's what they're saying in Financial Crimes."

Vàzquez stares at Torrent with his bulldog jowls pulsating; it's clear, however, that he is no longer seeing his subordinate. There is silence. One of the sergeant's two mobiles starts to vibrate and he seems to come back to himself.

"OK," he says, flashing a look at the phone. "Let's start with a visit to our Pakistani friend. Melchor, your turn. Let's tug on this thread and see what happens. The rest of us will wait."

Melchor nods and, slapping the table, the sergeant ends the meeting. Torrent rips a page out of his notebook and hands it to Melchor. On it is the Pakistani man's name, phone number and address: Joaquín Costa 13, ground floor; there is also an IMEI number: 36 866906 620391 3.

As Melchor drives into Barcelona, his phone rings: it's Vivales.

"Everything under control?" he asks.

Melchor tells him yes. They talk about Cosette, who started attending a summer camp the previous day.

"That girl does not take after her father," Vivales says. "The first day she's already made friends. But that's not why I called. Puig and Campà can make it for supper this evening. How does that suit you?"

"Perfect."

"Then we'll meet at home at nine," Vivales decides. "Shall I pick up Cosette this afternoon?"

"If you can, I'd be grateful. I'll probably be in Barcelona, but—"

"Say no more. OK, I've got to go. I'm on my way into court."

"Didn't you say you were going to take some time off?"

"Starting Monday." Melchor hears the lawyer talking to someone else: "'I'll be right there.' OK, then, see you at nine."

He leaves the car in an underground car park beside the Library of Catalonia, walks along calle Hospital and turns right onto Joaquín Costa. The air is filled with the intense aromas of spices and, on either side of the street, there is a diverse confusion of shops run by Indians, Pakistanis, Arabs and Sub-Saharan Africans. It's been ages since Melchor set foot in Raval, the former red-light district in the heart of Barcelona. Actually, he'd never frequented it much, not even when, still an adolescent, he sold drugs for a Colombian cartel and sometimes found himself there supervising the dealers who worked that zone. Now he's shocked by the dirt, the noise and the overwhelming number of tourists, and he wonders if the neighbourhood has deteriorated in recent years or if all that surprises him because, after so many years in Terra Alta, he is no longer a city boy; he also thinks that, during his angry delinquent youth, he would have laughed if anyone had told him that one day he would return to that twisted labyrinth of narrow, ancient, foul-smelling streets as a cop.

The ground floor of number 13 Joaquín Costa is occupied by a grocer's shop. Beside the door, almost hidden behind the cash register, a smiling old lady with dark skin wearing a multi-coloured sari encourages him to come in with a sort of bow, but Melchor simply takes the notepaper out of his pocket and reads out loud the name Torrent has written there. The old lady turns towards the back of the shop and, in an even louder voice, pronounces a name vaguely similar to the one Melchor had given her. From one end of the shop springs a round and shaven head, whose owner exchanges a few incomprehensible words with the woman and, while Melchor receives a WhatsApp message, which he doesn't read, walks to the entrance with an expression of surprise. The boy, whose skin is as dark as the woman's, is wearing a green shirt, dark red trousers and flip-flops. Melchor asks him if his name is Farooq Hoque; the boy says yes, and then Melchor asks him if his mobile number is 696519382. The surprise on the boy's face turns into apprehension.

"Why do you want to know that?" he asks, in impeccable Spanish. "Who are you?"

Melchor identifies himself and looks at the old lady, who clasps her palms together, bows again and smiles. Melchor guesses that the woman has not understood a word and, holding his hand out to the boy, asks for his phone. The boy hands it over without any hesitation, as if the device were on fire.

"That's not my number," he says, however.

Melchor verifies the IMEI number of the phone: the boy is not lying.

"Someone's using your name," he explains, handing it back. "Have you ever lost this phone?"

Visibly relieved, the boy says no. Melchor then asks if he frequents any internet cafés, and the boy says he does and mentions a place down the street. Melchor thanks the boy, nods towards the old lady, who is still smiling with a beatific expression, and leaves.

Outside the shop, Melchor sees the WhatsApp that he's just received is from Rosa Adell. "Hello, I hear you're in Barcelona," it says. "I'm going there for work tomorrow. Shall we have dinner?" Melchor doesn't even stop to wonder how Rosa knows he's in Barcelona: he knows news travels fast in Terra Alta. "Sure," he replies. "What time and where?" Rosa's answer arrives as he finds the internet café. "At 9.30 at La Dama," it says. "Diagonal and Enric Granados. OK?" Melchor types back immediately: "OK."

The internet café is called Internet Begum and is very near the ronda de Sant Antoni. It is a long, narrow place with no windows, offering several telephone booths, four computers and a photocopier; only two of the booths are occupied at that moment; four people are sitting at the computers. Facing the entrance there is a counter, behind which a full-bearded Arab man, who looks like a mujahid, types on his mobile phone and raises his head when Melchor approaches.

"Do you do SIM cards?" Melchor asks.

"Of course," the man answers.

"I'd like to get one in someone else's name."

The mujahid stops typing, puts the phone down on the counter and observes the recent arrival with interest.

"I don't mind paying," Melchor says. "I've got money."

"It'll cost you three times what a normal card costs."

"Only triple?" Melchor changes his tone. "OK, beardie, tell me who got you to make a SIM card in the name of Farooq Hoque."

He takes out the paper Torrent gave him again and shows it to the man, who doesn't even look at it.

"Are you a cop?" he asks.

"What do you think?"

The mujahid picks his phone up again and pretends to be concentrating on it. At that moment a woman wearing a purple headscarf who has just left one of the phone booths walks up to the counter, holding a small child by the hand. Melchor moves aside for her and, while she is paying, walks around the internet café, at the back of which is a cubicle where, hunched over a computer and some papers, a big, old, bald albino man is so absorbed in his work he doesn't even notice him. When the woman finishes paying for her call and leaves, Melchor goes back to the entrance.

"Haven't you left yet?" the man says.

Melchor leans on the counter.

"Can I ask you something?"

The other man fixes his gaze on his phone and does not respond. Melchor asks gently:

"Nobody's ever kicked the shit out of you, have they?"

Visibly upset, the bearded man looks up from his phone. Melchor takes it and moves it to a corner of the counter, turning it off first.

"Look," he continues, in a conciliatory tone, "let's make a deal. You tell me who you made that SIM card for, and I won't shut down your business or throw you in jail. What do you reckon?"

The mujahid has not yet decided how to reply when Melchor hears a French-accented voice behind him.

"Is there a problem, Tammam?"

Melchor turns around to find the big, almost bald albino from the back office, and a second later, with a joyful shock, recognises, beneath his aged features, Gilles, alias Guille, alias the Frenchman, the successful businessman turned librarian of Quatre Camins prison, who, almost fifteen years earlier, while serving his sentence for the murder of his wife and her lover, had transformed Melchor into an unrepentant reader of novels and changed his life for ever.

"Oh là là!" the Frenchman exclaims. "I can't believe it: who do we have here?"

"Careful, Señor Feraud," the mujahid warns him. "He's a *poli*."

The Frenchman's browless eyes narrow until they're just two slits.

"A what?" he asks, incredulous.

The mujahid repeats what he's just said and, without taking his eyes off his former fellow inmate, the Frenchman bursts into thunderous laughter, baring his shark's teeth.

"Do you remember me?" he asks.

Melchor nods, and the two men stare at each other for another second to the bewilderment of the Arab. The Frenchman is wearing a loose, white sports shirt, which disguises his Buddha's belly, but not his enormous, soft, milky arms; he is also wearing tracksuit trousers and rope sandals, and, judging by his reddened eyes, he seems tired. He must be well over seventy: the passage of time has lined his face a little but has not shrunk his body.

"Come on then, *flic*," he says, taking Melchor by the arm. "Let me make you a coffee."

They go to the far end of the shop, and, as soon as he gets inside the cubicle, the Frenchman prepares two cups of coffee in a Nespresso machine, chatting cheerfully in his excellent Spanish flecked with guttural French Rs. The cubicle is his office, a jumbled space where the old ex-con moves like an intelligent bear, without bumping into anything; it is separated from the rest of the business by grimy windows, badly lit by an adjustable table lamp and furnished with a desk heaped with papers, an ancient, cracked-leather armchair, a couple of wooden chairs and a laptop the screen of which shows an Excel spreadsheet. On top of the desk, beside the computer keyboard and a couple of open notebooks filled with numbers scribbled by hand, are a pair of reading glasses and a piece of foil speckled with crumbs.

"I was doing the accounts," says the Frenchman, perhaps apologising for the mess. "I sacked the accountant, who was useless. I'm looking for a new one, so I'm working more hours than there are in a day. Believe me, kid: a business that doesn't let you sleep in till eleven in the morning is not a business worth having."

He points Melchor to a chair, brings him a coffee in a plastic cup, then, with another in his hand, drops into the armchair, which groans under his many tens of kilos. For a few minutes, the two former prisoners catch up on each other's lives. Melchor is succinct and only partially truthful: he tells him that he's been living in Terra Alta for years and is only in Barcelona for a short while; but when the Frenchman asks him how and why he became a policeman, he shrugs and does not tell the truth: that he decided to become a policeman to find his mother's murderers, and that he decided it because he read *Les Misérables* while they were both serving time in Quatre Camins; nor does he tell the former librarian that the novel became his guiding light and turned him into a different person, and that he was responsible for him having read it. Suddenly curious, the Frenchman asks:

"You're not married?"

Melchor shakes his head.

"Well done," he congratulates him. His fatigue seems to have dissolved in the joy of the reunion. "And if you do commit the mistake of getting married, at least don't commit the mistake of getting divorced."

"I was married, but my wife died," Melchor feels obliged to reveal.

"Oh . . . I'm sorry."

"I have a daughter: her name is Cosette."

"Like Jean Valjean's daughter?"

"Exactly."

"How come?"

Melchor shrugs again.

"My wife liked *Les Misérables*," is all he says.

Sprawled out in that big old armchair overflowing with his immense corpulence, the Frenchman shakes his head with a mixture of surprise and satisfaction, and Melchor feels that it's not easy to reconcile that cordial seventy-year-old with the gruff, laconic and intimidating prisoner he knew in Quatre Camins, even though they both share the same shabby resemblance to a sperm whale. For his part, the Frenchman tells him that he regained his liberty seven years earlier and that, after spending a long time in Toulon, his native city, trying to make a living and reconcile himself with his country (without much success in either endeavour), he returned to Barcelona. There he worked at various places, including this very internet café, until he managed to buy it from its owner; now he has three, the second also in the Raval, and the third in Poble Sec, as well as a gift shop for tourists, selling childish trinkets.

"I'm rebuilding my empire," he concludes with irony-free pride. "The problem is I got divorced almost a year ago and my wife is bleeding me dry. Listen to me, Melchor: don't get married again."

The Frenchman then talks about his love life, which seems intense and varied – it wasn't his wife who divorced him, but he who divorced his wife, to go and live with another woman thirty years younger than him and from whom he soon separated – and then he gets back on to his businesses. He still hasn't finished with the subject when he stands up to make more coffee. Melchor declines the offer, but takes advantage of the pause to ask, as if it were the most natural thing in the world, if they falsify SIM cards in his internet café.

"Sure," the ex-prisoner answers, as naturally as he was asked. Without spilling a drop of coffee, he sinks back into his armchair, which is almost eclipsed by his mass. "I do them myself, I don't trust anybody with those. For a fake card I charge three times what I get for a normal one."

"The guy at the front told me."

"It's a good little earner, you know?" Immediately, the Frenchman stops himself from saying any more. Then he smiles, vaguely. "Oh yeah, that's right, you're a cop."

Still smiling, he takes a sip of coffee and sets the cup down on the desk, on top of the crumpled, dirty tin foil. When he speaks again, his smile has tightened into a sarcastic sneer.

"Hey, Melchor," he says, showing the palms of his hands. "You're not going to fuck me over for this, are you? You wouldn't do that to a friend?"

In reply, Melchor takes out Torrent's note again and hands it to him.

"Of course not," he says, trying to reassure him. "I just want you to tell me who you made a SIM card for in this name."

The Frenchman picks up his reading glasses, puts them on, reads the piece of paper. That done, he sets the glasses back down on the desk, hands the paper back to Melchor and lolls back in his chair with a sigh. Then he looks fleetingly around the internet café through the dirty or misty window, and finally he asks Melchor, with genuine curiosity:

"Are you really asking me to become an informer?"

"I'm just asking you to give me a name."

"Don't bust my balls, kid," the Frenchman blurts out, and Melchor recognises the exact tone of the first words he ever heard the old man speak in Quatre Camins, the night when, not long after he'd been sent to that prison, two other prisoners were attempting to get a rise out of him: "Julián, Manolito, if you don't shut the fuck up, I'll cut your balls off."

"You're asking me to turn informer," the Frenchman insists. "After twelve years in prison . . . How many years did you do? Two? Two and a half?"

"A little more than a year and a half."

"A little more than a year and a half," the Frenchman grumbles and, less irritated than perplexed, adds as if talking to himself or to someone who isn't there: "Twelve years toughing it out in that disgusting hole for this brat to come here now and ask me to drop my drawers . . . *Merde, alors*!"

Melchor admits to himself that the Frenchman is right, that he has violated a tacit rule of solidarity among prisoners, that he has disrespected his host without meaning to. But he does not apologise, and both men remain silent for a few seconds, like two old friends who don't need to talk to enjoy being together. After this lapse of time, Melchor stands up.

"Well, I've got to go," he says. "Thanks for the coffee."

Before he opens the office door he hears behind him:

"Do you know why I'm not going to give you the name of the person that card was for?"

Melchor turns around.

"You already told me," he says. "Because you're not an informer."

The Frenchman looks at him as if Melchor had tried to apologise.

"Apart from that," he says.

Melchor doesn't know what to say.

"Because if I give you that name word will get round," the Frenchman says. "And, if word gets round, goodbye business."

116

Melchor nods, even though he's sure his friend has not finished.

"Also," the Frenchman goes on, "that person has done nothing wrong."

"Are you sure?"

"Completely. I know her from the neighbourhood."

"People in this neighbourhood don't do bad things?"

"Not her. I told you I know her. Believe me. You know as well as I do: the only good thing about prison is that it teaches you to distinguish the real sons of bitches from those who only seem like sons of bitches. And, even though there are far more sons of bitches outside of prison than inside, this person is not a son of a bitch."

The argument, supposing it is an argument, does not convince Melchor, who nevertheless nods again. *It's a woman*, he thinks. Apparently satisfied, the Frenchman stands up from his armchair with a combined crunching of joints, leather and wood.

"Let's go," he says. "I'll walk you to the door."

As they walk past the counter, the mujahid, who is attending to a man on crutches, glances at them out of the corner of his eye. Melchor emerges into the burning sun of two in the afternoon while the Frenchman stands on the threshold, the door half-open.

"Come back whenever you like," he says. "Now you know where to find me." Suddenly he seems to hesitate, then walks out into the street, closing the door behind him and, in a confidential tone, admits: "I'm curious about something, don't answer if you don't want to." Melchor urges him to go on. "Did they find the sons of bitches who killed your mother?"

The question catches the policeman by surprise and, as he pulls himself together, he remembers that the only time the old man visited him in his cell in Quatre Camins was when he got the news that his mother had been murdered; he also remembers the only two things he said: "Now you're a man, son. Welcome to the club."

"Why do you ask?" Melchor says.

"Did they find them or didn't they?"

"They didn't find them."

"And have you looked for them?"

Melchor takes a couple of seconds to answer.

"No," he lies.

But he realises the Frenchman does not believe him.

While he eats lunch on his own, facing a television screen, in a cheap restaurant on calle Pinto Fortuny, Melchor thinks that he's been in Barcelona for two days and this is the second time someone or something has reminded him of his mother's murder. He also thinks of Javert, the inflexible policeman who inflexibly pursues Jean Valjean all through *Les Misérables*, and of the Javert who was born within him when thanks to the Frenchman he read *Les Misérables*. He thinks that at some point he had written off that private Javert, but the truth is he comes back time and time again, furious, unfailing and obsessive, as righteous as the day he was begotten, like an alcoholic falling off the wagon. And he thinks that, although his mother's murder might be a closed case for everyone (including himself, who years ago gave up on closing it), for the Javert he carries inside it is not, and that is why fate or necessity reopens it every time he returns to Barcelona, with all its toxic burden of guilt and pus and anguish and stench.

He is distracted from this ominous thought by the appearance of the mayor on the television. The screen shows her in a car park, in the open air, besieged by a thrusting forest of microphones. She is speaking, but, in the hubbub of the restaurant, her voice is inaudible. She smiles, but that smile looks very little like the one she offered Blai, Vàzquez and him at City Hall yesterday: it is a smile without shadows, assured and radiant, the smile of a professional seducer, which they'd barely caught a glimpse of the previous evening, when the mayor was a bundle of nerves. Then, as if illuminated by a spark of lucidity, Melchor realises that the mayor is not a politician: she's an actress. But a special actress. He has not yet managed to define what kind of actress she is when her image disappears from the screen, replaced by that of a newsreader.

Melchor has a couple of espressos, pays his bill and then heads to MediaMarkt on Diagonal Mar. There, in the mobile phone department, located on the first floor, he manages to find out the name and address of the person who bought the phone associated with the IMEI code Torrent gave him.

"They bought it three weeks ago," the manager says, handing him a copy of the receipt. "The phone was for their business. And so is the address."

The man offers Melchor the chance to review the footage recorded by the security cameras the day the phone was purchased, to try to identify the purchaser. But, after weighing up the offer, the policeman decides that it could take hours to look through the whole recording and in the meantime he might be able to find the phone's owner at their place of work.

"Could you get someone here to do it?" he asks the manager.

"If there's no other option . . ." The man resigns himself.

Melchor writes his phone number on the receipt.

"Do it, please." He tears off his number and hands it to the manager. "And, when you find them, send me a WhatsApp or call me on this number."

At number 6 calle Casp, headquarters of Radio Barcelona, Melchor asks the security guard at the entrance for Guillem Jarque. The guard requests some identification, asks if he has an appointment with Señor Jarque; Melchor says no and shows his credentials. The doorman takes a look at the document and another at Melchor. Then he speaks on the phone.

"Wait here a moment, please," he says as he hangs up and points to the lobby. "He'll be right up."

Ten minutes later, when he has grown tired of waiting, Melchor asks the security guard if there's a problem, and the guard says he can go right into the studios and ask for Jarque. Following this advice, Melchor goes through the metal turnstile, down a set of stairs, opens a door and almost runs smack into a skinny young man with horn-rimmed glasses and two days' growth of stubble; he is wearing a ZZ Top T-shirt and getting ready to leave.

"Excuse me," the guy apologises, panting as if he had been running. "Are you the cop who's looking for me?"

Melchor says he is.

"Come in, come in," the guy encourages him. "Sorry to keep you waiting. I was on my own and I couldn't leave. Do you want a drink? We haven't got anything but water, but . . ."

Melchor declines the offer.

"I have a couple of questions I'd like to ask you," he says.

"Sure, sure." The guy nods, gradually catching his breath. He talks very quickly, gesturing, blinking, his head and features seem to be in perpetual agitation. "Go ahead, ask whatever you want. Don't be shy. Are you working on a case? Can I ask you what it's about? No, of course not. Sorry. I'm a journalist, so my work consists of asking questions."

"Mine too," Melchor says.

The guy laughs dutifully.

"Yeah, yeah, of course, what an idiot. Forgive me again. It's just that . . . Well. I started working here three weeks ago, I'm in training, you know how these things are. And now you show up, a cop and . . . Anyway, as I said: ask whatever you want."

Melchor asks if he bought a mobile telephone from Media-Markt on Diagonal Mar three weeks ago. The journalist looks at him as if he'd just picked the winning number on the Bonoloto.

"Fuck, man, how do you know that? It was an awesome phone, I bought it because the one I had was shit and I thought that, if I was going to work at a good radio station, I had to have a good mobile. So—"

"Where is it?"

"What?"

"Where's your mobile phone?"

"I lost it. Or someone stole it."

"Did you lose it or was it stolen?"

"I lost it."

"Did you report it?"

"Of course. And I cancelled the SIM card."

"Where did you report it lost?"

"At the Sarrià-Sant Gervasi station, the one on Iradier. I lost the phone at the Putxet metro station. Do you want me to tell you how I lost it?" Melchor nods. "Well, you see, it was a couple of days after I started working here. I loved my new phone, I really did, and, while I was waiting for the train, I sat on a bench and started sending messages and reading newspapers. Until suddenly, I don't know why, I put the phone down beside me, on the bench, I must have remembered something or thought of something. I don't know. But the train came and the phone stayed on the bench, as soon as the doors closed and the train started to move I realised what I'd done and swore up and down and cursed my mother and all my relations. So I got off at the next station and ran back; but, of course: when I arrived, the phone wasn't there anymore. Someone must've taken it, I told you it was new, a latest generation wonder, no surprise that the first person who found it would keep it, rather than hand it in at the nearest police station, in this country we're not like that . . . what a disaster, right? I'm always losing stuff, if there was an Olympics for losers, I'd be sure to win a medal."

"Thanks."

"Is that all?"

Melchor says yes and holds out his hand.

"Wow, I thought you were going to ask me more stuff," the guy admits, shaking hands. "You can ask me all you want, you know? I've got some free time now, and I've always loved helping people. I hope what I told you has been useful, although I don't know, I'm pretty good at asking questions, but really bad at answering them, it happens with journalists quite a lot, don't you think? Are you sure you can't tell me what you're investigating?"

As soon as he emerges onto calle Casp, Melchor phones Blai, who doesn't answer; then he calls Vàzquez, whose number is busy. He hasn't yet reached his car when the sergeant returns his call.

"Everything OK?" Melchor asks.

"Everything's fucking terrible," Vàzquez replies. "The kidnapping of the Santa Coloma narco's wife is getting complicated. The Romanians are getting nervous."

"You want me to give you a hand?"

"No. You concentrate on the mayor, who keeps calling me. What a pain in the arse that woman is, God almighty! Any news on that?"

Melchor tells him what Guillem Jarque just told him and asks what's the quickest and simplest way to view the images from the security cameras at Putxet metro station, to try to identify the person who took the journalist's phone.

"Do we know the date and time the guy lost his phone?" Vàzquez asks.

"They'll be in the report at the Sarrià-Sant Gervasi station," Melchor says.

"Then you better go there now and look at the video footage," Vàzquez suggests. "Send me a WhatsApp with the guy's name and I'll call ahead so they have it ready for you. If you don't hear from me that means there's no problem."

"Great," Melchor says.

"Did you find out anything about the SIM card?"

"The Pakistani kid from the Raval has nothing to do with it," Melchor says. "They made the card out in his name in a neighbourhood internet café."

"And did you go there?"

"Of course. I tried to scare the manager into telling me something, but there was nothing to be done."

"I'm not surprised," Vàzquez says. "For the money they bring in, the bastard owners choose tougher and tougher managers all the time."

"That's what I thought," Melchor lies again, remembering the mujahid. "A real tough guy."

He parks in one of the spots reserved for patrol cars, at the door to the police station and, after identifying himself at the entrance, asks the duty officer if the footage has been prepared for him to view at the request of Sergeant Vàzquez from Egara. The officer looks at him uncomprehendingly, assures him he knows nothing and asks him to wait for a moment. The moment stretches out into several minutes, after which – and after several internal telephone calls – the officer tells Melchor that the footage will be ready in a few minutes, and invites him to wait inside. Melchor says he'd rather wait in the foyer.

He takes a seat and, once again, waits. As he was driving there up calle Casp Blai had returned his call and filled him in on the progress of the investigation. He had also had time to speak to Cosette, who had told him in detail about her second day at camp; for his part, he had told his daughter they'd be having dinner with Vivales' friends Puig and Campà that evening, and that he'd be home around nine. Now, while he's waiting, he sends a couple of WhatsApp messages. One to Vivales, whom he'd forgotten to ask on the phone if he wanted him to pick up anything for the meal. "No need," Vivales responds immediately. "Everything's under control." The second WhatsApp in response to one from the head of the telephone department at MediaMarkt saying he's found the purchaser of the phone he'd been asking about on the shop's security cameras. "Many thanks for the information," is his reply. "There's no longer any need for it."

It is after seven when a uniformed officer announces that the footage is ready. Melchor follows him down a hallway, they go up to the second floor in a lift, walk down another hallway and enter an office where a corporal, also in uniform, waits. He invites Melchor to sit in front of a screen showing a frozen image of a metro station, in one corner the timestamp reads 7.40. Melchor explains what he's looking for to the corporal who shows him how to fast-forward, slow down, rewind and stop the video footage.

"In the report it says he lost the phone around eight," the corporal says, with the mouse in his hand. "Here you have the footage from 7.40 to 8.40. A whole hour. If you need me, call me: I'm in the office next door."

Melchor thanks him and, as soon as he's left alone, gets down to work. The quality of the images is poor but adequate: at least good enough to make out the faces of the people swarming across the screen. He examines them closely, and although a couple of times he thinks he recognises the journalist among the crowds getting on and off the carriages, he does not identify him for sure until 8.12, at which time, when the metro train had just absorbed all the passengers who were waiting on the platform and was about to depart again, a man with the strap of his bag across his chest bursts across the frame and slaps the carriage door that has just closed in front of him, but Melchor only realises that it is the journalist when, after catching his breath with his hands resting on his knees, he sits on a stone bench that juts out from the wall of the recently emptied platform, takes out his mobile phone and starts to look at it. He's not very far from the camera, so he can be seen quite clearly. Gradually people begin to flow into the station, men and women on their own, couples or groups who, at first, stand or sit far away from the journalist. At some point the journalist puts his phone down on the bench, takes a diary out of his bag, or something that looks like a diary, and starts leafing through it. An old lady sits down beside him a short while later, on the other side from where the mobile phone is lying; then, a couple of children accompanied by their father sit beside the old lady, and then a bunch of teenagers appear in school uniforms and ties, stand next to the journalist and block the phone from view. Melchor tries to get a look at their faces, but they all have their backs to the camera and he can't. More people filter onto the platform, until, when it is packed with people, the metro appears and glides into the station. At that moment, the journalist stands up and, surrounded by the rest of the passengers, gets on the metro. Melchor looks at the stone bench: the phone has disappeared. He then understands that the journalist is mistaken; he didn't leave the phone on the bench for anyone to take. The journalist did not lose the phone: someone stole it.

The question is who.

Rewinding, Melchor freezes the moment when the journalist puts the phone down beside him. He looks again at the old lady and the two children with their father; it could not have been them: they're nowhere near the phone, but on the other side of the journalist. He sees the group of students again. He immediately notices details he hadn't picked up on the first time: the first is that they haven't come from outside, but from the other end of the platform; the second is that they surround the journalist on the flank where he has put down his phone, and that they do so without the journalist noticing, not him or anyone around him, by an enveloping movement that, for a second, strikes Melchor as rehearsed. He still can't see their faces, or he only manages to see them in such a blurry, partial way that it would be impossible to identify them, but he is sure it was them. He rewinds again, watches the few minutes that interest him once more, freezing the image over and over again. All in vain.

He goes to the office next door, knocks, and the corporal, who is typing at his computer, waves him in.

"Can I ask you one last favour?" The corporal nods. "I want you to have a look at something."

They go back to the office and Melchor explains what he's looking for and shows him the pertinent frames. The corporal, a man in his early fifties, tall, strapping and with very white hair, examines them a couple of times.

"Typical," he concludes after giving up, also incapable of identifying the students. "The gang of brats has taken the mobile. Later they'll fight over it or sell it and split the money. They're really good at it, looks like choreography, it's all the rage these days. The only strange thing is that they've reached these neighbourhoods, up till now it was only a thing in Hospitalet, Santa Coloma and places like that . . . Anyway, forget about it: you've hit a wall."

It's after ten by the time Melchor gets to Vivales' place. The lawyer and his bosom buddy Chicho Campà are sitting on the balcony waiting for him, with the table laid; each of them has a white apron around his waist and a glass of wine in his hand. Melchor apologises for being late.

"Don't worry, kid," Campà reassures him, shaking his hand and giving him an effusive pat on the shoulder. "There's no hurry."

Melchor asks after Cosette and Vivales says she had dinner at nine and that, since she was falling asleep, she had gone to wait for him in bed.

"But you might still find her awake," he adds. "Manel was reading to her."

Melchor goes into the bedroom he's sharing with Cosette and sees his daughter in bed, asleep in the faint light from the bedside lamp. Beside her, sitting on a wicker chair, with his suit wrinkled and tie loose, is Puig, also asleep, with a copy of *Michel Strogoff* open on his lap. Melchor folds the edge of the sheet under Cosette's chin, tucks the other end under her feet and then shakes Puig gently.

"What! What's up! What's up!" Vivales' friend starts awake and opens his eyes wide. "Where's the girl?"

"Relax." Melchor grabs him by the arm. "It's me. Cosette's asleep."

Still panting, Puig seems to calm down. Melchor turns off the bedside lamp and the two men leave the bedroom.

"Fuck, you gave me a fright," Puig says.

"Did she fall asleep quickly?"

"Quickly and angelically." Now they walk down a long hallway towards the other end of the flat. "She asked me to read to her, but in reality what she wanted was to talk about you. Do you know what she told me?"

"What?"

"That you're like *Michel Strogoff*, because the bad guys were after both of you. What do you think of that?" Melchor doesn't say anything. "She also asked me if I thought the bad guys were going to catch you."

"She really said that?"

"Word for word."

"And what did you tell her?"

"What could I tell her?"

"Don't start going on at Melchor, Manel," Vivales demands when they get to the kitchen, where he and Campà are finishing the dinner preparations. "We're here to eat and drink, not to yank each other's chains."

"I was only talking to him about Cosette," Puig apologises. "Fuck, the questions that girl asks."

"Children's questions are the only ones that are interesting," Campà says, stirring a chestnut sauce in a frying pan. "All the rest is verbal diarrhoea. Why do apples fall down from trees and not up? It's a child's question, isn't it? Well, look at the meal Newton made of that. OK, this is ready."

"Everyone to the table!" says Vivales. "Chicho's outdone himself today. And it's me telling you this, a man who has no rival when it comes to being stingy with compliments."

Campà has spent all evening in Vivales' kitchen, preparing

128

the meal, the first course of which is now awaiting them on the table on the balcony: three different salads – one with cheese and nuts, another of tomatoes from La Pera, anchovies from L'Escala and avocados, and another of endives with Roquefort – creamy squash soup, bacon-wrapped dates, grilled escargots and truffle cannelloni. It's not the first banquet like this since Melchor met Puig and Campà one distant dawn when, after spending the night talking with the Mexican magnate who had ordered the murder of the Adells (and thus tying up the final few loose ends of the case), he had gone to pick up Cosette at Vivales' flat and there found the lawyer's two old comrades standing guard over his daughter who Melchor had wanted to keep away from the dangers of Terra Alta (real or imagined), after her mother's murder. Puig is divorced, has two grown-up children and is one of three partners in a reputable architecture firm, Pere Chimal Arquitectos; he also lectures as an associate professor at the University of Lérida and at the Polytechnic, which obliges him to make frenzied commutes and attracts recurring sarcasm from Vivales, who knows the university barely pays him and does not understand or says he doesn't understand why he should work for free. As for Campà, he is head of the political sciences department at the Autonomous University of Barcelona, a confirmed bachelor and closet homosexual: he has never confessed his erotic inclinations to his friends and his friends have never let on they're aware of them. Furthermore, Puig and Campà are, physically and metaphysically, as different as night and day, or at least they appear to be: Campà wears glasses for short-sightedness, is tall, slovenly and almost as stout as Vivales – which earned them both the modest privilege, when they did their military service, of being assigned to the sapper squad – and wields a militant and snide scepticism, whereas Puig is short, restless, skinny, rather elegant and easily irritated. Vivales maintains that in those dramatic differences lies the secret to the cast-iron friendship that unites them.

When they're done with the first course, Campà puts his apron back on and, while the rest of them prepare the table for the second, finishes cooking his signature dish: sirloin steak in chestnut sauce. The three of them have grown used to Melchor drinking Coca-Cola with his meals (the first times they saw him do so, Vivales' friends gave him their condolences), but they wash down the meat with two bottles of Torres Gran Coronas Reserva. Later they make coffee and bring the full pot out to the balcony with a set of cups and saucers; Vivales also puts a box of Montecristo no. 4s on the table, a bottle of Jameson's Black Barrel, three thick whisky glasses and a full ice tray. While he pours the drinks, the lawyer reveals to his two buddies the real reason for the banquet: Melchor is interested in talking about the mayor.

"About ours?" Looking for the young policeman's eyes through the thick clouds of smoke, Campà takes his recently lit pipe out of his mouth. "The mayor of Barcelona?"

"Who else?" Vivales asks, after savouring his first sip of whisky and clicking his satisfied tongue against his palate; turning to Melchor, he adds: "They both know a lot about her, especially Manel: his office works with City Hall often."

"We know a lot about everything," laughs Puig, finishing his coffee. "Especially after the fourth drink."

Melchor has not told Vivales about the case that has brought him to Barcelona, but he has mentioned that it has some connection to City Hall in general and to the mayor in particular, and, although he expected at some moment he would bring the matter up, he had also hoped he could have done so in a subtler or less direct way. He has eaten too much and feels weighed down, a little uncomfortable, but the night is cool and on Vivales' balcony, in the company of his friends and surrounded by tall buildings and other balconies emitting sounds and laughter, music and conversations, it all feels pleasant; in fact, it's as if they aren't in the middle of a great city, but in the square of a seaside village. Campà asks Melchor what he wants to know about the mayor.

"I'd like to know what kind of person she is," Melchor answers.

"I don't know what kind of person she is," Puig rushes to explain. "But I do know what kind of politician she is."

"Is there a difference?" Vivales asks.

"You're right," Puig answers. "I've only met her once, and do you know what the first thing she did was when we were introduced?"

"What?" asks Campà, whose pipe is now fully functioning, which means that from here on in he will only take it out of his mouth to speak.

"Check out my package," Puig says.

"How disappointed she must have been," Vivales says.

"Are you sure your flies weren't open?" Campà asks.

"This afternoon, while I was having lunch, I saw her on TV," Melchor says.

"I bet it was her own channel," Puig says. "The municipal television station, I mean. She spends all day wiggling her arse on it. Before, in Barcelona, we had manipulated public television. Now we have public television converted into an instrument of propaganda for the mayor and her faction. Although maybe you didn't see her on the municipal channel but on 12TV. That's her ex-husband's station: another instrument of propaganda at her service."

"I don't know what channel it was," Melchor admits. "But she did seem like an actress."

"Got it in one," Campà congratulates him.

"All politicians seem like actors to me," Vivales says.

"They are," Campà says, setting his half-empty whisky glass on the table. "But they're not all as good as she is. That woman is a chameleon. If she goes on a right-wing radio station, she sounds right-wing; if she talks to a left-wing station, she seems left-wing; and, if she's on a moderate station, she sounds like a moderate. That's our mayor: a series of masks. The question is, what's behind all those masks. And the answer is nothing: the masks that hide her face *are* her face. That woman has fewer convictions than a mosquito; the only thing she believes in is accumulating power. Machiavelli would love her."

"That's probably why she likes to say that left and right don't exist," Puig ventures.

"Exactly," Campà agrees. "Saying left and right don't exist is like saying north and south don't exist: someone's either disoriented or they are trying to disorient. And in the case of the mayor, there is no doubt that what she is trying to do is to disorient. I've never seen a politician with such an ability to say what her audience is hoping to hear. That woman knows what people want before people know they want it. You don't have to look any further than how she became mayor."

"And how was that?" asks Melchor.

Campà takes a few seconds before answering, time for a couple of reflective puffs on his pipe. He's wearing a pair of shorts that are too loose and a *guayabera* that's too tight, with several grease stains here and there and a few breadcrumbs lodged in the ridges of his belly.

"It's incredible," he begins, pushing his glasses up with his middle finger. "People forget faster than ever, maybe because journalists forget faster than ever. They live for the present. They have no time to look back, and that's why they don't understand what's going on in front of them, even right under their noses. How is it possible that nobody remembers that the day before yesterday this woman was the refugees' champion? And, if anyone does remember that, heaven help them: how is it possible that nobody reminds her, now that she has turned into the scourge of immigration? How come nobody asks her why she's changed? What happened to make that woman say about this matter, and about so many others, the exact opposite of what she said just a few years ago?"

"Fuck, that's true," Vivales realises. "I'd forgotten."

"So had I," Puig confesses; like the lawyer, he has a cigar in one hand and a glass of whisky in the other. "She seems like two different people."

"Well, she's not," Campà says. "They're the same person, she just says different things. Or opposite things. And why does she say them?" The mayor's answer is still ringing in Melchor's head: *I've changed because the world has changed.* "Because she knows people want to hear them," Campà says, taking another puff on his pipe before continuing: "I think she started to realise it after the Islamist attacks in 2017. It's often said that what has changed Barcelona from top to bottom is the Procés, but it's not true."

"Depends what you mean by the Procés," Puig goads him.

"I mean what needs to be understood," Campà explains, didactically and rather sharply. "The ludicrous attempt to obtain the secession of Catalonia by any means despite the opposition of more than half of Catalan voters, which the autonomous government began in 2012 and that culminated in 2017, with the autumn insurrection, the fraudulent independence referendum and the illegal declaration of independence . . ." Puig seems satisfied with the clarification, and Campà goes on: "It's often said that what has changed Barcelona from top to bottom is the Procés, but it's not true. The Procés has changed almost nothing, not in Barcelona or in Catalonia or anywhere: the only thing the Procés has changed is something very tiny, very anecdotal, so that nothing essential would change at all. That's precisely what it was for. That's why it was launched by those who have always called the shots here, using the people as cannon fodder. But no: what truly began to change this city were the attacks. The attacks and the feeling of uncertainty that followed them. Suddenly people were talking non-stop about murders, robberies and rapes, as if there had never been any here before. Suddenly people started saying this was the most violent city in Europe. Suddenly citizen anti-delinquency patrols began to appear. And, most of all, suddenly we, who as children had never seen an Arab anywhere, realised we were surrounded by Arabs. By Arabs and Africans and Chinese and Pakistanis and every kind of people. And we also realised that not all of them wanted to acclimatise here or were ready to bow their heads and say yes, bwana, to whatever we ordered them to do. My friend . . . !" Campà exhales smoke, takes a sip of whisky and leans back in his chair with the glass resting on his crumb-sprinkled *guayabera*. "Probably nobody realised that a profound change in the Barcelona mentality was begin-ning then, a change that later, with the Covid crisis, became even more evident . . . No-one noticed except that woman. The proof is that six or seven years later she plonked herself down in City Hall with a hard line on security, an Islamopho-bic and anti-immigration rhetoric that wrong-footed everyone, especially since it didn't appear to be what it was: it seemed like a progressive but brave and politically incorrect approach that advocated an unabashed prioritising of citizens' safety. And that's why she triumphed. Before you were talking about the municipal television station, and there you see her every day showing boats full of immigrants prepared to invade us, terrifying people with the phantom of mass migration. And there you have as well, on the same station, on the radio and in the newspapers, ideologues in the mayor's pay, Rabasseda, Boronat and company, former radical leftists or radical nationalists vociferating daily from their media pulpits on the urgent need to preserve the threatened values of Western culture, Europe's Christian roots and I don't know what other rubbish, a supremacist cocktail made out of a bit of Spengler, a little dab of Huntington and a good shot of the other Camus – Renaud, the bad one – and his theory of the great replacement, theory being the operative word. Anyway, this woman was able to guess before anyone which way the wind was blowing and knew very well how to use the most powerful instrument of control a politician has in her grasp: fear."

"This woman and her husband," Puig specifies. "Or her ex-husband." Turning towards Melchor, he explains: "They separated a year or so ago, after she was re-elected."

"Daniel Casas," Vivales says. "That's his name. His family is one of those Chicho was talking about, one of the ones who've been running the show for generations. People have always said that he was the brains behind the mayor's career, that he made all her important decisions and so forth. And it has always been said that the mayor was a puppet. His and his family's."

"In other words, if you're right and the mayor is an actress," Puig reasons, "in this play Casas was the producer and stage director. And the mayor the star."

"You're forgetting a fundamental character," Campà reminds him.

"You're right," Puig admits, pointing vaguely at his friend with the glowing tip of his Montecristo. "Enric Vidal. And he is definitely a character."

"The deputy mayor?" asks Melchor, who is following the conversation with all his attention and mild astonishment.

"The one and only," Campà says. "They say he is the power behind the throne at City Hall, that he is the one who's really in charge. Though I don't believe it."

"You don't?" asks Puig, sounding surprised.

"No," Campà says. "Same as I don't believe the mayor is a puppet of Casas and his family, or no more than Casas and his family are puppets of hers. And I say the same thing about City Hall. The one in charge there is the mayor. There and in her party. Don't be fooled. Vidal thinks he's very smart, and so does Casas, but the truth is she's the smart one. So smart that she makes them think they're the smart ones, that they're the ones who rule. So smart that she's better than anyone at acting dumb. She's the real political animal, the one with the killer instinct that authentic politicians have. No doubt about it . . . Hey, I'm not saying that Vidal has no influence at City Hall. He's got loads." Campà downs his whisky and explains: "In Barcelona's municipal government, the deputy mayor has always had a lot of power, the mayor's right hand and the person who ran the internal machinery of City Hall. Now it's still like that but improved and expanded, among other reasons because the current mayor gave Vidal something from the start that, as far as I know, no deputy mayor has ever had, the ability to combat the psychosis of insecurity that she herself created and that swept her into office."

"You're referring to the security powers," Puig guesses.

"Exactly," Campà says. "But it's not just that. Vidal has expanded that area monstrously as well. I'll give you an example that will interest you." Vivales picks up the bottle of whisky and starts to generously refill the glasses. "Traditionally, the Guardia Urbana had a very small information-gathering service. It was in charge of the mayor's security and not much else; the rest was up to you lot, the Mossos. Well, Vidal has created a very powerful force, employing who knows how many police officers, effectively a bodyguard at his and the mayor's exclusive service. And they get up to all sorts of tricks."

"The Vidal Boys," Melchor says.

"Has word of their exploits reached even Terra Alta?" asks Vivales, putting another bottle of whisky on the table.

"No," Melchor admits. "But it was one of the first things I heard about when I arrived here."

"I'm not surprised," Puig says. "They're people to watch out for, Vidal's troublemakers, and the mayor's and her husband's. They're very versatile: they'll beat people up, bribe cops, judges and journalists, dig up dirt on everyone and their mothers . . . So, who's going to have the nerve to mess with them. The most dangerous is the one in command, Juan María Lomas is his name, Inspector Lomas, although everyone calls him Hematomas, need I say more. I don't know about you, but I haven't been afraid of the police since the Transition, but with these guys I'm not so sure."

"Now all you need to know is that Vidal and Casas are best friends," Vivales tells Melchor. "To complete the triangle for you."

"They've known each other their whole lives," Puig tells him. "Vidal's family is another one of those who've always been in charge here. By the way," he adds, looking back and forth from Campà to Vivales, "have you heard that he and the mayor have fallen out—"

"What do you mean, have we heard?" Vivales scoffs. "It's in all the newspapers!"

"What I've heard," Puig says, "is that the mayor's amicable separation from Casas is a cock-and-bull story, that they've been fighting like rats in a sack, and that she's not getting along with the other one either, so much so that they're not speaking, or only when they can't help it."

"That's what everyone says," Campà agrees.

"Well, you know what I say?" Puig asks. "I don't believe a word of it."

Vivales asks him why.

"Because they're the perfect trio," Puig says, getting up from his chair, cigar in hand: he has taken off his tie and rolled up his shirtsleeves; his eyes are feverish from the alcohol and he is sweating. Sheltering behind their respective whiskies, Vivales and Campà listen to him attentively. "Let's see. That Casas and the mayor should separate is normal, the strange thing is their having been together so long, everyone knows they each have their own things going on the side, especially the mayor—"

"You're not going to tell us again about her checking out your package," Vivales warns him. "Those are hallucinations of yours, Manel. You're hot for her."

"Especially the mayor," Puig repeats, squeezing his eyes closed for a moment, as if afraid of losing the thread of his reasoning. "And now she's preaching chastity, the return to traditional family values and the need to have children to preserve Christian civilisation so that the Muslims won't overrun us and all that xenophobic shit."

"Just like when she was an activist preaching free love and bragging about her lesbian experiences," Campà goes on. "This woman has made a political argument out of her own life. She used to preach left-wing morals and now it's right-wing morals. What matters is to issue moral precepts."

"It's true," Puig accepts. "But now, forget all of that and consider what she's achieved in such a short time with her two associates. They've created a party that has changed Catalan politics from top to bottom as well as the agenda of Spanish politics; they govern with an absolute majority in City Hall and all the polls say that, if they stood in the regional elections, they'd win. What more could they want? Why would they fight among themselves? Why would they change what's working, and working fucking brilliantly?"

The question floats for a few seconds in the summer air of the balcony as Puig stops gesticulating. Then, with his eyes fixed on Campà, happy at last to be able to contradict him, he says:

"Because politics isn't like structural calculations, Manel, my friend. If politics were rational, you'd be right. But it's not. Don't forget hubris." He turns to Melchor. "You know what the Greeks called hubris?"

"The arrogance that leads men to challenge the gods," Melchor says.

"More or less," Campà says. "And the gods punish them for that arrogance. That's what happens in Greek tragedies and that's what tends to happen to politicians when they gain power, especially if it's with a crushing majority, as was the case with the mayor."

"If I've understood you correctly," Puig recapitulates, still on his feet, with his cigar or what remains of his cigar in his hand, "what you mean to say is that, no matter how many successes the star has achieved by working with the director and producer, no matter how well things have gone thanks to their support, in the end what she wants is to free herself from them and from all those who have helped her, and set up her own company."

"You have understood perfectly," Campà says approvingly. "Except that your simile doesn't entirely work, because the mayor is not merely the star of the show. She might make

139

everyone believe it, starting with the journalists and political analysts. She probably made Casas and Vidal believe it, because it was in her interest that they believed it, because she needed them, even if only because politics is expensive, and they and their families have money, while she's just a normal, ordinary girl, born into a working-class family and raised in La Salut . . . But I repeat: that woman is much more than an actress, even though she's an extraordinary actress and, if she so desires, she'll get rid of them, supposing they don't see her coming and get rid of her first, of course . . . In any case, this sort of thing has happened in politics since the world began: a nobody takes power helped by the powerful, power forges the nobody into a charismatic leader (it's what power almost always does, no matter how stupid the nobody might be) and the charismatic leader gets rid of or tries to get rid of those who helped them up. Since the world began."

As Puig polishes off what's left of his whisky and his cigar, Campà offers examples of the phenomenon he's just described, some distant and others closer to home. When he gets to Carlos Puigdemont, the accidental president of the Catalan autonomous government who unilaterally declared independence in 2017, Puig interrupts again, and after a short time the dialogue spills over, by way of some unexpected meandering, into a debate over the quality of democratic education in Catalonia, a matter on which, just for a change, both friends entirely agree – they both judge it to be terrible – although they don't seem to, because Puig stands up several times more to emphasise his points of view, sweating buckets and addressing most of his remarks to Campà, who returns his gaze with one eyebrow arched and his pipe in his mouth. After a while, as he refills the whisky glasses, Vivales intervenes in the heated discussion and, pointing at his two friends, says to the policeman:

"I hadn't told you before because it's embarrassing, but Ortega and Gasset here are two upright citizens who believe in democracy."

"And you don't?" asks Melchor, who has never heard the lawyer talk politics, except to rail against politicians.

Vivales is surprised and stops pouring.

"Are you joking?" he asks in turn, looking at Melchor with his unmistakable stony face. "How could you think I'd believe in a system that gives the right to vote to an individual like me?"

Astounded, Puig and Campà look at each other for a second, and in the next second celebrate their friend's witticism by knocking their glasses together with a double guffaw. Vivales joins in with the toast reluctantly. Puig is the first to resume their dialogue.

"To get back to our mayor," he says in a reflective tone, as if suddenly free of the effect of the vast amount of alcohol that has been knocked back, "I saw the disaster coming straight off the bat. Do you know when? When she arrived in City Hall and the first thing she did was abolish Colau's housing law. The one that said all developers had to reserve thirty per cent of all they built for public housing. I was never a fan of Ada Colau, who was also a first-rate actress, you all know that; but that thirty per cent thing was well done. And, as soon as this woman killed it, I said to myself: here come business-friendly policies; in other words, gird your loins, a government of thieves is on its way."

"As you can see –" Vivales turns to Melchor again – "as well as believing in democracy, Manel is a dangerous red."

"In a pig's eye!" Puig gets riled up again, gripping the arms of his chair as if to hold himself back from throttling the lawyer. "Red yes, and proud of it; now, when it comes to dangerous . . . But I'm just a damned social democrat, man, which is as harmless as can be. The thing is, in these times we're living in, we social democrats seem like dangerous reds."

"For once, and without allowing it to serve as a precedent, I have to admit that Manel is right," interrupts Campà, who has spent almost the whole night agreeing with his friend. "This municipal government is run by a gang of thieves."

"Are you serious?" Melchor asks.

"Completely," Campà replies. "Before, in Barcelona, or in Catalonia in general, the ones who robbed hand over fist were in the Generalitat; now City Hall robs us as well." Since his pipe has gone out he produces some sort of tiny metal arrow and, using it like a spoon, begins to empty the ashes from the bowl of his pipe into the ashtray while, addressing Melchor, he goes on in a professorial tone: "Look, what has happened here is the following. When we got democracy started up again, Catalan nationalists installed a patronage-based kleptocracy. In other words, the regional government stole from the citizens and divided the spoils between the governing party and the families of the governing party, starting with the president's party. As for the rest of Catalonia, they bought off half of them with favours, perks and sentimental blackmail; anyway, the old lie: all for the fatherland and the rest of that piffle." He finishes scraping out his pipe and continues: "As for the other half of the people, they didn't notice or didn't want to. Most were immigrants from other parts of Spain and, even as they were having their pockets picked, it didn't occur to them that it was anything to do with them, that this Generalitat was for pure-bred Catalans, that they were just passing through. What a load of shit . . . But that's how things worked until the Procés, and they still work like that, because, as I said, the Procés was organised precisely for that reason, so things would carry on working in the same way. The problem now is that City Hall also works that way."

"Didn't it work that way before?" Vivales asks, with a sceptical look on his face.

"No," replies Campà, who has left his pipe and reamer on the table, beside a fastened leather tobacco pouch. "Or not entirely. Of course, there was corruption at City Hall, but not like there is now, systematic and generalised, as it's been from the start at the Generalitat. Furthermore, the municipal administration used to be quite competent, and worked quite well, but in a very short time it has become as bureaucratised and politicised as the Generalitat. Or more so."

"I can testify to that," Puig says.

"Is it true what Vivales says," Melchor asks. "Do you do a lot of work with City Hall?"

"My studio does quite a bit. It's what we're known for. We build a lot of public housing, though a lot less than is needed."

"No, for pity's sake!" Vivales begs, blocking his ears with fingers. "Not your public housing sermon, please. I'd rather be tortured to death."

Puig smiles like a little boy caught stuffing himself with sweets.

"It's true the subject interests me," the architect apologises. "In fact, I've been trying to write a doctoral thesis on post-war public housing for many, many years, and—"

Vivales interrupts, pretending to whisper to Melchor:

"Now he's going to say nice things about Franco."

"Hey, Chicho, what was that line of Machado's?" Puig asks, then answers his own question: "The truth is the truth, whether it's Agamemnon who speaks it or his swineherd. Was that it?" Campà nods, absorbed in the task of refilling and lighting his pipe. "Look," continues Puig, "one thing the dictatorship did well was to create public housing. It's the fucking truth, whether we like it or not. He built a lot, and some of it is really good. Right here, in Barcelona. Emigrants from the rest of Spain, poverty-stricken people who lived in caves, in Somorrostro or in Montjuic, moved into homes. Very precarious, sometimes of poor quality, inconveniently located, but housing, after all. Many unfortunate lives were saved. And one of the bad things that's been done since democracy was restored, is to forget about public housing. The right to housing even features in the constitution, for fuck's sake!" Puig threatens to get angry again, but he remains in his seat; he has mopped the sweat from his brow and neck. "It's very simple, Melchor: in Spain we have public healthcare and education systems that work reasonably well, but we don't have a public housing policy worthy of the name. What do you think?"

"Very bad," Vivales replies, with an elaborate gesture of infinite tedium, collapsing on the table with his cheek leaning on his right hand.

"And what's more important?" Puig asks again. "Cure people and teach them to read and write or give them shelter and a roof over their heads?"

"Having a roof over your head," Vivales repeats, as if he were reciting the Catholic catechism.

"And whose fault is it that we don't have public housing comparable to healthcare or education in this country?" Puig asks.

"Rampant capitalism," Vivales answers. "That is, it's the property developers' fault, who think only about making money." The lawyer seems to snap out of his rote lethargy and opens his arms wide as if asking for clemency. "You see how I know your fucking communist public housing sermon from A to Z?"

"I'm afraid to say that Manel is right about this," Campà chimes in, his pipe working all out again. "The public housing situation in this country is shameful, everyone knows it. But it's not fundamentally the developers' fault. It's the politicians', who don't dare confront them, especially since some of them are banks, and the parties are in debt to the banks up to their eyeballs. How are you supposed to stop someone in their tracks when you owe them a ton of money? How are you going to get them to forgive your astronomical debts if you don't make things easy for them and do them favours?"

"Another unbridled red," Vivales complains. "The kid here asked you to tell him about the mayor, not to put the world to rights."

Puig and Campà ignore the lawyer's reprimand and embark on an abstruse debate on the financing of political parties, which according to them is the beginning and end of corruption in Spain – corruption beyond repair, they agree, because it could only be repaired by those who live off it, in other words the parties themselves – until the lawyer calls them to order again.

"I repeat," he says to Puig as he pours more whisky, "what Melchor is interested in is your relationship with City Hall."

"Chicho summed it up very well before," Puig concedes, taking a sip of Jameson's as he focuses on Melchor again. "What has happened is that, with this mayor, City Hall has begun to function the way the Generalitat functions. Almost the way Francoism functioned. My father was also an architect, and he told me that in the sixties, during the time of Mayor Porcioles, a witticism went round the trade about two municipal officials who signed off on the construction licences:

'If you want to build on a terrace, call Soteras
If you want to build today, call Borday.' "

The couplet elicits a giggle from Campà and half a smile from Vivales. "It's not the same now, but almost. At our office, we see it daily. In the past the public tenders were clean; now they're rigged: the same firms always get them, the mayor's friends and their henchmen, who are the ones who fund her party. Political positions have multiplied and been filled by incompetent people who are faithful to those in power, who have replaced the bureaucrats who ran City Hall, most of whom were decent people. This is not the nostalgia of an old man in his sixties, you know, Melchor? It's reality. The result is that our municipal government has completely collapsed, ceased to function, and the city is going downhill at top speed. Correct me if I'm wrong, Chicho."

"You're not wrong," says Campà, shaking his head while taking the pipe out of his mouth. "In politics, creating something that works is very difficult, but destroying it is easy. The proof is that in less than four years these people have undermined something that everyone took for granted was working and that, whoever was in power, was going to go on working. That's the problem with democracy: as soon as you take it for granted, you're putting it in danger."

Vivales pours the fourth round of whisky and, after they return to the matter of corruption ("It's not all the fault of politicians," Campà says. "Of course not," Puig rejoins, getting worked up again. "It's ours. In this country, someone who pays taxes when they could get away with not paying them is seen as a dickhead." "And rightly so," says Vivales. "Fuck that shit."), the conversation veers off to their military service. Melchor is not surprised by that turn: he knows from experience that, on these nocturnal musters, the three friends always end up reminiscing about the time they first got to know each other; he also knows that this is the moment to leave them to it.

He says goodnight, heads to his room, gets into bed and starts reading stories for the Terra Alta High School's literary prize, though he soon gets bored and picks up Eça de Queirós' *The Illustrious House of Ramires*. Half an hour later he leaves the novel on his bedside table and, after one last look at his daughter, who is sleeping peacefully beside him, turns off the light.

After a prolonged period of tossing and turning on the bed, whole phrases and images swirl through his head, unconnected snippets of a day refusing to end, and, when he finally does slip into a doze, he is awakened by voices from the other end of the flat. He gets up, walks down the hall without switching on the light and stands in the dining-room doorway, protected by the darkness, spying on the balcony, where the three friends are singing at the top of their voices, pitilessly out of tune, indifferent to the silence surrounding them, Puig and Vivales seated with arms around each other's shoulders, Campà standing in front of them, brandishing his pipe like a conductor's baton. The song goes:

> You are tall and slim,
> like your mother,
> a salty brunette
> like your mother.

Melchor feels envious.

The next morning he gets up at 7.15 and, after having breakfast with Cosette and driving her to the community centre for camp (Vivales has stayed in bed, wrestling with his hangover), he heads for Egara. As he passes Blai's office door, which is ajar, he hears the voice of the former head of the Terra Alta Investigations Unit, raps on the door and leans in. Sitting opposite Blai is Sergeant Vàzquez.

"Come in," the inspector orders him. "You're just in time."

Something bad has happened: both his superiors have it stamped on their faces.

"Last night the mayor called me again," Vàzquez tells him without further ado. "The bad guys have been in touch with her again."

"Another letter?" Melchor asks.

"No," the sergeant says. "This time it was by phone."

"And?"

"Now they want more than just money."

Melchor waits for Vàzquez to fill him in. Blai does instead: "They want her resignation."

2

"We must have watched the video of the mayor in the cabin in La Pleta de Bolvir, that was where we normally watched what we filmed in the place on León XIII . . . Although the truth is I don't recall having seen it until recently. I might be mistaken, but I don't remember it. What I am sure of is that the mayor was one of the last ones before something happened that made us stop hunting girls and filming ourselves with them."

"What was that?"

"An incident . . . A thing that happened . . . Anyway. Actually, it has nothing to do with what we're talking about."

"Does it have to do with you and your friends from Esade?"

"Yeah. And with the films from the place on León XIII, but—"

"Then it has to do with what we're talking about."

"I shouldn't have mentioned it."

"We agreed you'd tell me everything."

"I will, don't worry . . . Sure you don't want a little whisky?"

"Positive."

"OK, well, I'll have a little more. And before we go on, let me tell you something. Something important . . . Since I got here, I've started reading, I was alone and far from Barcelona and with no visits from anyone but Marga, who has only come to see me a couple of times, so I've had nothing else to do but read, read and surf the internet and watch TV . . . Well, not long ago, in a book I bought in a supermarket, I read a sentence I loved. I can't remember who the author was, but it said more or less the following: 'There is as much difference between us and ourselves as there is between us and others.' Something like that . . . What do you think? I believe it's true . . . I don't believe in individual identity. I believe we are one single person, but we contain multitudes."

"Your wife told me more or less the same thing."

"Herminia? Have you been talking to her?"

"The day before yesterday. And she told me something similar to what you just said."

"What did she say?"

"That failure turned you into a different person, nothing like the man she had known. That it poisoned you."

"She's right. Herminia is almost always right . . . Whichever way you look at it, I am no longer the same person who married her, or the same one who studied at Esade and made friends with Casas, Vidal and Rosell and went out with them on Saturday nights looking for girls to take to the place on León XIII . . . I'm not. I have the same name and I have more or less the same face as him, but I'm not the same person. I'm not that guy, and that guy isn't who I'd been up till then, the proof is that shortly after starting at Esade I abandoned my old friends from La Salle and didn't see them again. Not that I had so many, but . . . Anyway. Actually, I think that, back then, when we were at Esade, I aspired to be a different person, I wanted to be like my new friends, that's for sure, I wanted to become like them . . . I wanted that or my father did and I wanted it through him or him through me . . . I don't know if I'm explaining it right . . . My poor father, who was desperate for me to form part of the Catalan elite that my Esade friends belonged to, or that's what I thought, the elite that had the immortal magic and authentic power of money, those people he hated and admired because they were the only sovereign, independent ones, the rest of us were a gang of slaves, and that is what my father absolutely did not want, for me to be a slave like the rest, he wanted me to be a free man . . . What I'm trying to say is that in those days I secretly felt like an impostor, I also felt like a swine, of course, but most of all I felt like an impostor, a fraud, that's why I'm now disgusted by what I was, and it seems incredible that I wanted to be that person, and that's why I'm almost glad deep down to have to tell you this story that I've never told anyone, to see if I can free myself once and for fucking all of what I was . . . For that and because it's the only way those bastards will ever pay for what they've done . . . Though I know it's very difficult."

"I've given you my word that I'll do what I can to make sure they pay."

"Those people never pay, they always get let off, always get away with it . . . It's a universal law."

"We'll see about that . . . Tell me something: when did you first meet them?"

"In 2007. When I started studying at Esade. Why?"

"Because the crimes can still be prosecuted."

"I hope they do pay for them. I hope their lives get fucked up the way they fucked mine up . . . But I'll believe it when I see it."

"You were going to tell me what happened with the mayor. You said that it was a short time before an incident that . . ."

"Yes, it must've been in the autumn of our third year, the last year I spent at Esade, in any case I'm sure it was before

151

the December exams, I know because when the exams started I stopped going out on the weekends and shut myself up to revise . . . My friends also stayed in to study, and with more reason than me, as I hadn't failed any courses the previous semesters, but they had, especially Rosell, who was always the worst student of the three. So they were all forced to study more than me . . .

"By then the group's habits had changed a bit, I mean our Saturday night hunting habits . . . Vidal and Rosell had girl-friends, two girls from rich families, Carme and Eva were their names, they'd known them their whole lives, and they used to come out for dinner with us and then to the Sutton, on calle Tuset, the Up&Down had closed the previous year, when we were in our second year. When we left the nightclub we'd try to get rid of them, which wasn't always easy, sometimes we did and sometimes not . . . When we managed to escape, we'd go on the prowl, but not to the same places anymore. We kept going to where we thought it would be easiest to hook up and where we felt safest, especially the dance clubs on the outskirts, but we'd also started going to the nightclubs, music venues and after hours clubs in the old town in the city centre or in Gràcia or Sants, places that closed very late or didn't close until dawn or noon the next day, and where the customers were quite different from those in the outlying nightclubs . . . That night, as I remember it, after Vidal and Rosell took Carme and Eva home with some excuse, the four of us were to meet at Bikini, a night-club on Diagonal. We didn't find anyone there, it wasn't a place where you could easily pick someone up, so we went from bar to bar in the old town, in the plaza del Pi and the plaza Real and along the Rambla, and, when we'd already resigned ourselves to an empty bed, we got to the Paralelo and went into a dive that was still open for a nightcap.

"Don't ask me what it was called because that's the only time I went there and I don't remember . . . What I do remember is that it was very close to the old Arnau Theatre and when we arrived they had the shutters on the door half-closed. I also remember that the place was small and narrow, there was barely room to move, the music was at full volume . . . Inside we joined a group all or almost all of them students from the University of Barcelona, middle-class kids, though we only found that out later. Casas and Vidal immediately spotted a girl, or maybe she spotted them, whatever the case they started talking and flirting while Rosell and I also mixed with the group . . . It was late, the place was theoretically closed and, after a while, at the near-deserted bar with no music, there was just the four of us left along with the girl and a very drunk friend of hers who I'd been talking to for a while. Both seemed willing to come with us, but we didn't even consider that possibility . . . We'd never taken two girls at once to the place on León XIII, and rightly so: after all, it's much harder to dominate two women than one on her own.

"So we did what we'd done before in similar situations . . . It was a strategy that was so well oiled that we only needed to look at each other to put it into practice. Casas left with the girl and the rest of us said goodnight to her friend and went to get the car. We didn't have to wait long . . . Casas arrived with the girl, who didn't seem surprised to see us there without her friend. She asked about her and we lied, said we'd tried to convince her to stay with us, but she'd told us she was going home because she was tired and woozy and she'd had enough. That said, the girl got into the car without any more questions. She didn't even ask where we were going . . . Up to this point, everything was going more or less as normal, more or less as it had on so many other nights, the girls never or almost never suspected us, and this one didn't have any reason to either. Who could imagine that those four posh kids lost on Paralelo, young, pleasant and polite, could be a danger to anybody . . . ?

"But none of us could have imagined what happened next.

"The girl behaved with absolute composure from the moment she walked into the place on León XIII, or when she got into the car with us . . . at least that's how I remember it, with complete self-control, as if she'd only had one drink, or as if what she'd had to drink had no effect on her."

"Had you put something in her drink?"

"No. The idea was to give it to her when we got to León XIII and wait for it to take effect. That was the protocol we followed when the girls weren't out of it or drunk or drugged on arrival and we ran the risk that things might get complicated . . . The thing is, while my friends showed the girl around the place and prepared the scene, I escaped to my hiding place, and I wasn't set up to record yet when, much earlier than expected, they came into the room with the walls plastered with movie and rock star posters, the room where we always filmed. Don't ask me why they got there so quickly. I don't know . . . But what I do know is that, according to what my friends told me later, the girl barely tasted the drink with the Rohypnol they made for her. And don't ask me to go into details about what happened later, judge for yourself when you see the video, as I said I only remember having seen it recently and, the truth is, it seemed strange, on the one hand it's more or less like the rest of the videos I filmed, I mean that it's one of those things that makes you feel profoundly embarrassed for the people you're watching, one of those things a person wishes they'd never seen because those who watch are tainted . . . But, on the other hand, there's something strange about that footage, a sort of added obscenity or insult or perversion, a shameful supplement of degradation or indecency and, at once, why should I lie, something exciting, something tremendously exciting, although maybe that's only for me, I don't know, the thing is if I had to describe what that video contains with a single phrase I'd say that it's not the rape of one woman by three men but the rape of three men by one woman . . . I know it sounds crazy, among other reasons because there is no trace of violence in the images, at least the violence that tends to be associated with rape. But you're a cop so you know very well that no violence is needed for rape, intimidation is enough, and that's the sense I had while I was filming, the same one I had years later, when I saw those images, or saw them again, I mean the feeling that the woman was intimidating my friends, that, while she was kissing them and taking off their clothes and caressing them and sucking them and encouraging them to penetrate her, my friends were paralysed, stunned, not knowing what to do except let things happen, except meekly enjoy what she was doing with them, unable even to look at each other or say a word or even move without her guiding them, as if they were about to fall off a cliff or as if they were three clowns who had blanked on stage, in the middle of a show, and want to escape but don't know how . . . Anyway, I'd never seen anything like it, and I never have since . . . Well, guess who that girl was."

"You're not going to tell me it was the mayor."

"Surprised, aren't you?"

"A little. Do you think that what you've told me also explains why she's so afraid of anyone seeing that video?"

"I don't know. But, if I were her, I wouldn't want anyone seeing it at all."

"And if you were one of your friends? It doesn't seem to matter to them . . ."

"If I were one of my friends, I wouldn't want anyone to see

155

any of those films, except for that one . . . That one I wouldn't really care about. They come off like a bunch of puppets, sometimes they seem as if they're under a spell, but nothing more, I'm telling you they seem more like victims than violators. She however is a different story, judge for yourself when you see the video, everything I could tell you will be unnecessary . . . Well, except for one thing, and up till then I'd never done what I did that night."

"What's that?"

"Masturbate while filming."

"You'd never done that? Hadn't those gang rapes aroused you before?"

"No . . . at least not the way that one did, that's what I was trying to tell you before . . . I mean, before that there was arousal, but it wasn't the sex that excited me, it was the violence. I mean I didn't get off on seeing my friends fucking those strangers, what excited me was seeing my friends fucking the girls who resisted fucking my friends, or who weren't aware they were being fucked . . . Something like that. But that time, with the mayor, it wasn't like that, the important thing that time was the sex, not the violence, that's why I started touching myself and ended up coming against the wall almost at the same time as my friends came all over the mayor . . . That's the last thing I remember of that night . . . No . . . I'm lying . . . I remember something else, and it's that when we went outside the mayor seemed surprised to see me show up again, I remember dawn had broken and that, when she recognised me, she smiled as if teasing and asked: 'And where did you get to?'

"For the whole of the following week none of us spoke of what had happened at the place on León XIII, and no-one mentioned the girl. This wasn't at all unusual . . . We never talked about those weekend revelries, or we only talked about them when we went up to the cabin in La Pleta de Bolvir to watch the videos, which, as I told you before, we did every once in a while, for sessions that could last whole weekends, I don't remember very well, or I only remember them as if they were hallucinations or dreams. The rest of the time, as I say, none of it existed, it was actually as if it occurred in a parallel time or on a different planet, or in a place where the rules of normal life did not apply . . . That's the impression I had, I think that's how my friends felt, and in a certain sense maybe it was true. Which doesn't mean it didn't affect us . . . Sometimes it did affect us, but in a particular way, in a slow and subtle, almost secret way, which only in time ended up being visible.

"That's what I think happened with what happened that night . . . For a start, everything went more or less as it had up till then, but when the Christmas holidays ended I began to notice strange things. At first I didn't register them or I didn't think they were important, or I thought they were just coincidences, until I realised that something was going on . . . I don't know if I already told you that my friends drove to Esade every morning and that, when I made friends with them, they started picking me up at the corner of Bonanova and vía Augusta. From there, taking the Vallvidrera Tunnel, we'd be in Sant Cugat in a quarter of an hour (I would take the metro as far as Sarrià) . . . Well, anyway, Casas and Vidal suddenly started driving to Sant Cugat separately, each in his own car. Sometimes Vidal and Rosell would pick me up at Bonanova and vía Augusta, and other times Casas and Rosell would drive me. There were mornings when it was only Casas who would come by, or just Vidal, or even Rosell, and there were also mornings that I'd have to get to Sant Cugat the way I had before I made friends with them, on a Ferrocarriles Catalanes train, and then walk up to Esade, where to top it all Casas and Vidal began to sit separately in class, stopped going everywhere together, avoided each other ... All this created a tremendous problem for me, because I didn't know which one to stick with. If I hung out with Vidal, I felt I was being disloyal to Casas. And, if I hung out with Casas, I felt I was betraying Vidal ... Rosell had the same problem, or that's what I think, although he never mentioned it to me and I never mentioned it to him, surely because we both sensed that a problem does not really exist until it's named and that, until it's named, it's only a phantom problem, a false problem ... I don't need to tell you that the four of us stopped going out together on Saturday nights, all of a sudden and with no explanation the weekend revelries ended. At first, I asked several times what had happened, but no-one answered me or they answered evasively or vaguely or with lies, until I stopped asking. Finally, one Saturday night, just before the Easter holidays, we went out together again. I don't remember how or why or who organised the outing, but I thought that, whatever the problem might be between Casas and Vidal, it had been resolved.

"Big mistake ... The night was so short. During dinner, Casas and Vidal got involved in one of those absurd arguments where people are in theory arguing about one thing when it's clear that in reality they are arguing about something else, even though nobody knows exactly what it might be, apart from those who are arguing, and sometimes not even them ... Rosell and I tried to mediate between the two of them, ease the conversation somewhat, change the subject, but it was impossible and, when we'd finished dinner, things had got so poisonous that only Casas, Rosell, Carme and I went to the Sutton Club. Vidal left with Eva, and I didn't see him again until after the holidays.

"Only then did I find out what was going on ... It was

Rosell who told me, one afternoon when just the two of us were driving back from Sant Cugat in his car. What he told me left me stunned. First he asked me if I remembered the mayor, he didn't call her that, obviously, I don't know what he called her, but I said I remembered her, how could I not . . . Then he told me that, after the night we met her and took her to León XIII, she and Casas had started to see each other in secret. I asked him how he knew, and he said Casas himself had told him . . . 'Seems strange, doesn't it?' Rosell said. 'A bit,' I said, though actually it didn't seem that strange to me. Rosell said: 'Well, wait. That's nothing.' Then he told me that, after going out with the mayor several times, Casas broke up with her, but a few days or weeks later he changed his mind and called her and started going out with her again . . . 'And now comes the good bit,' Rosell said. The good bit was that, when Casas started seeing the mayor again, Casas discovered that she and Vidal had also been going out together, or maybe it was the mayor who told him . . . I mean, what Casas found out was that Vidal and the mayor had been seeing each other while he was seeing the mayor, that they'd been seeing each other when he dumped her and that they were still seeing each other, when he had started seeing her again . . . This discovery didn't bother Casas at first, according to Rosell it even amused him, at least that's what he'd said. But after a while he stopped liking it, especially because it was Vidal with whom he had to share that girl, and also because he was sure that Vidal knew as well, in other words, because he believed they both knew that the other knew, but neither had the courage to tell the other. Casas didn't say this to Rosell, but Rosell had no doubt about it . . . I didn't ask if Casas had spoken of the matter with Vidal, much less if Rosell thought both of them had fallen in love with the mayor: the first because I was sure that if he'd spoken to Vidal, Rosell would have told me; the second, because it seemed obvious. But, when Rosell dropped me off at Sarrià that afternoon and I took the metro home, I was already convinced that the friendship between Casas and Vidal had been shattered and that, without that friendship, everything was going to be different.

"I was wrong again . . . A few days later, one morning when I was waiting for Vidal and Rosell at the usual time at the corner of paseo de la Bonanova and vía Augusta, instead of just the two of them in the car, they pulled up with Casas, just like old times. I was dumbstruck: but I got in the car as if it were no big deal, and as if it were no big deal we drove to Sant Cugat and went into Esade, and from that morning on we became inseparable again, the former camaraderie and jokes and laughter and rivalry and complicity all returned, between Casas and Vidal as well, especially between them, and they suddenly seemed more in tune with each other than ever. I didn't know why, but the bad blood between them had disappeared overnight, and over the days that followed I asked Rosell several times if he knew what had happened, but he always told me he knew nothing and was more surprised than anyone . . . Later we found out or guessed that Casas and Vidal had both split up with the mayor, that both of them had stopped seeing her almost at the same time, although I never found out if that was just by chance or if it was the result of some kind of agreement between the two of them, which is what I sometimes tended to think. Other times I thought the opposite. And other times I didn't know what to think . . . Anyway, things got back on track, as they say, everything went back to being more or less how it had been before the mayor came onto the scene, even the prowling at the end of our Saturday night revelries . . . Though neither lasted much longer, I mean neither the prowling nor partying went on for much more than another month or two at most. Then we stopped going to the place on León XIII, not long before we started to prepare for our final exams . . ."

"And not long after the incident you mentioned earlier, no? The one that made you stop prowling for girls and filming yourselves with them."

"Yes."

"Are you going to tell me about that now?"

"I told you it has nothing to do with the mayor."

"I'll decide if it has anything to do with anything or not. If you don't tell me, there's no deal."

"I'll tell you. Calm down . . . But first let me tell you about something that will be of more interest . . . It happened around the same time, and this did change everything, at least for me, starting with my relationship with my friends. It was much more decisive for what you're interested in. Do you remember the case of the phantom cards?"

"Phantom cards?"

"That's what a journalist nicknamed it, and from then on everyone knew it as that . . . Haven't you heard about it?"

"Vaguely."

"It's incredible. Though I don't know why I'm so surprised, that's how things work . . . One day a scandal is on the front pages of all the papers, fills the news bulletins on radio and television, saturates social media and the next day no-one remembers it. Except for the people who've been swept up in it and had their lives destroyed, of course . . . They do remember, they remember for ever. But the rest, the pack of hounds, no, they forget immediately, they're too impatient to go for the jugular of the next victim."

"This scandal affected the mayor?"

"The phantom cards? No. It was my father who was affected

by it . . . And me as much as him. Or more . . . Do you want me to tell you how?"

"If it's connected to the blackmailing of the mayor . . ."

"It's connected alright."

"Go ahead."

"It all started before my final year at Esade, I wouldn't be able to give you an exact date, maybe the previous year, or even the one before that. The first spark of the case flickered when a journalist from Madrid published emails from the director of a savings bank about some credit cards that, according to the journalist, were to cover the private expenses of the institution's executives and consultants. Back then, as I think I told you, my father was a member of parliament in Madrid, a socialist, and the party had named him a consultant to that institution, a partially public bank, which had advisers from the left- and right-wing parties and unions. I'm not talking about executives but consultants, I mean, members of the administrative board, people who made collective decisions as to how the bank was run and such: how much they should invest in this or that economic sector, how much in charitable work, stuff like that . . . The thing is, when I asked my father about those emails, he told me not to worry, that it was true that, like all the rest of the bank's consultants, he had a card for business expenses and one for personal expenses, but that was part of his salary as a consultant, a common practice in the finance world, and the leaking of the emails and their publication in the newspapers was just an attempt to erode the power of the prime minister, who had appointed the director of that bank, and to cause a political and economic scandal where there was no scandal, neither economic nor political. Don't worry, he repeated. This is going to dissolve like a sugar cube in water. They'll end up apologising to us.

"I don't know if he was deceiving himself or trying to deceive me . . . My father, as I've told you, was not a banker but a trade unionist, that was his world, he didn't know what kind of shady deals banks made, their common practices or uncommon ones, he knew nothing about any of that, and he paid a high price for his ignorance . . . A little while after we had that chat, the Anti-corruption Prosecutor asked a high-court judge to investigate the seventy-eight directors and consultants of the institution who had used company cards to cover personal expenses and, almost at the same time, it was announced that the bank was in technical insolvency, everyone had known for a long time that it was in serious trouble, but now it was announced that it had to be bailed out with taxpayers' money, that many customers would lose their savings and hundreds of workers would be left jobless.

"That's how my father's ordeal began, and it was also my family's and my ordeal, the beginning of the cataclysm . . . As soon as he could, my father repaid everything he had spent down to the last euro and swore to anyone who asked that he had committed no irregularity, that the bank's directors had assured them that those cards had been approved by the government and were perfectly regulated by the institution, all of which, according to what the secretary had told him, was a way of paying their consultants in kind, and regardless he had always respected the spending limits that had been imposed and he was sure the bank declared its revenues to the Treasury, because he had been told that by the bureaucrats responsible.

"He swore to everyone who asked, as I said, starting with the journalists and ending with the judges before whom he had to testify, but it was all futile . . . During the summer of my last year at Esade, my father was forced to resign from all his posts, vacate his seat in parliament and was expelled from the party, and months later, when the trial ended, he was sentenced to two and a half years in prison, although he only served ten months . . . All this was dreadful, but it was not the worst part. The worst part was the public lynching . . . Since the accused belonged to all or almost all the parties and unions across the political spectrum, the phantom cards scandal was presented in the media as a flagrant indication of general corruption among the political, economic and union elite of a corrupt democracy, and the accused were found guilty by the press long before the judge found them guilty. No-one was interested in going into subtleties, distinguishing between the bank's directors and those who were simply advisers, between those who had used the cards according to the regulations they'd been given and those who'd done as they pleased and used them for anything they felt like; all they wanted to talk about was the money one director spent in strip clubs and brothels and another on a trip to Bora Bora, as if all the rest of the accused had done the same . . . As for my father, I told you before that in Catalonia in previous years he'd become known as the scourge of right-wing nationalist corruption, so the media (especially the nationalist and right-wing media, funded by the right-wing nationalist government) exhibited his sentence like a trophy, the perfect symbol of the hypocrisy of the left, denouncing theft with one hand while robbing with the other.

"It was a horrible time, the worst I've ever gone through in my life, and I've been through some tough times, believe me . . . I remember, for example, both times I accompanied my father when he testified at the trial in the high court. At the door a group of people were waiting, waiting for him and waiting for all the rest of those implicated, who filed by, almost all hurrying through with their heads bowed . . . I don't know who those people were, the ones waiting at the entrance, people harmed or supposedly harmed by the failure of the bank, I imagine, or just bystanders, curious people with nothing better to do than to go and hurl insults and eggs and tomatoes at my father and the rest of the accused, what do I know . . . But I assure you they did not resemble humans, they resembled beasts, bloodthirsty hyenas, in those days I learned something I never forgot, and it's that there is nothing as dangerous as someone who is or believes himself to be a victim, nobody turns more easily into an executioner than a victim, supposing those people had actually been real victims, it seemed obvious to me that they were not there to demand justice but to demand vengeance, and they were not shouting and throwing things at the accused to shame them or because they despised them but because they, those who were yelling, had not been able to do what the accused had done, or what they'd imagined they'd done, and that made them furious . . .

"To add insult to injury, my mother had fallen into a terrible depression since the scandal broke, and shortly before the judge passed sentence she had a stroke and had to be admitted to hospital, with one side of her body paralysed. That's how she spent the years she had left, depressed and paralysed and never leaving the house, first in my charge and later, when he had served his sentence, under my father's care. As you can imagine, I left Esade . . . What was I going to do? My mother ill, my father accused and pursued and then in prison, my family ruined. We didn't even have enough money to cover tuition fees . . . And did anyone help me? Don't make me laugh. In those circumstances nobody lends you a hand, unless it's to push you the rest of the way under. My father had become a leper, and lepers are kept at a distance, along with their families . . . And, above all, don't ask if my friends helped . . . They could have, you'll say . . . Who, if not them, right . . . ?

They and their families, who had the magic of money and power and would have been able to help us easily, after all I'd done for them they could have asked me, at least, if we needed help, shown some concern . . . Did they ask? Were they concerned about our situation? My father's, my mother's, mine? Don't make me laugh . . . Of course not . . . Not in the least . . . People are like that; the rich, especially, are like that. I told you before they're made of different stuff. For them the rest of us don't exist, or we only exist according to their interests. When we no longer interest them, we stop existing. Bam. Never seen you before in my life. Full stop.

"That's what happened then . . . Although my friends knew about the cataclysm from the start (how could they not, everyone knew), they didn't open their mouths, didn't say a single word or make the slightest comment, they did not lift a finger to help me, didn't even call me when college started again in September and I didn't turn up, they acted as if they knew nothing, they behaved, as I said, as if I didn't exist, as if I'd never existed . . . How I would love them to pay for that."

"Ingratitude is not a crime."

"No, but it should be . . . Anyway, they won't even pay for their crimes."

"We'll see about that."

"It's late. Aren't you tired?"

"No."

"You're not sleepy?"

"No."

"I am."

"We have to continue."

"Yeah . . . OK . . . Give me a minute. I have to go to the toilet."

3

The mayor has summoned them to meet her at four in the afternoon in El Botafumeiro, an exclusive restaurant ensconced in the heart of the working-class neighbourhood of Gràcia. The idea of meeting far away from City Hall, however, had not been hers but Vàzquez's, who did not want to go back there. "The fewer people who see us in that bordello, the better," the sergeant had said. "We don't want some wise guy suspecting something."

El Botafumeiro is still quite busy when they arrive. One of the mayor's bodyguards tells them that his boss's lunch has not finished, and, since there's no room at the bar, they decide to wait outside, under the blue awning that shades the restaurant's door, flanked by two golden lamps in the shape of Galician incense-burners. They wait there for a while, preoccupied and silent, watching the crowds overflowing the pavements of Gran de Gràcia, and the river of cars, buses, motorcycles, bikes and scooters proceeding noisily up to plaza Lesseps, and, in the middle of all that racket, Melchor suddenly thinks he can read Vàzquez's mind: he knows he is obsessed with and nervous about the kidnapping of the wife of the drugs trafficker from Santa Coloma, and for a moment remembers him again in the warehouse in Molins de Rei, sitting on the floor in the pooling blood, cradling the decapitated head of the Venezuelan narco's daughter in his lap, shrieking, his face drenched with tears, and he feels like telling him that it wasn't his fault and he shouldn't torture himself anymore because as long as there's remorse, there's guilt.

At that moment one of Vàzquez's mobiles rings, and he takes a few steps away out into the burning sunshine, forgoing the protection of El Botafumeiro's awning.

"That was Verónica," the sergeant tells Melchor, when he returns to his side. "The girl from the press office. She wants to see us right away."

"Both of us?"

"Both of us. We're meeting her near here, in the Roure Bar. We'll go as soon as we've finished with the mayor. Her office is in Les Corts, but she's coming up here. She says she has to talk to you as well. You know each other, right?"

They know each other. Verónica is the press liaison for the Mossos d'Esquadra and, a few months after the Islamist attacks in 2017, she drove to Terra Alta to ask him a favour: the Catalan public television station was preparing a feature on the attacks, and they wanted to interview him; of course, he would appear with his back to the camera, and the technicians would distort his voice to make it unrecognisable; she had already spoken to Commissioner Fuster, who had given the proposal the go-ahead, as long as Melchor agreed. Melchor did not. The press officer insisted: she argued that with the chief of the corps, Major Trapero, charged by a judge of the National High Court for his role in Catalonia's attempt to secede from Spain in the autumn of 2017, and with the whole force depressed and troubled by the events leading to the October declaration of independence, the feature was essential just then; she assured him that nothing could lift his colleagues' morale as surely as the memory of their conduct during the Islamist attacks and no-one exemplified their conduct better than he did. It was all in vain: Melchor flatly refused to appear on the programme.

"I told Cosette I'd pick her up from camp at five," he says.

"Well ask someone to go in your place," Vàzquez says. "Verónica needs to speak to you urgently, that's what she told me."

Melchor phones Vivales, and they talk about the previous night's dinner (the lawyer tells him that his friends went home at dawn), and, for the second time in the last three days, Melchor asks him if he'll collect Cosette. Vivales says he will.

"Sorted," Melchor says.

Now they do find a seat at the bar in El Botafumeiro, which empties out gradually as they drink a coffee. When the moment comes, the mayor's assistant leads them to a private dining room, where a couple of waiters are taking the tablecloths off a long oblong table. Around the table are nine soft armchairs and over it hangs a chandelier from which a cluster of golden metal teardrops dangles. It is a windowless room, with a large mirror at the back and several oil paintings of maritime scenes decorating the walls, which are covered in dark crimson wallpaper. The assistant asks if the two policemen would like anything to drink.

"We've just had coffee," Vàzquez answers.

Then the assistant asks the waiters to bring another coffee for the mayor, a bottle of mineral water and three glasses, and asks Melchor and Vàzquez to wait. A few minutes later his boss appears.

"Sorry to have kept you waiting," she says in greeting. "I've been shut up in here for more than two hours with people from the Chamber of Commerce and I needed to freshen up."

She shakes hands with them both and holds on to Melchor's for a few seconds, while he remembers that, at their initial interview, the mayor had been much more standoffish.

"The other day I had no idea who you were," the woman admits. "Had I known—"

"Have you told anyone you met with us?" Vàzquez sounds alarmed.

"Don't worry, Sergeant," the mayor reassures him. "It was Commissioner Venebre, who was kind enough to call to see how everything was going, who told me about your colleague."

The mayor praises Melchor's conduct in Cambrils, and while she strings out two or three clichés about the growing threat of Islamist terrorism, she gives Melchor the impression she feels a great admiration for him, immense gratitude, as if he were the most important person in the world to her at that moment, and it suddenly occurs to him that a great part of her appeal stems from this: not from what she is but what she makes others think they are to her. He also remembers one of the things Chicho Campà said last night, on the balcony of Vivales' flat: "That's our mayor: a series of masks. The question is what lies behind all those masks. And the answer is nothing." The mayor is still absorbed in her anti-Islamist homily when there is a knock on the door: it is a waiter with the coffee and water.

"Please, sit down," the mayor says.

Melchor and Vàzquez take seats facing the woman, who scrolls through her phone until the waiter leaves and the three are again alone. Then she hands the device to Vàzquez.

"There's the number they called me from," she says. "And the time. I'll tell you the truth: I'm now very worried."

"I understand," he assures her, looking avidly at the screen of the phone.

"No, you don't understand," the mayor says. "They gave me

170

ten days to hand over three hundred thousand euros and resign. If I don't, they'll release the video."

Vàzquez looks up from the phone.

"Ten days?" he asked.

"Until Saturday." She nods. "Not this one, Saturday week."

The sergeant shows Melchor the screen.

"I think it's a payphone," he says. "Text Cortabarría and tell him to trace it. No, better not tell him anything . . . I'll do it." Then he turns back to the mayor: "If we had a tap on your phone, all this would be much easier."

Vàzquez rapidly tries to explain, rationalise his request, but the mayor cuts him off ("Out of the question") and the sergeant shows the palms of his hands in a gesture of apology. The mayor says:

"What we have to do is pay up and put an end to this affair as soon as possible."

"Paying will put an end to nothing," Vàzquez says. "I told you already. And I beg you not to get nervous. That's what the blackmailers want."

"I'm not nervous. I'm scared."

"That I understand as well," Vàzquez assures her.

"Do not tell me again that you understand."

The mayor's reply is followed by an embarrassed silence. Vàzquez blinks several times, grinds his teeth, juts out his chin; Melchor recalls once more the kidnapping of the Santa Coloma trafficker's wife, and for a second fears his colleague might explode. Luckily, the woman apologises.

"Sorry," she says. "I told you I was scared."

"Don't worry." Vàzquez points to her cup of coffee. "Drink that and tell us about the call, please."

The mayor inhales and exhales deeply, picks up her coffee cup and takes a sip. She is wearing a pair of ivory-coloured

171

trousers and a lilac silk blouse, with a chain from which hangs an onyx cameo that hides her cleavage; it is obvious that, as well as freshening up, in the bathroom she has taken the opportunity to touch up her make-up. Behind her, a seascape depicts a handful of fishermen in their boats under a strange silvery dusk, while a flock of seagulls glides above the waves like a miniature squadron of fighter planes.

"I received the call last night," the mayor says. "At home. It was late, I was about to get into bed, I don't usually answer the phone if I don't recognise the number, and much less that late. But this time I had a premonition."

"Did you recognise the voice of the person who called?" Vàzquez asked.

"No."

"Was it a man or a woman?"

"A woman."

"From here or a foreigner?"

"From here."

"Any idea of what age she might be?"

"None."

"Go on, please."

The mayor swallowed the rest of her coffee.

"I tried to remain calm," she went on, crossing her hands on the table: slender hands, bony, with long fingers and purple nail polish. "I said what you told me to say. That lots of people go around saying they have sex tapes of me and threatening to make them public. How could I know she really had one. That I was only prepared to negotiate if she demonstrated that she had it." A pause. "Do you know what she said?"

"What?" Vàzquez asked.

"She said I was trying to trick her, that everything I had said was a lie and that nobody had ever tried to blackmail me

172

with any sex tape. And then she proved that she did have the video."

"How?"

"She told me what was on it."

"She described the images?"

"She told me where and when it was filmed."

"She could know all that and not have the video."

"Yes. But she has it."

"You're sure?"

"Completely."

Vàzquez and the mayor stare at each other as if silently measuring each other's intellect or capacity for resistance. Melchor understands that articulating her anxiety is dissipating the mayor's initial nervousness and restoring her self-confidence. One of Vàzquez's two mobiles vibrates on the tablecloth; the sergeant barely glances at it.

"Tell me what is on the video," he asks.

Slightly disconcerted, the mayor turns towards Melchor, and then back to the sergeant. Then she sighs, pours some water into one of the glasses and drinks it. Melchor notices that her hands are not trembling.

"The film is from when I first met my ex-husband," the woman says.

"When was that?" Vàzquez asks.

"Almost twenty years ago. We were both still studying, I was finishing my degree, I'm a couple of years older than him. I'd gone out for dinner with some of my classmates and, since it was Saturday, we had quite a lot to drink and the night went on longer than we'd intended. Dani showed up in one of the bars, very late. He was with some friends. Anyway, one thing led to another and we ended up at some place his family owned, near avenida Tibidabo. That must be where we were filmed."

"How do you know?"

"From what that woman told me."

"The blackmailer?"

The mayor nods.

"Did you realise you were being filmed?"

"Of course not."

"Did your husband?"

"No. I don't think so. I don't know. In any case, he never said anything about it."

"Was it just you and your husband who were filmed?"

"No."

"Who else was with you?"

"I told you already: friends of my husband's."

"What friends?"

The mayor does not answer immediately; indecisive, she looks at Melchor again, as if seeking refuge in him, or an escape route. In any case, she finds neither.

"Enric," she finally says. "Enric Vidal."

Vàzquez is also slow to react.

"Your deputy mayor?" he asks, perplexed.

The mayor nods again.

"He's a very good friend of my husband." And she adds: "Same goes for Gonzalo Rosell. The People's Party spokesman . . ."

"At City Hall."

"Yes."

"Rosell is also a friend of your husband or he also appears in the film?"

"Both."

Vàzquez seems not to believe what he's hearing. Obviously uncomfortable, he clears his throat, and, out of the corner of his eye, Melchor notices that he turns discreetly towards him, and avoids doing the same.

"Anyone else?" the sergeant asks.

"Anyone else what?" the mayor answers.

"Does anyone else appear in the video?"

"No."

"Did the blackmailer tell you that as well?"

"I experienced that myself, nobody needed to tell me." Impatient again, the woman huffs, crosses and uncrosses her arms, flutters her hands at the level of the seascape that hangs on the wall behind her. "Look, don't get all prudish with me: this is what people do when they're young," she continues, taking it for granted that everyone knows what things she's referring to. "The other day I warned you, I did a lot of silly things back then, we've all done them and, if some people didn't, too bad for them. But we don't have to make too much of them. The question is—"

"We're not the ones making too much of them." Now it's Vàzquez who interrupts. "You are."

"It's just that for a normal person they're no big deal," she replies, "but, for me, they are. This is what I wanted to tell you: a man's political career could survive a film like this, but not a woman's. And, much less, if that woman is me. Don't you understand?"

The question silences the room for a few seconds, during which Melchor is reminded again of last night's dinner at Vivales' place: "And now she's preaching chastity," Manel Puig had said, referring to the mayor, "the return to traditional family values and the need to have children to preserve Christian civilisation so that the Muslims won't overrun us and all that xenophobic shit." The sergeant does not seem convinced by her arguments and, after responding in the blink of an eye to the message that just pinged on his mobile, he changes the subject.

"How long did you speak with the blackmailer for?"

"Four or five minutes, no more. Long enough to know she wasn't bluffing. And there's something else." The sergeant shoots her a questioning look. "I got the impression that the resignation is only a way of pressuring me. That it's not the main thing. The main thing is the money."

"Where did you get that impression?" Vàzquez asks.

"I don't know. From how she was talking, I suppose: she didn't speak the same way about the two things. That's how it seemed to me. That's why I think it would be better to pay once and for all and negotiate so they hand over the tape in exchange for the money and stop pestering me. And so we don't make things even worse."

In his two interviews with the mayor Melchor has kept quiet and concentrated on deciphering her non-verbal language; but now he can't contain himself.

"Things are not getting worse," he says.

The woman looks at him less with interest than shock: this is the first slightly articulate phrase she has heard him complete.

"Four days ago, these people asked me for three hundred thousand euros," the mayor reminds him. "Now they're asking for the same three hundred thousand euros and my resignation. Explain to me why things have not got worse."

"Because it's likely they've wanted you to resign from the beginning," Melchor explains.

"Why did they not demand it then?" the mayor asks.

"I don't know," Melchor admits, before venturing: "To throw us off track. So as not to give us any clues to their identity. So we won't suspect who the blackmailer might be."

"It's possible," Vàzquez backs him up. "And it's also possible there are two different blackmailers: one who wants the money and another who wants you to resign. That would explain the impression you had on the phone. And that would be good for us, because we could provoke conflicts between them and take advantage. Can you think of anyone in particular who would like to see you resign?"

The woman's expression of interest and astonishment suddenly gives way to sheer incredulity.

"Are you joking?" she asked with a slightly forced laugh. "Do you have even the vaguest idea how politics works?"

"I mean anyone related to the video," Vàzquez hastens to clarify.

The clarification freezes the laughter of the mayor, whose right hand reaches for her onyx cameo and caresses it with her thumb and index finger, allowing a second's glimpse of the fleshy depths of her cleavage.

"I don't know," she says, dropping the cameo.

"There is something I'd like you to clear up for me," Melchor interrupts again. "If your husband and his two friends were participating in the orgy, who filmed it?"

As if she had not understood the question, or as if she needed time to process it, the mayor asks him to repeat it; Melchor rephrases it, substituting the word "orgy" with the word "party".

"There was another person," the mayor says. "Another friend of my husband's. He was part of the group but didn't participate in that bit."

"Could he be the one who filmed it?" Vàzquez asks.

"He could be," the woman admits. Nobody has entered the private dining room, but she looks towards the door and keeps looking at it for a moment. Then, turning back to the two detectives, she continues: "I don't know who he was, he was only there that night. Dani never mentioned him to me that I recall . . ." She extends her arms in a resigned or powerless gesture. "Anyway, I still insist that we have no choice but to pay."

"I'm not saying we shouldn't," Vàzquez concedes. "But it's still early. Look, as you know, the blackmailers demanded to be paid in moneros, and the people from the Financial Crimes Department assure us that, using that type of payment, we have a chance to catch them. It's not certain but there's a chance. In any case, we should exhaust other means first."

"For example?"

The sergeant displays the number the blackmailer had called from on the mayor's mobile screen and, while he copies it down, says:

"We'll see what this turns up." He gives the mayor's device back to her and adds: "Of course if we had a tap on your phone—"

"Don't waste your time," she cuts him off. "You're not going to convince me." The mayor looks at her watch.

"Anything else?"

"Yes," Melchor says. "How do you get along with your ex-husband?"

The mayor's eyes drill into him with a mixture of surprise and vexation, as if he has just disappointed her immensely. But then, unexpectedly, she gives him a charming smile.

"We get along well," she assures him. "Very well, I'd say. We've been married for five years, we have a daughter, we get along well. We separated by mutual consent."

Thinking that three affirmations equal a negative, Melchor asks:

"And with Enric Vidal?"

"What about Enric?"

"Do you also get along well with him?"

"I do."

"That's not what people say."

The woman shrugs, still smiling.

"Don't believe everything people tell you," she says. After a pause she announces: "OK, I have to go."

She stands up and the two policemen do the same.

"It's best if you leave first," Vàzquez offers his own bit of advice, shaking her hand. "We shouldn't be seen together."

"As you wish." She says goodbye to Melchor, walks to the door, grasps the handle and looks back at the two men. "Remember there are only ten days left."

"Don't worry," Vàzquez says. "Trust us."

The mayor nods again.

As soon as the mayor leaves the room, Melchor blurts out:

"Vidal is involved in this."

"What?" Vàzquez asks, blinking furiously.

"The deputy mayor is blackmailing the mayor," Melchor says. "Or he's working with the blackmailers."

"How do you know?"

"I don't know: I sense it. And so does the mayor. Why do you think she gave the case to some hack detectives and then to us?"

The sergeant sits back down again and, after a few seconds of silence, seems to catch on.

"Right," he says. "If she didn't sense that Vidal was mixed up in the matter, she would have taken the case to her own people."

"Exactly. She brought it to us because she doesn't trust them. And she doesn't trust them because she thinks their boss is knee deep in it."

Vàzquez pounds the table with his fist and two empty glasses fall over on the cloth.

"Bloody hell," the sergeant grumbles. "It's true."

"It's at least possible," Melchor clarifies, righting one of the fallen glasses. "I think that, before, she only suspected, but now she's sure."

"Why do you say that?"

"Because of the face she made when you asked her if anyone who appears in the video might be interested in her resignation. That's when something clicked."

As if thinking out loud, Vàzquez concludes:

"So, her own deputy mayor wants her resignation."

"If he's mixed up in this, for sure."

"We're not getting carried away, are we?" the sergeant suddenly reconsiders. "Are we complicating things more than we need to?"

"Not at all," Melchor insists. "There are those who think Vidal is hoping to replace his boss. And they have good reason to think that. It's even possible that the mayor's ex-husband wants rid of her, and he's in the film too."

"Which probably means that her ex-husband is also one of the bad guys," the sergeant reasons, abandoning his brief stint as devil's advocate.

"Maybe. After all, he and Vidal are lifelong friends. Like the other one. What's his name?"

"Rosell." Both policemen remain silent for a moment, and Melchor notices that Vàzquez has an almost imperceptible tremor in his left cheek, as if he'd developed a tic. "There's one thing that doesn't fit," the sergeant admits. "If the mayor sensed from the start that Vidal was involved in the matter, why didn't she tell us? Why doesn't she tell us now? Out of fear? Vidal and his people don't go in for half measures, that's for sure. But—"

"I don't know," Melchor also admits. "One way or another, what's certain is we have to talk to him as soon as possible."

Vàzquez opens his eyes wide.

"To Vidal?"

"To him, the ex-husband and the other one."

"So they know we're on to them? No way."

"They don't need to know we're on to them. Only that we're after whoever's blackmailing the mayor."

"And if it's them who are blackmailing the mayor?"

"We have to run that risk. I'd be willing to sacrifice the element of surprise in exchange for a good conversation with those three."

"Remember there's a fourth. Although we don't yet know who he is."

"OK then, with those four."

Vàzquez seems to be thinking it over: his mouth is tight and, under the dark circles of fatigue or insomnia, his left cheek is still trembling.

"Be patient," he says to Melchor, refusing his suggestion. "We're going to explore this avenue first."

"At least have these three followed."

"Are you crazy? I don't even have enough manpower for the basic essentials and I'm going to put them to work on this?"

"Ask Blai. He'll give you backup. I'll take care of Vidal. Tell him we need some people to keep an eye on the other two?"

Vàzquez doesn't devote much time to considering Melchor's suggestion.

"Well, I'll think about it." He stands up. "Let's go, Verónica must be getting tired of waiting."

The meeting is in the Roure, a bar near El Botafumeiro that's been going for years. So, after going back out into the hot chaos of Gran de Gràcia and walking a hundred metres towards

Diagonal, they turn right at the first side street and carry on to the small plaza where the café is. They don't see the press officer straight away among the few couples chatting under the old ceiling fans – artefacts retired as cooling instruments and recycled as relics attesting to the establishment's long history – but, once they've passed a bar loaded with traditional tapas, they recognise her sitting at the back, waving her arms like windmill sails to get their attention.

"What a coincidence, Vàzquez!" Verónica says to the sergeant while pointing at Melchor. "I've been wanting to talk to this man for so long; I call you and it turns out he's thrown in for free." She plants a couple of kisses on the cheeks of each policeman and, while she clears a place on the table amid the confusion of papers, she adds: "Sit down, please. And forgive this mess: I always carry my office around with me."

She's a petite, dark-haired, lively woman in her mid-thirties, wearing a pair of faded jeans and a dark green T-shirt; she wears her hair up and gestures profusely. She has barely sat back down again opposite the two policemen when the waiter appears. Melchor and Vàzquez don't order anything; she, who has just finished her cortado, orders another.

"So, tell me." She turns to Melchor with an open smile. "What brings you to Barcelona?"

"He was missing us," Vàzquez jokes.

"Really?" Verónica asks.

"I'm just here on assignment," Melchor explains. "I'm not staying long."

"And you'll go back to Terra Alta?" Verónica asks.

Melchor nods. The press officer huffs with an expression of infinite boredom.

"I don't know what you see in that place, *chico*. Have you been there, Vàzquez?"

"No."

"You're not missing much, I can tell you that. It's the back of beyond!" Trying to ingratiate herself with Melchor, she adds: "Mind you, I'm not saying it wouldn't do for a romantic weekend." Before immediately correcting herself: "Of course, for a romantic weekend, a bunker would suffice . . . Honestly, though, what a good time you could be having here in Barcelona. We'd give you five-star treatment. You know that, don't you?"

The waiter's arrival saves Melchor from answering. Still pondering the advantages that a transfer to the capital would unlock for him, Verónica takes a Canderel dispenser out of her handbag, drops two tablets the size of lentils into her cortado, puts the dispenser back in her bag and begins to stir the coffee with a spoon.

"Anyway, as for what we're doing here: do you know Isaki Lacuesta?" Melchor shakes his head. "You've never seen any of his films?" To Verónica's astonishment, Vàzquez also says no. "Well, you don't know what you're missing, my darlings. He's a fantastic director, who makes fantastic films and who, well, anyway, I'm speechless. I knew him a lifetime ago, when I worked at the *Diari de Girona*. We had a bit of a thing. Not much of one, unfortunately. Well, I'll spare you the details." She passes a hand in front of her face, like a magician's or a flamenco dancer's flourish. "So, he wants to direct a movie about the 2017 attacks."

Perhaps hoping to weigh Melchor's reaction, Verónica pauses and takes a sip of her drink; not a single muscle moves on the policeman's face.

"But, of course," the press officer finishes, "he's only going to do it if he can count on you."

Melchor smiles politely.

"I already told you I don't want to be on TV," he reminds her.

"But this isn't TV, man!" Verónica exclaims, taking his hand with one hand and patting it with the other. "It's cinema. It'll be a documentary, nothing whatsoever invented, nothing. Why would he? And it'll be great. You'll see. You don't know Isaki, he's a star. If anyone can turn this story into something awesome, it's him."

Verónica continues to sing the praises of the director and invites Melchor to consider the value the film could have for the force or for the morale of the force; she repeats, refining and updating, the arguments she used years earlier, when she tried to convince Melchor to appear on that Catalan television programme; she also adds some new ones: according to which, Melchor has turned into a "transversal and supra-partisan" symbol over the years, representing the best that the Catalan police can be.

"Don't you get it?" Verónica insists: she had let go of Melchor's hand, but she takes it again. "There are boys who arrive at the Police Academy and the first thing they do is ask about you."

"No shit," says Vàzquez, whose facial tic has accelerated.

"I'm telling you," Verónica reaffirms, giving Melchor's hand another pat. "And we have to take advantage of that. After all we've suffered in recent years . . ."

The press officer resumes her charge, as if she were facing her last chance to convince Melchor. She is still cycling through her arsenal of arguments when Vázquez interrupts her, pointing at his colleague:

"If you're going to give him a blow job, let me know and I'll leave you two alone, eh? I've got work to do."

"I'm serious, Vàzquez," Verónica scolds him.

"So am I," Vàzquez says.

Verónica laughs joyfully while coquettishly batting away the sergeant's comment ("You're just jealous"), but it takes her a second to recover her poise. She takes another sip of her cortado and renews her offensive, turning back to Melchor.

"There is another reason for you to agree. You could give your version of events."

"I gave it to the judge," Melchor reminds her.

"I don't mean just the attacks," Verónica clarifies. "I mean events in general."

Melchor looks at her uncomprehending. The woman leans forward, her ribcage on the edge of the table, and her breasts spill onto the wooden surface. Vàzquez struggles in vain to keep his eyes off them. The press officer asks Melchor, "Don't tell me you haven't read Javier Cercas' latest novel?"

He is about to apologise, and explain that he doesn't read contemporary novels, when Vàzquez interrupts:

"What novel?"

"I can't believe this." Verónica sighs. "You don't watch Isaki's films, or even read novels that talk about you. But, my darlings, what world do you live in?"

Vàzquez repeats his question.

"A novel about Melchor," Verónica explains. "Well, about Melchor or about a guy with Melchor's name who resembles Melchor quite a bit . . . it's called *Even the Darkest Night*. Have you really not heard anything about it?" The two cops maintain a slightly embarrassed silence; the woman goes on addressing the sergeant: "Cercas says he based the story on Melchor, though he also says that everything in the novel is made up, well, that he invented the story from start to finish. But there are those who say that that's a lie and that it's all true, I mean, that your colleague here told his story to Cercas and he

185

did nothing more than write it down. Do you know this guy, Melchor?"

Melchor assures her he does not.

"Shit, what a mess," says Vàzquez, scratching his shaved head.

"You see?" Verónica says. "Another reason to help Isaki with his film: to refute the lies and confirm the truth. In Cercas' book, I mean. Because there must be some truth in it, don't you think?"

Melchor doesn't answer.

"I'm confused," Vàzquez admits. "If I wasn't on duty, I'd knock back a stiff drink right now." Impatient and a little irritated, he adds: "Tell me something, Verónica, is this the only thing you wanted to talk to us about?"

Straightening up in her chair, the woman sighs again, pleads with Melchor to reconsider the offer and smooths her wrinkled T-shirt.

"No, honey; this is just the good bit." The press officer drinks the rest of her cortado and asks straight out: "Are you two investigating the mayor being blackmailed?"

The sergeant is startled.

"Who told you that?"

"Roger Galí," Verónica answers. "A journalist from *Ara*. Don't ask me where he got it because I have no idea. The only thing he told me is that there were rumours going around that the mayor is being blackmailed with a sex tape and that you are on the case. Is it true or not?"

"Goddamn it all to hell," Vàzquez swears. "This is all we need."

"Is it true or is it not?" Verónica insists.

"Of course, it's fucking true. What I don't understand is how this could reach the ears of a journalist. Unless . . ."

"Unless someone saw us going into City Hall and started snooping around," Melchor finishes his sentence.

"Shit," the sergeant says.

Silence.

"Maybe it's someone testing the waters," Melchor speculates. "Maybe someone has an interest in getting the matter out in the open. Or in us knowing that it could come out."

The hypothesis floats over the table while Melchor and Vàzquez exchange glances. Verónica asks:

"What the heck are you two thinking?"

The sergeant answers with another question:

"What did you tell the journalist?"

"What could I say? The truth: that I didn't know the first thing about it. That I'd try to find out. That I'd let him know."

"You have to stop him," Vàzquez begs her. "If he publishes, we're royally fucked. If the criminals find out we're on to them . . ."

"I'll do what I can," Verónica promises. "Though it won't be easy. *Ara* is going through a rough patch, for a change, they say it's on the brink of closing down, except that this time it seems like they're serious. So an exclusive like this is going to suit them down to the ground."

"You have to stop him," Vàzquez repeats. "However you can."

"I'll manage." Verónica nods. "But hurry up, please: I'm telling you this thing is red hot. And, if it's miracles you need, go to Rome. You get it, right?"

Vàzquez nods too. Vaguely satisfied, Verónica looks for a second at the chaos of papers on the table and seems a little lost, as if she doesn't know where to start in fulfilling her promise. Vàzquez takes advantage of her indecision to announce:

"Well, if there's nothing else, we'll make a move. I'm drowning in work and I have to get back to Egara."

They wrap up and, as the two policemen walk out into the six o'clock heat, Verónica pays for her coffees. They say goodbye in the plaza, where the press officer has parked her motorbike. Helmet in hand and sitting astride her bike, Verónica recovers the joyful mood with which she'd greeted them. Finally, she launches one last appeal on behalf of Isaki Lacuesta and asks Melchor to think over his film project.

"I'll call you in September, or I'll come and see you in Terra Alta," she announces. "Maybe I'll get inspired and show up with a date. Are you single, Vàzquez?"

"And unencumbered," the sergeant replies instantly.

Verónica winks at Melchor and puts on her helmet.

"Well, maybe I'll come and see you with this hunky guy." She laughs. "Meanwhile, don't forget about me."

Vàzquez tells her not to forget them and, as he watches her drive away down Riera de Sant Miquel, he says:

"She's so nice, isn't she?"

When Melchor gets home he finds Vivales reading a stack of documents and Cosette playing with a friend from the summer camp, a girl called Sandra who has her teeth armour-plated with braces and a good-looking, witty mother who does not go unnoticed amid the chaos of arrivals and departures from the community centre. Sandra's mother comes to pick her up soon, and Melchor talks to her for a few minutes. Later, while Cosette is watching TV, Melchor and Vivales prepare dinner and, when it's ready, Melchor leaves his daughter and the lawyer eating by themselves and walks to La Dama, a restaurant hidden in an old modernist building on Diagonal.

A waitress leads him to a dining room where Rosa Adell is waiting for him, sitting on a red velvet sofa, with a martini in hand. They say hello with a kiss, and Melchor sits down opposite his friend while the waitress asks him if he'd like an aperitif. He orders a Coca-Cola and, when she leaves, says:

"You shouldn't have booked such an expensive place."

"Well, I'm paying, so it's my choice," Rosa says.

"Are we celebrating?"

The woman raises her martini glass in a solitary toast, takes a sip and asks:

"How about your homecoming?"

"Barcelona is not my home," Melchor corrects her. "My home is Terra Alta."

Rosa smiles. They are sitting at the back of an elegant room. Behind Melchor, a stylish, elderly, Japanese couple are having dinner; to his left a window looks out onto Diagonal, although the sheer curtains that cover it reveal only a shapeless glow. Rosa Adell is wearing a white cotton blouse, with a black brooch in the shape of a miniature eagle with outstretched wings: the logo of Gráficas Adell; she has added a subtle touch of colour to her full lips and her deep, oval eyes, and the light from the lamp hanging from the wall behind her gives her mature skin a hint of gold. Looking at her, Melchor feels very fortunate that this beautiful, cultured and educated woman honours him with her friendship, and that she has set aside the commitments that have brought her to Barcelona to have dinner with him, an ordinary policeman fifteen years her junior; he also thinks what he often thinks when he sees her: that Rosa is the same age that, if she were alive, Olga would be.

"How's the capital, then?" she asks.

While Melchor explains as far as he can why he's in

Barcelona, the waitress brings his Coca-Cola and two menus and Rosa requests another martini with a gesture. Melchor is surprised by the request. Rosa drinks, but very little and almost always wine, and the policeman wonders if she's having two cocktails on an empty stomach because she needs to perk herself up. What for, he wonders. He also wonders if she has found something out since Saturday, or if something has happened (something related to her ex-husband or Salom, for example, something related to the Adell case or to those responsible), and if that is the real motive for the dinner.

"And you?" Melchor asks.

"Me what?"

"What are you doing here?"

The woman exhales, sounding both bored and tired.

"Work hassles," she says.

While they share a starter (Santoña anchovies and bay scallops au gratin), Rosa tells him about a novel by Don Winslow called *The Cartel*. It's a regular scene between the two of them: a reader of contemporary novels (especially, crime stories), Rosa tries to infect Melchor with her enthusiasm for one of her recent favourites. Without much success. After Olga's death, Melchor's literary tastes experienced a sort of regression, and since then the policeman has gone back to feeding exclusively on nineteenth-century novels, just as he did before he met her; he never tells Rosa that, when it comes to crime stories, he has more than enough at work, and so he makes an effort to listen to her, also without much success. So, while she talks about DEA agent Art Keller and drugs kingpin Adán Barrera, Melchor drifts off into thinking about the blackmailing of the mayor, though he only notices he's stopped paying attention when he catches Rosa Adell looking at him with a half-smile.

"What are you thinking about?" she asks.

"Nothing."

"It's impossible to think of nothing," she objects. "Besides, has no-one ever told you you're a very bad liar?"

Of course, Melchor is on the verge of answering. *Olga*.

But he doesn't.

Their main courses arrive which they share as well (Mediterranean sea bass with ratatouille and scallops with cauliflower purée and a beef reduction), and, while Rosa begins to divide them up, Melchor asks:

"Do you know the mayor?"

"Of Barcelona?"

Melchor nods.

"Does the case have to do with her?" Rosa asks in turn.

"What case?"

"What case do you think? The one that's brought you here, the one you were thinking about while I was telling you about *The Cartel*."

Still serving, Rosa gives him an ironic look.

"Do you know her or not?" Melchor insists.

"I had lunch with her once. It was a business meet and greet. Or something like that. I had just taken charge of Gráficas Adell."

"And?"

The answer comes only after Rosa has tasted the sea bass.

"Frankly, I thought she was a fake."

Melchor recalls Chicho Campà and asks:

"You mean she only says what people want to hear?"

"More or less. And also that she doesn't have anything serious to say, but she says it very well. The secret of success in politics, no?"

The conversation later swerves to Cosette and Rosa's four daughters, who are all much older than Cosette and have moved away, though they regularly visit the family home in Terra Alta. This is another frequent topic of conversation between them and, although it interests him more than crime novels do, Melchor has to concentrate to avoid losing his train of thought again. Only then does he notice that he's never seen his friend this content as long as he's known her. He wonders if Rosa has at last begun to overcome the unhappiness that swooped down on her five years ago, when her parents were murdered; then he wonders if he is also starting to overcome his and, as if he already has the answer, he takes advantage of the first opportunity to announce some news: when a librarian's position opens up in Terra Alta, or somewhere around Terra Alta, he's going to apply for it.

"If I get it, I'm leaving the force."

Rosa looks at him in shock. She knows that, for the past three years, Melchor has been studying librarianship, but she always thought he was just doing it out of interest, or for the same reason he puts fresh flowers on Olga's grave every Saturday, as a way of staying loyal to his dead wife; but she never imagined that he intended to earn his living as a librarian.

"Are you sure?"

"Totally."

They share a dessert as well: a tarte tatin.

As soon as they leave the restaurant, Rosa takes Melchor's arm and asks him to walk her home. She has drunk almost an entire bottle of wine (a verdejo from Rueda recommended by the sommelier), but she's not drunk, or doesn't seem to be. They walk along Diagonal, turn right onto paseo de Gràcia and walk towards the sea. The night is warm and the conversation flows easily, and at a certain point Melchor starts to think his intuition has failed him and his friend did not invite him to dinner in order to give him some bad news.

He's not wrong. Rosa Adell stops at the entrance to the Hotel Majestic, on the corner of paseo de Gràcia and Valencia.

"I'm staying here," she says.

A little surprised, Melchor looks at the front of the hotel with its three stone arches flanked by dwarf cypresses in huge metallic flowerpots and its modernist iron and glass canopy. The entrance is deserted but for the uniformed doorman, in his derby, who wanders around with his hands behind his back, pretending not to notice them. Melchor has taken for granted that they are walking down to Rosa's daughters' flat on calle Pau Claris, where she usually stays when she visits Barcelona.

"You're not staying with your daughters?" he asks.

"No," Rosa answers. Her lips curve into a mischievous, almost childish expression, as she lowers her gaze to the hexagonal paving stones adorned with floral motifs. "The truth is I'm not in Barcelona for work." Looking up, she adds: "I lied. The truth is that I've only come to see you."

Then she approaches Melchor and, like a teenager in love, indifferent to the metropolitan hustle and bustle around them, grasps his cheeks and finds his mouth and kisses him. When she pulls back, her eyes shine in the luminous night.

"Do you want to come up to my room?" she asks.

Melchor understands then that this is the news Rosa was saving for him, the latest news from the Adell case, and also understands why Rosa had needed to drink to deliver it. He looks away and meets the gaze of the doorman, who immediately averts his eyes. Then he looks back at Rosa. *Olga is dead*, he reads in her eyes. And also: *She died five years ago*. And also: *But I am alive*. Melchor understands that Rosa is right. Suddenly he remembers: *As long as there's remorse, there's guilt*.

"I can't," he hears himself say. "It wouldn't work. I'd

disappoint you." He falls silent, doubts for a moment, and adds: "Besides, you deserve something better than me."

As soon as he has said it, he regrets having said it, because he feels that, for Rosa, those words are adding insult to the injury of his refusal; but he doesn't know how to rectify it. The owner of Gráficas Adell sighs and smiles again.

"There's nothing better than you, Melchor," she says: her eyes are no longer shining as they were before. "But maybe you're right. I shouldn't have suggested it."

Rosa says goodnight and walks away towards the hotel. She has not yet crossed the threshold when, just as she draws level with the doorman, she turns back towards the policeman, who has remained standing still on the corner, watching her go. The doorman looks at them as if caught in the crossfire.

"Will you let me tell you something?" the woman asks.

To the doorman's relief, Rosa takes a few steps back, away from him, and stops a couple of metres from her friend.

"Don't kid yourself, Melchor," she says, pointing at him with an admonishing finger. "You'll always be a cop."

When he gets home, he finds Vivales sunk in his favourite arm-chair, beside the open door to the balcony. The television is on and he's watching an old black-and-white western. Melchor sits down beside him and asks how Cosette is.

"All under control," says Vivales. "Out like a light hours ago."

He's wearing enormously baggy boxer shorts and a white T-shirt with red polka dots that emphasises his prominent gut, and his legs, thick and hairy, rest on a pouffe; to his left, on a small table, is a watered-down glass of whisky. On the television screen James Stewart is teaching a group of students composed of boys and girls, a black hired hand, several farm labourers and Vera Miles, under the satisfied gaze of an obese sheriff. The black man is reciting the second paragraph of the Declaration of Independence of the United States: "All men are created equal."

"Bollocks," the lawyer murmurs, as if arguing with himself. "And then they say that Ford was a racist."

Melchor is not a big cinema buff, but, thanks to Vivales, who adores westerns (and who is in the habit of watching a film every night), he knows who John Ford is; also, that this film is called *The Man Who Shot Liberty Valance*.

"How'd it go with the rich heiress?" the lawyer asks.

"Fine."

Vivales talks without missing a detail of what's happening on the screen, and Melchor remembers a scene from another western. A cowboy is astonished to discover that he likes a woman and, to sort out his feelings, he asks the owner of the saloon: "You ever been in love?" "No," comes the answer. "I've been a bartender all my life." A few seconds later, Melchor asks Vivales if he has heard of a novel called *Even the Darkest Night*.

"What?" says Vivales.

John Wayne has just burst into the schoolroom, covered in dust, bringing urgent bad news – Liberty Valance and his men are heading into town intending to kill James Stewart – and Stewart adjourns the lesson and takes off into the countryside in a horse-drawn waggon to learn how to shoot. John Wayne follows him, stops his waggon and offers to teach him how to use his pistol. Melchor asks the question again and adds the name of the novel's author. Vivales answers that he hasn't heard of it.

"It's about me," says Melchor.

On John Wayne's instructions, James Stewart is setting up three paint cans on three posts. When he finishes putting the last one up, John Wayne shoots the three of them while laughing at the gullibility of James Stewart, who runs up to John Wayne and, furious and covered in paint, knocks him to the ground with one punch, provoking a guffaw from Pompey, his black servant. Vivales, who never laughs, laughs. Melchor wonders if he's laughing at John Wayne or at him. The lawyer quickly clears things up.

"What?" he asks again.

Vivales turns towards him for the first time, a trace of laughter still lingering on his face.

"The novel," Melchor says. "It's about me. That's what I've been told."

The lawyer tries to take in his words without success.

"A novel about you?"

"Yes," Melchor answers. "It's called *Even the Darkest Night.*"

Vivales shakes his head, sceptical, while his lips form the shape of a circumflex accent and a breath of a breeze sneaks past the balcony door to alleviate the heat of the room for a second; then the lawyer takes a sip of whisky and the film once more monopolises his attention. Melchor looks at the time on his phone: almost one. He looks at the TV screen again and tries to decipher what's going on there. Before he manages it, Vivales turns back to him.

"Do you want us to sue him?" he asks.

"Who?" Melchor answers.

"This Cercas guy."

"Sue him? What for?"

"What do you mean what for?" Vivales says. "For invasion of privacy, an attack on your honour, public scandal. I don't know. Any excuse is good for filing a lawsuit. This Cercas must be some kind of lowlife, but we'll get something out of him. I'm telling you."

Melchor looks at Vivales, thinking he's joking.

"Shall we sue him or not?"

He realises he's not joking.

"It's late," Melchor says. "I'm going to bed."

As he stands up he recognises the scene on TV: desperate, with tears in her eyes, Vera Miles is begging John Wayne to save James Stewart, who is preparing to face Liberty Valance in a duel without knowing how to fire a revolver.

"Wait." Vivales sits up to reach for the remote control. "I'm going to bed too."

"Aren't you going to watch the end of the movie?"

"I know it by heart. Besides, on Friday I'm in court and tomorrow morning I've got to prepare for it."

The lawyer turns off the TV and, with a groan, rises from his armchair. The two men straighten up the dining room a little, turn off the lights and leave a couple of dirty glasses in the kitchen sink. As they walk to their respective bedrooms, Melchor asks Vivales about Friday's trial, and the lawyer explains that he's defending a guy accused of abusing his wife. Melchor asks the name of the guy; Vivales answers Alexis Rosa.

"I don't know how you can defend people like that," Melchor lets slip.

They're at the doorway of the room he's sharing with Cosette. In the gloom of the hallway, Melchor smells the whisky on Vivales' breath and hears the gravelly sound of his breathing. The lawyer lowers his voice so he won't wake the little girl.

"And I don't understand how a cop like you can ask me a question like that," he says.

"You're not telling me the guy's innocent?"

In reply, Vivales lays a kind hand on Melchor's shoulder and, with real curiosity, asks:

"Innocent of what?" Then he explains: "As far as I know, the lad's a nasty piece of work. But by now you should know that I would be capable of defending Jack the Ripper. Not just Jack the Ripper: Liberty Valance. And do you know why?" He doesn't wait for a reply. "Because even the biggest son of a bitch in the world has the right to have someone defend him. Otherwise there can be no justice." There is silence and Melchor realises that Vivales is looking him in the eye; he is glad it is too dark for him to see. "Or were you innocent when I defended you?" Taking his hand off his shoulder, Vivales concludes: "Each to his own, son: you devote yourself to chasing bad guys, and I'll devote myself to defending them."

Melchor gets into bed thinking that this is the first time in his life Vivales called him son.

At eight-thirty in the morning he drops Cosette off at the community centre, and is about to get back into his car to drive out to Egara when he thinks he should send a WhatsApp message to Rosa Adell, but he can't think what to write and doesn't write anything. At that moment Vàzquez rings and orders him to stay in Barcelona.

"I know where they called the mayor from," he says. "Didn't I tell you it was a payphone?" He gives him an address in the Raval. "Head over there, see what you can find out." Then, talking faster and faster, Vàsquez says, "There's news on the Santa Coloma kidnapping, things are coming to a head, I've been getting ready to intervene all night."

"Do you want me to come and give you a hand?"

"No need," Vàzquez says. "Blai is behaving himself and for once I have enough people. You carry on with the mayor's thing; we can't leave her in the lurch, especially with so little time left till the deadline. Do you need anything?"

"No," Melchor says. Then he immediately corrects himself: "Yes, actually. When you can, find me an address. A guy called Alexis Rosa."

Vàzquez gets him to repeat the name, then asks:

"And who is he?"

"I'll tell you later."

He walks to the Rambla, enjoying the morning's fleeting coolness and, when he reaches the Liceo metro stop, he turns right on calle Sant Pau, carries on walking and, right at the corner of the Rambla del Raval, he discovers a payphone built into the wall.

He spends the rest of the morning sniffing around the neighbourhood. First of all, he explores the immediate surroundings of the phone until he finds two establishments that have security cameras facing the street: the first is a security firm; the second, the cashpoint of a branch of the Banco de Santander. Neither of the two cameras focus directly on the payphone, but Melchor wants to see the images recorded by each of them two days earlier, at the time the blackmailer called the mayor. The bank manager puts up no objections; the person in charge of the security firm, however, is more reluctant, but also ends up agreeing. Melchor examines the two lots of footage carefully: he does not detect anything suspicious in them. Nor does he get anything out of interrogating employees and owners of the nearby shops, bars and restaurants, several residents of the building where the phone is and a homeless man he finds sleeping in a corner, curled up on top of a sleeping bag, camouflaged by his dog. He goes up and down calle Sant Pau a couple of times as well as the adjacent side streets, trying to reconstruct the blackmailer's hypothetical route. At some point he is even tempted to go back to the Frenchman's internet café, which is very close, and ask him again about the client he duplicated the SIM card for using Farooq Hoque's mobile phone, but he quickly decides that it would be futile or counterproductive and rejects the idea.

At noon someone from Egara sends him Alexis Rosa's address. An hour later he calls Vàzquez a couple of times in quick succession and sends him a couple of WhatsApp messages, but the sergeant does not answer; Blai doesn't respond to his messages either. Then he decides to run an errand.

He gets onto the metro at plaza de Cataluña and takes Line 1 in the direction of Hospital de Bellvitge. Nine stops later he gets off at Torrassa and walks to calle Orient. There he looks for number seven, finds it, rings the intercom of a flat on the third floor. Nobody answers and he goes to a café right across the street.

It's past lunchtime and he is ferociously hungry, so he sits beside a big window and orders a salad, a steak and a Coca-Cola. He eats without taking his eyes off the entrance of number seven, where he sees a middle-aged couple, a punk-looking girl and an old lady dragging a shopping trolley emerge. At about four, when he is about to call Vivales to explain that something has come up again and ask him if he can pick up Cosette, he sees a man in his fifties with curly ginger hair go in the front door. Without rushing, he pays for his meal, leaves the restaurant, crosses the street and rings the same bell. This time there's an answer.

"Alexis Rosa?" Melchor asks.

"Yes," a male voice says.

"I'm here on behalf of Domingo Vivales," Melchor lies.

"Who?" the man asks.

"Domingo Vivales," Melchor repeats. "Your lawyer. Open up, please. It's important."

The door opens.

That night, after he has been reading *Michel Strogoff* to his daughter for a while, she asks him if they are going to stay in Barcelona for a long time; Melchor tells her no, not long.

"How long?" Cosette insists.

"I don't know," Melchor admits. "Are you not having a good time here?"

"Really good."

"So then?"

Snuggled up next to him, Cosette shrugs and makes a face. Melchor asks:

"Would you like to go home this weekend?"

"I'd love it."

They agree to spend the weekend in Terra Alta and, a little while after Cosette falls asleep, Melchor receives a WhatsApp infested with capital letters and exclamation marks in which Vàzquez informs him that they've freed the Santa Coloma narco's wife that evening, that they're celebrating in the Nicosia, a bar in Sabadell, and that he should come out and celebrate with them. Melchor sends his congratulations and says he'll see him tomorrow morning at Egara.

The next morning, in Egara, the party is still going, or that is the impression Melchor gets when he arrives. The Abduction and Extortion office is packed with colleagues who have barely slept, drinking orange juice and coffee and devouring croissants, pastries and cupcakes; there are also some civil guards and National Police officers among them. In the centre of the hubbub, smiling from ear to ear, euphoric and exhausted, Vàzquez is in full flow, and, when he sees Melchor, he hugs him and explains how the previous night's operation went down in a matter of hours. Under Blai's supervision, at five in the afternoon a force of more than fifty officers had burst into a villa in Sant Vicenç dels Horts, near Barcelona, where they found the narco's wife, terrified but unhurt, and that in total they had arrested five individuals, four in the villa in Sant Vicenç – two Romanians and two Spaniards – and another – Algerian – in a flat in Sant Joan Despí. At a certain moment, Vàzquez interrupts his tale to answer a phone call.

"Congratulations are arriving from the ladies, boys," the sergeant announces, winking with complicity at his colleagues and looking for a quiet place to talk. "It's Verónica, the stunner from the press office."

When the sergeant returns to the group, the smile has disappeared from his lips, replaced by a surly sneer.

"How fleeting is joy . . . !" he says. "There's a story about the mayor in *Ara*."

All the members of the unit rush to their computers and mobile phones. The article, in effect, takes up the whole front page of the digital edition of the paper, with Roger Galí's byline. In order to justify the four-column headline ("Sextortion at the plaza de Sant Jaume"), he has padded the article with gossip about the mayor's sex life and political skulduggery at City Hall: the only piece of concrete news the hack contributes is that the city's ruler is being subjected to sexual blackmail and that the Mossos d'Esquadra have opened an investigation into the case. Melchor has not yet finished reading the article when his ringing phone makes him suddenly aware of the silence reigning in the office. It's Blai.

"Have you seen *Ara*?" he asks.

"I'm looking at it," Melchor answers.

"The chief inspector is fuming," his friend growls. "I want you and Vàzquez in my office right now."

The sergeant is not bothered by receiving a superior's order through a subordinate, and, as the celebration disintegrates and Vàzquez and Melchor leave the office, he asks if he found out anything about the payphone the blackmailers used to call the mayor.

"Nothing," says Melchor, thinking that Cosette was going to have to do without her weekend in Terra Alta.

The one who's really fuming is Blai, who receives them in his office like a caged animal, pacing to and fro in front of the window that overlooks Egara's central courtyard.

"Well," he says when he stops cursing the press, the chief inspector, his bad luck and the world in general. "Now what?"

With Melchor's help, Vàzquez improvises a hurried summary of the situation. The tic in his cheek is back, his lips tremble and Blai has to ask him a couple of times to speak more slowly. When the sergeant concludes his explanation, there is silence and, before anyone can react, his phone rings.

"Here she is," Vàzquez announces, after looking at his phone.

The sergeant takes a deep breath before answering and, for a couple of minutes, Melchor and Blai watch how, seized by a sudden serenity, their colleague listens to, agrees with and attempts to calm the mayor, asks for a few minutes to consider the options and promises to call her right back.

"Now she's really scared," Vàzquez tells them, as soon as he finishes the call. "She wants to pay no matter what."

Silence takes over Blai's office again, but this time it is Melchor who breaks it.

"I don't think that's such a bad idea," he says, sure he's

translating into words what his colleagues are thinking. "If the guys from Financial Crimes are right, paying would give us a chance to catch the criminals. It's time to try it out."

Blai stares at Melchor; then he turns to Vàzquez and asks for his opinion. The sergeant takes a few seconds to answer, during which time he blinks as if his eyelids had caught the tic from his cheek.

"I don't think it's a bad idea either," he confesses. "No matter what, we have to change our strategy. We don't have much time left, and we've lost the advantage of secrecy. Of course, we could interview the three tenors right now. After all—"

"The three tenors?" Blai interrupts him.

"Our three suspects," Vàzquez clarifies. "The three who appear in the video: the husband, Vidal and the other guy."

"Rosell," says Melchor.

"That's it," Vàzquez says. "We could pursue them, after all, now they know we're on the trail of the blackmailers. But I wouldn't. Not yet. I'd play the pay-out card first. It's simpler and quicker. This might be the moment to use it, as Melchor says. If it works, fantastic. If not, we start interrogating them."

Blai has been listening to the sergeant's arguments while striding back and forth in front of his office window, through which dazzling sunlight pours in. Once Vàzquez has finished talking, the inspector stops, looks at him and then at the wall to his right, exactly where he's hung the photo of his family, with his wife and four children wearing hiking gear and climbing a rocky headland in Terra Alta; as he contemplates the bucolic image, the inspector's mind seems to go blank for a moment.

"Not another word," he finally decides, emerging from his abstraction. "Let's try paying. Melchor, go to Financial Crimes right now: tell them to start to look for the moneros and, as soon as they have the mayor's money, to buy them and pay what has to be paid. Better this afternoon than tomorrow, if possible. Tell them to let me know as soon as they know anything." He points to the sergeant: "And you tell the mayor to get the money ready. And to call me when she has it. If she can't get hold of me, tell her to ring Melchor. And when you get off the phone with her you go home, take a shower and get into bed. You look like you haven't slept in a week." Vàzquez starts to protest but Blai cuts him off: "That's an order."

Melchor spends the rest of the morning with three members of the Financial Crimes department, who shortly before noon tell him that it will be very difficult to get hold of enough moneros to pay the ransom in less than forty-eight hours. The news irritates and relieves him: it irritates him because it puts the case on ice for the weekend; it is a relief because, unless Blai tells him otherwise, he and Cosette can spend the weekend in Terra Alta. Blai does not tell him otherwise.

"Don't worry," is what the inspector says, after his compulsory rant against the Financial Crimes people. "Off you go. I'm on duty this weekend. As soon as I hear anything, I'll call you."

Melchor picks up Cosette at the community centre, and they buy a couple of sandwiches and eat them as they drive down to Terra Alta. When he turns off the Mediterranean motorway, and onto the main road, they call Vivales. The three of them talk hands free for a while and, before ending the call, Melchor asks the lawyer about that morning's trial.

"It's been postponed," Vivales says. "Yesterday the guy fell down the stairs of his building and he's in hospital with a couple of broken ribs. Clumsy bugger."

Melchor spends the weekend wondering whether or not to call Rosa Adell, and ends up not calling her. Cosette is barely at home: she plays football, goes swimming, watches films with her friends, and on Saturday night she sleeps over at Elisa

Climent's house. Melchor goes out for a run every morning in the countryside and spends the rest of the time reading at home or sitting by the door of the bar in the plaza, with a coffee or a Coca-Cola. At midday on Sunday, while he is finishing *The Illustrious House of Ramires*, having spent the morning reading manuscripts for the short story competition, Blai calls to say that the Financial Crimes people managed to get the moneros together last night and first thing that morning paid the ransom.

"And?" Melchor asks impatiently.

He has walked away from the terrace of the bar, seeking to shelter from the murderous July sun in the shade of the mulberry trees in the centre of the plaza.

"Nothing doing," Blai answers. "It seems these guys are genius hackers: they've connected their telephone to take the money, but they've camouflaged the IP address thanks to an application called TOR, and to top it off they've connected to that application through a VPN."

"A what?"

"A virtual private network. A sort of tube or tunnel that connects you directly to the server without allowing anyone to have access to your transactions, so the communication becomes private. That's what I've been told. In short, the guys are armour-plated, so we're not getting anywhere that way."

Blai falls silent and, while Melchor watches the cheerful midday bustle on the terrace of the bar from a distance, he imagines his colleague, alone and downcast by the bad news in the Sunday desolation of the Egara complex, with his wife and kids two hundred kilometres away in Terra Alta. He asks:

"Have you told Vàzquez?"

"I've called him a couple of times, but he's not picking up. You try. Tell him we'll start interviewing the three tenors tomorrow."

"I'll call him right away."

Another silence; for a moment, Melchor thinks Blai has hung up. Then he hears:

"We've got six days left, *españolazo*. We have to sort this out before then, whatever it takes. We're not going to tolerate any crooks deciding who can be mayor of Barcelona and who can't, are we?"

Part Three

Part Three

1

On Monday morning, after dropping Cosette off at the community centre, Melchor goes into a café on calle Córcega, orders a double espresso and begins a round of phone calls. First he calls Vàzquez, who does not answer; he's lost count of how many times he's tried in vain to get hold of him to convey Blai's order from yesterday: they have to interview the only three suspects they have as soon as possible. So, after calling Vàzquez without success, Melchor rings Casas, Vidal and Rosell.

He does not manage to get through to any of the three, but he does speak with their secretaries. The first tells him that Casas has not yet arrived at his office, asks for his name and the reason for his call, she also asks for his phone number, but Melchor assures her he will be back in touch. Vidal's and Rosell's secretaries are more forthcoming; as soon as Melchor identifies himself as a policeman, they both find space in their bosses' agendas: Vidal will see him at midday on Tuesday at City Hall, and Rosell, who is out of town, on Thursday afternoon. He is saying goodbye to Rosell's secretary when a call comes in from Vàzquez.

"About time," Melchor complains. "I've been calling you all weekend. Where did you get to?"

Nobody answers; Melchor hears someone breathing with difficulty on the other end of the line.

"Vàzquez?"

"I'm here," the sergeant says.

He speaks with a thin thread of a voice. Alarmed, Melchor asks:

"Are you alright?"

"Not really."

"What's the matter?"

Vàzquez's answer takes a few seconds; Melchor understands that something's wrong. The sergeant asks:

"Could you come over here?"

"Where are you?"

Vàzquez gives him his address in Cerdanyola.

"I'm on my way."

"Melchor," the sergeant stops him, before he can disconnect. There is silence. "Promise me you won't say anything about this to anyone."

"Anything about what?"

"Anything at all. I'll tell you later. Promise me."

Melchor promises.

It takes him almost three-quarters of an hour to get to Cerdanyola, passing Nou Barris and Santa Coloma de Gramenet. En route he gets calls from both Blai and Cortabarría, but he answers neither of them because he thinks they'll both ask him about Vàzquez and he won't know what to tell them; he also gets a call from the mayor's ex-husband's secretary and she tells him that he's in luck: her boss can see him that very afternoon, at four, at the head office of Clave Barcelona.

"Perfect," Melchor says. "I'll be there."

Vàzquez's place is in a building on the corner of a pedestrian street in the centre of Cerdanyola, calle San Ramón, right above a baby clothes shop. Melchor rings the intercom bell; nobody answers, but the door opens with a click. He walks up three flights of stairs, and when he gets to the third floor he sees one of the doors is ajar, he has a bad feeling and takes his pistol out of its holster. Holding the weapon in his hands, he pushes the door open and goes in. There is an almost hermetic gloom in the front hallway, but as Melchor walks up the hall it dissipates until, in the dining room, a few rays of light transform it into semi-darkness. Melchor is feeling the wall in search of a switch when he hears:

"Don't turn on the light."

It is Vàzquez's voice, coming from the shadows, and, while Melchor puts his pistol back in its holster, he makes out the sergeant in the darkness: he is sitting on the floor at the far end of the dining room, bare-chested, with his back against the wall and his legs stretched out as if he were exhausted. The slats of the blinds let in a faint light, and there's a smell that suggests confinement and filth. Melchor approaches Vàzquez, whose head seems to be collapsed on his left shoulder, and crouches down in front of him.

"Don't worry, Melchor," the sergeant murmurs, sitting up a little. "Don't worry. I'm fine."

He doesn't look it. In fact, he looks terrible: he's panting, trembling and sweating profusely, his lips chapped and several days' growth of beard devouring his face: his eyes shine, feverish and reddened.

"What's happened?" Melchor asks.

"Nothing," Vàzquez answers. "Don't worry. Sometimes it happens. I'll be fine. I just need to take my pills and—"

Vàzquez cannot finish his sentence: a convulsive crying fit

overtakes him. Not knowing what to do, Melchor tries to touch his shoulder, but, before he can complete the gesture, the sergeant throws his arms around his neck. He stays like that for a while, clinging to him and weeping. He stinks. After what seems an eternity (during which Melchor tries to digest the astonishment that the man sobbing in his arms like a frightened child is the toughest guy he knows), the sergeant pulls back, leaving Melchor's hands damp and his shirt soaked. Vàzquez looks at him now with his eyes wide open, still trembling but forcing himself to appear calm, and tells him again not to worry.

"How long have you been like this?" Melchor asks.

"Only a couple of days."

"How many?"

"I don't know. Two or three."

The last time Melchor saw Vàzquez was three days ago, in the Abduction and Extortion office, when, after a night of partying, he and his men were still celebrating the happy outcome of the Santa Coloma kidnapping. Melchor remembers the sergeant being very nervous, very agitated, talking very fast, and he asks him whether he has slept or eaten at all over the weekend; the sergeant stammers a response, and Melchor doesn't want to imagine what might have happened during the last fifty or sixty hours in that gloomy, rank and soulless flat. He stands up.

"Let's go," he says, grabbing Vàzquez by one armpit. Vàzquez bats his hand away.

"Where to?" he asks.

"To a hospital," Melchor says. "You have to see a doctor."

Vàzquez shakes his head emphatically.

"You don't understand," he mutters.

"What is it I don't understand?" Melchor asks.

Vàzquez raises his hands to his head and rubs them over his

face, as if he wanted to wash it; then, with his eyes popping out of his head, he looks at Melchor.

"I'm bipolar," he says. "They diagnosed me when I was in hospital, after what happened in Molins de Rei."

Melchor crouches back down in front of Vàzquez.

"I have periods of euphoria and periods of depression," the sergeant explains. "Up and down, up and down, first one then the other. I know how this works now, I'm used to it, so normally I control it, but this time . . . I don't know, it got out of hand. Last week I began to feel euphoric, I noticed it, things were going up, but I was sure I could keep it under control and I didn't take my pills . . . I don't work well when I take my pills, you know? They dull me, don't let me think. And with the shambles of the kidnapping . . . I didn't want that to happen again, I couldn't let that happen again. You can understand, Melchor. You understand, don't you?"

Melchor again sees Vàzquez sitting in a pool of blood, on the cement floor of the warehouse in Molins de Rei, with the decapitated head of the Venezuelan narco's daughter in his lap, screaming his head off like a lunatic, his face bathed in tears. *As long as there's remorse, there's guilt*, he thinks.

"The only thing I understand is that you're all fucked up," Melchor says. "And I should take you to a hospital."

"Are you crazy? If you take me to a hospital they'll admit me. If they admit me they'll find out at Egara. And if they find out at Egara it's over: or do you think they'll leave the unit in the hands of a nutcase?"

Melchor has no option but to admit to himself that the sergeant's logic is impeccable.

"They'll retire me," Vàzquez answers his own question. "They'll send me home. And what am I going to do at home, eh? What do I do? Feed the pigeons? I'll shoot myself. I swear, if they send me home, I'll shoot myself. On the other hand . . ." He straightens up a bit, tries to wipe the tears and snot off his face. "On the other hand, if you lend me a hand . . . Believe me, Melchor, I know how to fix this without resorting to doctors or hospitals; it's happened to me before; I just need to take my pills and eat and sleep properly for two or three days. Trust me."

Not knowing what to say, for a couple of seconds Melchor stares at the filthy, broken man who is begging for his help sitting on the floor in front of him. His eyes have grown accustomed to the gloom now, his nose to the stench.

"What do you want me to do?" he asks.

Melchor spends the rest of the morning working at Vàzquez's place, coming and going. The first thing he does is squeeze a glass of juice out of some old oranges he finds in the fridge, prepare a bowl of cereal with milk and make sure the sergeant consumes them both along with a 300 mg tablet of Lithobid, 10 mg of Zyprexa and 2 mg of Trankimazin. Next, after washing him and cooling him down a bit with a sponge, airing out his bedroom, tidying up and changing the sheets on his bed, he helps him into it and stays by his side until he falls asleep. Then he finishes cleaning up the flat – leaving both the sergeant's phones out of his reach, on silent – calls Blai and tells him that Vàzquez has had to go to Seu d'Urgell urgently because his mother has fallen ill.

"For fuck's sake," Blai curses. "After sending half his people off on holiday? And why didn't he call me to tell me?"

"I don't know: all I know is that his mother lives in a farmhouse out in the sticks where there's no coverage, so don't bother trying to call him," says Melchor, before hurrying to change the subject. "By the way, this afternoon I've arranged to meet the mayor's ex."

"Casas?"

"And tomorrow, Vidal."

"Great. That just leaves Rosell."

"I've got a meeting with him on Thursday. He's away."

"Can you talk to all of them on your own?"

"Sure. As long as you do me a favour."

"What favour?"

"Do you think we could tap their phones?"

"Out of the question. There's no way any judge will authorise that."

"Then have them followed. Until Rosell gets back, just the two of them."

"OK. I don't know where I'm going to get the people, but consider it done."

"If you need to, you can count on me."

"I will need to. And, by the way, where are you right now? I haven't seen you this morning either—"

"Blai? Blai? Shit, you're breaking up."

Melchor leaves Vàzquez's flat carrying several bags of rubbish, drops them in the bins, goes to the pharmacy and, with the prescriptions the sergeant has given him, gets three bottles of pills, one of each of the medications he's already given him, to which he adds a box of Symbyax 25 mg. Then he goes to a supermarket, buys mineral water, cereal, fruit, vegetables, bread, milk, cheese, packets of soup and tins of food, returns to the flat, makes a couple of salads and a couple of soups and leaves them in the fridge.

It's almost three in the afternoon when he finishes. Vàzquez is still sound asleep.

*

He finds a parking space in an alley between Bonanova Church and the ronda de Dalt, walks down to the plaza de la Bonanova and follows the avenue until he comes to the pasaje Güell. It is a private little street, quiet and protected by a large wrought-iron gate, open at that moment. Melchor walks through it, and recognises on the left, embedded in a wall beside a door, the logo of the consultancy firm Casas runs, a blood-red square with fourteen white letters: CLAVE BARCELONA.

A young woman wearing intellectual-looking glasses and a brown leather mini-skirt opens the door, shows him to a waiting room and, pointing to a sofa and telling him to wait for a moment, asks if he'd like a coffee. Melchor realises at that moment that he has had nothing to eat or drink since breakfast, accepts the offer and sits down. To his right, on a partition, the consultancy's logo is repeated relentlessly, as if trapped between two facing mirrors; on his left the wall is almost entirely taken up with a single phrase written in English: "It is likely that something unlikely will happen."

His coffee has not yet arrived when Casas appears.

"Sorry to keep you waiting," he apologises, smiling and stretching out an obliging hand. "At this stage of the summer people think only of their holidays . . . But, tell me, have you been offered anything to drink?"

Shaking the man's hand, Melchor says yes he has. Casas asks his secretary to bring the coffee into his office and, while the two men walk down the hall, says he regrets that he cannot spare him as much time as he'd like, to which Melchor responds that he only needs a couple of minutes.

"Incidentally," Casas says, stopping short, now inside his office, and looking Melchor in the eye, "allow me to say that it is an honour to meet you. It's not every day that the hero of Cambrils comes to call."

The policeman is not surprised that Casas has guessed the reason for his visit – after the feature in *Ara*, the blackmailing of the mayor is no longer a secret, nor is the fact that it is under police investigation – but he is that Casas knows who he is. How has he found out? From the mayor herself?

"Do you know something?" His host offers him a chair facing a designer desk on which sit a halogen lamp and a laptop, and takes a seat opposite him. "I am of the opinion that all societies need heroes, and ours more than most: guys that people can feel proud of, mirrors they can see themselves in. And here, in Catalonia, we have so few . . . But tell me, don't you live in Terra Alta? What are you doing in Barcelona?"

"I've just come up for a few days," Melchor explains. "I'm here on assignment."

"Well, you should stay. What the hell is there in Terra Alta? This is where things happen, man, living in a village is like burying yourself alive." There is a knock at the door; the secretary comes in and sets a tray with a nickel silver coffee service down on the desk. "Of course, taking into account how you've been treated . . . And I'm not just referring to the government, which should have erected a monument to you. I mean Catalonia in general. If we were Americans, there would already have been a couple of films and a couple of series out about the events in Cambrils, and David Fincher and Christopher Nolan would have come to blows over the rights. Here, however, we have to settle for a little novel by Javier Cercas. What a disaster, God in heaven, where's our self-esteem. And then there are those Catalans who want us to be independent. Sugar?"

Melchor says no. The secretary has left after pouring the coffee.

"By the way, I suppose you're sick of being asked," Casas

goes on, passing Melchor his cup, "but, what did you think of the novel? The Cercas one, I mean."

Melchor gulps down the coffee and puts the cup back down on the tray while registering the jolt of caffeine in his empty stomach.

"I haven't read it," he admits.

Casas gazes at him as if he had begun to levitate. He's only a few years older than Melchor, very thin, medium height, athletic build, with lively, curious blue eyes and the slightly mocking smile of a perpetual adolescent, sure of being liked; he has a deep tan and dresses with upscale informality: white Hermès polo shirt, J Brand jeans and Lotusse loafers. Stunned, he runs a hand over his very short, very dark hair.

"I can't believe it," he says. "Someone writes a novel with you as the main character and you don't even read it? Though you're not missing much, frankly. What happens, for those of us who have read it, is that our curiosity is piqued, we want to know what's true and what's false. Logical, right? I've talked about it with a few people . . . Have you heard of Lluís Bassets? He's an old friend of my father's, a journalist at *El País*, you've probably read him. Anyway, Lluís knows this Cercas guy and he says he's a fucking troublemaker. I mean, when he says that everything in his books is true, it's all false; and when he says that everything is false, it's all true. So, since Cercas says everything in this book is made up, everyone thinks it's all true." He laughs openly, showing his perfect teeth. "But I don't think so. I mean there are things in the book I don't buy. I don't know. That before you joined the police you were in prison for drug trafficking, for example. Or that you were the one who solved the Adell case. And much less do I believe what it says about your mother . . ."

Once again anguish constricts Melchor's throat.

"What does it say about her?"

"That she earned her living as a prostitute," Casas says. "And that one night she was killed and her body was dumped in a vacant lot in Sant Andreu. That did happen, of course, I remember it very well because it was a very famous crime, much talked about. But that woman . . . anyway, I'm sure she wasn't your mother. Was she?"

Casas waits for Melchor's response with interest. Melchor take a deep breath and shakes his head.

"I knew it," Casas exclaims, slapping his desk in elation. "The guy must've followed the case in the press, like we all did, and, when he was writing the book, decided to saddle your mother with the story of that poor woman. He's got a lot of nerve, that Cercas, what a way to trick people . . . But, anyway, I don't suppose you're here to talk about novels, but about what *Ara* published. More coffee?"

Melchor remembers the impact the first cup had on his stomach, but he's so hungry he accepts a second. Casas serves him and then pours a cup for himself. In a quite different tone he warns the policeman: "I should advise you that I know nothing about that matter."

The anguish in Melchor's throat gradually melts as he tries to concentrate on the interview.

"That's not what your ex-wife says."

"What does my ex-wife say?"

"She says you appear in the video with which they are blackmailing her. And she's sure it was made the day you two met. Apparently, you, Enric Vidal and Gonzalo Rosell appear in the footage. As well as her, of course."

Casas nods without conviction.

"She told you that?"

"Yes."

"How can she be so sure?"

"I don't know, but she is. You know the video she's talking about, don't you?"

Casas curls his lips into a disdainful sneer.

"I have an idea. Does that make me a suspect?"

"Who said anything about you being suspected of anything?"

The two men stare at each other for a second. Casas forces an uncomfortable smile and takes a sip of coffee. Apart from the laptop and the halogen lamp, on his desk there is a metal tin bristling with pens, pencils, felt-tip pens and an immaculate stack of papers; behind him, a large Tàpies hangs on the wall, dominated by a real sock, wrinkled and stuck to a canvas where broad grey, black and brown brushstrokes predominate, suggesting a volcanic or intergalactic or post-nuclear landscape, or perhaps simply a landscape on the outskirts of a large metropolis; to his right, a large window overlooking the pasaje Güell lets floods of burning light into the air-conditioned room. As he sips his coffee and again feels it hit his stomach, Melchor asks:

"Have you seen the video?"

Casas nods again.

"Once, ages ago, shortly after we made it. It was a bit of foolishness. I don't know why Virginia's so worried."

"Have you talked about it with her?"

"No. But we were married and I know her as well as I know myself. Tell me, what do you think that video contains?" Casas opens his arms wide, as if it were absolutely outrageous, and then takes the drama out: "What's it going to show? A damned teenagers' orgy. Log on to Youporn and you'll see hundreds of them. Do you think something like that could end a politician's career?"

"The mayor thinks so."

"Well, she's mistaken."

"And the blackmailers, too?"

"Them too. Look, Virginia is not a politician, she's not cut out to be a politician. She never was. She really only got into politics because she married me, because I convinced her to, because it was useful to me; if it hadn't been for that, she would have done something else, carried on working with refugees or something like that. That's the truth." Taking a sip of his coffee, he runs his tongue over his lips – thin and well defined – and adds: "I'll tell you something else. We Catalans don't know how to play politics. We know how to do some things, but not politics. We're terrible at it. And do you know why? Well, because political power has not resided in Catalonia for centuries. We're not very familiar with it, we don't know how to manage it, and deep down it frightens us. And when we have it, we get drunk on it. Sure, power always intoxicates, but, if you've never tasted it, it intoxicates you much more. Do you remember the Procés? It seems like centuries have passed since all that, doesn't it? Well, the Procés was in part, a very large part, the result of an intoxication with power . . . But we were talking about something else, weren't we?"

"We were talking about your ex-wife," Melchor reminds him. "Did power also go to her head?"

"In a very bad way," Casas replies. "And municipal power isn't even real power. Real power is still where it always was, and Virginia doesn't know what it is. Maybe she's starting to sense it, but she still doesn't know. And, even so, she is drunk on it. In any case, video or no video, my ex-wife hasn't got much of a future in politics. I'm telling you."

"She hasn't got much of a future because she's separated from you?"

"Of course."

Casas raises his eyebrows twice in quick succession, as if he doesn't want Melchor to take what he's just said seriously, or not too seriously.

"Does your wife's intoxication have to do with your separation?" the policeman presses.

"Could be." Casas shrugs. "In the life of a couple everything has to do with everything. But, if what you're asking me is whether that was the cause of our separation, the answer is no."

"And what about the infidelities?"

Now Casas smiles, although it is obvious the question has not pleased him.

"What infidelities?" Before Melchor can answer, his host clicks his tongue and explains: "Look, Virginia and I have had a lot of fun together and we've made a lot of things together. Including a daughter. We set up a political party and won an election and the office of mayor. Not bad, don't you think? And at a certain moment we decided to separate. Why? Well, because everything ends and, when a couple ends, the best thing to do is separate. Without guilt. Without resentment. Without delay. In other words, if you've got it into your head that I have something against my ex-wife and want to destroy her, forget it. I don't hate Virginia." Casas looks towards the window and stares at the street being punished by the hot afternoon sun. For a second he seems lost in thought; then he looks back at Melchor. "And even if I did hate her. As Michael Corleone says, 'Never hate your enemies: it affects your judgment.'"

"Does that mean the mayor is now your enemy?"

Casas is about to answer when his mobile rings. He takes it without apologising and, his brow slightly furrowed, listens for a few seconds. "I'm with a visitor," he says. "Give me five minutes." And he hangs up.

"It means that, even if Virginia was my enemy, I would not

hate her," he corrects Melchor, picking up the thread of the conversation as if nothing had interrupted it. "But she is not even my enemy: in this life one has to choose enemies who are on one's level, and Virginia, frankly . . . Anyway. What is true is that she is no longer my protégée."

"Who is your protégé now?"

The question seems to disconcert Casas.

"Is this of interest to your investigation?"

"That depends. Is Vidal your protégé now?"

Casas laughs again, but this time his laughter sounds a bit forced.

"What an idea!" he exclaims. "As if Enric needs anyone's protection! But if the question is whether I am going to support his political career—"

"That's what I'm asking."

"I don't know." Casas shrugs, traces of laughter still on his face. "He hasn't asked me to. And if he does ask I don't know what I'll do. What I do know is that I've distanced myself from the party and he has not, and I also know that, until further notice, Enric is still Virginia's right-hand man, and I don't think she'd know what to do without him . . . Listen, Enric and I have known each other our whole lives, we're like brothers. And, yes, of course, I know he has political ambitions; I should hope so: a politician who's not ambitious is no politician. But, between you and me, I don't know if he's the best person to replace Virginia, I don't think so, he's spent too much time inside City Hall, he's very visible in municipal politics, if I had to choose right now I would not hesitate to pick someone new, fresher and more malleable, someone like Virginia was a few years ago, if the tables turned even Virginia herself could . . ." Casas turns pensive again for a moment, during which the canvas hanging on the wall behind him catches Melchor's attention again: he suddenly thinks Tàpies' sock has fallen down a little, slid down the surface of the painting and is no longer where it was before. "Anyway, the fact is that right now Virginia is not even my political adversary. I have nothing against her. Besides, she is still my daughter's mother. I still love her. And, since I still love her, I would never do anything to harm her. You understand, don't you?"

Melchor nods, but as he does so, he realises that he does not believe a word of what Casas says. Trying to disguise his mistrust, he asks:

"Do you know anyone who would? Harm her, I mean."

Casas shrugs again.

"Many people, I suppose. The more power you have the more people hate you. It's the way of the world. But, going back to the video, that seems more like a joke. Believe me. And now you're going to have to forgive me because—"

"I still have a few more questions."

Casas had been on the verge of standing up, but he stays bolted to his chair. It is the first time during the interview that he seems annoyed. However, a moment later, he is smiling obsequiously and encouraging Melchor to continue.

"Do you know who made it?" the policeman goes on.

"The video?"

"Yes. If you, Vidal, Rosell and the mayor appear in the images, someone must have filmed you. The mayor mentioned some friend."

"Of course. Ricky Ramírez was his name. Virginia's right: he was the one who filmed us. He was at Esade with us."

"The mayor says she only ever met him that night."

"Could be. Actually, we weren't close either, I only knew him for two or three years, no more. Then I lost track of him. And a couple of months ago I found out he'd died.

I heard from Enric, who did keep in touch with Ricky. Ask him."

"Do you know what happened to the video? Do you have any idea who kept the film?"

"No. I always thought it had been lost."

"Did you all know you were being filmed?"

"Yes."

"Everyone?"

"Well, everyone except Virginia."

"Did she know afterwards? I mean, did she find out later that you had filmed her?"

"No. I don't know. It's possible that I might have told her later, but I honestly don't remember. As I said it's not something we attached any importance to."

"Did you make other videos like that?"

"No, of course not. What for? It was improvised, a kids' experiment or a bit of hooliganism, if it even went that far . . ." He opens his hands in a gesture that combines impatience and apology. "Anyway. Are we finished?"

Melchor is not finished, but he understands he's not going to get any more out of that interview and he says yes.

Casas sees him out and, walking down the hall, recovers the cheerful ease with which he welcomed him, apologises again for only being able to afford him a little time, reiterates that every society needs heroes and regrets the ingratitude theirs has shown to Melchor, urges him again to return to Barcelona and, by now in the waiting room, wishes him luck and gives him his mobile number.

"Call me whenever you like," he says in farewell, shaking the policeman's hand enthusiastically. "I'm here should you need me."

He says something else too, but Melchor doesn't catch it

because he gets distracted by the phrase – repeated over and over again – that covers the wall in front of him: "It is likely that something unlikely will happen."

He calls Vàzquez as soon as he gets out onto paseo de la Bonanova and starts to walk towards the alley where he parked his car. The sun is still very high, it's very hot and he's no longer hungry. The sergeant answers after a couple of seconds. Melchor asks:

"How are you?"

"Better. I just woke up."

It's not his usual voice, but nor is it the ghostly voice from that morning. Melchor says this to himself and at that moment is struck by the suspicion that someone is following him.

"Have you been asleep all this time?" he asks.

"It's what I need. Sleep, eat and take my medication."

Melchor stops abruptly outside the La Salle School, looks to his left, towards the courtyard and neo-gothic facade and the handful of palm trees that partially hides it, and his suspicion hardens into certainty. He keeps walking.

"Have you eaten?"

"No."

"I filled up your fridge. And I made a couple of salads. Do you want me to come by?"

"There's no need. Go pick up your daughter. She gets out of camp about this time, doesn't she?"

"Yes."

"Have you talked to Blai?"

"I told him you're in Seu d'Urgell, with your sick mother. He fell for it."

"Great. How's everything else?"

"Really good. I've just spoken to a psychopath and I have a son of a bitch tailing me."

"What?"

"Don't worry, man. It's a joke. Do me a favour and get better, OK?"

He's about to take the phone away from his ear to disconnect the call when he hears:

"Melchor."

"What?"

Vàzquez does not reply straight away. Finally he says:

"Thanks, man."

Melchor walks up the street that skirts around the Bonanova church, turns left then right and, when he turns left again, he stops and waits around the corner, his body pressed back against the wall, totally still. A few seconds later his pursuer appears, and without a word Melchor trips him, throws him to the ground, twists one arm behind his back, grabs him by the neck with the other hand and smashes his head against the pavement. The guy utters a stifled cry and Melchor bangs his face against the ground again: once, twice. Then he turns his victim over and kneels on his chest, without letting go of his neck: his face is bloody and his nose battered. Melchor asks:

"Who are you? What do you want? Why are you following me?"

Spluttering something, the man tries to protect himself with his arms, but Melchor interprets that defensive gesture as an offensive gesture and punches him in the face.

"Enough now, fuck!" the guy moans. "Stop hitting me! I'm a cop too."

Melchor looks him in the eye and does not believe him. He holds his closed fist inches above the man's face, like a hammer poised to deliver another blow.

"I'm telling you I'm a policeman, for fuck's sake," the guy repeats, in exasperation. "In the Guardia Urbana."

Melchor lowers his arm, but his gaze still demands an explanation. Panting, but calmer, the guy spits blood onto the pavement.

"We're colleagues, *coño*," he explains, with a sour and pained expression. "I was ordered to follow you."

"Who by?"

"My boss. Inspector Lomas."

Melchor realises the guy is telling the truth. He lets go of his neck, takes his knee off his chest and stands up. Still lying on the ground, the guy touches his face gingerly.

"Shit," he swears. "You've broken my nose."

"You work for Hematomas?" Melchor asks. "The boss of the Vidal Boys?"

The police officer leans up on one elbow and spits out more blood. He's quite a bit older than Melchor; he's very pale and almost bald. He seems exhausted, lacking even the strength to stand up.

"That's what they call us," he grunts, resigned. "And that's what they call him. In this fucking job nobody escapes their nickname."

"Did they tell you why you had to follow me?"

"What do you think?"

"Answer me or I'll beat the shit out of you."

"No, they didn't fucking tell me! And I didn't ask either. I just do my job."

Again Melchor believes him. Suddenly aware that they're in the middle of the street, he looks one way and then the other, but he doesn't see anyone. He crouches down by his pursuer again.

"Listen to me," he says. "Tell your boss not to send anyone

else to follow me. Tell him that, if he wants to talk to me, he knows where to find me. OK?"

The guy nods.

"Good." Melchor stands up again. "And don't ever spy on a colleague again."

"I only do what they order me to," the guy replies. "Same as you."

Melchor thinks he's right; then he thinks he's not.

"Go on, go take care of that face," he says, pointing at him. "You're a mess."

The next morning, at the door of the community centre, Sandra's mother insists on picking up Cosette at the end of the day and taking her home, so the two girls can play together; and because he has an interview set up with Vidal that afternoon that could go on for a while, Melchor accepts her offer.

As he's driving towards Egara he resists the temptation to phone Vàzquez, because he thinks he'll still be asleep and that what he most needs is rest. He and Torrent are the first to arrive at the Abduction and Extortion office; Cortabarría shows up a few minutes later. They are the only members of the unit on duty – González and Estellés are on holiday, as are two members of the evening shift – and Melchor tells them that, due to family problems, Vàzquez has had to travel urgently to Seu d'Urgell, where he'll be for a few days, and that before leaving he'd called him to ask him to pitch in that week when the unit was down to the bare bones, dismantled and leaderless, and gave him instructions. So, over the course of the improvised meeting, they redistribute the work at hand, and Melchor immediately realises they can't spare more than two members of the unit for the mayor's case, which is insufficient even for tailing Casas and Vidal. During the meeting he receives two phone calls. He doesn't answer the first, which is from Vàzquez, but he does answer the second, which turns out to be from Vidal's secretary, who apologises because the deputy mayor will not be able to see him at City Hall at three-thirty, as they had arranged.

"Something's come up," she says. "He's got to do a press interview for a foreign newspaper. He'll do that after lunch at the same restaurant where he has a business meeting. I don't know what time he'll finish. At four or four-thirty. If you don't mind waiting, perhaps he could give you a few minutes after that."

"I don't mind," Melchor says. "Where's his lunch?"

The secretary gives him the name of the restaurant; Melchor assures her he'll be there at four and, when his meeting with Torrent and Cortabarría finishes, he closes the door of Vàzquez's office and calls the sergeant, who says he's feeling better and will be back at Egara in a couple of days.

"There's no hurry," Melchor lies. "Nobody's missing you here: you should see how happy the gang is with no boss."

Melchor hears a sort of croaking, which could as easily be a cough as a laugh; he supposes it is a cough.

"You're a bastard," Vàzquez says.

"And you're a wuss."

He goes to Blai's office, but finds it closed, nor does Blai answer his phone. He sends him a WhatsApp: "Are you operational?" Blai responds immediately: "Traffic jam. Meet for lunch?" "OK," Melchor texts back. "But early. At four I have to be in Barcelona." They arrange to meet at two in a restaurant called Clotilda.

He spends the rest of the morning dealing with paperwork and reading about Daniel Casas, Enric Vidal and Gonzalo

Rosell. Around one-thirty he leaves the office, and before two he is in Clotilda, a restaurant in Sabadell where, years ago, during his first stint at Egara, he sometimes ate with Vàzquez and other colleagues from the unit. Blai has reserved a table in the cellar, a sort of private dining room with no phone reception, and, when he sits down there, Melchor understands that his friend has done so on purpose, to disconnect from the constant demands of his mobiles. Blai shows up just after two-thirty.

"Sorry, *españolazo*," he says in greeting, with a pat on the cheek. "I've had a crazy morning."

He immediately calls over a waiter, asks for a beer urgently, points to Melchor's empty glass and asks if he wants another; Melchor nods.

"One Coca-Cola and one glass of beer," Blai says. "And bring us a menu, please. We're in a hurry."

"*Volando voy*," the waiter sings softly.

"I bet you can't guess who I just ran into," Blai says as soon as they're alone.

He is radiating joy.

"Gomà?" Melchor says.

Blai's eyes open as wide as saucers.

"Shit, how'd you know?"

"Because you only look that happy when you run into Gomà."

The inspector lets out a loud laugh. Melchor feels that day to day, at the Egara headquarters, Blai wraps himself in a straightjacket of hyper-responsible seriousness, obsessed with being worthy of his post, and only when he's on his own with his old colleague does he relax and turn back into who he is, or at least who he was in Terra Alta.

"No shit," Blai responds, delighted.

The waiter returns with the drinks and menus. Blai keeps

him there while he takes a sip of his beer and scans the day's menu. In the end, both men order the same thing: green salad and steak with potatoes.

"Well, I'm not going to lie to you either, kid," Blai then tells him; he projects a tone of exaggerated satisfaction, tucking his thumbs into his armpits rippling his fingers as if he were playing an invisible piano at a dizzying speed: "I love having him there, bogged down by his deputy inspector's stripes, rabid with envy because I'm head of the Central Jurisdiction of Personal Investigation while he's bored stiff in the stolen car unit. The bastard was so cocky, such a prick . . . But, wait, I haven't told you the best bit. Do you remember Pires?"

Four years earlier, Sergeant Pires was Deputy Inspector Gomà's assistant in the Territorial Investigations Unit at Tortosa and, as such, had been in charge of writing up the affidavit for the Adell case. Melchor says that yes, he remembers her.

"And you remember that Gomà left his wife for her, don't you?" This time Melchor cannot reply, because Blai jumps the gun. "Well, now she's left him. Pires left Gomà, I mean. Can you believe it? Gomà leaves his wife for Pires and Pires leaves Gomà for . . . Well, that I don't know. She must have left him for being mediocre, a failure, a dickhead, she must've thought he was going to have a great career and there he is, unable even to pass his inspector's exams. Pickled prick, eh?"

Blai goes on insulting Deputy Inspector Gomà until the waiter appears with the salads.

"Anyhow –" he changes the subject while dressing his salad and starting to eat – "what did you want to talk about? How's the mayor's case coming along? How did it go with Casas yesterday?"

"Well," Melchor answers, "when I said goodbye to him, I told a friend I'd just been with a psychopath."

Blai chokes on a piece of lettuce. Melchor gives him a couple of thumps on the back.

"A psychopath?" Blai manages to repeat; he wipes his mouth with his napkin and looks at his subordinate with distrust.

"That's what I said to my friend," Melchor repeats. "It just came out."

Melchor's expression combines uncertainty and disgust.

"I don't know." Contradicting himself as he goes, he explains: "He has a very high opinion of himself. He believes his ex-wife is mayor thanks to him, and that without him she's nothing. He says he still loves her and doesn't want any harm to come to her, but I don't believe him. And I don't believe he has nothing to do with the blackmail. In short: we have to get him under surveillance as soon as possible."

"Have you got enough men?"

Melchor tells him he does not.

"We're up to our necks. At most I've got two I can use. In any case, until Rosell gets back, I could make do with another two."

"I'll see what I can do."

"Yesterday you said to count on it."

"That was yesterday and this is today. But don't worry: I'll take care of this."

For a few seconds they remain silent, conscientiously eating their respective salads. From the other end of the restaurant a dense noise of cutlery and conversations reaches them, but neither man looks up from his plate.

"There's something else," Melchor says.

"What's that?"

The initial joy has disappeared from the inspector's face, which now displays a very concentrated expression. Melchor takes a sip of his Coca-Cola and wipes his lips with his serviette.

"Yesterday I caught a guy tailing me," he says. "He was from the Guardia Urbana. One of the Vidal Boys."

Blai's expression changes again: now it is one of open concern.

"How do you know?"

"Because I talked to him."

"To the guy who was tailing you?"

"Yeah. We exchanged views. He told me his boss had ordered him to follow me."

"Hematomas."

Melchor nods. The waiter appears with the two plates of steak and potatoes and takes away the empty salad plates. Once he's gone, Blai grumbles:

"Fuck, man, this is getting complicated. Those people are dangerous."

"Didn't seem like it to me."

"Well they are. Besides, if I report this upstairs, there could be a huge fucking scandal: the Guardia Urbana putting the Mossos d'Esquadra under surveillance. Fuck."

Hunger gets the better of them and they set about their steaks.

"Don't report it . . . And look on the bright side," Melchor suggests after a while. "This means Vidal wants to know what we're doing, and if Vidal wants to know what we're doing he must be involved somehow."

"Not necessarily," Blai objects; he is speaking, swallowing and cutting at the same time. "It wouldn't be the first time Hematomas acted on his own initiative and at his own risk."

"In a case that affects the mayor?" Melchor questions. "I don't think so."

"I can believe anything about that character."

They go back to eating in absorbed silence. When Melchor finishes, he looks at his watch.

"I have to get going," he announces. "I've arranged to see Vidal at four." He urges Blai to take his time, leaves a twenty-euro note on the table and stands up, adding: "See if you can sort out the surveillance this afternoon."

"Don't worry."

"And tell the ones tailing Casas and Vidal that we want an exhaustive report on their movements."

"I'll tell them."

As he's passing his friend, Melchor touches his shoulder to say goodbye. Blai pins his hand for a second.

"And do me a favour," he says, looking up firmly. "Be careful."

Two men stand guard on a small patch of ground outside the door of La Balsa restaurant. Melchor recognises one of them, who he's seen in photographs: pale, strong, short, with a moustache and a bit of a gut.

"Well, well, look who we have here," the man says. "You're Marín, aren't you?"

Melchor walks up to him.

"And you're Hematomas, right?"

The man's countenance clouds over.

"Don't they call you that?" Melchor says. "Sorry, I must've been misinformed."

"Where are you going?" Inspector Lomas asks.

"To see your boss," Melchor answers. "Didn't he tell you?"

Lomas ignores the question.

"He's busy," he says.

"Don't worry." Melchor continues on his way. "I've got time, I can wait."

The head of the Vidal Boys stops him with a hand; Melchor looks at the hand, not the inspector. Also, for the first time, he notices the man with him, much younger than Lomas and quite a bit taller; he seems focused, tense and watchful.

"Yesterday you beat up one of my men," the inspector reproaches him.

"That's outrageous," Melchor exclaims. "Here in the capital you call the slightest little thing a beating."

"He's got a broken nose."

"Really? I'm sorry. But the fault is yours: if you hadn't ordered him to follow me, he'd still have it intact."

Lomas observes him with equal measures of annoyance and suspicion.

"I'm going to give you a piece of advice," he finally says. "For free."

"Thanks," Melchor says. "You know something? I'm really bad at giving advice, but I'm good at taking it."

"Don't play the fool with me."

"Sorry," Melchor says, knowing that the more lightly he takes this man, the more dangerous he'll be; nevertheless, unable to resist, he adds: "And the advice?"

Lomas looks disconcerted. He glances sideways at his man, as if afraid of looking bad; then he turns back to Melchor.

"That was the advice," he clarifies.

"That I shouldn't play the fool with you?" Melchor smiles. "Ah. I hadn't caught it."

Before the inspector can reply, Melchor moves his hand aside and keeps walking. He's on his way up the restaurant steps when he hears behind him:

"Marín."

He turns around. Lomas walks over to the bottom of the steps; his companion follows.

"You're getting yourself into trouble," the inspector says. "You know that, don't you?"

Melchor half-closes his eyes with a fatalistic or resigned air. "Don't say I didn't warn you," Lomas threatens.

The restaurant nestles on the slope of Tibidabo within the stone walls of a nineteenth-century pool. Melchor walks into a vast elevated dining room with a tropical feel, dominated by a bar, a marble fireplace, large windows, the wooden ceiling supported by beams. At that hour the dining room is empty, but on the terrace, under a white canvas awning, a few tables are still occupied; someone waves to him from one of them.

"Señor Vidal is expecting me," he explains to a waiter who approaches with a quizzical look.

The deputy mayor of Barcelona is sitting in one corner of the terrace, with a lit cigar in one hand and a glass of whisky in the other; across from him sits a tall, slim, smiling, blond man, who stands up when Melchor arrives, and shakes his hand.

"Sit down, sit," Vidal invites him, pointing with his cigar to the chair next to the man's. "My friend Mr Burton and I have finished. Now we're talking off the record, which is always better, isn't it, Dennis?"

"That's right," Burton says.

"Would you like anything?" Vidal says to Melchor. "A coffee? A drink?"

"Nothing, thanks," the policeman says.

Vidal waves away an approaching waiter.

"Mr Burton is the *Guardian*'s correspondent in Spain and he's writing a book about Barcelona," Vidal tells Melchor. "I was just telling him something my father often repeated: 'Catalans who don't want independence have no heart; those who do want it, no head.'"

"Can I really not quote that?" asks Burton, who has a closed notebook in front of him.

"Quote it if you like," Vidal concedes magnanimously. "But

don't attribute it to my father, may he rest in peace. They'll think he was an inveterate cynic. Which is what he was, of course, but . . ." Vidal takes a sip of whisky. "Look, Dennis, we cannot have ideals, or even ideas. Political ideas, I mean. That is a luxury we cannot allow ourselves."

"When you say 'we', who are you referring to?" the correspondent asks.

"Who do you think I'm referring to?" the deputy mayor answers. "Us. Those who run things. Those who have money and power, supposing they are two different things. Ideas are for intellectuals, ideals for the poor; but, in our case, it would be irresponsible. Especially in a place like this."

"I'm afraid I don't follow you," the journalist admits, scrutinising Vidal after writing something down in his notebook.

Melchor is also observing him. He is the same age as Casas, but he looks quite a bit older. In part, perhaps, due to the way he dresses, which reminds Melchor of an ageing diplomat, with his fine, loose-fitting, dark grey suit, blue striped shirt and deep red silk tie; and in part, also, due to his serene and tidy way of talking, his excess weight and his luxuriant greying beard. He doesn't seem to mind the humid heat that condenses under the white canvas awning, only rarely stirred by a warm breeze, because he hasn't even taken off his jacket. A sweat stain soaks his shirt, he has loosened the knot of his tie and his hair is a bit dishevelled.

Vidal rubs his chin with the same hand that holds his cigar, and savours another sip of his whisky, gazing pensively beyond his interlocutors towards the far end of the terrace, which seems besieged by jungle vegetation.

"We were talking about the Procés before," he reminds the journalist, who nods emphatically. "Well, the Procés is a good example of what I mean: In 2012 we were sunk in a terrible crisis, the worst in a century, and we were having a very bad time. Very bad. What did we do? What we had to do: get the people out on the street, with our own means and with the inestimable help of our government, to put as much pressure as possible on Madrid, put them between a rock and a hard place and force them to solve our problem. I don't need to tell you that we're not *independentistas*, nor have we ever been, because we've always been people with heads; *independentismo* is another one of those luxuries we can't allow ourselves. But, what better way to pressure Madrid? And what faster and easier way to get the people out on the street?"

"Are you saying that you people set up the independence movement?"

"Not the independence movement. There have been *independentistas* in Catalonia for more than a century: people with a lot of heart and not much head, as my father would say. What we set up was the Procés, that is, we transformed a minority claim into the claim of almost half the country."

The correspondent from the British paper contorts his mouth into a doubtful expression.

"Frankly, I find it difficult to believe that, for almost a decade, you people managed to singlehandedly get a million people out on the streets demanding independence," he admits. "Even if they were idiots."

"They are idiots," Vidal affirms. "There's not the slightest doubt about it. Individually, there are some who are not. A few. But, en masse, carried away by feelings, passions and flags, then yes, without exception. Probably including you and me, dear friend, if it came to it. Let's hope it never does. In any case, to be on the safe side, I have taken the precaution of never attending a demonstration in my life, supposing that those for the Procés were demonstrations."

"Were they not?"

"Are you kidding? Of course not. They were parades. Don't you remember? Everyone in uniform, everyone in their place, ready for whatever the organisers ordered them to do, everyone knowing their role, everyone ready for the cameras to film them . . . How is that a demonstration? And that's why they were so useful to us. The people, believe me, do what they're told, especially if you have money and political power on your side, as we do, and on top of that you've got television, radio, newspapers, social networks and everything they've got to have. It's easy to get people out of their houses, especially now. The problem is getting them back in again."

"Was that the problem with the Procés?"

"Exactly. The problem is that it got out of hand. You'll see." He takes another sip of whisky, sucks on his cigar and exhales a cloud of smoke that hangs in the summer swelter of the terrace. "We had our guy in the Generalitat, Artur Mas. A good kid. Heir to the patriarch Pujol and the family messenger boy. One of ours, even spoke Spanish at home, like we do. But things got messed up and Mas was thrown out of the presidency and that left Puigdemont, an insignificant provincial nobody who has neither power nor prestige. We all took it for granted that Mas would control him without any trouble, but we were mistaken. Because Puigdemont is a believer, a Taliban who takes entirely seriously what to us was just a game, a decoy, a strategy destined to bring us out of the financial crisis unscathed. But he wasn't like that: he was ready to go where he didn't need to go, or he was more afraid of not doing it than doing it. Anyway, a disaster."

"It hasn't gone so badly for you."

"That's true, although it could have gone better. But don't forget that our interests align with those of Catalonia. Those of

Catalonia in general and of Barcelona in particular. And, if Barcelona and Catalonia don't do well, we don't do well, even if we do relatively well. I'm not sure I'm explaining myself. In any case, the idea of the Procés, as I was saying, was good. Good and most of all necessary. Indispensable, I would say. And it's precisely for that reason what we're doing now at Barcelona City Hall is so important, and what we're going to do tomorrow in the Generalitat, or at City Hall and the Generalitat at the same time: fix the disaster. We provoked it and we will fix it. Don't you think that's the responsible thing to do?"

The *Guardian* journalist seems to think it over for a moment, gives Melchor a fleeting glance, somewhere between ironic and interrogatory, and turns back to Vidal.

"That could be," he accepts. "Though there are people who think the opposite."

"There are always people who think the opposite," says Vidal.

"There are people who think that what you lot are doing now is substituting one culprit for another," the journalist hastens to clarify. "Before, Madrid was to blame for all your troubles; now, all your troubles are blamed on immigrants."

The observation seems to have caught Vidal off guard. For a couple of seconds he swirls what's left of his whisky around in his glass, concentrating on it.

"Rather unfair, don't you think?" He looks up with a mischievous but also hurt expression and savours another sip of whisky without taking his eyes off the correspondent, as if trying to say without words what he cannot say with them. "Anyway, as they say, it takes all kinds."

Vidal puts the cigar in his mouth and, while the journalist smiles as if he has understood, the column of ash that has formed at the end of it collapses onto the whiteness of the tablecloth.

"Well." The journalist stands up. "You'll have other things to talk about. And I should get going."

He picks up his notebook, thanks Vidal for his time and shakes the policeman's hand. He reaches out to shake the deputy mayor's hand as well when he also stands up.

"I'll see you out, Dennis," Vidal says.

The journalist says there's no need, but the politician insists and the two men walk towards the exit, one of the politician's hands resting on the correspondent's shoulder. Melchor checks his phone; various WhatsApp messages have arrived. One is from Vivales, asking if he should pick up Cosette. "Don't worry," Melchor texts back. "I've arranged to pick her up later from a friend's house." Another message is from Blai. "Vigilance sorted, at least until Rosell returns. Tomorrow evening you start with Vidal, OK?" "OK," Melchor replies, and adds: "I'm still with him." "And?" Blai writes. "A gangster," Melchor writes. "A psychopath and a gangster," Blai sums up. "Watch your back." Melchor goes back inside the restaurant and catches sight of Vidal at the entrance, conversing with Inspector Lomas. He writes a message to Vàzquez: "How're things?" He's barely sent it when he hears Vidal's voice behind him:

"What a prat, eh?"

The deputy mayor sits back down on the other side of the table.

"You mean Hematomas?" asks Melchor, knowing perfectly well who he means.

"I meant the journalist," Vidal answers, as if he hadn't heard his subordinate's nickname. It's obvious he's been to the men's room: he has washed his face, brushed his hair and straightened his tie a bit; the sweat stain, however, is still on his shirt, large and dark. "These Englishmen have been telling us what we're like for centuries, and they've ended up thinking they know us better than we do. They come with their answers already determined, so you tell them one thing and they print the opposite. No matter what you tell them, they write whatever they want. Of course, that happens with all journalists, don't you think?"

"I don't know," admits Melchor, who at that moment receives a WhatsApp from Vàzquez. "Excellent," he reads, at a glance. "Nobody's ever interviewed me," he says, looking back at Vidal.

"Well, you don't know how lucky you are," Vidal congratulates him. "Being interviewed is like offering to take it up the arse: you spread your legs and hope it'll be as God wishes. If the journalist is smart, you come off smart; if they're stupid, you come off stupid. And, since most journalists are fools . . . Believe me: there's nothing worse than a journalist. Except for a politician, of course."

A waiter arrives with a tray on which there is a bottle of Lagavulin, an ice bucket and a bottle of mineral water.

"Are you sure you won't have anything to drink?" Vidal asks while the waiter pours him a generous shot of whisky.

"No thanks," Melchor answers. "If you don't mind, I'll get to the point; I don't want to waste your time."

"Don't worry," Vidal says. "You're not going to waste it. Besides, I'm more interested in talking to you than you are to me."

"Is that why you had me followed?"

The deputy mayor raises an eyebrow, but rather than look at Melchor he looks at the waiter, who has picked up an ice cube with a pair of tongs and is holding it just over the lip of the half-filled whisky glass. Vidal nods and the waiter drops the ice cube in and leaves.

"I ordered them to follow you because information is power," Vidal says. "And my job is to manage power." He waits for a moment while he takes a sip of whisky and watches

Melchor's reaction, as if he suspects the policeman might not have understood. He puts the glass down, leans forward, resting his elbows on the ash-covered tablecloth, laces his fingers together and locks eyes with him. "Look, Melchor, I understand very well what's going on with you. You've heard what people say about me, what journalists write about me, my notoriety, and you've believed it. And you believe that I am involved in Virginia being blackmailed."

"Who told you that? Casas?"

"No-one needed to tell me, man. I know it. As soon as you found out that I appeared in that video, you made up your mind. But I'm going to tell you something: it's not true. I am not involved, nor is Dani and much less Gonzalo. In fact, we are just as vulnerable to blackmail as Virginia."

"And why aren't they blackmailing you?"

"Oh, that I don't know. Probably because they know we wouldn't allow ourselves to be, at least not with that video. But, before you ask me more questions, let me tell you something: the rumours about me are true. To put it a better way, they're partially true. Rumours are always like that, aren't they? A mixture of truth and lies. Only, if you add a truth to a lie, the result is always a lie. If you see what I mean."

"Perfectly. And what is the truth of this lie?"

A spark appears in Vidal's pupils that Melchor does not know whether to attribute to the alcohol or the sudden and undisguisable joy certain people get when asked the exact question they need to win an argument, or simply to show off. The deputy mayor stubs out his cigar in the ashtray, where another butt lies dead.

"Have you read Montaigne?" he asks.

Melchor shakes his head.

"Oh right, you only read novels," the other says. "Well, I

read him every day. Just two or three pages, no more. But every day. And he's damn good. He seems to only talk about himself, but in reality he talks about everything, and like nobody else does. Of course, I don't read much, because I don't have a lot of time, but . . . When it comes to politics, everyone goes on about Machiavelli, and I'm not saying he's bad. But Montaigne is much more serious, much more radical, much better. For example, he says the public good demands to be betrayed, lied to and murdered, and that's why politics needs to be in the hands of stronger people with fewer scruples, people able to sacrifice their honour and conscience for the wellbeing of the country. What do you think, eh? I've never assassinated anyone, of course, but I've done more or less all the rest. And do you know why? Because I do not deceive myself, because I know very well that in politics we have to do things that no-one wants to do, we have to get our hands dirty, deal with the devil if necessary. That's why, if there is a hell, all politicians will end up there. That's reality, and anyone who doesn't know that should not go into politics, because they don't know what power is." Melchor tries to butt in, but Vidal gets ahead of him. "And, yes, I know there are those who say we Catalans don't know how to wield power, that we don't know what it is, that it scares us and that's why we're bad at politics."

"That's what Casas told me yesterday," Melchor manages to get in.

"He always says that," Vidal says. "And do you know why? Because his father said it. And my father too. And the entire Catalan economic elite for more than a century. But it's not true. It probably used to be, but it's not anymore. Now power is not just held by states; cities have it too. I would almost say that cities have more power. Tell me, what's more important, Barcelona or Catalonia, which isn't a state, but almost, because it has almost as much power as a state? Barcelona has a thousand times more. And we wield power, yes we do. Real power. Or at least we're learning to wield it. The first person to understand this was Margaret Thatcher, and that's why she abolished the Greater London Council: she didn't want the city to fly solo, regardless of the country, and she kept it on a short leash so it wouldn't overshadow her. And that's what Jordi Pujol did here to Barcelona. Or what he tried to do."

"Why are you telling me all this?" Melchor asks; it's the question he's been trying to ask for some time.

"To deal with this matter as soon as possible and get down to what interests me," Vidal replies. Since Melchor does not appear to have understood, the deputy mayor unfolds his hands and sits up a bit, but doesn't take his elbows off the table. "What I'm trying to say is that I might be a son of a bitch, I'm not saying I'm not. But I'm not blackmailing Virginia. Think about it. What would I have to gain?"

"Get her to resign and take her place," Melchor hastens to say. "And, while you're at it, end her political career."

Vidal clicks his tongue, shaking his head with a condescending half-smile.

"You disappoint me," he says. "I'd been told you were smart and sensible, but now I see they were wrong. Don't you see what you're saying makes no sense whatsoever?"

"So why did the mayor not ask you to investigate the blackmailing?"

"That's something you should ask her. But, since you're asking me, I could give you several answers, among them being that we are not a judicial police force and therefore not authorised to investigate things like this."

"Don't make me laugh."

"That was not my intention." Vidal makes an effort to sound

sincere. "And don't misinterpret me: I'm not saying our relationship is at its best right now. Virginia's and mine, I mean. That is public knowledge. Some things have become unnecessarily complicated and her divorce ruined others . . . But, there's a world of difference between that and blackmailing her to force her out of politics. And while we're at it, if I wanted to blackmail her, believe me, I wouldn't do it with that video; that's kids' stuff, one of those stupid things people do when they're young . . ." A spark of sarcasm dilates the deputy mayor's pupils, and Melchor guesses what's coming. "You did a few yourself, didn't you?"

"I don't know what you're talking about."

"Sure you do," Vidal contradicts him, leaning back in his chair. He picks up his glass of whisky and swirls the liquid; the ice cube has almost completely melted. "I'm talking about the Javier Cercas novel."

Melchor shrugs.

"I haven't read it," he confesses. "But, from what I've heard, it's all made up."

Vidal opens his eyes wide, and then laughs; afterwards he lifts his glass to his damp, full lips and takes a long sip.

"Is that what you've been telling people?" he asks, still savouring the whisky. "I understand. But don't try it on me, please. It strikes me almost as a lack of respect."

For a couple of seconds Melchor holds the deputy mayor's gaze.

"Are you threatening me?" he asks in reply.

"But how could that occur to you, man?" Vidal is scandalised, or pretends to be. "All I'm doing is explaining what's out there. Tell me something: do you remember Isaías Cabrera? Until recently he was a Mossos sergeant in Internal Affairs. He told me you know each other."

Melchor does not need to dig too far into his memories; Vidal, for his part, does not need to hear Melchor's reply: he can read it on his face.

"He's been working for me for a while now," the deputy mayor informs him. "And he's delighted. Talk to him, if you want. He's the one who told me that the thing about you being in prison is true. That you worked as a gunman for Colombian narcos. And some other things that your bosses and colleagues don't know, or that they know, but prefer not to know, and that demonstrate that this Cercas guy, lo and behold, has less imagination than they say. But, anyway, this is not what I wanted to talk about. Believe me: I couldn't care less what you did or didn't do when you were a kid. What I wanted to explain was something else. As long as you've finished with your interrogation, of course."

"I haven't started yet," Melchor says.

Vidal opens his arms hospitably.

"Then what are you waiting for?"

For some minutes they talk about the video. Melchor asks the deputy mayor the same questions or almost the same questions that he asked Casas on Monday, and he receives the same or almost the same answers, just burdened with fewer doubts and vacillations, which instils in the policeman the suspicion (or rather the conviction) that, in the intervening period, the two old friends have agreed on a version of events, between themselves and perhaps Rosell as well, supposing Rosell is just as involved in the operation, which does not seem at all improbable. At a certain point Melchor mentions the name of the person who filmed the video:

"Casas told me he lost sight of him after you finished your degrees, but that you kept in touch with him."

"He exaggerates. Or you misunderstood him: actually, I've

only seen Ricky again in the last few months." Vidal exhales, narrowing his eyes. "He's a sad case. Dramatic, even, I would say. We knew him back when we were students. Then he was an intelligent guy, brilliant even, though a bit childish. He dropped out before finishing his degree and fell off the radar, we didn't hear anything more about him. Until, suddenly, not long ago, he reappeared, got back in contact with us, first with Dani and then with me. In reality, he came to ask us for help. I did my bit, or I tried to; Dani didn't. He didn't tell you that? Well, it's true. And I don't hold it against Dani that he didn't help him, because Ricky is a self-destructive guy, and one of those people who ask you for help, but make it obvious that they hate you for having to ask you, and hate you even more if you give it to them . . . So, a classic case. I don't know if he was always like that or if failure turned him into what he is. The fact is that, when Ricky showed up again, he was ruined, desperate, a total, unmitigated failure. I did what I could to help him, believe me, I tried to treat him as well as possible, for old time's sake. Because I was fond of him. Because, deep down, I'm a sentimental guy. For whatever reason, but I did try to help him." He cuts the motionless heat of the terrace horizontally with a flat, emphatic hand. "It was all in vain. But I continued to see him, and in the end I was at least able to help him die. I mean, when I found out he'd died, I paid for the funeral and the burial, because he didn't have a pot to piss in. Literally. The coroner said he'd had a heart attack, but I wouldn't be surprised if he took himself out. I would have done, if I'd been in his shoes."

"Did he have any family?"

"No. Not that I know of. Only a couple of neighbours came to his funeral. A sad story, as I said."

The deputy mayor has allowed his mood to be infected by

his childhood friend's bitter end; or that's the impression he gives, his gaze fixed on the tablecloth, as if seeking, in its ash-tarnished whiteness, justification or consolation for that disastrous fate. Until he seems to wake up, notices his interlocutor, brings his whisky glass to his lips again and asks in a different tone of voice:

"Well, are you finished now? Any more questions?"

"No. For my part we're finished."

"Great," he says with satisfaction, as if recovering from a moment of weakness. "Now it's my turn. I have a proposition for you."

Before seven Melchor goes to pick Cosette up from her friend Sandra's house. Sandra's mother answers the door; she is agitated, her hair's a mess and she reeks of alcohol. The woman invites him in and, after allowing him to exchange a few words with Cosette, who is playing with Sandra in her room, asks him to have a drink. Melchor turns down the offer, but the woman disappears into the kitchen, returns with half a glass of gin and starts talking about her husband, from whom, Melchor (who only half-understands what she is trying to say) deduces, she is separated. After the woman has been badmouthing her husband for a while, Melchor asks her if he hits her. "Hit me?" she asks, in surprise, but without caring whether the girls hear her or not. "If he hit me I'd cut his balls off with a chainsaw! That's for sure. I'd hit him with everything I could get my hands on! The fucking bastard!" At that moment the woman bursts into tears and Melchor tries to comfort her until, without knowing how, he finds himself in her bedroom, a situation she takes advantage of to put a hand on his crotch while attempting a seductive smile, which provokes Melchor's unconcealable pity. When she sees his reaction, the woman takes her hand away, backs off, mutters an apology and, caught in a mixture of desperation and embarrassment, stifles a cry and throws herself down on the bed, mumbling unintelligible reproaches and self-pitying curses while crying her eyes out. Not knowing what to do, unable to leave and abandon her in such a state, Melchor sits on a chair and waits in silence. The woman gradually begins to calm down, but at some point a loud fart resounds in the bedroom, between sobs, like a note from a cornet.

"Well," Melchor says, making a lot of noise standing up from the chair, to cover up the reverberation as much as possible and try to spare the woman that last humiliation, "Cosette and I should get going."

The two of them are making dinner when Vivales arrives. They eat on the balcony and, after the two men wash up while Cosette watches cartoons, Melchor reads *Michel Strogoff* to his daughter for a while. Then he waits for her to fall asleep and, once she does, returns to the living room. Vivales is resting in his usual chair, facing the blank TV screen.

"No film tonight?" Melchor asks.

"Not today," Vivales answers, pointing to a pile of documents on the floor. "I have things to do."

"I thought you were on holiday."

"I thought so too." Vivales stands up. "I forgot that slaves don't get holidays."

The lawyer leaves the living room while the policeman, with an iPad in hand, takes a seat beside his armchair. Vivales returns straight away, carrying a bottle of whisky, a heavy crystal glass and a bowl of ice. Melchor is concentrated on his iPad, looking for information relating to Ricky Ramírez. He can't get it out of his head that Casas lied about him. He told him that he hadn't seen him since their student days, but, according to

253

Vidal, that is not true: recently, Ramírez asked him for help and he refused to give him any. Why had Casas lied about it? Or had he simply forgotten about that request for help? Who was Ricky Ramírez? Was he the one who kept the video with which the mayor was now being blackmailed? And, if that's the case, who ended up with it after his death and is now using it? Despite having died a few months ago, does Ramírez have any direct relation to the blackmail, seeing as he was responsible for the filming? And what about his death? Is it related to the case?

"Today a client came to my office," says Vivales, sitting next to Melchor again, picking up a piece of ice with his fingers and dropping it into his glass with a tinkling sound. "A small-time crook, but one to watch out for, just out on probation. Thanks to yours truly, all modesty aside. Well, to celebrate I offered him a whisky and asked him how he liked it. Do you know what he answered?" Vivales puts on a voice even more gravelly than his own: "With lots of smoke and lots of whores!"

Mumbling to himself ("This is the benefit of my work: always learning new things"), the lawyer pours himself a good splash of whisky; Melchor doesn't bat an eyelid, too absorbed in his iPad to register the lawyer's anecdote. The latter, settled back into his armchair, asks:

"How was your day?"

A little impatient, Melchor looks up at Vivales and is tempted to ask him to be quiet and let him continue with his reading but says instead:

"I had a job offer."

The lawyer wrinkles his brow.

"From Enric Vidal," Melchor continues.

"The mayor's mangy dog?"

"The same. He has suggested I work for him."

"You're kidding."

"He insinuated that in four days I'd be in charge of the Vidal Boys. In two, rather."

"You'll have told him he can suck your dick."

"I told him I'll think about it."

Vivales looks at him with a mixture of incredulity and sarcasm and leans back expectantly while Melchor puts the iPad down on the floor. He doesn't want to worry the lawyer more than necessary, so he adds that he told Vidal he'd think about it in exchange for not having Hematomas' men follow him anymore, and that Vidal had agreed.

"Do you remember what Campà said the other day?" Melchor asks. "Well, I don't know if it was Campà or Puig."

"Same difference," Vivales says. "What Ortega says, Gasset says too. What was it he said?"

"That it was possible that Vidal and Casas were trying to set the mayor up. Remember?" Vivales nods. "Well, it's true."

"You're not talking about the blackmail story that *Ara* published, are you?"

Melchor says yes, explains to Vivales why he is on assignment in Barcelona and sums up what he's discovered since his arrival in the capital. The lawyer listens with maximum attention. When Melchor is finished, Vivales reflects for a few seconds.

"And are you sure Casas and Vidal are behind the extortion?" he asks.

"No," Melchor answers, picking the iPad up off the floor. "But I think they are. Others too, perhaps. Rosell, for example. Apparently, he's also in the video."

"And have you also spoken with him?"

"No. I'm seeing him on Thursday."

Vivales nods again, but doesn't seem too convinced. Melchor's thoughts turn once more to Ricky Ramírez.

"Be careful," the lawyer warns him. "Those are dangerous people."

"That's the second time someone's told me that today."

"So you see what I mean."

The policeman nods as well. Then he looks at the screen of his iPad, which has gone black; he touches it with a fingertip and it comes to life again.

"Well," Melchor shuts down the exchange. "Enough chit-chat."

2

"What were we talking about?"

"The case of the phantom credit cards. Although I still don't know what it has to do with the mayor."

"Well, it does."

"You told me that, when your father was disgraced by that whole business, no-one helped you."

"Does that surprise you? Not me. If a person is sinking, nobody reaches out a hand; and, if they do, it's to push you all the way under. That's how things work . . . Deep down, my friends only did what anyone would do: distance themselves as fast as possible from the outcast. And I was as much of an outcast as my father. It's true that when I didn't show up at Esade in September, they could have called me, could have asked why I wasn't in class, taken an interest in my father or in me . . . But they didn't. They hadn't done anything up till then, and they didn't do anything at that moment either. We had been inseparable, but they didn't lift a finger . . . Of course, I didn't try to keep in touch with them either. And do you know why? Well, because the worst thing about becoming an outcast is that you accept without protest your outcast condition. You become ashamed of yourself, close in on yourself, the only thing you want to do is hide in a corner and lick your wounds like a dog after a beating . . . So maybe I shouldn't blame my friends. But I do blame them, you better believe I blame them, and at that time I blamed them even more, maybe because I suddenly realised that I hadn't wanted to see the obvious, that I had never been one of them, that they only pretended I was, that they'd always seen me as a subordinate, not even a spectator or a witness, that's what Rosell was to Casas and Vidal, for them I was just a servant, a lackey, and the worst thing was that I had been that because I wanted to be, without anyone forcing me, I had been their servant because I wanted to be like them, in the hope of integrating myself into their circle, of belonging somehow to the magical elite of power and money . . . And that's why I'd done so many things that disgusted me, or that were disgusting me now, when they were done and could not be undone. And it was when I realised all this that I began to feel revulsion, an all-consuming revulsion. And that was when I swore to myself that I would get revenge on all of them for having drawn out the worst I had inside, for having turned me into a monster . . . That's what I've tried to do now, even though it's gone wrong."

"Maybe it didn't go so wrong."

"It went fucking atrociously wrong."

"They can still end up paying for what they did."

"I hope so, but I won't hold my breath . . . It will be me who pays, not them. It's always the same ones who pay. I told you before, it's a universal law."

"And I told you I'd do all I can to make sure they pay."

"Yeah. That's why I'm telling you all this, although . . . Hey, are you sure you don't want a little whisky?"

"I'm sure. Go on."

"You should join me, if I wasn't drinking alone, I'd talk

more . . . I'll go on. As I was saying, when the phantom cards case blew up, we were ruined overnight, my father was no longer being paid his salary and he had to return the money he'd spent and start paying lawyers, so I left Esade and moved to the University of Barcelona, which is much cheaper than Esade. I also started teaching a couple of mathematics classes at a private academy owned by a guy who owed my father a favour, I did have a bit of luck there, at least I found a job quickly, even if it was a shit job, and it gave my mother and me something to live on until my father got out after ten months in prison, by which time I had finished my degree, with great difficulty, but I got through it. Around that time I started looking for other ways to make money, and that was when I first heard of bitcoin, and when I began to mine them – anyway, I'll tell you about that later, let's stick to my father for the moment . . .

"His return home improved things and made them worse. On the one hand, he was no longer locked up and I no longer had to go to Madrid to see him, in the Soto del Real prison, with the expenses of travel, hotel and meals that entailed, not to mention the carer who had to look after my mother while I was away, and who also had to be paid . . . But, on the other hand, my father came out of prison a different person, a shadow of what he had been, a sort of ghost. And, even though he knocked on every door, and asked and humiliated himself and begged, it took him a long time to find a job . . . Or maybe it wasn't so long, but it felt like that to me, it seemed to go on for ever. First, because now I had to support my father as well as my mother. Second, because the guy who owed my father favours must have decided they were even and didn't renew my contract at his academy and I had to start earning a living giving private lessons in every subject imaginable at home (my luck had run out, it never lasts long for me). And third, because, in short, until then it had been a nightmare living alone with my mother, who couldn't take care of herself and did nothing but stare at the television screen without turning it on and moan, but with my father at home the nightmare multiplied, imagine what it was like living with the two of them, seeing the man who until recently had been everything to me, as if he were God almighty, become a shadow of his former self, a diminished, intimidated and broken old man, who never stopped complaining and hardly dared go outside . . . They were dreadful months, the three of us shut up in that claustrophobic flat in Ensanche, for which on top of everything else we could no longer afford the mortgage, the three of us simmering on the low flame of our own misfortune . . . Until, finally, an old colleague of my father's, a socialist councillor at Torredembarra Town Hall, took pity on him and got him an administrative job in his town's department of Social Affairs, and with the salary he earned he rented an apartment and took my mother to live there.

"I protested, or rather I pretended to protest, but not much . . . The truth is I was thrilled to be free of my parents; that sounds awful, I know, but the truth almost always sounds awful. It's not like I stopped seeing them altogether, I phoned them now and then and went to spend the day with them in Torredembarra once a month. So I didn't abandon them, at least not entirely, but I was able to get out from under the crushing weight of having to support them and live with them, the very picture of defeat, a picture that was very difficult to live with . . . But then things began to straighten out a little. I managed to sell my parents' flat for a good price, paid off the mortgage and rented a small flat near plaza Joanic in Gràcia. Then I found work at a food company, stopped tutoring, fell in love with a colleague and a short while later married her, a church wedding, which my father, who was not a believer, cried all the way through, gripping my mother's wheelchair . . . Anyway . . . The following years were good. Marriage agreed with me, my wife . . . You said you talked to her the day before yesterday, didn't you?"

"Yes."

"She probably hasn't got a good word to say about me, in the end it was really bad. But at first it wasn't, we were happy then, at least I was happy, I don't know what she told you . . . Herminia is a wonderful woman, who really loved me, I have wonderful memories of her. She was an economist, as I said, we worked together, I liked my job more than she liked hers, but she didn't complain, I got promoted in the company and started earning a decent living without much stress. Everything was going well, but it wasn't enough for me. I had always dreamed of setting up my own business, because I thought that was the only way to be independent, so, after mulling over the matter for a long time, I finally decided to set up a courier service . . . Why the parcel trade, you'll wonder. Well because it was the sort of business that was on the rise at the time, and also because one of my wife's cousins had been the manager of a company in the field and encouraged me to set up my own. My wife supported me too, and even my in-laws, they invested part of their savings in the business and underwrote several lines of credit. The 2008 financial crisis seemed like water under the bridge by then and there was fresh optimism in the air, and, since I was confident in my management abilities (I'd always wanted to run a company, that's what I'd studied), I soon arrived at the conclusion that the business could work . . .

"I was right. For the first two or three years it did, in fact it worked quite a bit better than we'd all expected. To begin with, that was a blessing, of course, but we soon turned the blessing into a curse, because the euphoria emboldened us and led us to make some mistakes that at first seemed inconsequential but were not. Things soon went wrong, in part due to those mistakes, and in part because my wife's cousin and I did not see eye to eye, and after a while, having fought desperately for months to survive, it all fell apart; first we had to suspend payments, then the company went bankrupt and in the end I felt as though my house had caught fire and collapsed on top of me and I had been buried beneath a mountain of rubble.

"That was when I understood what it means to fail . . . I had experienced my father's disgrace as a failure, but it had not been a failure; or, it had been my father's failure, not mine. That was why my father could not get up again once he'd fallen and I could (although I'd only risen in order to fail more and fall harder, to fail entirely). What I mean is that real failure is not inherited or shared: it is exclusive and owned, non-transferable. Furthermore, in Spain you only fail once. There are no second chances for us. Unless you're protected by your family's immortal money, in our country someone who fails seriously fails for ever. Spanish failure is like that: serious, soiled, inglorious failure, failure without redemption. That's why all that syrupy romantic mythology about failure that they sell in films makes me sick, all that sentimental rubbish about the dignity and glamour of failure . . . In failure there is no dignity or glamour or anything anybody might want to buy, and those who buy it, like those who sell it, don't know what it really means to fail, at least to really fail in Spain. That's how it is, believe me – the rest is verbal diarrhoea.

"All this to tell you that my life went literally to shit. We had to close the business and dismiss the employees, who took us to court; some of our suppliers accused us of fraudulent bankruptcy. It went to trial and, although I miraculously escaped being sent to jail, in the end I was up to my neck in debt, debts so big I could never pay them, and that I wouldn't pay if I could: it would be like feeding sharks, who never tire of feeding and end up eating you alive . . . I bet you've heard that said many times, right? That the business world is like that, a world of sharks. Well, it's true: out there, if you don't devour, you get devoured, in that world there is no compassion. People should know this and drop the fantasies, and then everything would go much better . . . Anyway, I've lost my train of thought again. Where were we?"

"The bankruptcy of your courier company."

"Oh yeah. I was saying that I escaped getting sent to jail by the skin of my teeth. But I was left drowning in debt. Anyway, I managed to keep my wife from appearing in court through great sacrifices . . . I am proud of that, to tell you the truth, although it didn't save my marriage. I have nothing to reproach my wife for, by the way: her parents were left without a cent, the banks seized their assets, and she suffered so much that the love she had for me dried up and died and must have left her with nothing but that bitter, foul aftertaste that failure leaves . . . In short, I was desperate, and when a person is desperate, he does the stupidest things. One of the many I did was to contact my old friends from Esade.

"During the trial I had met lots of the kind of people who swarm around courts and lawyers' offices. I'd heard about new kinds of businesses, very promising businesses, they said, cryptocurrencies, online betting, things like that . . . I wanted to make up for the disaster of the courier company and became obsessed with the idea of proving that I wasn't a failure . . . By then online betting was regulated in Spain, but still very lucrative, so I started investigating that seriously. I made friends with a couple of guys, two very young banking employees who worked for an online betting shop in their spare time but had ideas of their own; they were sure there was a lot more to be made there and wanted to set up something to get into that business seriously . . . They explained their plan to me and proposed I participate in it, and I convinced myself that it was a good idea and that all I needed was an associate with capital to put up the initial investment, not a very big investment but sufficient to get going."

"And you thought that associate could be one of your old friends."

"Exactly."

"You hadn't had any news of them in all that time?"

"I hadn't talked to them, but of course I'd heard news of them . . . In Barcelona it's impossible not to hear about them. Money is discreet, and Catalan money even more so, but those families are too grand to hide easily. So, sure, every once in a while I heard talk about them . . . And, if I'm honest, nothing I heard or read surprised me too much, I wasn't even surprised that my friends had ended up going into politics directly or indirectly, I told you politics had always interested them, as it has always interested those of their class, as an extension of business, I mean. That said, when I tried to get back in touch with them, only Vidal had gone into politics, he was already at City Hall at the time, I think he was the socialist councillor for the district of Sant Gervasi, while Rosell had left his family business, he'd just been named president of Barcelona Global, I don't know if you heard about that, it was a shady operation set up by the rich of Barcelona to promote the city and then it turned into a lobby to try to prevent its decline after the flight of capital following the independence putsch of 2017 . . . Although, to be exact, it wasn't Rosell who had left his family business, it was the family business that had left him, his younger brother Martín had just taken control of the family holding company and had kicked him out on his arse, so the presidency of Barcelona Global was one of those decorative positions where you put people you don't know what to do with.

"Rosell was in fact the first one I called, but I didn't even get to speak to him. At Barcelona Global they told me he was out of the country and would be gone for some time . . . Something similar happened with Vidal. I remember I called him several times at his office at City Hall, but he was either not there or had just left or was on the phone or in a meeting, and even though I left my name and telephone number and asked them to have him call me, he did not call. At that stage I should have understood that none of my old classmates wanted to see me or talk to me, but I was too obstinate and I called Casas . . . And this time my obstinacy was rewarded. I had heard a lot about Casas over the years, much more than about Vidal or Rosell, because he was the one who appeared in the media most often, even though he was the one who tried hardest to avoid it, or precisely because of that . . . Casas had lived in New York for quite a while, had married a Japanese woman, had divorced her and returned to Barcelona, starting a newspaper and going after radio and television franchises that the Generalitat eventually granted him. Also, it was a while since he'd founded his consultancy Clave Barcelona, and thanks to that he'd started to acquire a reputation for being the mastermind or promoter behind a few up and coming politicians."

"Was he already married to the mayor by then?"

"They had just married. They were actually the couple of the moment in Barcelona, and that was before she became mayor of the city, practically before she'd gone into politics. The two of them didn't even need that to be the apple of the

265

press's eye ... It took nothing for them: a successful entrepreneur, the heir to one of the country's biggest fortunes, young, handsome and intelligent, marries a girl from a humble family who happens to be a human rights campaigner, don't forget that back then the mayor had recently founded Home Refugees, becoming something of a celebrity, almost like a sexy, young, secular, Catalan and very left-wing Mother Theresa. Do you remember?"

"No. And it's hard to imagine, seeing her now."

"Precisely. People have forgotten, but that's what she was like then. And those who do remember must think it was her husband's influence that changed her."

"And wasn't it?"

"I don't know. And, frankly, I couldn't care less. The only thing I know is that politicians are neither right-wing nor left-wing: they're just politicians. The only thing they're interested in is power. They couldn't give a shit about anything else."

"Was your father like that too?"

"My father was an exception ... That's why he ended up the way he did ... Besides, I already told you, he wasn't a politician, he was a union leader."

"Let's get back to the mayor. Tell me something: did you recognise her? I mean, when you saw her again, did you identify her straight away as one of the girls from León XIII?"

"Not straight away, no ... Look, I don't have a very good memory, but the faces of those girls are not something I can forget, I think I could recognise them all ... Though maybe I'm exaggerating. Even so, why would I associate that famous activist with one of those unfortunate victims? It's true that, the night she spent in León XIII, the mayor turned out to be quite a special one, so special that the word 'unfortunate' didn't really apply, much less the word 'victim' ... And, it's also true that the first time I saw her again, I don't remember where, it would have been on TV or in some newspaper, there seemed to be something familiar about her, like she was one of those people you know, or you've crossed paths with, but you don't know how you know them or where from.

"Until she got together with my old friend and, overnight, she started showing up in celebrity magazines. Then, all of a sudden, everything came together in my head, I remembered the night in the place on León XIII and what happened later between her, Casas and Vidal, or what Rosell told me had happened . . . And it's strange: this didn't surprise me either. Quite the contrary, I felt that this fluke, which seemed so implausible, or so absurd, was neither absurd nor implausible, maybe it wasn't even a fluke, I mean, perhaps it was the most logical thing in the world that those two should wind up together, just because they seemed so different and because they had met in such an unusual way . . . Anyway, I know that's a stupid and self-serving thought and that, after the fact, it's easy to find logic in the most illogical things, but that's exactly how I felt. If I didn't tell you, I'd be lying. But I was going to tell you about something else . . ."

"You told me you were looking for an associate for your online business and that you had more luck with Casas than with Vidal or Rosell."

"At least I managed to speak to him . . . Of course, I called him on his own phone, not at his office, someone had given me his number. At first, he couldn't place me, he didn't recognise my name, or he pretended not to, but he quickly remembered or pretended to remember, we had a brief friendly exchange and then he asked me what I wanted . . . I lied. I said I didn't want anything, that I saw him in the press every once in a while, that I'd been meaning to phone for ages, that I'd got hold of his mobile number by chance and had wondered if he'd like to go for a coffee with me, for old times' sake. At first he hesitated, but, just when I was convinced he was going to fob me off, he suggested we go out for lunch the following week at a restaurant called Santa Clara, in Pedralbes, near the Barcelona Tennis Club . . .

"I spent the whole week waiting for the lunch, but in the end I arrived late for it. I did it on purpose, I wanted Casas to think I was a busy man and not impatient to see him . . . By the way, I don't know if I've told you already, but Casas can be charming, a cheerful, affectionate and funny guy. He can be, and that afternoon he was, he welcomed me with open arms, he looked healthy and was in a very good mood, seemed happy to see me . . . At some point he said he regretted that I had disappeared inexplicably from his life and put it down to the thoughtlessness of youth that he had never called me or tried to get in touch with me when, at the beginning of our final year, without warning, I failed to return to Esade. He didn't mention my father's tribulations, as if he hadn't been aware of them, and I lied when he asked about my life after Esade . . . But all that took just a moment, the rest of the time we spent joking around and telling anecdotes and, as I laughed heartily, I felt that we really had been friends and that I'd missed him, felt nostalgic for our friendship, told myself I'd been unfair to my old friends, that I'd been fooling myself, deceiving myself, my friends were not responsible for my failures and disappointments, nor for my misdeeds, the only one responsible was me, it was unfair that I blamed them for all my woes, and much less that I'd wanted revenge . . . Thinking all that made me feel good, so good that I had a feeling that encounter could be a step change signifying a new stage in my life. Or something like that . . . I also loved that Casas managed not to talk about his successes during the whole meal or shrugged them off as unimportant, that he treated me as if he were not the epitome of triumph and I of failure."

"Did you talk about his wife?"

"No. Not that I recall . . . And it doesn't surprise me: I bet he had forgotten I was with them the night we met her . . . Anyway. When it came time for coffee we ordered two whiskies, and while we drank them, I remembered my father's advice: 'Surround yourself with good people and you'll become one of them.' And that was when I decided to talk about the business proposal. I hadn't gone with that intention, at least not exactly, my idea was to sound out Casas, see how he was doing and stuff, but at that moment I saw him so well disposed towards me that I must have felt I couldn't let the opportunity pass by . . . No sooner said than done. I told him about the online gambling proposal, explained how it worked, mentioned my two associates ('two experts' I called them), set out the idea of setting up a new gambling platform, said we just needed a fourth associate to invest a modest sum of money (modest for him, although I didn't say this) and assured him that we would do the work and that, in exchange for his small investment, he would receive profits that would not be spectacular at first, because we didn't want to run unnecessary risks, but with time, and as confidence in the project grew, I was convinced would be at the very least substantial . . . I remember that, while I was talking, I had the impression that the alcohol was making me eloquent. I asked for a paper napkin, did a few figures, and when I finished I handed it to him. 'It can't fail,' I said, with the emphatic influence of the whisky. 'It's a sure thing. That's why I want to offer it to you.' I fell silent and then rounded it off: 'And because I love the idea of us working together and being friends again.'

"I finished speaking convinced that it was impossible Casas would reject my proposal. He took the napkin and looked at it for a while, as if he wanted to make sure the numbers were correct or as if what I had jotted down were not numbers but an enigma or a treasure map . . . Then I started to have doubts, I got anxious, I must have felt I'd let myself get carried away again by my damned optimism. I asked: 'Well, what do you think?' 'Do you want me to tell you the truth,' he answered. I said yes. Then he said: 'The truth is it seems like a fantastic idea.' 'Really?' I asked. 'Really,' he answered. I punched the table euphorically and started praising the virtues of the project, praising myself, I slipped up a bit from pure joy . . . Finally, I said: 'Well then, we'll count you in, yeah?' It was a rhetorical question, of course. But only for me, not for Casas: the proof is that he answered no. I thought he was joking . . . I asked: 'What do you mean no? Didn't you just say you thought it was a fantastic idea?' 'And it is,' he said. 'But it's not for me. It's a great idea if what it's about is just making money.' I tried to smile, then asked: 'And what are businesses for?' And he answered: 'To make money. But not just any old way. Not at any price.' That's what he told me, literally, and then he said, although the betting business was a good, even great business, it was also a shady business, and that he was not prepared to get his hands dirty.

"What to think of that . . . ? Incredible, isn't it? I don't know where the Casas family fortune comes from. From the slave trade, I imagine. Or from the war, from exploitation and crime, which is where great fortunes come from. But there you have this fucking son of a bitch, who belongs to one of those criminal families and spent his youth raping women, accusing me of a lack of ethics for wanting to earn a living with a legal gaming business . . . I had learned a long time ago that the rich are the only ones who don't care about money, because they already have it. What I didn't know is that, in addition, they love giving lessons in morality.

"I've forgotten the rest of the afternoon's conversation . . . Well, I've chosen to forget it. I only remember that, when we finished, a chauffeur was waiting for Casas outside the door of the restaurant, and that when we said goodbye I was drunk and had a piece of paper in my hand and a feeling of absolute filth, as if someone had just vomited all over me . . . The piece of paper had the name, address and telephone number of the manager of the Barcelona branch of a Swiss chocolate firm with headquarters in Berne, one of the Casas family's holdings, or in which the Casas family had a majority share. My friend had encouraged me to call this number because, he said, he thought they could use someone like me there, so I suppose, after he turned down my proposal, I must have told Casas about my economic situation or my employment situation . . . The drunkenness lasted as long as drunkenness lasts, but the filthy feeling lasted much longer, it stayed with me for weeks, I hated myself for having turned to Casas, for letting myself be taken in by him again and bringing my old servile instinct back into the light, that former repugnant self who wanted to endear himself to the magical and transcendent elite of power and money, I hated myself because I had been stupid enough to hand Casas the opportunity to humiliate me three times in a row and in the most savage way possible: first, rubbing my face in his success and my failure, so obvious they didn't even need to be mentioned (though I only realised that much later); second, giving me a lesson in applied ethics; and, third, demonstrating how charitable he could be with disgraced friends . . . Whatever the case, during those weeks I dithered many times over whether to call the number Casas had given me. But, even though I was even more desperate than before, I reached the conclusion that the job awaiting me at the subsidiary of the chocolate factory could only be another form of humiliation. So, pride overcame need and I didn't call.

"That was the last time I saw Casas. Five years ago now, and I think it must have been in the middle of 2020, during the coronavirus pandemic, shortly before I spent some time in hospital and hit rock bottom . . . What made me hit bottom was bitcoin, that's what ended up dragging me down entirely. Remember that I told you I'd started mining bitcoin when my father was in prison?"

"Yes."

"At that time we were destitute, as I told you, so I needed money however I could get it and bitcoin seemed like a good way to make some . . . That was a time when cryptocurrencies were still pretty unknown in Spain. In fact, I began to use bitcoin in complete innocence, I didn't really know what it was, nobody or almost nobody really knew, it was just spoken of as a long-term project, that it was the money of the future, that people could make huge fortunes from it . . . Another very attractive thing back then was that you could make bitcoins at home, with your computer and with very little money, simply by connecting to the Bitcoin Network, which paid you a commission to keep it going. They called it mining. So, when I was living with my mother and father and earning a living by tutoring, I started mining bitcoin and in a very short time I mined more than a thousand. Do you know how much that would be at current exchange rates? Millions of euros. But back then bitcoins had no value, it wasn't even known if they ever would . . . The thing is that after a few months of mining, my computer packed up, and I no longer had access to my bitcoins, which turned into sleeping bitcoins, bitcoins that exist but you can't use. That pissed me off, of course, although what really annoyed me was discovering later, when I was married, that bitcoin could now be exchanged for euros . . . That was a fucking drag, that really pissed me off, I suddenly realised that I had a fortune in bitcoin, except it was as if I didn't because it was buried in my old computer. So I tried to dig it out, until I realised that I couldn't, that it was totally impossible to recover it.

"I told you that was what really pissed me off, and if it didn't piss me off more, if it didn't totally fuck me over, it was because I was too wrapped up with the courier company project . . . The madness started later, when the company went bankrupt and everything went to shit and, as I told you, I tried to make up for the disaster any way I could and demonstrate to everyone that I could triumph, casting about in the dark for a good business, although never for a second did I forget about my buried bitcoins, increasingly angry at being denied what was mine, so furious that, in the end, shortly after the failed attempt at launching the online betting business, I decided to get seriously back into bitcoin and recover however I could the fortune I'd lost.

"That was the biggest mistake of all, the definitive mistake . . . over the years that followed I lived trapped by a sick obsession, spinning around in a whirlwind with no way out: I became a regular on the forums specialising in cryptocurrencies, made a name for myself as a bitcoin guru, I bought devices from the United States, to get back into mining, devices that never arrived or, by the time they arrived, were already obsolete, I made ruinous investments, I don't know how many times I was swindled . . . Who knows . . . But the worst thing was that, while all this was going on, the price of bitcoin was rising unstoppably and I was blinded by the poisonous idea that there were tons of bastards getting rich around me and that the goose that lays the golden egg was slipping through my hands . . . The anxiety of that rollercoaster was addictive but exhausting and it was destroying my nerves, so at a certain moment I managed to get out of it and began to operate as an intermediary, which was much simpler and calmer, much less risky as well: I confined myself to buying and selling bitcoin, charging a commission to buyers and another one to vendors. I knew I couldn't get rich doing that, of course, but at least I had a calmer life and could make a living until the opportunity I was waiting for appeared.

"It arrived when I met the intermediary of a Galician drug trafficker who used bitcoin and began to work with him . . . I met him on an internet forum, Bitcointalk it was called. The work was the same as ever, except that, since the intermediary couldn't tell me where the narco's bitcoin came from, everything had to be done under the table and my profit margin was much higher. The business was working marvellously until one day, when I was just about to close a transaction for that client, the official price of bitcoin dropped sharply, in a matter of seconds it went from twelve thousand to six thousand euros, and the buyers backed out . . . I explained to the narco's intermediary that the operation had fallen through and I couldn't pay him what we'd agreed, but he answered that he didn't want to hear anything about it and I should fend for myself. 'I already told my client his bitcoins were worth a hundred and fifty thousand euros,' he warned me. 'If I tell him they're worth half that now, he'll kill us both. So, get a move on and find that hundred and fifty thousand.' I couldn't find it, of course, and one day, arriving home, I met three guys who took what money I had, destroyed everything they could get their hands on and gave me such a beating that I spent two weeks in hospital.

"That's how my relationship with bitcoin ended. And that's

how I hit rock bottom . . . I left my flat in Gràcia, rented a cheaper one in the Raval and met Marga, who lent me a hand and helped me get back on my feet . . . My father died not long after that. My mother had died a few years earlier and since then he'd been depressed and ill, or more depressed and ill than he was when he got out of prison. He was still living in Torredembarra, but his pension didn't stretch to any home help coming in to clean the apartment or cook a couple of times a week, so I helped out as much as I could. That's why I was so surprised after his death to find that he'd been paying for a safety deposit box in a Santander bank in Barcelona for all those years, and I put it down to forgetfulness or a mistake.

"But it was neither . . . I found out when I went to cancel the safety deposit box after I'd sorted out my father's affairs, emptied his apartment and taken the two or three things I wanted to keep. The box was in a branch of the Santander on calle Calabria, very close to our old flat in Ensanche, and when I opened it, I got the surprise of my life. Do you know what I found inside?"

"What?"

"My inheritance."

"Your inheritance?"

"That's right. What was in that safety deposit box, I guessed at first glance, were all the videos we'd recorded in the place on León XIII . . . Imagine my surprise; for a while I was unable to believe my eyes. I had completely forgotten about that, I thought the tapes had disappeared years ago. It never occurred to me that my father would have them . . . When I emerged from my stupor I told myself that, if my father had kept that material for all that time, paying money he didn't have to rent that box, it was because he knew the videos were valuable, because he thought he could get some benefit from them."

"And that was when you decided to blackmail the mayor?"

"No, that was when I decided to blackmail all of them. Casas, Vidal, Rosell. All of them . . . Well, actually, all except the mayor, that wasn't my idea."

"Whose idea was it?"

"I'm getting to that. But first I'd like you to understand how I felt when I made that discovery. Think about it . . . My father had died, I'd been horribly beaten, had given up on the idea of getting rich overnight, had even stopped buying and selling bitcoin and was getting by dealing marijuana and doing the books for a couple of neighbourhood acquaintances. And right then, at the worst moment of my life, when I thought I couldn't fall any further, my father gave me a gift from beyond the grave, the possibility of sudden wealth, at the very least a chance to sort out my life and settle some scores with my old friends from Esade . . . I thought that justice would finally be done, that I had in my hands what I needed to fulfil my dreams. Imagine how I felt . . .

"In any case, by then I was very cunning and I was aware of the risks I would have to run, so I tried to take every precaution . . . My intention was to blackmail the three of them, as I said, one after the other, but I started with Casas because he was the only one who didn't have a political post and he seemed the most vulnerable to me: Rosell had become a People's Party councillor at City Hall after being at Barcelona Global and getting the kind of reputation there that people who are good at nothing tend to get in politics (the reputation of a prudent, reasonable, conciliatory man), and Vidal had left the leadership of the socialist group, had joined the mayor's party and held the position he holds today . . . So I got hold of Casas' personal email address, created an anonymous account and sent him a message from an internet café saying that, if he didn't want a video filmed on León XIII to be made public, he should leave three hundred thousand euros in hundred-euro notes in a specific place on the Carretera de las Aguas. I was sure that my friends thought that those videos had disappeared years ago, just as I had until my father's death, and, even though I took into account that Casas might suspect who his blackmailer was, I also counted on him not being able to prove it, and most of all I counted on him paying to get rid of the problem as quickly as possible . . .

"What I didn't count on was what actually happened.

"One afternoon, shortly after sending that message to Casas, I found two guys at the door to the building where I was living. They forced me roughly upstairs and into my flat and began beating me, and I thought the Galician narco had discovered my hiding place and sent his thugs to finish the job . . . They were still beating me when two other guys appeared and ordered them to stop. The two guys who were beating me left and the other two stayed. One of them was Hematomas, the other was Vidal.

"It had been almost twenty years since Vidal and I had last seen each other, but he didn't even pretend to be pleased about the reunion. I was grateful. 'What's up, Ricky?' he asked. 'Long time no see, eh? Remember me?' I was lying on the sofa, very much the worse for wear, and Vidal asked Hematomas to go to the kitchen for a glass of water. The inspector brought the water from the kitchen and, while I sat up and drank it, Vidal asked me again if I remembered him. I told him I did. I must have also asked him what he was doing in my flat or why he had come to see me or something like that, because he said, 'Don't play dumb, Ricky, I'm here because you're not satisfied with swindling people selling bitcoin and dope. On top of that you have to blackmail your old friends.' I tried to defend myself.

'I don't know what you're talking about,' I said. Vidal clicked his tongue and looked annoyed, and Hematomas started to punch me. When he got tired, Vidal asked me if I knew what he was talking about now, and I spat out some blood and said yes. 'What a disaster, Ricky!' he said then: he was talking as if he were carrying out an unpleasant task or a painful duty. 'Having to see each other like this, at our age, after so many years . . .' He was fat and his face was puffy and red, as if he'd just come from a banquet where he'd had too much of everything . . . It was May, but he was wearing a trench coat, jacket and tie. Beside him, Hematomas was still mopping his brow from the beating, but he didn't seem furious or tired: he seemed bored. While he let me recover, Vidal kept talking. 'What I don't understand is how you could believe you would get away with it,' he said. 'As if tracing an email weren't the easiest thing in the world, no matter how anonymous it might be, and the internet café it was sent from, no matter how public. You're a bungler, Ricky, just like your father . . . That's how it went for him. And that's how it's going for you.'

"Reminding me of my father at that moment is what you call kicking a guy when he's down . . . I felt like crying, but I didn't want to give that bastard the satisfaction so I held back my tears. 'Look, Ricky,' he said, when he thought I was in a condition to process what he was going to say. 'I have a lot of work and very little time, so I'm asking you please not to waste it. OK?' I moved my head up and down: what else could I do? . . . 'Great,' he said then. He picked up a chair, sat in front of me and got to the point while Hematomas listened, standing behind him, with his hands in his pockets, without looking at us, as if it was nothing to do with him. 'Don't worry,' Vidal began. 'I'm not going to ask you how many videos you have from those days. Or where you've got them stashed . . . I don't care about any of that. There's only one thing that interests me: have you got the video of Virginia?' The question took me by surprise, but naturally I immediately knew which video he meant and, since I was no longer in a position to play dumb, I immediately answered yes. 'Great,' he said again. 'Congratulations. You've won the lottery. I'm going to make you a proposal so you can get out of the hole you've got yourself into. Listen carefully.' Vidal explained that I had chosen the wrong victim, that I shouldn't have tried to blackmail Casas but rather the mayor, and that what I should do was threaten to broadcast that video if she didn't pay me double the money I'd demanded of Casas. That's more or less what he told me.

"The expression on my face must have said it all . . . As you can imagine, the last thing I could have expected is that the deputy mayor of Barcelona, the mayor's own right-hand man, should ask me what he was asking me . . . Then Vidal said: 'I suppose you're wondering various things. The first being what interest I might have in your blackmailing my boss. The second is what guarantees are there that you will get to keep the ransom. And the third is what guarantees do you have that Virginia, or whoever, isn't going to catch you trying to blackmail her the way I caught you trying to blackmail Casas. Right?' I didn't say anything, but my silence was easy to interpret . . . Vidal went on: 'The first question I'm not going to answer because it's none of your business, but the other two I am.' To answer the second question, Vidal explained that, once the mayor received the threat, three things might happen. 'The first,' he said, 'is that she pays without complaint, thinking the problem will be solved just like that. Between you and me, knowing her, I think that's the most likely.' The second possibility consisted of the mayor giving him responsibility for resolving the problem, as Casas had done, in which case the problem would be resolved, because he would convince her that it would be best to pay and be done with it. And the third possibility was that she would bring in the Mossos d'Esquadra to resolve the problem, as you're the ones who, he said, in theory should take charge of solving a case like this. Vidal also assured me that the second option was not very likely, because he and the mayor had not been getting along for some time and because it was likely she would suspect he was directly or indirectly involved in the blackmail . . . That left the third option, the Mossos, and, Vidal told me, if the mayor talked to you guys, I didn't have to worry either, because he and his men would help me. 'We caught you straight away,' he said, 'but the Mossos won't catch you, because we'll teach you how to do things, we'll supervise everything, so you won't get caught. And we aren't bunglers, are we, Lomas?' The inspector had tired of standing and had sat down behind him, looking gloomy with his head hanging, and he said no: it was the only word I heard him pronounce that afternoon . . . Vidal stared at me and I figured he was trying to see if he had convinced me. I held his gaze until he brought out the argument he'd saved for last. 'There is another reason I'm sure no-one's going to catch you,' he said. I asked him what it was, and then Vidal smiled and I suddenly recognised my friend from twenty years earlier in that wolf-like smile. 'It's impossible to catch a dead man,' he answered."

3

Sitting in his car, Melchor types an address (passeig de les Acàcias, 18, Rupià) into the satnav of his phone and pulls out of the Egara complex.

The previous night he had been scouring the internet until very late for information on Ricky Ramírez. He didn't find much. Essentially he had discovered that in 2015 he founded a courier company called Mercurio, in which he figured as managing director, and in 2019 he had to close it due to bankruptcy; he was married to a woman called Herminia Prat; he later worked buying and selling bitcoin and everywhere online he is referred to as a business management graduate of Esade, though Vidal had assured him (and had no reason to lie to him) that Ramírez had abandoned his studies without finishing. There weren't many mentions of him, however, in recent years, and he didn't find any reference to his death, which didn't surprise him. He also looked for information on Herminia Prat. He barely found two mentions. One said she was a teacher at the Torroella de Montgrí art school, in a small town in Ampurdán; the other, that she had created or contributed to creating, in that same region near the French border, an association called Artistes a Cel Obert that promoted relationships between ceramicists and artists in other disciplines.

So that morning, as soon as he got to Egara, he'd called the art school in Torroella de Montgrí, but no-one answered and he imagined it was closed for the summer holidays. However, he tried calling again around ten and a woman answered. Melchor asked for Herminia Prat; the woman said she wasn't there and probably wouldn't be until September, when classes resumed. Melchor asked for her phone number and the woman said she wasn't authorised to give out teachers' contact information. Melchor revealed that he was a police officer. "Has something happened?" the woman asked in alarm. "No," he reassured her. "I just need to talk to Señora Prat." Without any further questions, the woman read out her phone number, email address and home address. "She doesn't go out much in the summer," she informed him. "If you go this morning, you're sure to find her." Melchor said thanks, hung up the phone, picked it up again, dialled the number he'd just written down. No-one answered. After a while he called again, with the same result. Finally, he went to see Blai, told him he wouldn't be able to follow Vidal and asked him to find a substitute. "Don't piss me off, *españolazo*," Blai protested. "Hadn't we agreed you'd take the second shift?" Melchor explained that he'd found the ex-wife of the man alleged to have been behind the camera of the video of the mayor and couldn't get through to her on the phone. "But I have her address," he went on. "She lives in a village in Ampurdán. I was told that if I went there this morning, I'd be able to talk to her." Not without first swearing his head off, Blai agreed to find someone to cover his watch, but before Melchor could get out of his office he asked: "Has it not crossed your mind that those three might have nothing to do with this?" "Many times," Melchor admitted. "But I don't

believe it." "Because?" Blai asked. "Because the simplest explanation is almost always the best," Melchor said. "And I want to
at least rule it out. Besides, it's Wednesday, we've got three days
before the deadline those bastards gave us expires and I've got
nowhere else to look." He added: "And you?" Blai looked at him
in silence for a second; then, he grumpily pointed to the door.
"Go on, get out of here," he said, "before I change my mind."

It's not yet half past twelve when Melchor gets on the
motorway heading towards France. Three-quarters of an hour
later, he takes the Gerona North exit, drives through Celrà and
Bordils and, just after the crossroads at La Pera, turns left and
then almost immediately right into Rupià. It's a tiny village
of old stone houses clustered around a Romanesque church,
accessed by one long straight street that leads to an intersection
of narrow streets. Guided by his satnav, Melchor takes the little
street on his left, drives along beside a dried-up stream and,
when he arrives in front of some swings, identifies the house
he's looking for: the last one.

It is a few minutes before two, and the village seems deserted
under the unforgiving July sun. Melchor peeks over a gate that
leads into a garden: recently mown lawn, an acacia tree, an
olive tree, honeysuckle, jasmine and vines, a small, well-tended
vegetable plot; also two different-sized buildings, and in the
small one, beyond the half-open door, a woman who just
then, as if she sensed she was being observed, turns towards
Melchor. The woman leaves what she is doing, picks up a cloth
and, while she wipes her hands, gestures for him to come in.
Melchor walks across the garden on a path made of planks (a
dense cloud of scent envelopes him as he passes a jasmine) and,
when he reaches the door to the small building, he says hello,
apologises for the intrusion and asks if the woman is who he
thinks she is. The woman says she is.

"I'm a police officer," he introduces himself. "Could I speak to you for a moment?"

Herminia Prat stops wiping her hands. She smiles vaguely, as if dazzled by the glare of the sun; more than surprise, her smile reveals curiosity.

"It's about your ex-husband," Melchor explains as he finishes walking over. "Ricky Ramírez."

The clarification changes the woman's face, the features of which seem to crumble. She's not much older than him, but she looks as if she is: her long hair is grey, almost white, and she has a freckled face scored with wrinkles and an air of fatigued fragility. She is small, very thin, with a dull look in her eyes, and breasts that barely register under the red-flowered print of her dress marked with clay and paint. A bracelet of blue stones dangles from her left wrist.

"He died a few months ago," Herminia tells him.

"I know," Melchor replies. "That's why I want to talk to you."

The woman wipes her hands with the rag again, perhaps not so much out of concern for hygiene as to calm her anxiety. She speculates:

"If it's about money—"

"It's not that," Melchor interrupts. "It's about a case I'm investigating. An important case."

The woman's face looks more curious than anxious again; her opaque eyes no longer scrutinise Melchor as if he were an intruder.

"I should tell you that once we divorced we hardly ever saw each other," she explains. "In fact, when he died, I hadn't seen or heard from him for almost a year."

"That doesn't matter."

With a gesture of indifference or reluctance, the woman invites him in.

Melchor goes inside a rectangle illuminated by windows that overlook a vast expanse of trees and wheat fields, where the motley order of a ceramicist's studio reigns. Two worktables occupy the centre of the space, overhung with fluorescent lights and surrounded by unmatched chairs; beyond stand two large kilns, one blue and the other grey, and a manual rolling mill, designed to compress and stretch the clay. To the left of the entrance, beside an old fridge with a dusty radio on top of it, there is a metal potter's wheel, a cupboard with drawers brimming with colour samples and a shelf crammed with plates, vases, bowls on steel points and slightly Daliesque sculptures representing nightmarish beings: witches, dragons, centaurs, unicorns and griffins. There are two more shelves on the opposite wall. One of them contains clay pieces not yet fired (cups, bowls, teapots, plates); the other, plastic bottles full of coloured glazes. Only a small fan aimed at the worktables mitigates the stifling heat of the room a little.

"Is this how you earn your living?" Melchor asks. "With ceramics, I mean."

"Of course," Herminia answers, washing her hands at the sink. "Does that seem strange?"

Melchor doesn't say anything; he keeps observing, almost fascinated, the handcrafted profusion that surrounds him. On either side of the sink, on a stone ledge that juts out from the wall, there are two scales to measure the glazes, pigments, oxides and dyes with which she makes the colours, and several bowls bristling with tools and instruments: knives, scissors, brushes, tongs, cutters, pens, pencils, sponges, rulers, set squares, triangles, rags and awls.

"I used to make a better living," Herminia tells him, as if Melchor's silence was answer enough. "This is a district of ceramicists, there's always been a lot of competition in the area.

La Bisbal ceramics, you know . . . I didn't move here because of it, but I've liked making ceramics since school, and this is the ideal place to learn. A few years ago, I made lots of pieces and they sold very well, at tourist shops, local festivals and street markets, all over the place. There are not so many people buying these days, and those who do, shop at IKEA and places like that, at ridiculous prices. I can't compete with that, so I produce very little. For years I made quite a bit of money with those little figurines people put on baptism, communion and wedding cakes, you know what I mean?" Melchor, who's never seen those figurines, or had never noticed them, makes a vague gesture, which could be a nod but isn't. "I made thousands of them, commissioned by a wholesaler. But that ended too. Or almost. Now I only make figurines for anniversary cakes for couples who've been married for twenty-five or fifty years. When these people die off, adios."

Herminia turns off the tap, picks up a clean cloth and dries her hands again.

"So what do you live off now?" Melchor asks.

"Do you really want to know or are you just asking to earn my trust, like the cops in films?"

Melchor doesn't feel like answering with a lie and Herminia turns off the fan.

"Come with me."

Following the woman, Melchor leaves the workshop, walks back along the path of planks and into the house, the ground floor of which turns out to be a single spacious room, with a hippie feel and completely white walls, which is both living room and kitchen. Herminia points to a sofa covered in a bone-coloured blanket, opens the fridge and offers him a beer. Melchor says no thanks and the woman asks what she can get him.

"Just water," he says.

Herminia takes a jug of iced water out of the fridge and pours a glass for Melchor; then she opens a small bottle of beer, sits in a chair facing him and, dropping the formalities, encourages him to talk.

"I'm interested in knowing what kind of relationship your husband had with Virginia Oliver," Melchor says.

The woman takes a sip of her beer from the bottle; Melchor drinks some water.

"The mayor?" Herminia asks.

"Yes."

"None that I know of."

"He never mentioned her to you?"

"No." She hesitates for a moment. "Not that I recall."

"And what about Enric Vidal?"

"If you mean the politician . . ."

Melchor nods.

"Yes, he did talk about him," Herminia admits. "Him and his friends."

"Daniel Casas and Gonzalo Rosell?"

"That's them."

"They were also friends with your husband, right?"

"That's what he said, I never met them. But yes, he talked about them a lot, especially at the end, when, well, anyway . . ." The woman moves her hand as if cleaning the air of spiderwebs. "He'd known them at Esade, as a student, but, as far as I know, after that they lost touch. Why are you interested in this?"

Melchor apologises: he cannot tell her.

"You say your husband talked a lot about those friends," he goes on. "What did he tell you about them?"

Before answering, Herminia draws up her legs and bare feet and curls up in the armchair like a cat, with the beer bottle pearled with humidity in her hands. Her toenails are painted pink, and there is an ironic look of dejection on her face, as if Melchor were interrogating her about a misfortune she'd already written off. Behind her, a door open to the garden lets in a warm breeze, which explains why, although there are no cooling apparatuses in the room, it's much less hot here than in the workshop. Herminia takes another sip of her beer.

"Depends when," she explains. "At first he spoke very highly of them. Of them and of his years at Esade. He was very proud of having studied there and having had those friends. Or that's the impression I got. Of course, back then I was so naive . . . But no, it's true, when we first got to know each other, he'd use any excuse to talk about his friends, to tell those anecdotes of his . . . We all knew more or less who they were, of course, them or their families. I suppose, in part, he dazzled my parents that way, and obviously he dazzled me: he seemed like a prince who had arrived from an unknown galaxy, from a place where things were better, I don't know, shinier and easier. I imagine that everyone who falls in love feels something like that, don't they? But that was only at first, when we met."

"How did you meet?"

"We worked together at a food company." Herminia says a name, which Melchor doesn't recognise, and she moves around in her chair looking for a more comfortable position. "They made sliced bread. It was my first job, straight out of college. I studied economics, you know? I couldn't care less about economics, to be honest, but my family insisted I study something useful and . . . Anyway, I already told you I was very naive back then. The thing is we got married and set up our own company, a courier company called Mercurio. At first it went well, but then things started to go wrong and everything went bust. And when I say everything, I mean everything." At this point the woman's voice seems to break and she looks away towards the kitchen window. The big window frames a still stretch of ripe wheat and, beyond, the gentle profile of a succession of hills covered in vegetation. The woman clears her throat and turns back to Melchor; she has not cried, at least her eyes are not wet. "Before you asked me how I earned my living . . . I teach classes to children. I do other things too, but that's what I like most. And do you know why?" Melchor suppresses the urge to tell her she's straying from the point. "Because I've never learned as much about ceramics as by teaching it. About ceramics and everything else. The children, of course, learn as well, and they learn things that some adults never learn. For example, that one thing is what you try to do, what you imagine, and what you come out with is something else, and that you have to accept what comes out, you have to see the good side and think that maybe it's not what you wanted, but it's possibly even better than what you wanted, because what you wanted was not good. That's what happened to me: I never thought I'd be living the life I have."

"And what happened to your husband?"

"That can also be explained by ceramics," Herminia replies, and Melchor wonders for a moment if he's talking to a madwoman, so mad that it's almost impossible to detect her madness. "Making a ceramic piece consists of taking a portion of clay and transforming it into something else," the woman continues. "The clay is the same, but the thing is different. And that's what happens to people a lot of the time. At first we are a certain way, but later we turn into someone else. We have the same name and the same face, but actually we're not the same person anymore."

"Is that what happened to Ricky?"

"Exactly. What happened to him is that he was poisoned by

failure, which turned him into a different person. A horrible person, obsessed with money, ill over money, or the lack of it. This is not unusual either, don't you think? When things are going well, people aren't usually bad; they turn bad when things go badly. And, as well as becoming bad, they start blaming everyone else for things going badly for them."

"Are you telling me that, even though he no longer had any relationship with his friends from Esade, he blamed them for his failure?"

"Them and everyone else. Except for himself, of course: he blamed me, he blamed my family, he blamed the few friends he had, and even those he didn't have anymore. You can't imagine what that was like. No-one who hasn't lived through it can imagine what it was like."

As if trying to enable Melchor to imagine it, Herminia tells him of court cases, swindling lawyers, unpaid debts, sacked workers, family rows and creditors pounding on their door, insulting them over the phone and shouting at them in the street.

"A nightmare," she says. "I was pregnant and I lost the baby, and then the doctors told me I couldn't have children. I sank into a two-year depression. Fortunately, I had some cousins who were living near here, in Verges, who got me out of that hell. If it hadn't been for them . . ."

The woman's voice breaks or seems to break again, and again she looks away from Melchor, who thinks that Herminia has not written off her misfortune, that there are misfortunes that take eternities to write off.

"Once I left Barcelona I hardly saw him," she goes on after a few seconds, without resentment, looking back at Melchor and brushing a quick finger under her eye; she swallows the rest of her beer and leaves the empty bottle on the floor, beside the armchair. "By the time we split up I almost didn't recognise the man I'd fallen in love with in Ricky. It was, as I said, as if he were another person. A broken, egotistical man obsessed with his failure and blinded by money, a man who bad-mouthed everyone."

"Including his Esade friends?" Melchor asks.

"Them most of all. Daddy's boys, spoiled mediocrities, rich fucking brats who never had to make any effort, who had everything handed to them. That's what he started to say about them when things began to go wrong. Well, that was the least of it. He hated them as if they'd really done something to him. On top of that he was drinking a lot . . . Anyway, half the time I didn't even listen to him, to tell you the truth, I was fed up by then."

"Do you know if he saw them again?"

"His friends? No. I don't think so. I don't know." She pauses for a couple of seconds, staring at Melchor, but he realises she is not seeing him, just her own thoughts. Then, coming back to reality, she goes on: "What I do know is that he got involved in the world of cryptocurrency. Well, in fact he'd been into it before, when we were still together, it was an old project of his, back then I saw it as a sort of training, but then he got in deep . . . He was buying and selling bitcoin. He did strange deals. Or he tried to . . . He didn't want a steady job, he wanted to make easy money, strike it rich, as he used to say. But the fact is he never emerged from the pit. Every once in a while, he'd phone me, and sometimes we'd meet for coffee when I went to Barcelona to see my parents. I remember the last time I saw him." She lowers her feet from the armchair, picks up the little bottle and seems about to stand up; but she doesn't. "It was almost a year ago. One day he called me and said he'd been admitted to Valle Hebrón Hospital and he needed me. So I went to see him. I found him in a bed, with his face bandaged and a broken leg and a broken arm. I asked him what had happened and he explained something about an accident. I believed him, of course, but later I found out it was a lie: he had actually been beaten up. That day I met his girlfriend."

"He had a girlfriend, did he?"

"I met that one. Maybe he had others. He told me he was in trouble and he asked me for money. It wasn't the first time he'd asked, but he looked so bad that I gave him some, not that it was much, but it was quite a bit considering my subsistence economy. And I never saw him again."

"Did he pay you back?"

"No."

"Do you know the girlfriend's name?"

"No." Herminia seems to hesitate. "Although . . . Hang on a minute."

She stands up with the bottle in her hand, leaves it in the kitchen and goes up a wooden staircase to the second floor. Melchor checks his WhatsApp inbox, where messages are accumulating from Vivales, Blai, Cortabarría and Vàzquez, who announces that he's ready to come back to work the following day. He has answered three of them when he hears Herminia coming back down the stairs.

"You're in luck."

She hands Melchor a piece of paper torn out of a spiral notebook, with a name, a phone number and a bank account number. It is a woman's name: Marga Isern.

"Can I keep it?" Melchor asks, waving the paper.

"Of course," Herminia says. "Ricky gave it to me so I could deposit money into that account, and so I could call his girlfriend if there was any problem. I kept it in my diary."

Melchor puts the paper away, but Herminia does not sit back down.

"Well," the woman says, "I'm going to make some lunch. Do you want to stay?"

Melchor thinks the woman is making the offer to be polite, and that he has bothered her enough. So, he stands up, thanks her and says he has to get going. The woman does not insist but, as she sees him out, tells him to come back and see her or call if he needs anything else; Melchor reads out the number they gave him at the Torroella de Montgrí school and asks if it's hers.

"Yes." Herminia nods. "But I turn it off when I'm working."

They have reached the end of the path and the woman opens the garden gate. As they shake hands, the smell of jasmine reminds Melchor of something.

"There are rumours that your husband committed suicide," he says, choosing his words carefully. "You know that, don't you?"

Unexpectedly, Herminia laughs, and Melchor glimpses for a moment, in that clear, guileless laugh, which revealed a couple of dimples in those freckled cheeks, the girl she must have been before the ordeals she went through with Ricky Ramírez began.

"That's crazy!" she exclaims. "I didn't go to his funeral, as I didn't find out he'd died until after the cremation, but I can assure you of one thing: Ricky was not suicidal. He was a survivor. He would have lived under a bridge rather than kill himself. I guarantee you that."

As he drives out of Rupià, Melchor dials Marga Isern's number, but a tinny voice tells him that it is no longer in service. Then he calls Cortabarría and asks him to look up two things: Marga Isern's contact details and Ricky Ramírez's death certificate. Then he spends a while going over his conversation with Herminia Prat in his head and, as he drives towards Barcelona, he decides to call Vàzquez, but at the last minute he changes his mind and calls Blai.

"Don't fuck with me, *españolazo*," exclaims Blai when Melchor sets out his theory.

"I'm not saying it's true," he stresses. "I'm saying it's possible." Then he summarises: "Ricky Ramírez hated their guts, tried to blackmail them and they caught him. That gave them the idea of blackmailing the mayor, and the material with which to blackmail her. And they got rid of Ramírez so he wouldn't annoy them."

"Brilliant," Blai admits. "Too bad you don't have a single shred of proof."

"That's true," Melchor agrees. "But Ramírez was the one who filmed the video, so, if someone might have kept it, it would be him. Also, he dies and gets cremated super fast, and on top of that Vidal tries to convince me he committed suicide, which his wife thinks is a joke . . . In short, I don't think it's such a long shot."

Blai doesn't say yes and he doesn't say no. Melchor gives him time to think it over; after a few seconds, he asks:

"Blai, are you still there?"

"You're missing something," the inspector says.

"What's that?"

"The woman who called the mayor."

Melchor slows down suddenly, takes out the piece of paper Herminia Prat gave him and checks on his phone to see if Marga Isern's number is the same number the blackmailers used to call the mayor, or as the SIM card the Frenchman made in the name of Farooq Hoque. Neither of them match.

"Don't worry," Melchor finally says. "I'm looking for her."

Before he reaches Barcelona, he gets a call from Cortabarría to say he's found Marga Isern's address.

"Write it down," he says.

Melchor memorises the address, Cortabarría adds:

"We also have a photo of the woman. A couple of years ago she got caught selling marijuana. Interested?"

"Of course. Can you send it to me on WhatsApp?"

"Right away."

"Great. What about the death certificate?"

"We're working on it," Cortabarría answers.

Marga Isern lives in a building on ronda de Sant Antoni. Melchor double-parks right in front of it, gets out of his car and buzzes the woman's intercom, but no-one answers. Walking back to his car, he sees another car pulling out and hurries to take its place. It is a perfect observation point and, sitting behind the wheel, the policeman scrutinises the entrance to the building at the same time as the mugshot Cortabarría has just sent him, a photo of a woman around forty years of age, very thin and wearing a sweatshirt, straw-coloured hair, frightened face and reddened eyes. He has been looking at it for a while when he feels a pang of hunger. He walks over to a nearby bar, orders a hotdog and a bottle of water and goes back to the car. As he eats, he remembers that the Frenchman's business is very near there, and he has, at the same time, a hunch and an idea. He finishes eating on the walk to the internet café, and before going in throws the empty water bottle into a bin.

The mujahid is still behind the counter, absorbed in his mobile phone, but he looks up and says something to Melchor as he walks past. Melchor pretends not to hear: he goes straight to the Frenchman's office, walks in without knocking, and greets him with the first thing that pops into his head ("Hadn't we agreed that a business that doesn't let you sleep in till eleven is no business worth having? And what about a siesta?") and the Frenchman looks up with a bad-tempered expression. When he recognises Melchor, however, his face brightens and, taking off his reading glasses, he laughs fiercely and invites him to sit down. Melchor drops into a chair while the Frenchman rants about his customers and makes two cups of coffee in his Nespresso machine. When he hands Melchor his, he asks:

"So, what brings you here?"

"Nothing." Melchor shrugs and takes a sip from the paper cup. "I was working nearby and I had some free time."

"Pull the other one, kid," the Frenchman says, leaning back in his armchair with his coffee in his hands. Then he asks: "Did you find what you were looking for the other day?"

It's the question he was expecting, though it has arrived sooner than he expected, which he interprets as an advance confirmation of his hunch. He answers:

"What's that?"

"Do me the favour of not playing dumb with me, would you?" the Frenchman scolds him. "It's disrespectful."

Melchor gestures an apology.

"Sorry," he says. "What did you want to know?"

"If you found out about the SIM card for the Pakistani name?"

"Oh, that's right," Melchor pretends to remember. "Of course, I found it. For what it was worth. You made it for a woman who lives around the corner, on ronda de Sant Antoni. Her name's Marga Isern."

Petrified by surprise, the Frenchman looks at Melchor for a second with his cup suspended a centimetre from his mouth; then, without taking his eyes off his old prison mate, he drinks his coffee in one gulp, leaves the cup on the paper-strewn desk and asks:

"How did you find out?"

Melchor leans his face towards the Frenchman and winks.

"Because you just told me."

He finishes his drink and stands up while the Frenchman laughs again.

"You son of a bitch!" he exclaims. "You tricked me."

"Easy, pal," Melchor says, as he searches for a space to leave his empty cup and ends up putting it inside the Frenchman's. "This stays between me and you."

He thanks him for the coffee, but, before he can open the office door, the Frenchman says his name. Melchor turns around: his old friend and mentor is still sprawled in his chair, with his eternal cetacean air; there is not a trace of laughter left on his face, now dominated by a scowl.

"That girl has done nothing wrong," he says.

"How do you know?"

"Because I know. I told you I know how to tell the bastards from those who aren't. And that woman is not a bastard. She's unfortunate. A poor wretch who gets by however she can. Nothing more. On top of that her boyfriend died two months ago."

"Did you know him?"

"Enough to know that he was dangerous."

"Do you know how he died?"

"No idea: you think I know all the neighbourhood gossip? He died and that's all. From one day to the next. That's all I know. And that woman couldn't hurt a fly."

Melchor looks at the Frenchman for an instant, and wonders if Marga Isern had also been his girlfriend, or something like a girlfriend; he's about to ask him, but decides that, at least for the moment, it's none of his business.

"Don't worry," he tries to calm him again.

And, before he can say goodbye, the Frenchman surprises him with another question.

"Are you busy this evening?"

Melchor looks at him uncomprehendingly.

"Let's have dinner," the Frenchman says.

"I'm sorry," Melchor says sincerely. "My daughter's expecting me."

"You must have someone you can leave her with." Combining this assumption with a pleading gesture, he insists: "Come on, kid, for old time's sake."

Back on ronda de Sant Antoni, Melchor buzzes Marga Isern's intercom again. This time there's an answer. He asks for Marga Isern.

"Speaking," she says.

"Police," he says. "Open up."

Silence.

"Did you hear?" says Melchor.

"What do you want?"

"To speak to you."

More silence.

"Have you got a search warrant?"

"I don't want to search your flat. I just want to talk for a moment."

"I haven't done anything. I don't have anything to talk to the police about."

"You're wrong. Open the door, please."

"What do you want to talk about?"

"Ricky Ramírez."

"I don't know who that is."

"Sure you do."

"He's dead."

"That's why I want to talk to you. I also want to talk to you about a SIM card you had made at the internet café in the name of a local Pakistani shopkeeper."

This time the silence is even longer. It is just past seven and the light has begun to fade. A flock of Japanese tourists, with a guide in front, walks along the pavement on the other side of ronda de Sant Antoni.

"Marga?" Melchor says.

The door opens with a metallic click, and Melchor climbs a dark and narrow staircase up to the third floor, where he finds one door ajar. He opens it, crosses a small landing and immediately sees the woman: she is in the kitchen, standing beside a sink full of plates, smoking. Visibly nervous, the woman turns towards Melchor and asks:

"What do you want?"

Melchor walks into the very small kitchen, lit by a fluorescent bulb that blinks almost imperceptibly; there is an unhealthy smell floating in the air, mouldy cheese or feet. Beside the sink is a gas cooker and a tiny fridge; against the wall, a table with a litre-and-a-half bottle of Coca-Cola, several dirty glasses, an overflowing ashtray (which says: SOUVENIR OF CALATAYUD), a packet of cigarette papers and an open pouch of rolling tobacco. There are no chairs in sight, but Melchor asks:

"Could we sit down?"

"No," the woman answers, taking an anxious drag of her cigarette. "Ask what you have to ask and get out."

She is as gaunt as she was in the mug shot, and has the same yellowish hair, although cut shorter; her face still looks frightened, but it's a fear she is trying to disguise with displeasure, almost indignation, at having him there, in her kitchen. She's not wearing a tracksuit this time, but a pair of baggy jeans and a red T-shirt that accentuates her flabby, voluminous breasts. She is not attractive, but Melchor thinks she was or might have been, and he decides to get straight to the point.

"You're in trouble," he warns her.

"Oh yeah?" Marga answers; her left leg is trembling rapidly. "What trouble? If you mean the SIM card . . ."

"That's what I mean."

The woman puts her hand in her back pocket, takes out her mobile and, with a defiant look, hands it to Melchor, who takes out the SIM card in a couple of seconds and sees that it is not the one he's looking for.

"Happy now?" the woman asks. "There's the door, get lost."

Melchor puts the phone back together and hands it to its owner.

"You and I both know you had that card made," he warns her.

"Who told you?" the woman asks. "The Frenchman?"

Melchor is silent. Then he lies:

"I don't know who you mean."

"Yes you do," the woman says. "The owner of the internet café. It was him, wasn't it?" Melchor is silent again. "Well, I'll tell you why he told you that: because he's a dirty old man who wanted to get me in the sack and I didn't let him. That's why. The bastard is getting his revenge on me."

Melchor does not believe her, but pretends to have doubts.

"The phone with that SIM card in it is being used to blackmail the mayor of Barcelona," he says.

"And what's that to me?" replies Marga.

Melchor takes a step towards her and she braces herself. The woman's left leg has stopped trembling. Melchor shows her the palms of his hands, as if to show he is unarmed, even though the opposite is true.

"You're making a mistake," he says. "If you help me, I can help you."

Perhaps because she has realised that Melchor is not intending to attack her, the woman pretends to smile, takes a quick drag on her cigarette and, having barely exhaled the smoke, turns to the sink to tap the ash into it.

"You don't say," she asks, turning back towards him.

Melchor lets his gaze wander around the kitchen: he notices that there is a cat curled up in one corner, beside an empty plastic bowl, watching him with incandescent eyes.

"I can prove that it was you who procured that card," he said. "That's enough to arrest you. Do you know why I'm not going to?"

"Why?"

"Because I don't think you got involved in this on your own. There's someone else. You're protecting somebody. Tell me who you're protecting, and I'll help you."

Marga Isern scrutinises Melchor, who feels the woman is trying to calibrate how sincere he is being. After a few seconds, she takes another drag on her cigarette, puts it out under the tap, leaves the soaking stub on the edge of the sink and confronts the police officer again.

"Are you done?"

"No." Melchor improvises a change of strategy. "Tell me about Ricky Ramírez."

"I already told you he's dead."

"How did you know him?"

"From the neighbourhood. He lived near here."

"What kind of relationship did you have with him?"

"The kind the Frenchman wishes I would have had with him."

"Do you know what he died of?"

301

"A heart attack."

"Are you sure?"

"That's what the doctor said."

"And if I told you it's not true?"

The woman falls quiet, as if a shiver is running down her spine. Her left leg is trembling even more rapidly than before.

"What?"

"I have reason to believe he was murdered," Melchor explains. "And that you are unintentionally protecting the people responsible."

Now the woman looks at him disbelievingly, or perhaps she is just perplexed. She steps away from the sink, pulls a stool out from under the table and sits down. She seems a little dazed.

"Why do you think that?" the woman asks.

"I can't go into details," Melchor answers. "But I'm telling you I have my reasons. Powerful reasons. And, if it's true these people murdered your boyfriend, they could just as well kill you when you're no longer useful to them. That's why you need my protection."

The woman has taken some tobacco out of the pouch and has begun to finger it as if she were going to roll a cigarette. Everything seems to indicate that she is still in a state of shock. Everything indicates that she is trying to assimilate the news, or rather the hypothesis, and for a moment Melchor considers telling her that he is sure she was the one who phoned the mayor demanding money and her resignation; but the next moment he decides he has pressured her enough, and now it's better to allow her to reflect for a while. So he takes a cigarette paper out of the packet and scribbles his mobile phone number on it.

"Think it over," he says, handing her the paper. "And let me know when you've reached a decision."

As he's leaving ronda de Sant Antoni he calls Blai, tells him how things stand and asks if they can immediately tap Marga Isern's phone.

"No fucking way," says Blai. "I'm not calling the judge now for a thing like that. Forget about the tap until tomorrow morning. If they let us, that is."

"Do you think they wouldn't?"

"No, I think they will, but . . ."

"Tomorrow morning might be too late," Melchor thinks out loud. "I bet you anything you like she's phoning one of the blackmailers right now."

"That may be so," Blai admits. "But I'll bet you anything that none of them is going to talk about this matter on the phone with her. At least not for long. Why don't you stay there and keep an eye on her. If you can't, I'll find someone else."

"I'll stay. I'm having dinner later in the neighbourhood."

"Cool. If nothing happens before then, call me and I'll send relief."

Melchor gets in his car and waits. When he's been sitting there for a while, without taking his eye off the front door of Marga Isern's building, he calls Vivales and says to have dinner without him.

"Have you got yourself into trouble or have you scored?" Vivales asks.

"Neither," Melchor answers. "Come on, put Cosette on the phone."

"She's playing with a friend," Vivales replies. "Don't bother her. By the way, the mother of this friend was asking for you. She said she wanted to apologise, but she didn't say what for. Do you want me to tell her anything when she comes to pick up her daughter?"

Melchor asks Vivales to tell the mother not to worry, that she has nothing to apologise for, hangs up and goes back to waiting, but has not yet found a radio station he feels like listening to when he sees Marga Isern come out. He gets out of the car and follows her. Walking at a brisk pace, she goes into the Raval down calle Joaquín Costa, and Melchor has a feeling she's heading for the Frenchman's internet café. She's not: she walks past the place with the sign saying INTERNET BEGUM and continues walking towards the Rambla and the Gothic quarter. As he crosses calle Ferlandina, Melchor's phone rings. It's Cortabarría.

"Are you still in the office?" Melchor asks him, his eyes still fixed on Marga Isern, who's walking about twenty metres ahead of him.

"No," Cortabarría answers. "But I asked Sudrià to call me as soon as he found something out about Ricky Ramírez's death certificate. I thought it was urgent."

"And it is," Melchor admits. "Tell me."

"It's all in order," Cortabarría announces. "He died of a heart attack. There's nothing strange about it."

"Are you sure?"

"That's what Sudrià says. Call him, if you want. Have you got his number?"

"No. But I don't need to. Thanks for the information."

When he hangs up, Marga Isern has just turned down calle Hospital. He speeds up to make sure he doesn't lose her, but when he turns the corner, she's gone. Cursing, he walks up and down through the crowds of tourists and residents and library users going in and out of the Biblioteca de Catalunya, until, about to give up, he catches a glimpse of her through the large windows of a bar with very high ceilings almost directly opposite the library. For a moment he thinks she's seen him, then immediately realises she hasn't; he thinks of going inside the bar and watching her from there, but immediately realises that would be too risky, so he moves away from the window and starts watching the entrance to the bar from a bench in a park across the street. He sits there for a while, watching people go in and out of the bar and occasionally approaching the window with extreme care to make sure the woman is still there and that no-one has sat down with her. He is considering the possibility that she only left her house for a change of scenery when he recognises the chubby, thickset man with a big moustache approaching the bar from the direction of la Rambla.

"Bingo," he murmurs.

It's Hematomas. Melchor hesitates a few moments, but finally decides he should run the risk. He goes into the bar, sits at one end of the counter, orders a bottle of sparkling water and pays. Marga Isern and Hematomas are sitting a few metres away, at a corner table, the woman almost facing him and the inspector with his back to him. Melchor hides behind a copy of *La Vanguardia* newspaper threaded onto a wooden holder and, with every possible precaution, takes a couple of photos with his mobile.

Marga Isern has already drunk a beer and, when the waitress arrives, Hematomas waves her away. In the midst of the music and conversation that resounds throughout the bar, Melchor cannot hear what they're talking about. But he sees them perfectly, especially the woman, who seems too bewildered or interested in the man sitting across from her to notice anything going on around her. At first, Marga Isern talks non-stop, very quickly and gesticulating, as if she had something important to tell Hematomas, who allows her to get it off her chest, or is perhaps genuinely interested in what she's telling him. Then the inspector speaks and Marga listens, interrupting him once in a while. She is very agitated, to the point that on a couple of occasions Hematomas grabs her wrist, maybe trying to calm her down. At a certain point the woman looks over towards the bar and raises a hand. Melchor rapidly covers his face with the copy of *La Vanguardia*. When he looks at them again, Marga Isern is pouring her second beer into a glass while talking, increasingly upset, and Hematomas grabs her wrist again, but this time the woman wrenches her hand away and, in doing so, knocks over the beer onto the table and into her lap, which seems to make her even more frantic. Then Hematomas takes her by the wrist again and murmurs something that suddenly calms her; more than calms her: Melchor has a momentary impression that the police inspector is a charmer and she a snake, or perhaps a rabbit caught in the headlights of a car about to run her over. From that moment on, Marga Isern listens to Hematomas without interrupting him, drinking what's left of her beer in little sips, as if she has finally been pacified and is ready to follow the instructions the inspector is giving her, supposing that the inspector is giving her instructions.

It's only a reprieve, or a mirage. Suddenly the woman stands up, says something to the inspector (or rather seems to spit words in his face) and rushes towards the door. Melchor sees Hematomas, sitting with his back to him, trying in vain to stop her, but then swiftly has to hide again behind the newspaper, which only allows him to glimpse Marga Isern rushing outside. The inspector follows her to the door; then, with bureaucratic lassitude, he returns to the bar, pays for Marga Isern's two drinks and leaves.

Melchor lets a few seconds pass then shoots out of the bar. He catches sight of Hematomas fifty metres ahead, making his way through the crowd towards the Rambla, but there's no sign of Marga Isern, and his only thought is to try going back the way they came an hour or hour and a half earlier, hoping to catch her returning home. It is not an unfounded hope.

Shortly after passing the Frenchman's internet café, Melchor comes out onto ronda de Sant Antoni and almost walks straight into her as she's waiting for the pedestrian light to change to green. Melchor backs off a few steps and then watches her walk across the street, along the opposite pavement and go into her building.

It is almost nine, the time he arranged to have dinner with the Frenchman, but he needs to take a moment to think about what happened and, seeking solitude, he locks himself inside his car. There, watching Marga Isern's front door, he reflects. In the past few hours he has accumulated a few answers and many questions. He is certain, for example, that Marga Isern is involved in blackmailing the mayor, but he can't prove it unless the Frenchman testifies that he rigged the SIM card at his internet café, which at the moment does not seem likely, or unless the woman confesses, which seems even less likely. He is also sure that Hematomas is involved in blackmailing the mayor, because he saw him with Marga Isern right after she spoke to Melchor and discovered that he had identified her, and he thinks it impossible that the meeting could be justified by motives other than the extortion plot. Now then, does Hematomas' involvement mean that Vidal is also implicated in the case? Not necessarily. As Blai surmised, the leader of the Vidal Boys could be operating on his own, without Vidal's orders or consent, and, after collecting the three hundred thousand euros thanks to the empty lunchbox trick on the beach at Gavà, he might have demanded the mayor's resignation (as well as another three hundred thousand euros) to deflect attention, in the hope that the police would take the political bait and believe it was all Vidal, who was plotting to take his boss's place. Which would explain why the deputy mayor had offered the leadership of the Vidal Boys to Melchor: he no longer trusts

Hematomas, maybe he even suspects that he is playing dirty tricks behind his back. None of this is impossible, Melchor tells himself. More than that: it suddenly seems likely. More likely, in any case, than the hypothesis he'd been developing up to that point, according to which everything was following a plan concocted by Vidal, Casas and perhaps Rosell to remove the mayor from her post and end her political career.

From this new viewpoint, the case looks different: Ricky Ramírez kept the video after filming it and, when he died from a heart attack, Marga Isern found it among his personal effects and told Hematomas about the find, who decided to use it for his own benefit, maybe because he knew or suspected that Vidal was looking to replace him and wanted to assure himself of a settlement equal to the services he'd provided. But here is where the questions begin to pile up: why did Ricky Ramírez not blackmail his old friends when he was still alive? Maybe he didn't dare, despite the resentment he harboured against them? Or did he think he couldn't blackmail them with that video, as Casas himself thought. Why not blackmail the mayor then? Was he not brave enough? In that case, why keep the video? In case he one day got up the nerve or was desperate enough to blackmail them? Had Ricky Ramírez really died of natural causes? Was it not relatively simple, especially for people like Vidal and Casas, to make a murder pass for a natural death? And, if the death had been a murder, why? What did Ricky Ramírez do to get killed? Try to blackmail them? Is Marga Isern implicated in his death? And, if she isn't, why is she protecting Hematomas (or Hematomas and Vidal, or Hematomas, Vidal and his two friends)? Does she realise what kind of danger she's in? Would she turn to Melchor for protection?

He looks at the time on the clock in his car, gets out and walks towards Joaquín Costa. The Frenchman's internet café is still open, though it appears empty (even the mujahid has abandoned the counter by the entrance); but appearances are deceptive: the former prisoner is still there, so buried in his papers that he doesn't even hear the police officer come in.

"What's up?" Melchor asks, bursting into his cubbyhole again. "Doesn't this joint ever close?"

The Frenchman is drunk as a lord by the end of the night, and Melchor has to take him home – a half-empty flat in an old building near plaza Urquinaona – and put him to bed fully clothed, because he can barely stand up. They had dinner at Amaya, a traditional restaurant on the lower part of the Rambla. The first part of the meal had been a tug of war. Melchor realised straight away that, just as he had suspected from the start, the Frenchman had invited him to dinner to find out why he was looking for Marga Isern and what she had done with her falsified SIM. For Melchor's part, he was also trying to pump the Frenchman for information, but the only thing he got from him was quite innocuous: that he'd met Marga at the internet café, with Ricky Ramírez; that both of them used it now and then, sometimes together and sometimes separately; that they both sold marijuana, though Ramírez actually made a living buying and selling bitcoin, and on one occasion he had suggested the Frenchman should buy some.

"Did you?" Melchor asked, not because he cared, but to keep the ex-prisoner talking.

"You take me for a madman or what?" answered the Frenchman.

Melchor remembered Herminia Prat and asked his friend if he knew that, not long before he died, Ricky Ramírez had been beaten so badly he ended up half-dead in a hospital bed.

"No," the Frenchman said. "But it doesn't surprise me. I already told you the guy was dodgy."

"Is that because of the marijuana or the bitcoin?"

"Not just that."

"Then why?"

The Frenchman tapped his right cheekbone with his index finger and said:

"I know a crook when I see one."

When he was on his third whisky and umpteenth plate of Montánchez ham with tomato bread and Padrón peppers, the Frenchman began to slag off his third ex-wife, who he claimed had robbed him. Then he went back to talking about Marga Isern.

"She pretends to be tough," the Frenchman said, his voice mushy with alcohol. "But deep down she's got a heart of gold."

Melchor nodded.

"That guy had her wrapped around his little finger," the Frenchman went on. "He did whatever he wanted with her. If it hadn't been for him . . ."

Melchor came to his aid:

"She told me you wanted to get her in the sack."

The Frenchman smiled with his cavernous white whale mouth.

"Did she tell you that? Damn!"

"Isn't it true?"

"Of course, it's true. Her and four or five other clients, I'd bed any of them. But you know women. They always choose the wrong man."

The Frenchman drank the fourth and fifth whiskies while holding forth, in an increasingly confused way, about the female clients of the internet café, and, when they got outside, Melchor came to the conclusion that his friend had invited him for dinner not just to try to convince him that, whatever she might have done, Marga Isern was no danger to anyone (from which he deduced that, as well as wanting to get her in the sack, he was as smitten as any teenager), but also, with the help of his company, to fight the slow poison of solitude that was killing him.

Now Melchor is walking unhurriedly to his car from the Frenchman's flat, inhaling the early morning air. He feels sleepy, tired and eager to go to bed, and the only thing he manages to think clearly regarding the blackmailing of the mayor is that perhaps the next day, after four or five hours' rest, he'll see it differently.

He is only partly mistaken. He's sitting behind the wheel of his car, about to start the engine, when he notices a woman come out of Marga Isern's building. He recognises her straight away: it is Marga Isern. As he opens his car door, ready to follow her on foot, he sees the woman get into an Opel Corsa parked very nearby, so he closes the door, starts his car and follows the Opel Corsa, at a prudent distance, to the plaza de la Universidad and then up Aribau to vía Augusta, where it turns left in the direction of Sarrià. Still following the Opel Corsa, Melchor exits the city on the C-16 motorway, passes Sant Cugat, Sabadell and Terrasa and continues in the direction of Manresa, when the traffic, which until then has been light, becomes even lighter, which obliges him to take extra precautions and drop back a bit from the Opel Corsa, to avoid arousing Marga Isern's suspicions. His sleepiness and fatigue, which had lifted as soon as he began the pursuit, return on the outskirts of Manresa; to dispel them he turns on the radio: he puts on music, he puts on a news channel, he puts on a programme about ghosts and flying saucers, and suddenly, as if he had fallen asleep and were dreaming, he finds himself wondering why he is following her in the first place. Luckily, a short time later the Opel Corsa pulls into a service station; Melchor waits, protected by the semidarkness of the entrance, while Marga Isern fills up with petrol and pays, after which, instead of getting back onto the motorway, she parks her car in front of the cafeteria and goes in. Melchor thinks he's in luck, he can also refuel and get a vending-machine coffee, but, when he gets back to his car, he feels his luck has run out: the Opel Corsa is no longer parked outside the cafeteria. He drives as fast as he can in the direction of Berga; finally, after a few anxious minutes, he recognises Marga Isern's car. Only then, calm once more, does he taste the coffee: it's cold and tastes like dish water, but it wakes him up.

It is past four-thirty in the morning when they drive into the Cadí Tunnel. On the other side, submerged in darkness, is the valley of Cerdanya. There, instead of turning right towards Puigcerdà, the Opel Corsa turns left in the direction of Seu d'Urgell. Melchor thinks of Vàzquez, of his mother's fake illness and how, in theory, Vàzquez will be back at Egara the following morning. He also thinks that he should let Vivales know he won't be home tonight. Driving with one hand on the wheel and his mobile phone in the other, he writes a WhatsApp: "Not sleeping at yours tonight." And sends it to the lawyer. He replies in seconds flat, as if he'd been sitting up waiting for him: "What's up?" Then, for an instant, a hare-brained idea flits through Melchor's head, which, during this infinitesimal lapse of time strikes him as the most natural idea in the world. That, since Vivales is awake, he could call him, talk to him and force an intimacy between the two of them he'd never felt able to seek, which, he thinks, would be easier to find at that improbable hour, many kilometres away from each other, both immersed in the darkness of their respective solitude (Vivales in the insomniac solitude of his eternal bachelor's bedroom, he in the solitude of a car driving through a remote mountain valley, following a tormented woman who is fleeing who knows where). Perhaps he could talk to Vivales of things they'd never talked about, Melchor thinks, of his mother and his childhood as an orphan and the son of a prostitute in Sant Roc, and all the spectral fathers who, like ghosts or flying saucers, unsettled the nights of his childhood – the man who strode down the hall with confident proprietorial steps, the one who walked on tiptoe as if trying to pass unnoticed, the one who coughed and spluttered late into the night like a hardened smoker or someone terminally ill, the one who sobbed inconsolably on the other side of the partition wall, the one who told ghost stories or the one who left at dawn in a long leather jacket – perhaps he could seek or force that intimacy and ask Vivales what he has never dared ask him, and that is if, despite the fact that Melchor has never been able to put a face to any of those invisible faces, he is, in fact, his father.

But it is just an instant. Once it's passed, Melchor types a second WhatsApp: "Don't worry. I've scored." Vivales answers again in seconds flat. "About time," he writes. "But take care, there are a lot of sly ones on the loose out there." Melchor replies with a round, yellow, smiling emoji.

The Opel Corsa does not stop at Seu d'Urgell, Vàzquez's hometown, but skirts round the city to head for Andorra. A short time later it crosses the border; Melchor crosses behind it. Dawn breaks. They drive along a road that snakes between rocky peaks, arriving in Sant Julià de Lòria as the town is waking up, and, before driving out of the town centre, the Opal Corsa turns off the main road and heads down a paved street that ends up degenerating into a dirt track that disappears up the mountain. Melchor, who turned off his headlights a while ago, so as not to attract suspicion, brakes near the last houses – a couple of identical, recently constructed, two-storey buildings – and, from there, watches as the Opel Corsa parks in front of a farmhouse. The woman gets out of the car, knocks on the door, which opens and she goes in.

Melchor waits a few minutes. Then he parks between two cars, in a place from which he can keep an eye on the house, gets out of the car and walks towards it. It's not old or big or luxurious, at least not at first glance, but it has a good chimney and a solid stone wall around the garden, in the middle of which stands a cherry tree. Melchor checks to make sure it only has the one entrance (a door without a peephole, he notices), although if necessary, he could get in by piling up stones beside a corner of the wall and jumping into the garden from there. Once he has inspected the terrain, he goes back to his car and, sure the woman must need to sleep as much as he does, and hoping no-one will leave the farmhouse in the next few hours, he reclines the driver's seat and closes his eyes.

His alarm clock wakes him three hours later, after a dense sleep, free of nightmares. He sees he has received several WhatsApps, including two from Blai, who asks for Marga Isern's phone number in order to request judicial permission to tap it; Melchor sends it to him. "Where are you?" Blai asks. Melchor doesn't answer and Blai doesn't insist. He gets out to stretch his legs and breathe in some pure mountain air, and he notices a bakery-café a few metres towards the town. He walks over, goes in, orders a cappuccino and takes it back to the car. Then, for more than two hours, he waits; no-one comes out of the farmhouse – in fact, only two or three cars and one motorcycle drive by on the dirt road. At some point Blai calls him, and again he does not answer. He doesn't want to speak to the inspector because he doesn't want to be obliged to give explanations, to tell him where he is and what he's doing: Melchor has no jurisdiction in Andorra, which means, in the event of needing to act, his superiors should have previously advised the Andorran police, who may or may not choose to lend a hand, which means that everything could get complicated or held up, and therefore everything could go to shit. Working on his own and at his own risk, however, he enjoyed total liberty to do or not do whatever he decided without delay, without seeking approval and without anyone knowing what he was doing: if things go well, perfect; if not, also perfect.

After a while he sees Marga Isern come out of the farmhouse; she is not alone: she is with a bearded stranger wearing jeans. They both get into the Opel Corsa and drive down towards town, passing right by Melchor, who, overcoming the temptation to spy on them out of the corner of his eye, hides his face while pretending to do something on his phone. Now he hesitates: he can let them go in the hope they'll be returning and take advantage of their absence to see if there is anyone else in the farmhouse and, supposing it's deserted, to search it; or he can follow them in his car. He decides it would be prudent to follow them.

So he turns around and drives after them. They take the first main road of Sant Julià de Lòria and then, joining a steady torrent of tourists, the road to Andorra la Vella; twenty minutes later they take avenida Meritxell, the busiest commercial street of the city. They drive between blocks full of shops, before turning off towards a shopping mall, where they leave their car in the car park. Melchor also parks, follows them into the supermarket and sees them take a trolley and start filling it up with provisions. That's when, camouflaged among the customers packing the aisles, flanked by multi-coloured panels brimming with retail goods, Melchor manages to get a little nearer to Marga Isern's companion, who up close turns out to be a guy of about forty, with curly hair and a bushy beard, wearing very baggy clothes and flip-flops. To blend in with the crowd around him, Melchor picks up a few items – sliced bread, cheese, chocolate-covered rice cakes, a tin of tuna – and goes to pay for them at a cashier's desk far from the one where the couple have queued up with their overloaded shopping trolley. He gets to his cashier before they get to theirs, but he does not want to pay too quickly, so he flips through an English tabloid on the cover of which is a photo of Elvis Presley with a huge headline announcing witnesses say that the singer is still alive and, more than ninety years of age, living in the foothills of the Rocky Mountains in British Columbia. Melchor reads the headline several times, until the cashier wrenches him out of his distraction.

"That's twelve euros fifty, sir."

As he sets off again behind the Opel Corsa, this time heading out of Andorra la Vella, Melchor calls Cortabarría, who tells him first off that Vàzquez is back. Melchor asks to speak to him.

"Wait a moment," Vàzquez says as he picks up the phone.

Melchor guesses that the sergeant needs time to hide away in his office. A moment later, he says hello and Melchor returns the greeting.

"How are you doing?"

"Brilliant!" Vàzquez says. "Ready to clean up the fucking streets. Thanks for covering for me, Melchor."

"Don't mention it," Melchor says. "Now it's your turn to cover for me."

"Whatever I can do," Vàzquez says. "Anything for the hero of Cambrils."

"Don't laugh, you bastard," Melchor says. "I need you to get me a photo of Ricky Ramírez."

"Who the fuck is that?"

Melchor explains, then mentions the photo again.

"It's urgent," he concludes.

"Count on it," the sergeant says. "I'll get the whole gang looking for one right now. We'll find something."

"When you find one, send it to me by WhatsApp. Another thing. We've put tails on the three tenors."

"Torrent was just telling me."

"I can't watch Vidal this afternoon, because I have an interview with Rosell."

"Don't worry. I'll send someone."

"And I can't interview Rosell, either."

"Don't worry. I'll go."

"Take Cortabarría with you. He's up to speed on all of it. The interview is at four, in Rosell's office at City Hall."

"OK. Anything else?"

"Yes. I won't be coming to Egara today."

"That I already guessed. Blai was looking for you a while ago. Can I ask where you are?"

"Sure. But I'm not going to tell you."

The photo of Ricky Ramírez shows up in Melchor's WhatsApp at four-thirty, by which time he has been parked again in sight of the farmhouse for several hours and is devouring his second consecutive cheese sandwich; there's a message from Vàzquez with it. "The guy has the face of a saint, but he's a nasty piece of work," it reads. "Tried for fraudulent bankruptcy, deception and once for trafficking marijuana." Referring to the interview with Rosell, he adds: "Pavarotti is keeping us waiting." Vàzquez is right: in the photo, which is also a police mug shot, Ricky Ramírez has an innocent look, which is almost always the kind that guilty people put on. He has no beard, but Melchor is almost certain it's him; he remembers Elvis Presley and suddenly, with a hint of euphoria he hastens to contain, he feels that everything fits.

He finishes gobbling up his sandwich, opens the rice cakes and eats a couple, looks for a radio station playing music. Shortly after five he calls Vivales, who has just picked up Cosette from day camp, and talks to his daughter for a while. She wants to know why he didn't come home last night; Melchor tells her it's because he's about to catch the bad guys. Cosette asks who they are.

"The usual ones," Melchor answers. "The ones who seem like good guys."

"Do bad guys always seem good?"

"Almost always."

"And do good guys seem bad?"

"Sometimes."

"Oh, that's hard."

They talk for a while longer, and when he says goodbye to his daughter he warns her that he won't be sleeping at home tonight either. "Tell Vivales for me," he adds. As soon as he hangs up, his mobile rings: Blai again; again he doesn't answer. Seconds later a WhatsApp arrives from the inspector. "Fuck you and your father, *españolazo*; answer your fucking phone right now," it says. "It's urgent." Melchor rings Blai.

"I've just spoken to Commissioner Vinebre," the inspector announces without saying hello. "The mayor is about to call a press conference. She's going to resign."

There is silence.

"Do you know when?" Melchor asks.

"Tomorrow. The ultimatum expires the day after tomorrow, so—"

"Who told Vinebre? The mayor?"

"No. Someone close to her. I don't know who. But she obviously doesn't want us to know."

"Go and see her. Convince her not to resign."

"That's what I was planning to do. I'm calling so you can give me some arguments. By the way, where have you got to? I've been looking for you all day."

Melchor doesn't answer, but he hides the omission among arguments against the mayor handing in her resignation. As he lists them, however, they all seem insufficient to persuade a person dominated by fear, so, when he says goodbye to Blai, he has little doubt that his former boss will fail. Moments later, the door to the farmhouse opens and Melchor sees Marga Isern come out with the man.

It's just past seven and the sun is starting to lose its strength. The man and the woman talk for a moment beside the car, kiss each other on the lips, then the man holds the driver's door open and the woman gets in, starts the engine and drives away from the farmhouse while Melchor watches her go. This time he does not hesitate. As soon as the man disappears back inside the house, he starts his car and follows the Opel Corsa, which this time does not take the road towards Andorra la Vella but the one for Seu d'Urgell. Melchor escorts her until just before the border, but, as soon as he realises that Marga is heading back to Barcelona, he turns around and returns to the farmhouse, parks in the same place as before and waits for night to fall. Then, when there is just a wisp of violet light left on the tops of the mountains that surround the valley, he gets out of the car, walks up to the farmhouse and rings the buzzer. There is no immediate answer, so he buzzes again. Finally a man answers.

"I'm from the Super U," Melchor announces in a vaguely singsong voice: it's the name of the supermarket where they'd gone shopping that morning. "You forgot a bag of groceries at the checkout."

The man is again slow to answer.

"We aren't missing anything," he finally says.

"Well, I've got your bag here."

"Leave it outside."

"Sorry, sir. I have to hand it to you personally."

The door opens and, before he can recognise the man, Melchor has already put the barrel of his pistol to his forehead while, with a finger to his lips, he orders him to keep quiet. In absolute silence, he grabs Ricky Ramírez by the back of his neck and aiming the pistol at his head after searching him and taking his mobile, Melchor goes through the house to make sure there's nobody else inside. It's big, but almost all the rooms are empty, and, once the inspection is finished, Melchor pushes Ramírez down onto the sofa. The latter understands that the end of the search equals the end of the prohibition on speaking, so, panting and with panicked eyes, as he rubs his sore neck he asks:

"Who are you?"

"Don't worry." Melchor puts his pistol back in its holster. "I'm a police officer. Nothing's going to happen to you."

Neither the promise nor the information seems to calm Ramírez, who does not stop panting or rubbing his neck.

"You're making a mistake," he defends himself. "I haven't done anything."

"Sure," Melchor says. "And I'm Mother Teresa of Calcutta. Where's the video? Did you bring it here or have you got it hidden away somewhere?"

"Video? What video?"

Melchor grabs a chair and sits astride it, crossing his arms over the back.

"Have you come from Barcelona?" Ramírez asks. "Did you follow Marga? If you're from Barcelona you can't arrest me, you have no authority to operate here. This isn't Spain."

"No," Melchor admits. "But you'd be surprised how well we collaborate with the Andorran authorities these days." He presents his mobile and puts it down on the table between them, where there is an empty ashtray and a couple of old books; then he completes his lie. "Let's go. I'll make a call and in five minutes we'll have them here. Do you want to see?"

Ramírez regards Melchor with the suspicion of a cornered animal. He looks dishevelled, slovenly, in grey striped pyjama bottoms and a white, frayed T-shirt; he is barefoot, and his toenails are long and dirty. He tries to pull himself together, catches his breath, sprawls out on the sofa, a cheap, uncomfortable piece of furniture more suited to a coastal apartment than a mountain farmhouse, with a wooden frame and armrests, and the seat, back and cushions covered in a garish print fabric. Like the rest of the house, the dining room reveals a dull, impersonal provisionality: the only furniture, apart from the sofa, are a few bland chairs, a prehistoric television and a graceless sideboard; a couple of conventional watercolours of alpine landscapes hang on the white-painted walls.

"You're making a mistake," Ricky insists.

Melchor sighs.

"Look, Ricky," he says, gathering his patience. "Can I call you Ricky?"

"Call me whatever you want."

"Well, look, Ricky," Melchor says. "Why do you think I followed your little friend? Why do you think I'm here? I'll tell you. I'm here because I know enough to throw the book at both of you."

"You have no idea about anything."

"No, I've got some idea. It may not be much, but I do know something. For example, I know that you and your girlfriend are blackmailing the mayor of Barcelona with a sex tape. That you filmed that video. That you almost certainly collected the first ransom payment and without the slightest doubt you collected the second, because it was paid to your girlfriend's mobile phone. Not the one she has with her now, a different one that you've taken the precaution of throwing away, or were told to throw away . . . Another thing. I know you're in contact with Inspector Lomas, the boss of the Vidal Boys, which means you're in contact with Enric Vidal and probably with Daniel Casas and Gonzalo Rosell, who also appear in the video. Do you want me to go on?"

Ramírez stares at Melchor as if trying to take in what he has just heard, but he soon turns away and looks around without focusing on any object, perhaps without seeing any. Turning back to the police officer, he says, defiantly:

"You can't prove anything."

"I can't prove that Vidal, Casas and Rosell are guilty," Melchor admits. "But I can prove that you, your girlfriend and Hematomas are. That's what they call—"

"Everybody knows that's what they call him," Ramírez cuts him off.

Melchor makes an effort to smile.

"Of course," he says. "Anyway, as far as I can see, you've got two options. Do you want me to lay them out?"

Ramírez remains silent as he folds his arms expectantly. It's obvious he has partially recovered his self-confidence.

"First option." Melchor holds up his mobile again. "Don't cooperate with me, I make a phone call and in ten minutes we have our Andorran friends here. In this scenario we charge you, your girlfriend and, with a bit of luck, Hematomas. In other words, you and your girl take the rap, and everyone else goes free." Melchor falls silent to await a reaction from Ramírez, who doesn't flinch. "Luckily, there's another option. It involves you cooperating with me and telling me everything. And when I say everything, I mean everything, from A to Z and back again, clearly and without tricks, so I can understand. As far as I see it, this option has two big advantages. The first is that, if you agree to it, I give you my word of honour that I'll do everything in my power to make sure you come out of this business as well as possible . . . Well, you and your girlfriend. More than that, depending on what you tell me, as long as I believe it and it turns out to be true, I might not even need to charge you two and you can get on with your lives."

Ramírez unfolds his arms and says:

"I don't believe you."

"Believe me."

"Why should I?"

"Because I don't believe you've organised all this on your own. Not faking your death, not collecting the ransom at Gavà beach, not any of it. Don't take it the wrong way, but this is all a bit big for you. Enormous. Let alone your girlfriend. With all due respect, this is not something a couple of poor fools like you would get up to. In short, I am ready to lend you a hand in exchange for your help in catching the ones who actually set this mess up."

Melchor stops talking, but Ramírez does not abandon his reflective surliness. His eyes are very light, and they observe his interlocutor apprehensively from a face hidden by his lank, untidy beard. He scratches it as if it itches.

"What's the other advantage?"

Melchor was expecting this question, so he smiles again, this time effortlessly.

"Do you really think your partners in crime are going to leave you alone when this is over?" he asks. "After all that's happened? Knowing what you know?" Despite the beard's partial camouflage, Ramírez's expression reveals that he has wondered the same thing; or that's what it looks like to Melchor. "Don't be ridiculous. As soon as the mayor resigns, they'll get rid of you and your friend. Whatever happens and whatever you have. Those people are like that, they're not going to take any risks with you two. You must know that."

Melchor guesses that Ramírez knows it, but doesn't want to know it or prefers to forget it, and that his words have just brought him face to face with reality again. He imagines the whirlwind spinning in his mind; he imagines the weakness in his legs, the fear gripping his stomach, his heart racing.

"Do you want a glass of water?" he asks.

Ramírez does not answer. Melchor stands up and goes to the kitchen, which turns out to be large and unexpectedly clean. He finds two glasses, fills them with tap water, and returns to the dining room. Ramírez drinks the water down in one gulp and asks in a demanding tone:

"How are you going to help me?"

Melchor reiterates what he has already said, expands on it while making sure not to make any rash promises; then he insists that he wants to help him. He adds:

"It matters as much to me as it does to you. Possibly more."

Ramírez nods: he seems to believe him. He sets his empty glass down on the table next to Melchor's, which is still full, and stares at them both, lost in thought. Then he scratches his beard again and after a few seconds stands up.

"I need a shot of whisky," he announces.

He walks over to the sideboard, returns with a bottle, pours two fingers into his glass and knocks it back. He pours again and takes a deep breath.

"I don't know where to start," he apologises, looking Melchor in the eye.

"Start at the beginning. Tell me about your partners. Tell me how you met them. What kind of guys they are. Take your time, there's no rush, I want to know everything."

Ramírez nods again and lets a few seconds pass while he tries to find a comfortable position on that uncomfortable sofa; his gaze wanders or clouds over, as if he had sunk into his memories in search of buried treasure. After a period of time that Melchor wouldn't know whether to measure in seconds or minutes, Ramírez takes another sip of whisky, scratches his beard again and looks up at him.

"All three of them are sons of wealthy families," he begins in a different tone of voice, as if he'd just put on a disguise. "Sons of bitches as well, of course, but mainly posh brats. They were born like that and they'll die like that . . . Rich people are another species. Have you never heard that? Well, it's the truth. I'm telling you. The world is divided between two types of people: the rich and the rest, including those who aspire to be rich, who are the majority. Here you have a perfect example, I was one of them."

Epilogue

1

"I froze . . . I was on the sofa at home, my body aching after the beating Hematomas and his boys had given me, and Vidal had just told me that I could blackmail the mayor and nobody would catch me, because it was impossible to catch a dead man. How was I supposed to take that . . . ? I tore my eyes away from Vidal's and looked at the inspector. He was still sitting behind his boss, head hanging and gloomy. Then I looked back at Vidal, who laughed. 'Don't worry, Ricky,' he said. 'Nobody's going to kill you. You just have to pretend to be dead. But you have to do it so well that it'll be like you really died . . .' That's where the second part of his plan to blackmail the mayor started, or rather my blackmailing the mayor for him."

"So it wasn't your idea to fake your death?"

"No, it was Vidal's. He had it all planned so I would have no choice but to agree. He even gave me the details of my death. He talked about an invented heart attack, a couple of corrupt bureaucrats, including a coroner, and a couple of employees at the municipal funeral home. He talked about the Vidal Boys, although he didn't call them that, of course, and he talked about my funeral and my burial, and he also talked about renting a place far away from Barcelona, outside Spain but not too far, in some discreet place where I could hide without problems, he hadn't decided where yet, he had various possibilities in mind . . . Most of all, he talked about a new identity and a new life. 'New and much better than the one you have,' he told me. 'That's for sure.' He looked around with pity and then went on talking: 'Look at where you're living, Ricky. Look at what you've turned into . . . Well, that's over. No more surviving in this hovel selling marijuana and fiddling about with bitcoin. With the money you'll get from the mayor you could start over . . . Reinvent yourself. Reset.' That's what he told me. I must have looked stunned, because Vidal went on: 'Don't look at me like that, Ricky. I'm serious. I'm giving you an opportunity, a golden opportunity . . . And don't think that what I'm suggesting is impossible, because it's not. Quite the contrary, it's easier than you think. Besides, nobody's going to miss you. Who do you think is going to miss you? The druggie you've been sleeping with? What's her name? Marga . . . ?' Here he fell silent, I didn't say yes or no and he turned towards Hematomas, who nodded. Then he continued: 'Don't worry about her. If need be, we'll bring her on board . . .' It suddenly struck him as a great idea. 'Sure,' he said. 'She could be useful. She'll be our contact, so you and I don't ever have to see each other again.' And he kept insisting. 'Think it over,' he said. 'An opportunity like this doesn't come around twice,' he also said. 'Starting over in a place where nobody knows you, with money and no past . . . Think it over carefully, Ricky . . .'

"That's more or less what he said, and I tried to do what he said, I tried to think, but I couldn't, everything hurt, I was too bewildered to think . . . Although not so much that I couldn't see that something didn't fit. I told him. 'What is it that doesn't fit?' he asked. 'What do you get out of all this?' I answered. And

I added: 'And what does Casas get?' Vidal smiled again . . . I thought he was smiling because I had guessed that he and Casas were in cahoots, but he was actually smiling because he'd just sensed he had got what he wanted. 'I was going to tell you later,' he said. 'But, since we're going to be partners, I'll tell you now. So you can see that I trust you.' What he told me was that, as well as asking the mayor for money, I would ask her to resign. I wouldn't ask that at first, so she wouldn't know from the start that was what it was really all about and wouldn't suspect him or Casas. The resignation would be demanded later, when she'd already paid the first ransom, or the second, we'd see about that afterwards, in any case when the play had ripened and she had seen that it was serious and wouldn't be expecting something like that and could be forced into a hasty decision . . . That's what Vidal told me, and that's when I knew what the real aim of the operation was: to kick the mayor out and install him in her place. He was the deputy mayor, the second in command at City Hall, so, if the mayor were to resign, he would be her logical replacement. Vidal would take her place and, with two years until the next elections, he would have enough time to consolidate himself in the office and win . . . That was the plan, that's why Vidal wanted to use me. Casas wanted to use me for the same reason, of course, he also wanted Vidal to be the new mayor, my intuition had been spot on, the two of them were in cahoots, but you didn't have to be a genius to understand that in his case her resignation would also have a collateral benefit, shall we say, it would serve to demonstrate that, without him at her side, she was nobody, she was nothing more than a poor vulnerable woman who had only been somebody because he had wanted her to be, and the proof was that, without him, her political career was over . . . In short, those two sons of bitches wanted to use me to demonstrate to everyone who was really in charge, and along the way they were again doing with me what they had always done: treating me as if I were their servant.

"All that made me sick, I felt bile rising in my throat and I was about to tell Vidal to go to hell . . . But I didn't . . . I didn't let myself get carried away by my first impulse . . . I swallowed my shame and fury and told myself I had nothing to do with this story, that the rivalry between those two and the mayor was their problem not mine, their little cockfight had nothing to do with me and, if Vidal's proposal was viable and suited me, it shouldn't matter who benefitted from it. The question was: did the proposal actually suit me? Was it viable? And, if it was, was I really ready to stop being myself, to change my life and abandon everything, leave Barcelona, disappear, start from scratch . . . ? I asked Vidal two final questions. The first, how long did I have to give him my answer. The second, if I had any alternative. Vidal had foreseen the questions, of course, and was ready with prepared answers. He told me he'd give me twenty-four hours to decide. He also said of course there was an alternative. 'The five years in prison the penal code dictates for the crime of extortion,' he said. 'Plus whatever you get for your marijuana and shady bitcoin deals. Don't worry, Ricky, I'll make sure you get the judge you deserve,' the son of a bitch added. And then he summed up: 'So that's your dilemma: years and years in prison or a new life, a quiet life with enough money to live on. You decide . . .'

"I don't remember how Vidal left, if he said goodbye or anything. What I do remember is that I spent the next twenty-four hours thinking. And I thought about a lot of things, but mostly about one. Do you know what that was . . . ? About Spanish failure, that kind of failure I was telling you about earlier, dirty and non-transferable, with neither glory nor redemption, without the slightest bit of glamour or the slightest bit of dignity, that deep and true failure, which I know so well . . . I thought, when you fail like that, you only fail once, like I told you, in Spain, when someone fails, they fail for ever. I also thought that Vidal was right, if I died nobody was going to miss me, I wasn't even sure Marga would miss me, in any case, I thought, if I accepted Vidal's proposal I could start again, with Marga or without her, I would have the privilege of a second chance, an incredible privilege in Spain, almost a miracle, Vidal knew it as well as I did, a privilege as incredible as a person getting to live after death, as incredible as a resurrection . . . I thought of these things and others. Until it occurred to me that perhaps Vidal's proposal wasn't an opportunity, but rather a trap. I mean, I thought what you said before, that these people don't fool around and that, after everything that had happened and knowing all that I knew, they wouldn't leave me in peace just like that."

"You thought of that."

"Of course I thought of that . . . I mean, I thought that, supposing Vidal's proposal were feasible and I accepted, as soon as the mayor resigned and Casas and Vidal had what they wanted, I would cease to be useful to them and on top of that would turn into a danger for them, I thought they could do with me what they wanted, including get rid of me without anyone missing me, because I would already be dead . . . That's why they had made me that proposal, I thought. And I thought they had me by the balls. That I was lost . . . that's what I thought . . . Until, after thinking it over a lot, I realised it wasn't true, not entirely at least, I realised that I would only be lost and in their hands if I no longer had the videos. Because the one with the mayor was devastating for her, but the rest of them were devastating for Casas and Vidal, and also for Rosell, and, while they were in my possession, I had them by the balls, not the other way around . . . That's what I thought at that moment. That the videos my father had left me were not just my inheritance. They were also my life insurance.

"That was when I came up with my plan, an alternative or parallel plan to Vidal's, the plan that would allow me to counteract and survive his . . . The first thing I did was talk to Marga . . . I told her everything. At first she screamed to high heaven, got very scared, and categorically refused to participate. But she finally understood that I had no other way out, and I convinced her that, with Hematomas and the Vidal Boys involved, she would be running a few risks, but she would be running a lot more if she refused to participate. So she agreed to help me.

"The rest you can probably imagine . . . Vidal was right about one thing: it's incredible how easy it is to fake a man's death. He was also right about something else: nobody missed me, nobody was sorry I was gone. Not that I know of . . . a few days after I told Vidal I accepted his proposal, I left my flat as it was, came here with a new identity card, a new passport and a temporary residency permit, and moved into this house. Since then I haven't left Andorra."

"Who decided you would come here?"

"I did. I thought it would be a good place to hide and to start a new life, thought it was far enough away from Barcelona that I wouldn't run into anyone I knew and close enough that Marga could come to visit once in a while . . . Vidal didn't object, and that was the end of our association, at least our direct association. I haven't seen or spoken to him since. I have his phone number, but anything we have to say to each other we say through Marga, who doesn't talk to him either, but to Hematomas or one of his men . . . I don't need to tell you that Marga has kept me informed about everything and helped me a lot, thanks to her I was able to get the videos out of the safety deposit box at the Santander and bring them here . . . Poor Marga . . . Hematomas and his boys have got her much more involved than I would have liked, she's had to do everything or almost everything, including threaten the mayor by phone, that was never in any plan, of course, and that's not all, they've used her so they wouldn't have to get their own hands dirty and could control everything from a distance, but, anyway, the idea was that Marga would also benefit from this, and in spite of everything she seemed happy, things were going well, we got the three hundred thousand euros from the first ransom and this week the three hundred thousand from the second, with that money we could have started over, here or wherever . . . But yesterday you showed up and she got scared. She called me, I tried to calm her down and told her to talk to Hematomas, but there was no other way, I finally had to tell her to come and see me. And I fucked it up."

"You didn't fuck it up."

"If Marga hadn't come, you wouldn't have caught us."

"I would have caught you anyway . . . And, if I hadn't, it would have been worse, your friends would have done away with you both."

"Maybe . . . In any case, I want you to know one thing. Marga hasn't done anything, except to help me. She isn't guilty of anything. It would be unfair for her to have to pay for . . ."

"I believe you."

"I haven't been lucky with women, well, rather it's the women who have been unlucky with me. They love me, but I don't know how to love them. Herminia said it's because I don't know how to love myself . . . It sounds like a phrase from a self-help book, doesn't it? But maybe it's true."

"Don't worry, nothing's going to happen to Marga. And I've

already given you my word that I'll do my utmost to make sure you come out of this as well as possible. And that your friends pay for what they've done."

"I'd be satisfied with that, at least with them paying for what they did . . . But the only one who'll pay will be me. Like I told you, the same people always end up paying. It never fails."

"We'll see about that. Tell me something, do you have the videos here?"

"In this house? No way. Didn't I tell you they were my life insurance . . . ? They're in a safety deposit box in a branch of Andbank, in Llorts, near here. They're no longer my inheritance, but . . ."

"They're still useful."

"They might be, but who for? Not for me, in prison you don't need life insurance."

"That's not true . . . But I'm not talking about you. I'm talking about me."

"I hope so. I hope they're useful to you . . . We'll see . . . I don't think so . . . What I think is that with or without the videos, those three will come out of this smelling of roses as they've always come out of everything . . . Anyway, now I have told you everything I had to tell you. I'm dead tired. I need to sleep."

"You haven't told me about the incident yet."

"The incident?"

"The one that made you stop going out hunting for girls. You said it happened just after you filmed the mayor. Besides, there is one thing I still don't understand . . . Why your father kept the videos you filmed on León XIII, how he got them."

"The two things are connected . . . The incident and my father."

"Oh, yeah?"

"Yeah."

"Well tell me . . . If you don't tell me, there's no deal . . . Is there a problem . . . ? You don't want to tell me . . . ? You've told me everything else, haven't you? Why not this?"

"Because this is different . . . I shouldn't even have mentioned it. I told you that already. I slipped up. It was an error."

"You mean the incident or what your father did? Was your father involved in the incident?"

"In a way."

"And why is it different? Why don't you want to tell me?"

"Because it's different. Because it's . . . anyhow."

"I don't think it can be worse than what you've already told me."

"Yes, it is."

"Then maybe that's why you skipped it."

"I don't get it."

"Maybe you want to tell me. Maybe you need to tell me . . . Whatever the case, now you have no choice. Remember our deal. Besides, if you don't tell me . . ."

"I'll tell you, you don't have to threaten me . . . Let me pour a little more whisky . . . Maybe you're right and . . . Anyhow, I suppose at this stage it doesn't matter, after all I'm dead, so what I tell you can't harm me, but it can harm my friends. And that's what this is about, harming them as much as possible, yeah?"

"I'm listening."

". . . I don't know how to tell you this, the truth is, I'm ashamed, or horrified to tell you. Besides, it seems so unreal . . . Or perhaps it seems too real, sometimes it seems it was the realest moment of my life, or even the only real one, the moment of truth. The truth about my friends and about me as well. It's not that I feel guilty for what happened. Well, not entirely . . . Although I suppose I do bear some responsibility, a person is not only responsible for what he does but also for what he allows to be done or what he witnesses and does not prevent, a person is also responsible for what others do and he benefits from, that thing about us only being responsible for what we do is what people who don't want to be responsible for anything say, not even what they do . . . Anyway.

"It happened in our third year, the last one I completed at Esade, when my father was still a member of parliament in Madrid and was at the peak of his career, although it was not long before the case of the phantom cards would erupt and everything would go to hell. Or maybe it already had erupted, but it hadn't yet swept everything away . . . Either way, it was a Saturday, a Saturday night that started out like so many others, perhaps the only difference was that it was just the four of us, as I told you it was quite rare in those days that we would go out on a Saturday night without Vidal's and Rosell's girlfriends. But the rest was more or less as usual. We met at Vidal's house, ate at Jumilla and then went to the Sutton . . . Now I remember another detail: we took Vidal's father's BMW, not any of my friends' cars, I remember because the BMW was a very big car with tinted windows, a whacking great car. But as I said, at first everything was the same as ever . . . Until we left the Sutton and Casas and Vidal suggested we take a hooker to León XIII."

"You didn't tell me you took prostitutes there as well."

"You didn't ask . . . In any case we didn't do it very often. Only when we had no other choice."

"And what does that mean?"

"It means we only took hookers there when we couldn't coax any of the others. Or when we felt like it . . . Because, of course, in theory, with hookers it's all different."

"You mean you didn't rape them?"

"In theory we paid them and that was that."

"And in practice?"

"In practice too. Although that night was different . . . As I was saying, Casas and Vidal suggested it, even though Rosell and I resisted, we ended up going along with it, those two had had a lot to drink, I suppose they didn't feel like looking around, or they just felt like doing it with a hooker . . . What do I know . . . We didn't go to a brothel, the prostitutes at those clubs wouldn't agree to leave the premises and come with us, at least that's what had happened to us once, I imagine they weren't allowed or they were scared or didn't trust the customers . . . We went to the Barça ground, which was nearby. There were hookers everywhere and lots to choose from, we drove around the outside of the stadium and Les Corts cemetery to look them over, and finally we chose . . . I remember that woman very well, there is not a single day that goes by that I don't think of her . . . She was about forty years old, still had a good body and must have once been good-looking, wore a lot of make-up, a brunette . . . Casas and Vidal were negotiating with her for a while, but, when it seemed as though they'd reached an agreement, the woman thought better of it and said no, and made some comment . . . I don't know what she said (or I knew and immediately forgot), but what I do know is that Casas and Vidal didn't like it at all, it enraged them . . . That, and the fact she said no to them.

"We didn't try to pick up a different hooker. We left the Barça ground and had a few drinks at some bar in Sants, I can't remember where, though I do remember that Casas and Vidal were still very pissed off at the hooker who'd turned them down. I also remember that they didn't even bother to flirt with the girls we ran into . . . The thing is, after a while, it must've been two or three in the morning, we got back into Vidal's father's BMW and, instead of going each to our own home, we went back to the Barça ground and straight away recognised the hooker from before, still prowling around there. 'There she is,' Casas said to Vidal. 'Pull up to that bitch, she's going to find out . . .' It was Casas himself who negotiated with her, doubling or tripling the offer he'd made before, and ended up convincing her.

"What happened next I remember better than I'd like, because you don't forget what you want to but what you can . . . At León XIII everything went really fast, as you can imagine we skipped the customary preambles and got to the point, a hooker is a sex professional, although what I ended up filming didn't have much to do with sex . . . At first it did, of course, it all started as group sex, I had filmed similar things, not too many, because the normal thing at León XIII wasn't group sex but group rape, which is what that quickly turned into, I think the woman guessed very soon what was coming, but she was experienced and must have thought, to keep things from getting out of hand, it would be best to try to keep up an appearance of normality with what was increasingly less normal, until she understood that it was impossible and tried to resist, complained, demanded explanations, screamed, struggled . . . But at some point she must have realised that she was just making things worse, because she shut up and let them do things to her, by then she must have figured that was the most sensible attitude in order not to come out of there too badly . . . It didn't help her at all. First the group sex turned into group rape and then the gangbang turned into something else, something I wouldn't know what to call, to tell you the truth, sometimes I've thought of what happened as if it were a macabre ceremony or ritual or carnival, as if we were some kind of evil coven, what is certain is that I was fascinated following it from my hiding place, spying on what was happening on the other side of the wall, not believing what I was seeing but never stopping the tape, hypnotised by that spectacle, I remember for example that woman on all fours, naked and crying, her hands and feet tied, terrorised, I remember my friends beside themselves, insulting her, yelling, punching and kicking and pushing her and spitting on her while sticking it into every hole or pissing on her, as if they'd gone crazy or as if they'd always been crazy and I hadn't noticed till then, I watched that sadistic delirium, unable to look away, as I said, fascinated, bewitched, although I don't think the possibility had crossed my mind that it could turn into a horror film, which is what happened when Casas, who had disappeared from my frame of vision, came back into view, naked and drenched in sweat, shouting with his face smudged and his eyes popping out of his head and a brick or a rock in his hand, I don't know where he got it, I guess he'd gone out to the yard to get it, the thing is he started to hit the woman with it, he hit her in the head until Rosell took the stone from him and he started hitting her as well, and then Vidal did, although I'm not sure about that, I might have invented that memory, what I am sure of is that, after a while, the woman was dead and her body was lying in an impossible position among the blood-soaked mattresses, with the rock musicians and movie stars looking down at her from the posters on the wall . . . She looked like a rag doll, or a broken doll . . . Why are you making that face? What are you thinking? I warned you that—"

"I'm not thinking anything. Go on."

"Hey, didn't you say you don't drink whisky? Pour me some too. There's another full bottle on the sideboard . . . I told you what I was going to tell you was horrific, but I thought you cops were used to it . . ."

"Go on."

". . . When I realised what had happened, I switched off the camera and stopped filming. My legs were trembling . . . I think for several seconds I tried to convince myself that I hadn't seen what I'd seen, that what had happened hadn't happened, that I'd dreamed it or something. Then, still shaking, I went to the room with the mattresses, and as I entered my friends seemed like survivors of a hurricane or a nuclear explosion . . . Or three terminal patients . . . Or three drug addicts unable to come down from an acid trip . . . I don't know . . . I remember Rosell was on the floor, curled up in a corner like a foetus and that I couldn't tell if he was crying or laughing. I also remember the look in Casas' eyes, it was an imploring look of panic and total incomprehension, a look of absolute defencelessness . . . In the room there was silence such as I've never heard since . . . Vidal was the first to speak. He pointed to the dead woman as if he'd just noticed her, with an absent expression on his face and the stone smeared with blood in one hand, and he said: 'We have to do something.' It was obvious that the three of them were out of action . . . I felt trapped, disgustingly complicit in that horror, but I was the only one who still had any mental clarity, any ability to react.

"This explains what happened next . . . This and my servile instinct, my eternal urge to be worth something to them, to be useful and earn their gratitude and affection, to one day belong to their circle . . . 'Surround yourself with good people and you'll become one of them,' my father had told me. And there I was, tied to my friends by that death, impossible to be more surrounded by them, and that's why I have sometimes wondered if, at that moment, that woman's death hadn't seemed like an opportunity to me, a chance to get my friends out of a tight spot and leave them owing me a big favour . . . It's possible I might have thought that, and made the decision I made for precisely that reason. The decision was to call my father. I said so to my friends. 'I'm going to call my father,' I said. 'He'll help us . . .' None of them said anything, yes or no, like I said, the three of them were out of it, so I did, I called my father.

"It was really late, my father was in bed and must have got a terrible fright . . . I tried to explain what had happened, told him who I was with, he listened without interrupting and, when I finished speaking, he asked me for the address. 'Don't move,' he said. 'I'll be right there.'

"As soon as I hung up I felt I'd made a mistake, because surely the first thing my father would do was call the police, but I also felt that it was too late to change things and, even if I called him back and told him not to come, he was going to come anyway . . . And do you know something? Many years later, the only time my father and I talked about that night, in his apartment in Torredembarra, shortly before his death, he told me that had been his first intention, that's exactly what he had thought he was going to do, and if he didn't it was because after I called him, while he was getting dressed as fast as he could to go to León XIII, he said to himself that, if he reported us to the police, the four of us would be tried and sentenced to many years in prison, and at the last moment he decided he'd rather carry the death of that woman on his conscience than the destruction of his son and three other kids who had their whole lives ahead of them, because the woman's death could not be remedied, while the destruction of four kids, our destruction, could . . . And that time in Torredembarra, he also told me something else. He told me that he often thought he had done the wrong thing, that he should have taken us to the police, that we should have paid for what we'd done, and that, after the phantom credit cards scandal ruined him, more than once he felt his downfall was punishment for his mistake . . . What do you reckon . . . ? My father was a fair man, he thought a person reaped what he sowed in this life and sooner or later you end up paying for everything . . . Or maybe he was a superstitious man. I am not."

"Go on."

"Either you don't drink at all, or you drink whisky as if it were water. There's no middle ground with you."

"Go on."

"There's not much more to tell . . . When my father showed up at León XIII he took charge of the situation. Without a single reproach. He just wanted to know what had happened, I told him about the video, or rather the videos, he asked us about the place (who it belonged to, who used it, what we used it for), he made my friends take showers, did what he could to calm us down and sent us all home while he stayed there . . . Before we left he told us: 'What happened here tonight never happened.' And he added: 'Do as I say and everything will be alright.'

"We did as he said . . . We never talked about that night again, from then on we acted as if it had just been a regular night out, it changed absolutely nothing, not between us or with others, it's startling, don't you think? How easily we can decide something that happened hasn't happened, even something as horrible as what happened that night . . .

"I don't know how my father cleaned the place on León XIII, I suppose he would have asked for someone's help, in those days he knew a lot of people, although I don't know, I don't actually know if he really cleaned the place, or if he had it cleaned, I simply imagined he did, I never knew for sure and I never asked him, not even the only time we spoke about the incident in his apartment in Torredembarra, in fact he didn't even tell me then that he'd kept the videos, maybe he didn't know how to tell me, maybe he also regretted having kept them, or maybe he wanted to surprise me with them when he died . . . Who knows . . . What's certain is that we rigorously kept the promise, so rigorously that we never took another woman to León XIII. We didn't even set foot there again . . . And I don't need to tell you that my friends never thanked me for what he'd done, not me or my father, never remembered that we'd got them off the hook that night, that without my father and me their lives would have gone to shit, that never entered their heads, not when the scandal of the phantom credit cards destroyed my father and I dropped out of Esade, they didn't spare a word or a gesture then either. Nothing . . . Logical, right?"

"Was the video of the murder among those your father kept?"

"No."

"How do you know?"

"Because it was the first one I looked for."

"And it wasn't there."

"No . . . Maybe it got lost that same night, the night I filmed it, I mean. Or maybe my father destroyed it to make sure no-one saw it, because he thought it was too dangerous. I'm telling you, I don't know. Either way it wasn't there. If it had been—"

"Vidal didn't ask about it?"

"No. He might not even know it existed . . . Or he didn't remember that I filmed it."

"Your father didn't tell you what he did with the woman's body?"

"No. All I know is what the newspapers said, that the following day her body was found on some waste ground in La Sagrera, near Sant Andreu . . . My father must have left her there, or whoever helped him."

"Do you know the name?"

"Of whoever helped my father?"

"The woman's."

"Of course. I'll never forget that. The newspapers didn't give a name, but I looked on the internet until I found it."

"What was her name?"

"Rosario Marín."

2

"If they haven't broadcast the video by now, I don't think they will," Blai says.

"Me neither," Vàzquez agrees.

"Of course, they most likely don't even have it," Blai goes on. "If they had it, they would have made it public. That would be the logical thing, wouldn't it? An ultimatum is an ultimatum."

"That's true, maybe they don't have it," Vàzquez concedes. "Maybe they're bluffing. Most likely."

"If they were bluffing, they hit the fucking jackpot," says Blai. "They've got away with two big payoffs."

"Most likely," Vàzquez repeats.

"What do you think, *españolazo*?" Blai asks. Before Melchor can answer, he adds: "And, by the way, where the fuck have you been? Here we all are going crazy with the mayor's business and you, meanwhile, have been doing bugger all. Can you tell us why you haven't even been answering your phone? Is that why I brought you up here? So you can skive off?"

Thanks to Vàzquez, who lends him a hand, Melchor dodges the telling-off and shows complete agreement with the former head of the Terra Alta Investigations Unit. He had arrived back in Barcelona at dawn, after staying up for three nights in a row, the second of which was spent listening to Ricky Ramírez's confession in his rented farmhouse in Sant Julià de Lòria, Andorra. And, after sleeping for a couple of hours, he had paid a visit to the mayor, had lunch with his daughter and Vivales and slept for a while until Blai woke him up to give him the news and summon him to an urgent meeting in Egara.

"Well, I've fulfilled my part of the bargain," Ricky Ramírez reminded him. "What are you going to do now?"

"Fulfil mine," Melchor assured him.

For several minutes his whisky-inflamed brain had not stopped repeating his mother's last words to her friend Carmen Lucas the night she was killed, fifteen years earlier, after she had refused to get into the BMW driven by her murderers: "A gang of rich kids out for a good time in papá's car."

"What I don't understand is why you're so sure the blackmailing of the mayor has nothing to do with the fire in La Pleta de Bolvir," says Blai, speaking to Melchor.

"Do we know yet if it was arson?" Vàzquez asks.

"Doesn't seem like it," Blai answers. "Everything points to a short circuit. But the whole house was made of wood and, with that heat, it burned up like tinder. And it was night, so it must have broken out when they were asleep, because no-one escaped. The house was in the middle of the woods, and by the time the fire brigade arrived it was just a heap of ashes."

"How many bodies did they find?" Vàzquez asks.

"Two, as well as those of the three tenors," Blai answers. "All burned to cinders. One of them was Hematomas. The other hasn't been identified yet."

"Hematomas must have gone up to La Pleta de Bolvir on his own," Vàzquez suggests. "The three tenors were in the same car. Torrent and Estellés followed them, but they lost them on the way out of Barcelona. Not surprising, since it was Friday afternoon and the Vallvidrera tunnels were at a standstill."

"How do you communicate with Vidal?" he asked Ricky.

"I told you already," he answered. "Through Marga, who's in contact with Hematomas. But I do have his phone number. Vidal's, I mean. If it's urgent, I can send him a message. If it's very urgent, I can call him. Though I haven't since I've been here."

"Well, call him now," Melchor pressed him. "It's very urgent."

"You haven't answered my question," Blai insists.

"Because I don't think any of them were involved in the extortion," Melchor answers.

"A few days ago, you did," Blai reminds him.

"I did," Melchor admits. "But not anymore."

"On Thursday I came to the conclusion that Rosell didn't have the slightest bloody idea of what I was talking about," Vàzquez says. "That's aside from the fact that he struck me as an idiot."

"He is an idiot," Blai confirms. "Or he was. Everyone knows it. But not Casas and Vidal, they were pretty sharp. And some of the clues did link them to the blackmail plot."

"For example?" Vàzquez asks.

"What do you want me to say to Vidal?" Ricky asked.

"Do you know if he still has the cabin in La Pleta de Bolvir, where you used to go on weekends to watch the videos?"

"No idea."

"Well, find out. And, if he does, ask him to meet you there. Tell him you have to see each other. Tell him you have to tell him something very important. Or rather, say you have to show it to him."

"Why? What for?"

"You tell him and let me look after the rest."

"He won't agree."

"I think he will. Tell him it's to do with the videos. Something you hadn't told him up till now, but now he needs to know. Something that has to do with blackmailing the mayor that he should know before the deadline you gave her to resign. Tell him it also concerns Casas and Rosell, and that he should arrange to bring the two of them with him. Tell him like that."

"For example," Blai says, "Marga Isern, Ricky Ramírez's girlfriend, got a SIM card made in the name of Farooq Hoque, the owner of a mobile—"

"It's not true," Melchor cuts him off. "The owner of the internet café lied to me. He's in love with her, but she barely acknowledges his existence and he wanted to get back at her."

"And Hematomas?"

"What about Hematomas?"

"You told me he and Marga Isern were meeting."

"And they were. But they weren't meeting about the mayor."

"How do you know?"

"Because Marga Isern has been one of Hematomas' informers for a while. He recruited her when she was in jail. It's common knowledge in the neighbourhood."

"Will you come with me to the cabin?" Ricky asked.

"Of course," Melchor answered.

"And what do you plan to do when we're there."

"Don't worry about it, that's my business. You do what I tell you to and forget the rest. If you do, I'll let you go."

"What?"

"You heard me: I'll let you go. I'll release you. And Marga too. And this time your friends won't get away with anything. They'll pay for what they did."

"I'm glad. But you gave me your word you'd do whatever it took for Marga and me to come out of this well, not that you'd let me go."

"I'm giving it to you now."

"How do I know you're not tricking me? How can I be sure of what you're saying?"

"You can't."

"Then," Blai concludes, holding back his satisfaction, "if there's no longer anyone blackmailing the mayor and we have no evidence linking the three tenors to the extortion . . ."

"It's over," Vàzquez finishes his sentence. "Now all we need to find out is who ended up with the money. But, good riddance to bad rubbish."

"Thank goodness the mayor cancelled the press conference she'd called to announce her resignation," Blai says. "I still can't understand. On Thursday, when I last spoke to her on the phone, I couldn't get the idea out of her head. Anyway, I suppose she went over what I'd said, after all, I do have certain powers of persuasion, don't you think?"

"Give me a good reason not to resign," the mayor demanded over the phone.

"If I hadn't seen the video," Melchor said, "I'd say that a sex tape couldn't do you as much harm as your resignation. And there's nothing to say that, even if you resign, they won't broadcast the video."

"Are you saying you've seen it?"

"Yes."

"When? How? Where?"

"That I can't tell you. What I can assure you is that tomorrow morning I can put it into your hands."

"Give it to me today at noon and I'll cancel the press conference."

"I'm sorry, I can't today. You'll have to wait until tomorrow. You'll have to trust me."

"Well, that's everything, isn't it?" Melchor asks. "I'm expected at home."

"Yes," Blai says. "I suppose so. Case closed, as Inspector Gadget would say. Right, Vàzquez?"

"Sure," Vàzquez agrees. "The hero of Cambrils can go back to the peace and quiet of Terra Alta, which is all he ever thinks about. Don't worry, we'll keep looking for the cash. Although, frankly, I think it's going to be pretty hard for us to find it now. Whoever they are, those bastards have no doubt buggered off, and who knows where they could be by now."

"When should I tell them to meet me at La Pleta de Bolvir?" Ricky Ramírez asked.

"Tomorrow night. Before the blackmail deadline runs out," Melchor answered.

"OK," the mayor agreed. "I trust you. Bring the video to my house tomorrow morning and I'll call off the press conference."

"I'll be there," Melchor promised. "In exchange you have to do me a favour."

"Name it."

"Don't tell anyone we've had this conversation."

"Not even your boss? He's been calling me."

"No-one. You and I have not spoken or seen each other. Nobody has given you the video. OK?"

"Are you really going to let me go," Ricky asked. "Are you sure nothing's going to happen to me?"

"Completely," Melchor answered.

"See you in Terra Alta, *españolazo*," says Blai.

"Give me a hug," says Vàzquez. "Take care of yourself."

"Swear it on what you hold dearest," Ricky said.

"I swear on my mother's life," Melchor said.

Melchor and Cosette spend the first week of August in El Llano de Molina, Murcia, staying with Pepe and Carmen Lucas, Melchor's mother's friend.

It is a happy week. Melchor takes a dog-eared copy of *Les Misérables* and the stories he still has to read for the Terra Alta High School literary prize. He hasn't reread Victor Hugo's novel since Olga's death, and from the first page it ensnares him again to such an extent that he abandons the stories and reads it all the time: when he takes Cosette to the municipal swimming pool, where she swims with the friends she made in the village the previous summer (and who still call her Cosé, which Cosette loves); in the afternoons, after having lunch with Carmen and Pepe, while Cosette watches a film or plays with her friends outside, and later, when the sun is a bit lower and he takes her to play football with the local team in a field on the outskirts, or in neighbouring villages; most of all he dives into *Les Misérables* at night, after reading a chapter of *In Search of the Castaways: Captain Grant's Children* – the Jules Verne novel they start after finishing *Michel Strogoff* – and after Cosette has fallen asleep, when he stays awake until three or four in the morning, following the exploits of Jean Valjean on tenterhooks, though he already knows them by heart. One night, while Cosette is just about to fall asleep after her daily dose of Verne, unmistakable sounds filter through the walls from Carmen and Pepe's bedroom.

"What's that?" the little girl asks in alarm.

"What?" Melchor answers, trying to play for time.

"That noise."

Melchor pretends to listen harder: the sound is still unmistakable, but now arrives mixed with unmistakable moans.

"What noise?" Melchor insists. "I don't hear anything."

Cosette looks at the bedroom ceiling with her lips pursed, as if she were thinking or rather as if she wanted her father, who doesn't take his eyes off her, to understand that she is thinking.

"Are Carmen and Pepe making a baby?" she asks.

Melchor feels all the blood in his body rush to his face and thanks the heavens that he's lying down in a bed. Mentally he pleads for the noise to cease while he tries to find an acceptable answer to his daughter's question, but none is forthcoming. He barely manages to request: "Come on, go to sleep. It's really late."

The next day, the last of their stay in El Llano de Molina, Cosette insists that Pepe should take her to play football, and, in order not to stay in the house alone, Melchor decides to accompany Carmen to the allotment garden she has on the edge of town and still works on daily. At first, he tries to help her, but, in view of his obvious clumsiness, she points to the tool shed and laughingly tells him to stop getting in her way and go and read that doorstop he never puts down.

Melchor obeys. He sits on the ground, with his back leaning against the wall of the shed, watching the woman work, until he tires of that and resumes his reading of *Les Misérables*. He has reached the famous episode in which Jean Valjean, carrying Cosette's suitor Marius – whose life he has just saved at the barricade of La Chevreuse – flees through the sewers of Paris pursued by Javert, and, when he has been reading for a while, he looks up, sees Carmen a few metres away and suddenly thinks that nobody deserves to know that justice has finally been done as much as she does, to know that her friend's murder has finally been avenged.

"Carmen," Melchor murmurs.

She pauses in her task and looks at him, a little out of breath.

She is leaning over a recently dug furrow, brandishing a large hoe.

"What?" she asks.

"Do you remember my mother?"

Carmen Lucas leans her hoe on the turned soil and, still panting, wipes the sweat off her brow with a forearm. Dusk is falling over the allotment, and a light the colour of old gold surrounds the woman, as if she were an angel. For a moment, Melchor feels he has already lived through this scene.

"Not a day goes by that I don't think of her," Carmen answers. After a brief silence she adds: "Why?"

As long as there's remorse, there's guilt, Melchor thinks. He still can't remember where he read this sentence, but he realises that, despite having killed five men that summer, he has not the slightest bit of remorse, or any guilt whatsoever, and he is amazed to have once felt guilty over Olga's death, for having thought for years that he had failed his wife. He hadn't failed her, he understands. He is not guilty of anything. And he also understands that Carmen does not need to know and he does not need to unburden himself, to Carmen or anyone else, that he should carry the weight of those deaths on his own and he can happily do so.

"No reason," he answers.

Two days later, when he goes back to work at the Terra Alta police station, it is more evident than ever to Melchor that he does not want to carry on being a police officer: after all, he tells himself, he only wanted to become one after reading *Les Misérables* in the Quatre Camins prison, in order to find his mother's murderers; now that he has found them, he also tells himself, there is no reason on earth to go on practising this trade. Shortly after reaching this conclusion, while hoping for a place to open up at the Gandesa library or any library in Terra

Alta or the surrounding area that he might apply for, Melchor gets a phone call from Manel Puig, Vivales' friend, who tells him that the lawyer has died.

"He's had cancer for two years," Puig explains. "Before the summer they diagnosed it as terminal."

"I didn't know," Melchor manages to say.

"Nobody knew. He called me and Chicho a week before he died, a few days after he'd been admitted to hospital."

"How strange. I talked to him a couple of times and both times he said what he always says: 'Everything's under control.'"

"And it was. But under the control of doctors, who knew he was dying. So did he."

Melchor leaves Cosette with Rosa Adell, who has offered to look after her while he's away, and goes to Barcelona. He meets Puig and Campà at the Sancho de Ávila funeral home; they greet him tearfully and take him out for dinner. During the meal they tell him about Vivales' last days.

"He wouldn't let us tell you he was in hospital," Puig says.

"He didn't want you or your daughter to see him," Campà backs him up.

"Was he that bad?" Melchor asks.

"Not at all," Puig answers. "He was getting excellent palliative care, cortisone shots, so he was feeling no pain. That was the problem."

Melchor looks at them without catching on.

"He forced us to bring whisky and cigars into his room," Campà tells him.

"On the sly," Puig says, unnecessarily.

"One day he got completely plastered," Campà continues sadly.

"He wouldn't take his eyes off the nurses' tits," Puig says.

"Disgraceful," Campà says.

"Can't take him anywhere," Puig says. "He made us look like arseholes right up to the last day."

"What most worried him was having a Catholic funeral," Campà changes the subject. "He told me a thousand times."

"Me, three thousand," Puig says.

"I didn't know Vivales was a believer," admits Melchor, who, try as he might, cannot get Ortega y Gasset out of his head.

"And he wasn't," Campà assures him. "He was an anti-clerical atheist, thanks be to God. But that was precisely why. He told me that he wanted to be sure that, before burying him, someone would speak well of him. He meant the priest, of course."

"Pure Vivales," Puig decrees. "Do you know what he said to me?" Campà questions him with an intrigued half-smile and Puig does an imitation of the unmistakable voice of the lawyer, gruff from alcohol and tobacco: " 'Most of all, none of that lay funeral bullshit, Manel,' he said. 'No-one's better at sending people to the next neighbourhood than priests: they've been doing it for centuries.' "

"That's pure Vivales too," Campà says.

That night Melchor stays in the lawyer's flat. Unable to sleep, he spends hours going through drawers. He is looking for photos of his mother, but he doesn't find any. Instead, he finds several photos of Vivales, alone or with strangers; also some with people he knows. He finds, for example, a photo from his own wedding taken at the door of the Gandesa Town Hall: he and Olga, visibly pregnant with Cosette, occupy the centre of the group, and beside them are Salom and his daughters, and Carmen and Pepe, whose shoulder Vivales has an arm slung over, smiling a big toothy smile; he also finds a photo of a very young Vivales, in a recruit's uniform and surrounded by a gaggle of comrades, among whom he thinks he recognises Puig and Campà. That morning he also discovers, in the early hours, that Vivales paid two hundred and fifty euros monthly to Caritas and another two hundred and fifty euros to Open Arms, an organisation that helps refugees. Pure Vivales, he thinks.

The next morning, he finishes organising the formalities of death with which Puig and Campà had begun to battle the night before. Behind a desk, an employee at the funeral home, as she fills in a form, refers to the dead man by his real name.

"Vivales," Melchor corrects her. "He was called Vivales."

The employee smiles with professional gentleness and shows the death certificate she has received.

"It says Perales here," she points out to Melchor.

"Yeah," Melchor agrees. "But put Vivales."

He orders the set menu at a nearby restaurant and, to kill time while waiting for the funeral, he goes for a walk around the neighbourhood. He loses track of time and when he gets back to the funeral home he thinks someone famous has died, some actor or politician, because the entrance is packed with people; until, making his way through the crowd, he realises that the majority are immigrants or very dodgy-looking locals – pimps, prostitutes, night people with unhealthy lifestyles – and he understands they have all come to the lawyer's funeral.

"This Vivales only hobnobbed with the *crème de la crème*," Puig murmurs, inspecting the turnout.

The funeral chapel fills swiftly, and many of those present resign themselves to staying outside. For his part, during the sermon the priest speaks highly of the virtues of the deceased, whom he hadn't known: he praises his proven integrity, his sacrosanct respect for the courts and his gallant and obligatory defence of the law; finally, carried away by the momentum

358

of his own panegyric, he ends up elevating him to the rank of "champion of justice". At some point Melchor senses that Puig and Campà, sitting beside him in the front row, are making inordinate efforts not to burst out laughing; at another point he stops listening to the priest. He then remembers the morning when, barely out of adolescence, he met Vivales for the first time in a visiting room of the Soto del Real prison, near Madrid, where he was awaiting trial for belonging to a Colombian drug trafficking cartel that operated throughout Spain, and that other morning when, years later, recently released much earlier than predicted, thanks to Vivales' legal tricks, he began to suspect that this impenitent swindler might be his father. He also remembers another occasion, this time in the visiting room of the Quatre Camins prison near Barcelona. By then it had been a while since his mother's murder and Vivales was paying the tuition fees for him to complete his secondary education at Catalonia's Open Institute, as well as taking charge of his defence without ever charging him anything, something he had done from the start; one afternoon Melchor, wary of such generosity, resolved to ask him why he was doing what he was doing for him, and Vivales, after asking if he wanted the truth or would rather have a lie, and warning him that he wasn't going to like the truth, sprung it on him: "Because you're a loser, kid. And if I don't lend you a hand, nobody will." And at that moment Melchor believes he finally understands, in an explosion of lucidity, right there, in the middle of Vivales' funeral, surrounded by all sorts of losers like him, that after all Vivales was not his father, or that he only was in his orphan's reveries, but that he was the closest thing to a father that it is possible to have.

When the ceremony ends Puig and Campà invite him to go out for a drink with their friends. Melchor thinks he will probably never see Ortega y Gasset again in his life, so he accepts, and the three of them go to a café down the street on Sancho de Ávila. There a group of men await them. They are Vivales' comrades from the 62nd Arapiles Regiment, where the lawyer had done his military service and, as Puig and Campà introduce him to them and one by one they give him their condolences, Melchor wonders if those old men are the young recruits from the photograph he found last night in Vivales' apartment. Then he orders a Coca-Cola and sits down with them. They are all drinking whisky, all telling stories, indiscriminately, of Vivales and of their military service, as if in their memories (or in their imagination) both were the same thing; some of them laugh to the point of tears. When one of them stands up and, obviously drunk, begins to sing the anthem of the Spanish infantry, and the others follow his lead, Melchor stands up without drawing attention to himself, pays for everyone's drinks and goes out for a walk.

The assembly hall of the Terra Alta High School is jam-packed. It's the afternoon before the first day of the new school year, and students of all ages, many of them accompanied by their parents, fill the seats and even the side aisles, some standing and others sitting. They've been in there for more than an hour, listening to speeches and music and watching the presentation of the four literary prizes, along with the twelve runners-up awards; it is half past one and everyone, some more some less, is hungry and eager for the ceremony to end as soon as possible. So, when the vice principal of the school and the event's host announces that, as a finale, a member of the jury will say a few words in praise of reading, a mutinous sound travels from one side of the hall to the other.

In the midst of the hubbub, Melchor stands up and climbs the steps to the stage like a man mounting a scaffold. There is no applause, the vice principal vanishes instantly and Melchor takes his place behind the lectern and takes a piece of paper with a few handwritten notes for his speech out of his shirt pocket. He is shaking like a leaf. In hopes of getting the ordeal over with as soon as possible, he swallows and, without waiting for silence, begins to speak.

"My name is Melchor Marín and I am a police officer," he introduces himself. "Many of you know me. I was one of the judges of the prize and that's why they've asked me to say a few words. Also because no-one else wanted to do it." Melchor raises his eyes a little: when he was planning the speech, he thought it would be good to start by saying something funny, so the kids would laugh; but nobody has laughed: perhaps what he said wasn't funny, or nobody heard him. The racket is still considerable, even though teachers are running up and down the aisles trying to shush people. "And also because I like to read novels," he goes on. "This seems to be unusual. I mean, it's unusual for police officers to read novels, probably because my colleagues think it's more useful and more entertaining to read about real things than about invented things. Maybe they're right, and that's why I understand that some of them, occasionally, make fun of me. At first, when I was young, that bothered me; now it doesn't anymore, because I realise that a man who gets annoyed by other people laughing at him is not a man." Melchor clears his throat, steals another glance at the rows of seats and senses that an almost perfect silence has taken over; for a moment he thinks something's happened, or that someone important has just come into the hall. "When I was young I didn't like to read," he carries on. "I liked to run wild, as everyone does." Here a few laughs can be heard: shy, isolated,

361

sardonic or awkward. "I discovered novels in prison, when I was your age, maybe a bit older. Prison is a very bad place, I don't recommend it." Now the laughter is wholesale, and, a bit surprised, Melchor waits for silence again. He starts the sentence from the beginning again and finishes: "But, sometimes, even in a very bad place good things happen. For example, Cervantes had the idea for *Don Quixote* in prison; well, that's what they say, I don't know because I haven't read *Don Quixote*. I'm probably wrong not to have, after all, everyone says it's a very good book. But, I don't know why, I've always thought that it wasn't for me, and another thing I've learned over the years is that a person should only read the novels that are meant for him.

"But let's go back to prison. I began to read novels because of a man I met there. He was called Gilles and the guards called him Guille, but, since he was French, the rest of us prisoners all called him the Frenchman. He's one of the best people I've ever met in my life, even though he was in prison for having murdered his wife and a friend of hers with a hammer. This summer I ran into him again, in Barcelona, and he was in love, which is the best thing that can happen to a person." Melchor pauses, notices his mouth is dry and understands that fear has dried it. Unfortunately, no-one thought to leave a glass of water on the podium and, in the midst of the silence, he tries to encourage himself by telling himself there's not long to go till the end. "The thing is, the Frenchman was the prison librarian and spent all his days reading. I wanted to be like him, so I started reading novels. At first I didn't like them that much to tell you the truth, but then I read *Les Misérables* by Victor Hugo. It's very famous, you might have heard of it . . . I read it because I saw it on the Frenchman's desk one day and it reminded me of my mother, who always complained about my bad marks at school by saying: 'If you want to end up as miserable as me, don't study.'" The laughs force him to stop again, but he doesn't dare look out at the audience and, as soon as the silence returns, he goes on talking. "So I read *Les Misérables* and everything changed. I'd love to tell you how it changed, but the truth is I don't know, I am unable to explain it. For years I thought it was because it was about me, but then I came to Terra Alta and met my wife, who told me that all good novels are about us. She was right, of course, when it came to books my wife was always right, her name was Olga and she was the librarian here next door, at the Municipal Library, some of you still remember her. Thanks to Olga I began to get involved with the library, take books to the swimming pool in the summer and things like that . . . Well, I think I've gone off track." During the two or three seconds Melchor is quiet, not a fly is heard buzzing in the hall. "Oh, yes, I was telling you that, according to my wife, all good novels are about us. And she also said that *Les Misérables* was no different, that it was not about me in particular. Of course, she only said that at first, then we got married and she changed her mind, began to think that maybe I was right and *Les Misérables* was a special novel, but not because it was about me, but because it was about us, about her and me. My wife and I were very much in love . . . Anyway, all this is very complicated, as you can see, and I'm not very good at giving speeches. Luckily, this one is coming to an end. So, to wrap up, I'll tell you something else I've learned from reading novels. What I've learned is that novels are useless. They don't even tell things as they are, but as they might have been, or as we wish they could be. That's how they save our lives." Melchor falls silent, as if pondering, and the auditorium waits expectantly, not sure whether he has finished or not; finally he adds, almost as if to himself: "Well, that's all I wanted to tell you: that novels are useless, except for saving lives."

Another even denser silence greets the end of the speech, a silence broken first by a solitary handclap, then by another and another, and soon by a thunderous storm of applause. Before Melchor can walk down from the stage, people rush up onto it to congratulate him: the other members of the jury, parents, teachers, a little group of spellbound students, to whom he doesn't know what to say. He has not yet finished expressing his thanks for all the congratulations and trying to answer the questions, when, in the almost empty hall, he sees in the distance Inspector Blai leaning against a column, watching him with his arms crossed and a sardonic smile on his lips. Melchor is last off the stage and, when he reaches the back, Blai uncrosses his arms and puts one of them around Melchor's shoulders.

"You're a sly one, *españolazo*," the former head of the Terra Alta Investigations Unit congratulates him. "What a way to get children eating out of your hand. And that thing about getting into novels in prison . . . Poor gullible kids."

Melchor continues thanking the stragglers who approach to congratulate him, and when the two police officers are alone again, he nods towards Blai and asks:

"And what are you doing here?"

His old friend takes his arm off his shoulder.

"Just enrolled Toni and Laura," he announces. "They start tomorrow."

"Here?"

The inspector nods. The two men look at each other and, before Blai speaks again, Melchor guesses what he is going to tell him.

"I've accepted the post as Terra Alta station chief," he says.

It's the best news Blai could give him, but Melchor doesn't bat an eyelid.

"I know," Blai attempts to get ahead of him. "You're thinking

I've accepted the post for the sake of the family, so my wife will stop giving me a hard time about Terra Alta and all that. Aren't you?" He shakes his head back and forth as if criticising Melchor wordlessly. "Bollocks. What do you think I am, pussy-whipped?"

Melchor says nothing.

"Don't make that face," Blai reproaches him again. "I'm being serious. I was fed up with Egara. All those stuck-up snobs . . . But they don't know their arse from their elbow, man! Besides, I couldn't handle being in it up to my neck every fucking day, no-one could stand it . . . Anyway, I don't need to tell you."

Apart from the two police officers, there is no-one left in the hall, except for a caretaker who, without taking a break from sweeping, asks them to go outside. So they do, and, after exchanging a few last words with a couple of teachers and a couple of members of the jury hanging around the door, they start walking towards the old part of Gandesa.

"By the way," Melchor says, "I bet you don't know who's coming this weekend." Blai questions him with a gesture. "Vàzquez."

"No way."

"He's coming with the press officer."

"Verónica? The one who's after you to make the film about the attacks?"

"The same."

"I thought you didn't want to do it . . . The film, I mean."

"And I'm not going to."

"So then?"

Melchor shrugs and keeps walking.

"She called me a few days ago, wanting to come and see me to talk about it. I fobbed her off . . . Until Vàzquez found out and begged me to agree, on the condition that he come with her."

Blai stops, Melchor does the same and the two men look at each other for a second; then the inspector bursts out laughing.

"You bastard!"

Melchor smiles a little, happy to see his friend happy, and they both start walking again. Melchor digs his hands into his trouser pockets.

"Well . . ." He sighs. "Welcome to Terra Alta."

"Yeah." Blai nods. "As my wife always says: there's nowhere like Terra Alta."

The phrase plunges the two men into an embarrassed silence, because it sounds like a flagrant refutation of all the previous claims of independence that have spilled out of Blai's mouth. Aware of the blunder, the imminent Terra Alta chief of police hurries to straighten out the slip.

"But one thing's for sure, *españolazo*," he warns him, with a sudden vengeful joy, gripping Melchor's shoulder and whispering in his ear, "you can start getting ready down at the station: I'm going to whip you all into shape."

On his way out of the cemetery, Melchor looks for Rosa Adell under the cross on the roundabout. She's not there, and the first thing he thinks is that she's away on a trip, that she's not in Terra Alta. Then he thinks that Rosa has forgotten that it's Saturday, or that she thinks he's on the night shift that weekend. Then, sadly, he thinks she has finally tired of waiting. And the strange thing is that she didn't get tired earlier.

He walks down avenida Joan Perucho to avenida de Catalunya and, just past the bus station, a red convertible pulls up beside him. Rosa Adell is behind the wheel.

"Where're you going, *poli*?" she asks.

Melchor moves closer to the car. Although autumn is about to arrive, it is a warm and radiant morning, and Rosa is wearing a white summer dress and white sandals; a pair of sunglasses hide her eyes. Since Melchor just looks at her, leaning on the passenger door, the woman asks:

"Do you plan on standing there like an idiot?" She reaches across and opens the door. "Come on, get in."

Melchor gets in beside her and Rosa Adell drives into Gandesa.

"Where's Cosette?" she asks.

"Everything's under control," Melchor answers: it's not the first time he's surprised himself repeating Vivales' catchphrase, as if he's inherited it. "She's in Arnes, playing football."

"And you're not going to watch her?"

"She doesn't want me to." Melchor shrugs. "She says when I go she gets nervous and plays badly."

They drive slowly around the edge of the plaza de la Farola while Rosa shakes her head.

"That girl's smitten with her father," she says. Then, in another tone of voice, she says: "By the way, I heard you were really good at the awards ceremony at the high school the other day."

"It was awful."

"Well, I heard that the people were delighted and that everyone applauded like crazy." She takes her right hand off the steering wheel and points with her thumb to the back seat. "And speaking of literature: look what I've got back there."

Melchor turns around and sees a book.

"Pick it up," Rosa encourages him.

Melchor picks it up. The book is a novel. The cover shows a man and his shadow walking across a sunlit square. He reads

367

the name of the author and the title: *Even the Darkest Night: A Terra Alta Investigation.*

"Have you read it?" Melchor asks.

"No. Have you?"

He shakes his head while Rosa comments:

"I've heard that it's about you."

"I've heard that too."

"Do you know the author?"

"I've never set eyes on him in my life."

"I've heard that everything in it is true."

"I, on the other hand, have heard that it's all lies."

Rosa smiles: the sun shines on her face, and the wind blows back her hair. Melchor thinks she's lovely when she smiles.

"Do you remember Vivales?" he asks.

"Of course," Rosa answers.

"He really liked westerns," Melchor explains. "In one of them there's a cowboy who's just discovered he's in love. But he doesn't understand what's happening to him, and asks the owner of the saloon: "You ever been in love?" The other man answers: "No. I've been a bartender all my life.""

Rosa bursts out laughing. Melchor smiles as he leaves the book on the back seat.

"Where are we going?" the woman asks.

"Wherever you want," answers Melchor.

They are driving out of town. Rosa accelerates.

Acknowledgments

I would like to thank the following people for their collaboration: Cristobál Fernández Zapata, Joan Llinares, Jordi Martí, Néstor Pavón and Montse Seró. Also Patrícia Plaja, director of communications for the Mossos d'Esquadra, Inspector Jordi Domènech, Sergeant Enric Martínez, Intendent Antoni Rodríguez and Commissioner Marta Fernández. But most of all Inspector Carlos Otamendi, who had the patience and generosity to read the manuscript of this book.

JAVIER CERCAS is a novelist and columnist for *El País*. He is the author of *Soldiers of Salamis* (which sold more than a million copies worldwide and won the *Independent* Foreign Fiction Prize among many others) and its companion volume *Lord of All the Dead* (which won the Prix André Malraux). His other books include *The Anatomy of a Moment*, *Outlaws* (which was shortlisted for the Dublin Literary Award in 2016 and was made into a film directed by Daniel Monzón) and *The Impostor* (winner of the 2016 European Book Prize). In 2015 he was the Weidenfeld Professor of Comparative Literature at St Anne's College Oxford, and his lectures there are collected in *The Blind Spot*. His books have been translated into more than thirty languages. He lives in Barcelona.

ANNE MCLEAN has translated Latin American and Spanish novels, stories, memoirs and other writings by many authors including Héctor Abad, Julio Cortázar, Gabriel García Márquez, Enrique Vila-Matas and Juan Gabriel Vásquez. She has twice won the *Independent* Foreign Fiction Prize, with Javier Cercas for *Soldiers of Salamis* and with Evelio Rosero for *The Armies*. In 2004, and again in 2016, she won the Premio Valle Inclán for her translations of *Soldiers of Salamis* and *Outlaws* by Javier Cercas. In 2012, Spain awarded her a Cruz de Oficial of the Order of Civil Merit. She lives in Canada.